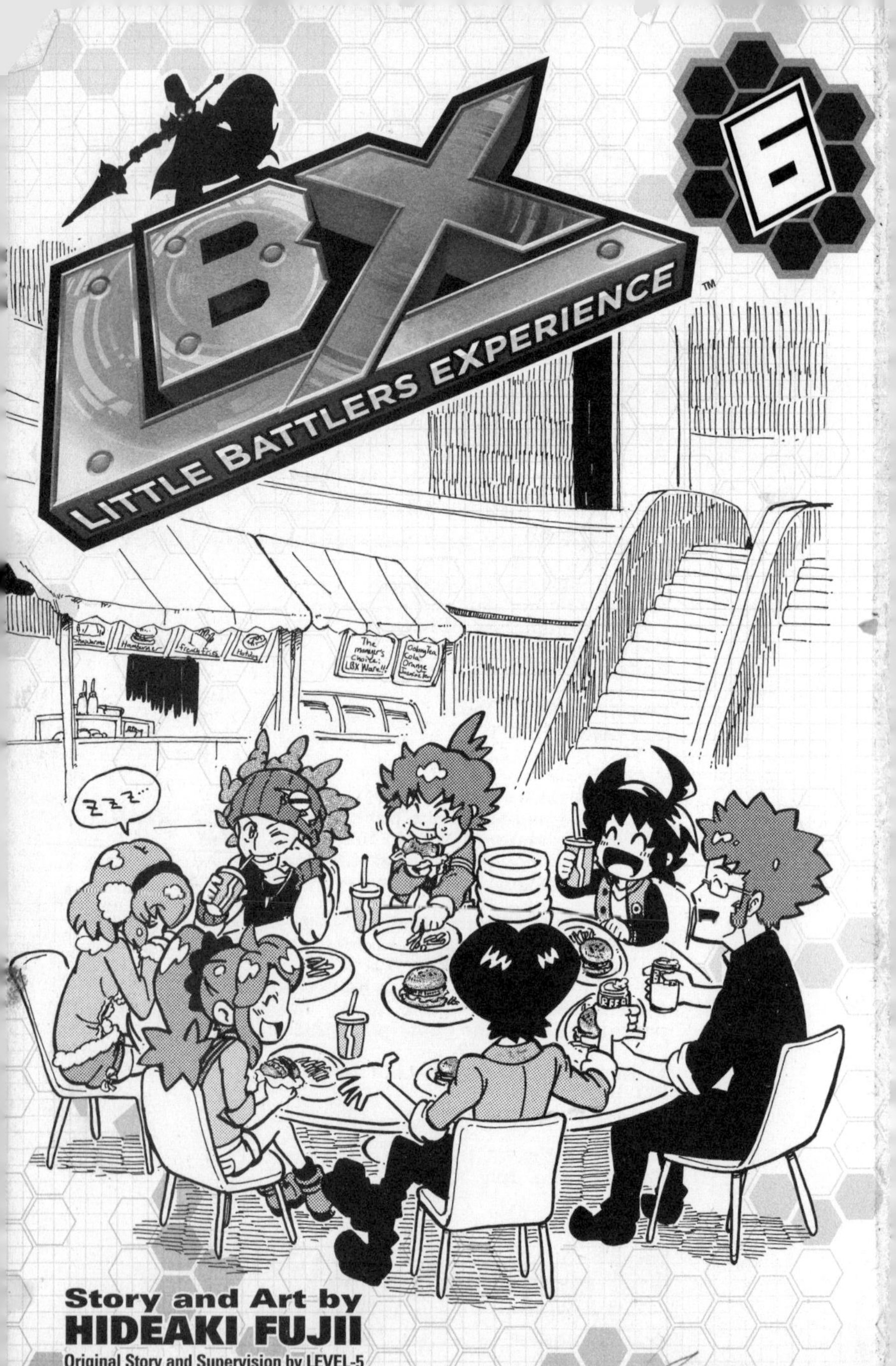
LBX
LITTLE BATTLERS EXPERIENCE™
6
Shawarma
Hamburger
French Fries
Hotdog
The manager's choice: LBX Ware!!
Oolong Tea
Cola
Orange
Z Z Z...

Story and Art by
HIDEAKI FUJII
Original Story and Supervision by LEVEL-5

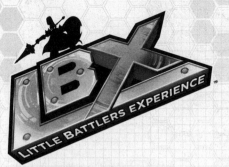

LBX Volume 6
WORLD BATTLE
Perfect Square Edition

Story and Art by Hideaki FUJII
Original Story and Supervision by LEVEL-5

Translation/Tetsuichiro Miyaki
English Adaptation/Aubrey Sitterson
Lettering/Annaliese Christman
Design/Izumi Evers
Editor/Joel Enos

DANBALL SENKI Vol.6
by Hideaki FUJII
© 2011 Hideaki FUJII
© LEVEL-5 Inc.
All rights reserved.
Original Japanese edition published by SHOGAKUKAN.
English translation rights in the United States of
America, Canada, the United Kingdom, Ireland, Australia
and New Zealand arranged with SHOGAKUKAN.

The stories, characters and incidents mentioned in this
publication are entirely fictional.

Published by VIZ Media, LLC
P.O. Box 77010
San Francisco, CA 94107

10 9 8 7 6 5 4 3 2 1
First printing, July 2015

www.perfectsquare.com

www.viz.com

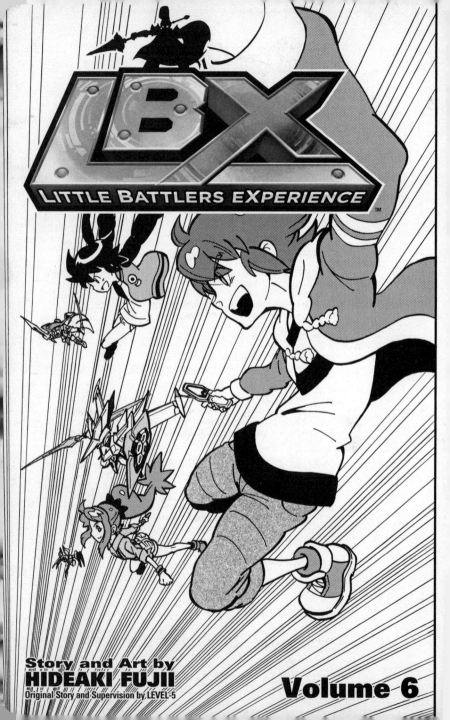

Story and Art by
HIDEAKI FUJII
Original Story and Supervision by LEVEL-5

Volume 6

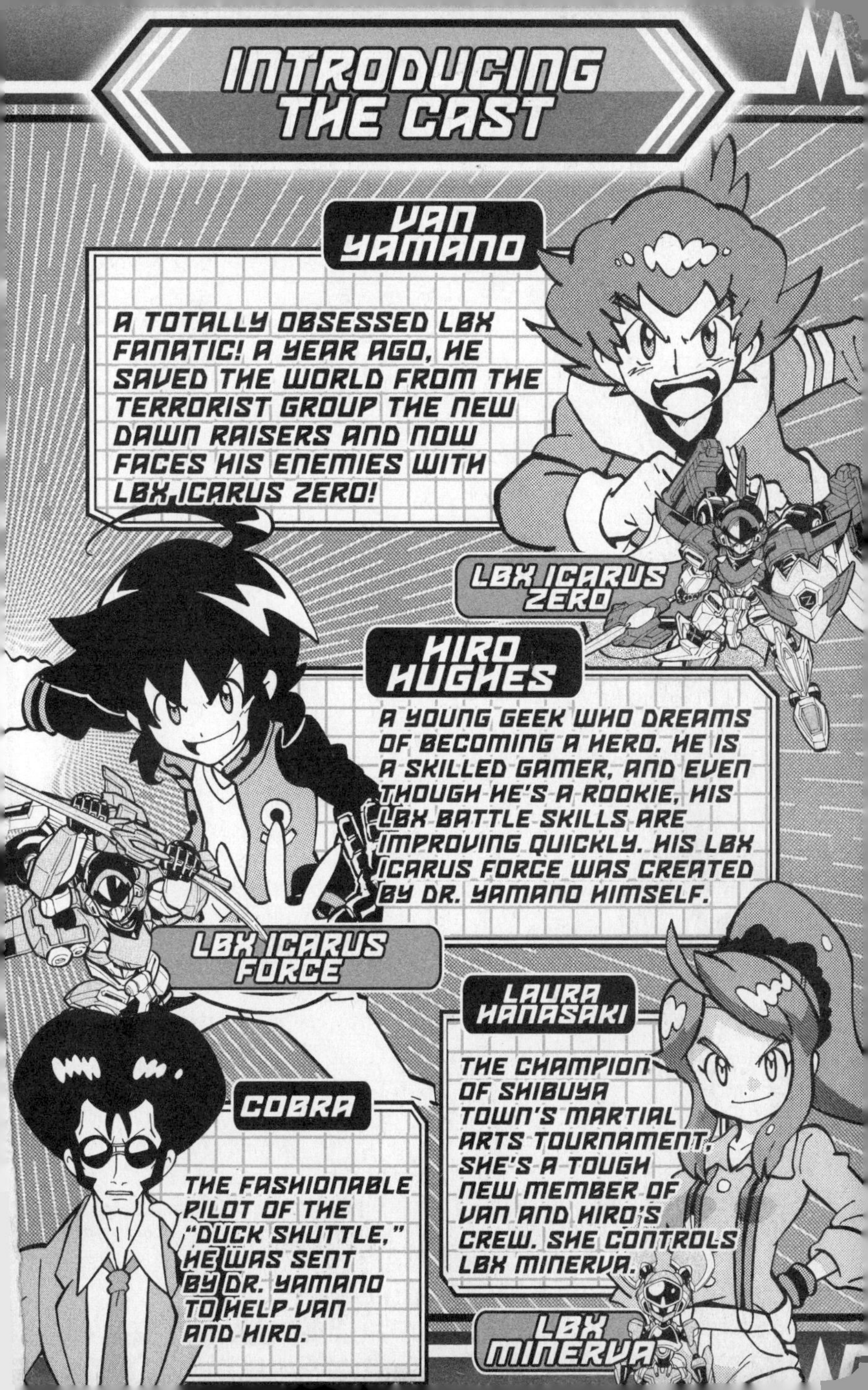
INTRODUCING THE CAST
VAN YAMANO
A TOTALLY OBSESSED LBX FANATIC! A YEAR AGO, HE SAVED THE WORLD FROM THE TERRORIST GROUP THE NEW DAWN RAISERS AND NOW FACES HIS ENEMIES WITH LBX ICARUS ZERO!
LBX ICARUS ZERO
HIRO HUGHES
A YOUNG GEEK WHO DREAMS OF BECOMING A HERO. HE IS A SKILLED GAMER, AND EVEN THOUGH HE'S A ROOKIE, HIS LBX BATTLE SKILLS ARE IMPROVING QUICKLY. HIS LBX ICARUS FORCE WAS CREATED BY DR. YAMANO HIMSELF.
LBX ICARUS FORCE
LAURA HANASAKI
THE CHAMPION OF SHIBUYA TOWN'S MARTIAL ARTS TOURNAMENT, SHE'S A TOUGH NEW MEMBER OF VAN AND HIRO'S CREW. SHE CONTROLS LBX MINERVA.
COBRA
THE FASHIONABLE PILOT OF THE "DUCK SHUTTLE," HE WAS SENT BY DR. YAMANO TO HELP VAN AND HIRO.
LBX MINERVA

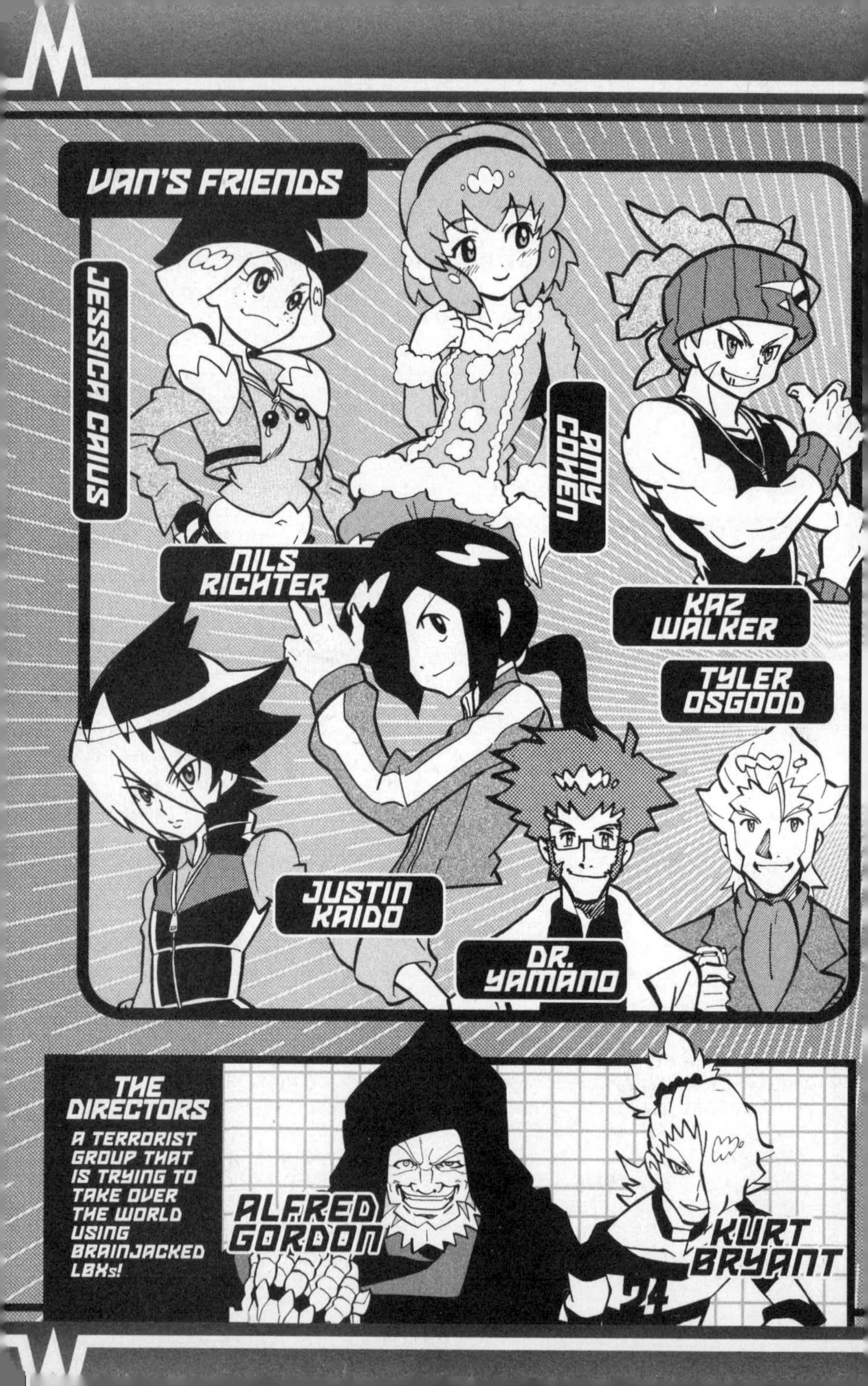
VAN'S FRIENDS
JESSICA CAIUS
AMY COHEN
NILS RICHTER
KAZ WALKER
TYLER OSGOOD
JUSTIN KAIDO
DR. YAMANO
THE DIRECTORS
A TERRORIST GROUP THAT IS TRYING TO TAKE OVER THE WORLD USING BRAINJACKED LBXs!
ALFRED GORDON
KURT BRYANT

TABLE OF CONTENTS

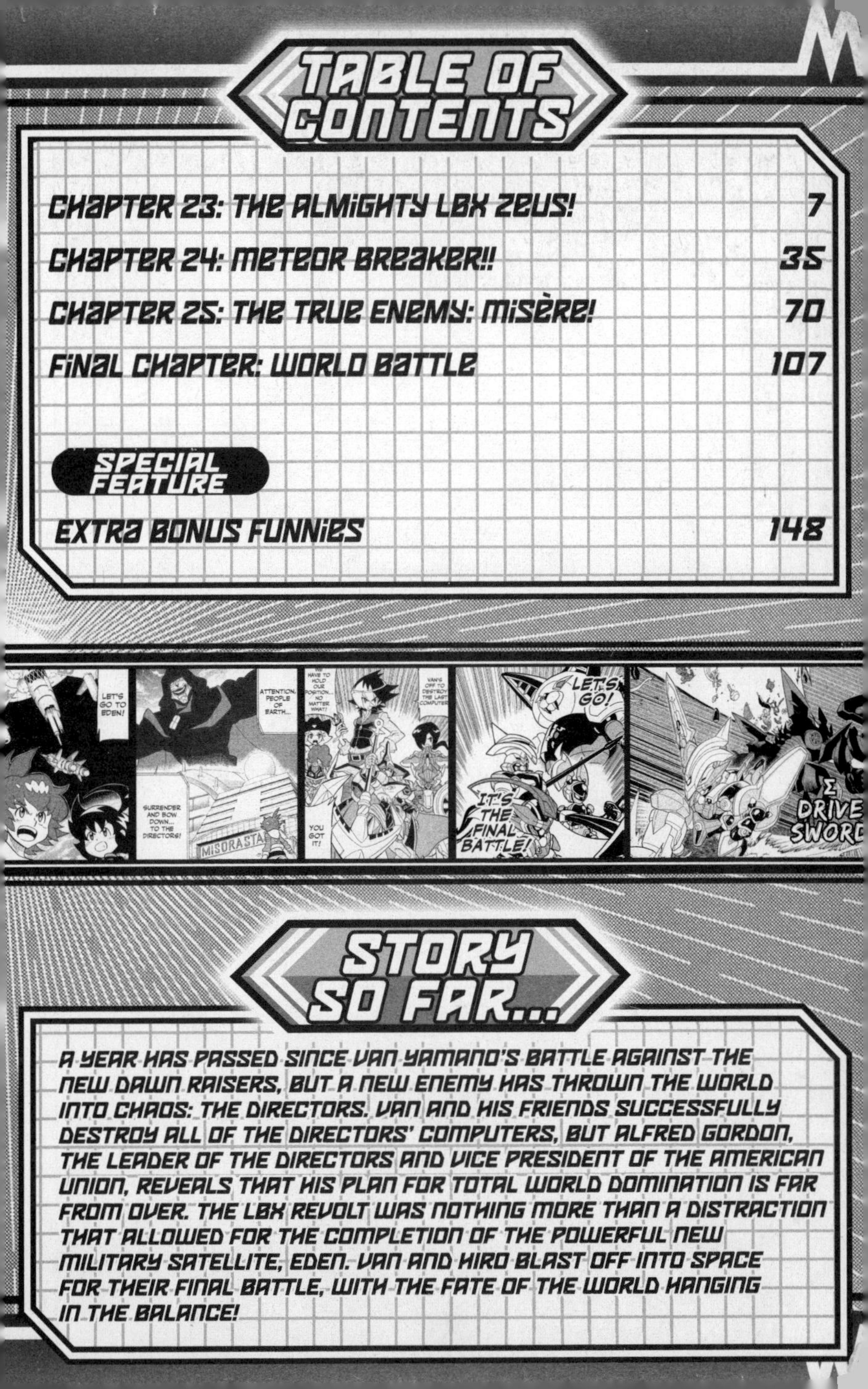

Σ DRIVE SWOR
LET'S GO!
IT'S THE FINAL BATTLE!
VAN'S OFF TO DESTROY THE LAST COMPUTER!
WE HAVE TO HOLD OUR POSITION... NO MATTER WHAT!
YOU GOT IT!
ATTENTION, PEOPLE OF EARTH...
SURRENDER AND BOW DOWN... TO THE DIRECTORS!
MISORASTA
LET'S GO TO EDEN!

STORY SO FAR...

A YEAR HAS PASSED SINCE VAN YAMANO'S BATTLE AGAINST THE NEW DAWN RAISERS, BUT A NEW ENEMY HAS THROWN THE WORLD INTO CHAOS: THE DIRECTORS. VAN AND HIS FRIENDS SUCCESSFULLY DESTROY ALL OF THE DIRECTORS' COMPUTERS, BUT ALFRED GORDON, THE LEADER OF THE DIRECTORS AND VICE PRESIDENT OF THE AMERICAN UNION, REVEALS THAT HIS PLAN FOR TOTAL WORLD DOMINATION IS FAR FROM OVER. THE LBX REVOLT WAS NOTHING MORE THAN A DISTRACTION THAT ALLOWED FOR THE COMPLETION OF THE POWERFUL NEW MILITARY SATELLITE, EDEN. VAN AND HIRO BLAST OFF INTO SPACE FOR THEIR FINAL BATTLE, WITH THE FATE OF THE WORLD HANGING IN THE BALANCE!

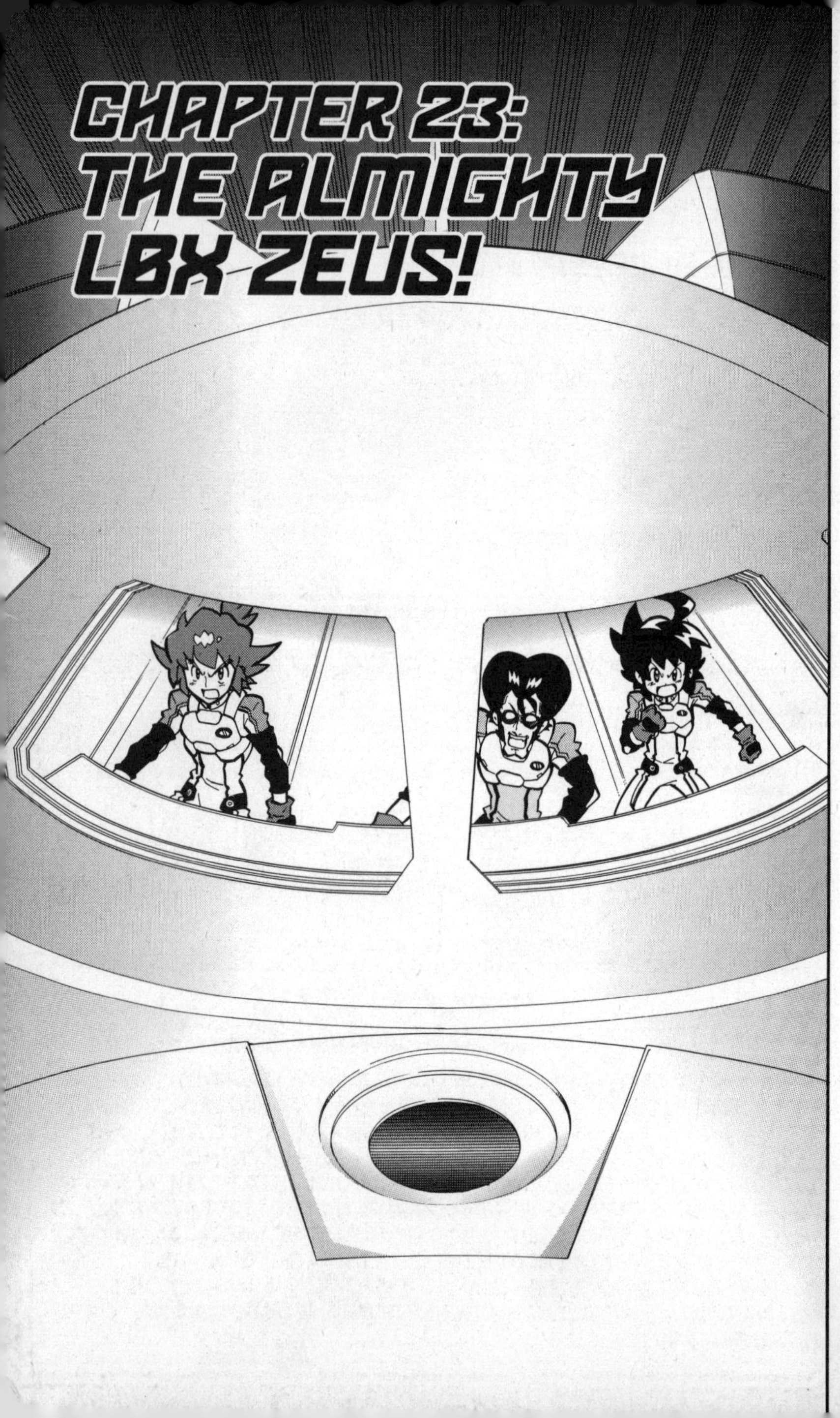
CHAPTER 23:
THE ALMIGHTY
LBX ZEUS!

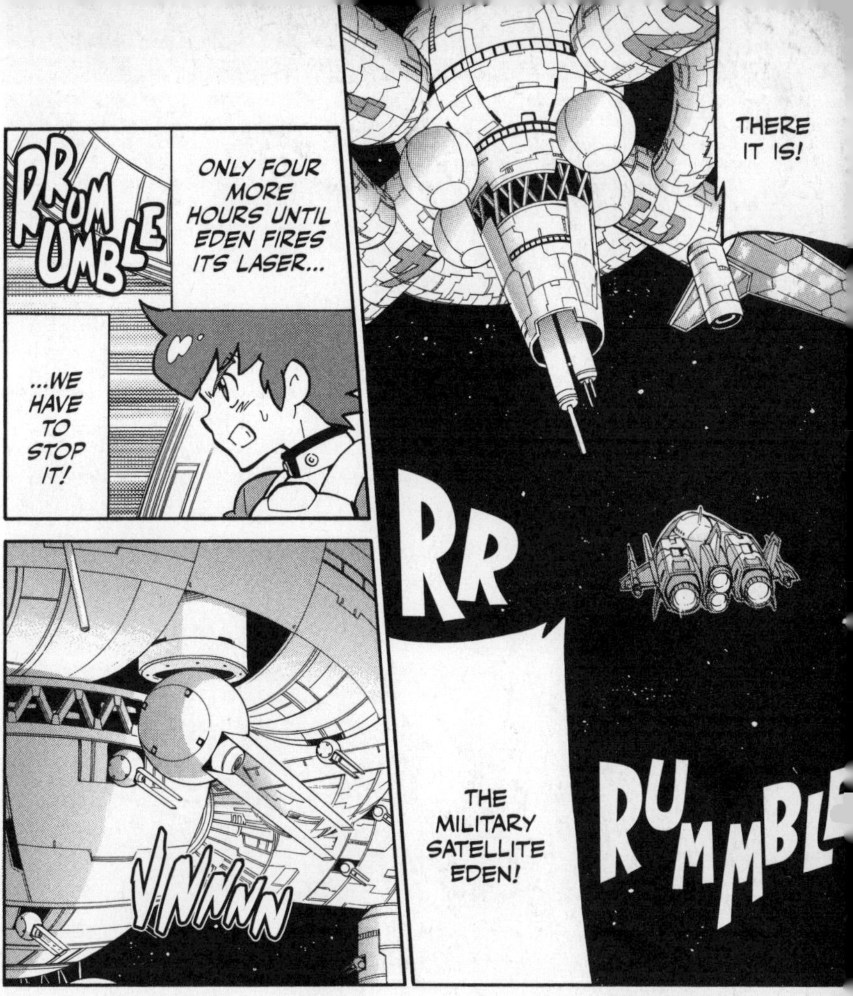
THERE IT IS!
RR
RUMMBLE
THE MILITARY SATELLITE EDEN!
ONLY FOUR MORE HOURS UNTIL EDEN FIRES ITS LASER...
RRUM UMBLE
...WE HAVE TO STOP IT!
VNNNNN

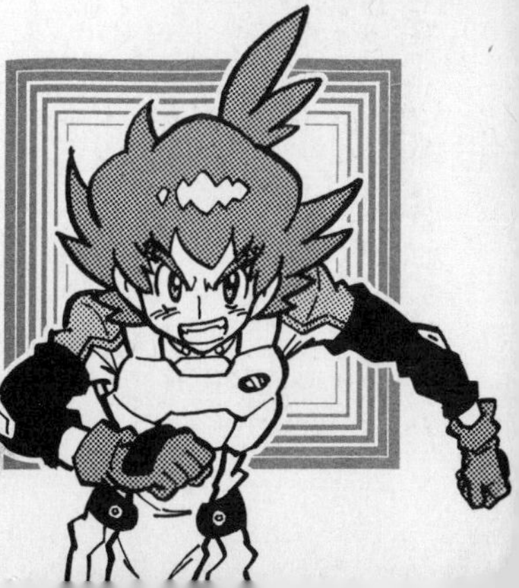

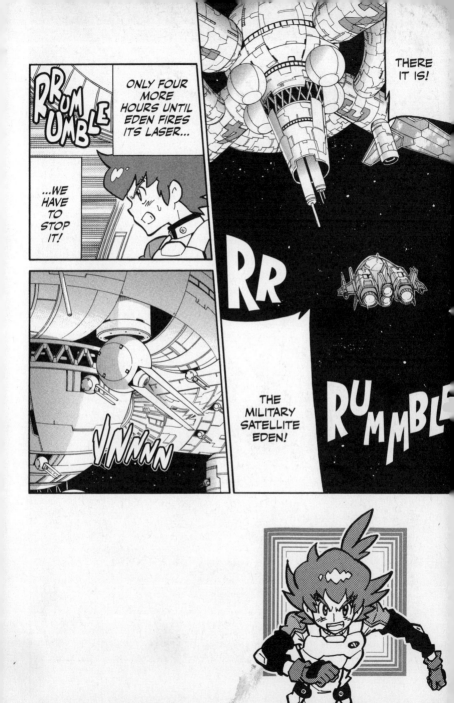

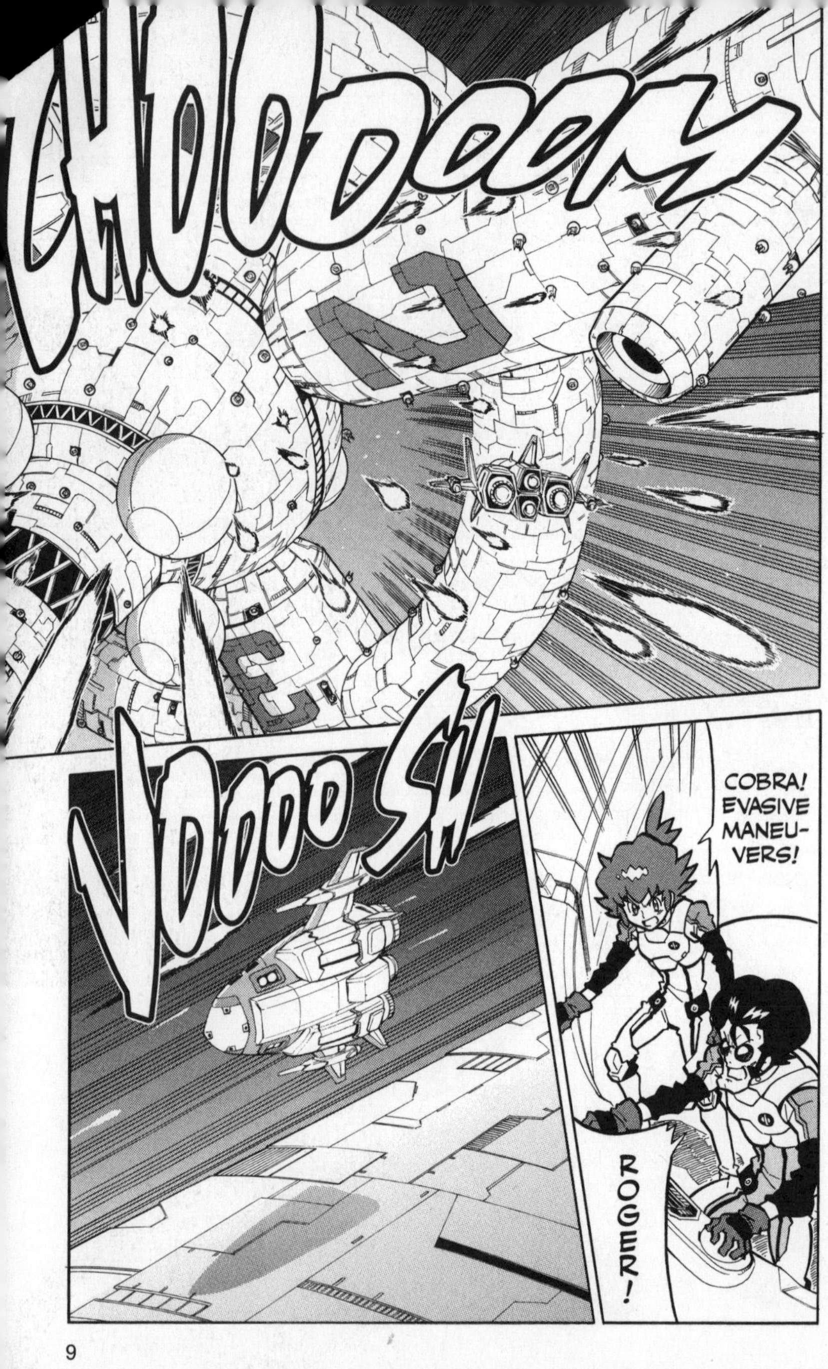
CHOOOOOM
COBRA! EVASIVE MANEU- VERS!
ROGER!
VOOOOSH

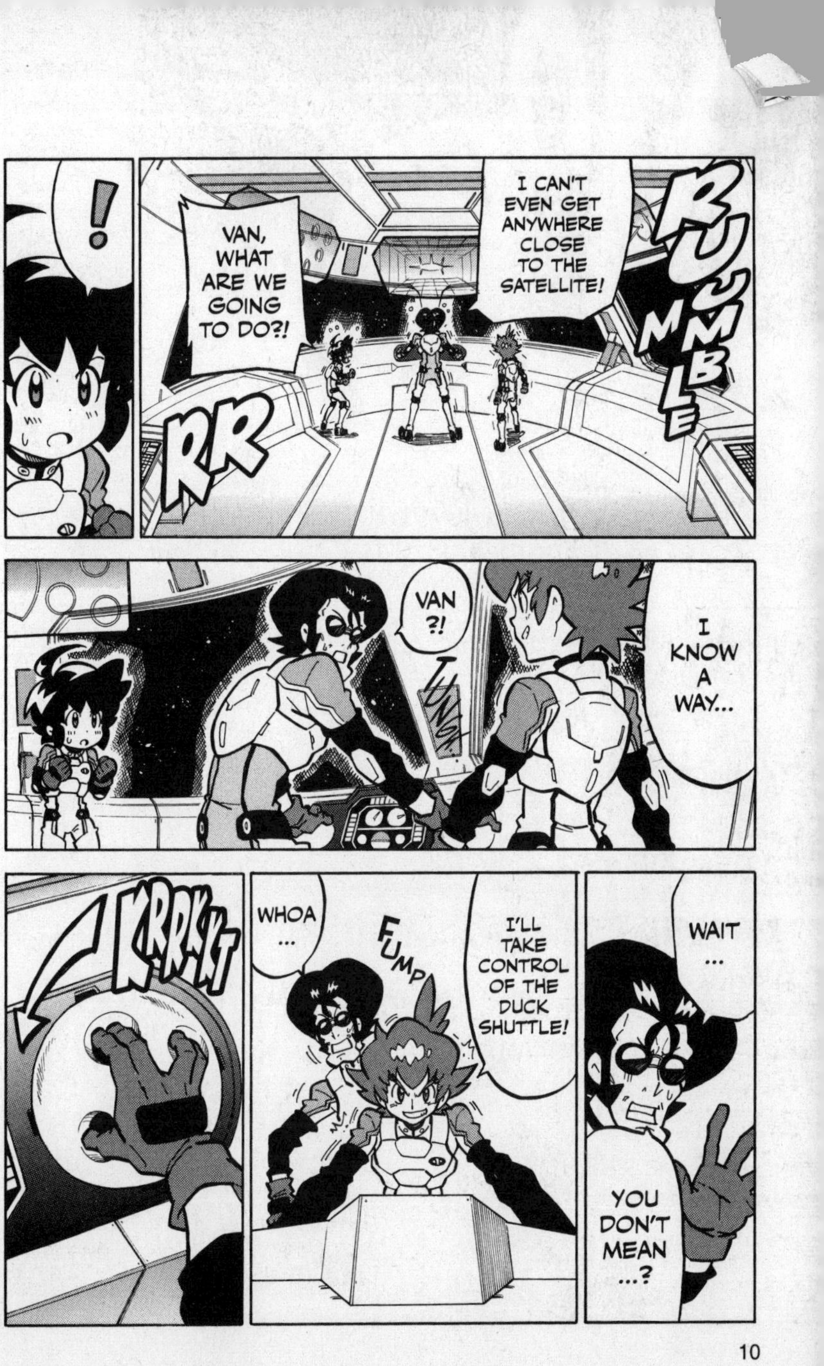
RUMMBLE
I CAN'T EVEN GET ANYWHERE CLOSE TO THE SATELLITE!
VAN, WHAT ARE WE GOING TO DO?!
RR
!
I KNOW A WAY...
VAN ?!
WAIT ...
YOU DON'T MEAN ...?
I'LL TAKE CONTROL OF THE DUCK SHUTTLE!
FUMP
WHOA ...

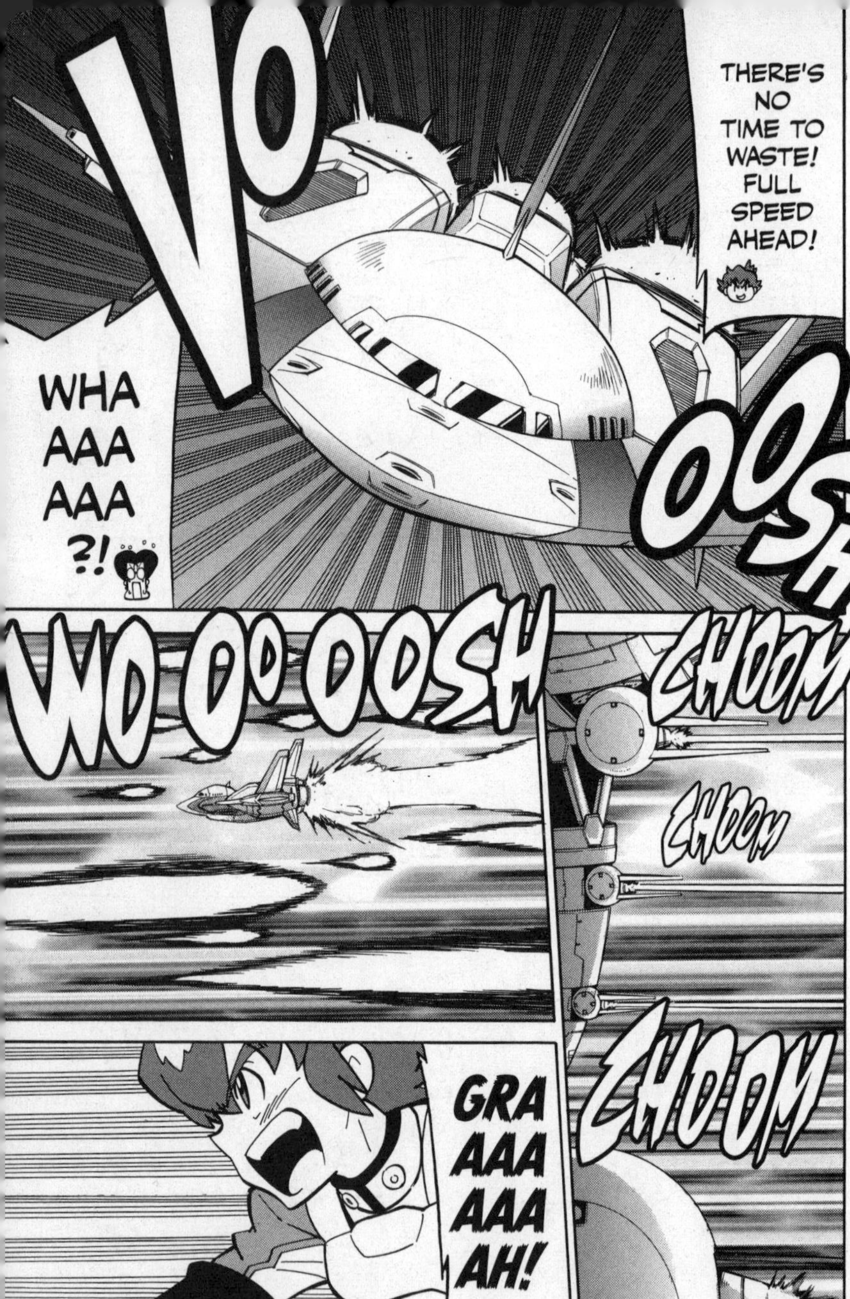
THERE'S NO TIME TO WASTE! FULL SPEED AHEAD!
VO
OOSH
WHAAAAAAA?!
CHOOM
CHOOM
CHOOM
WOOOOOSH
GRAAAAAAAAAAH!

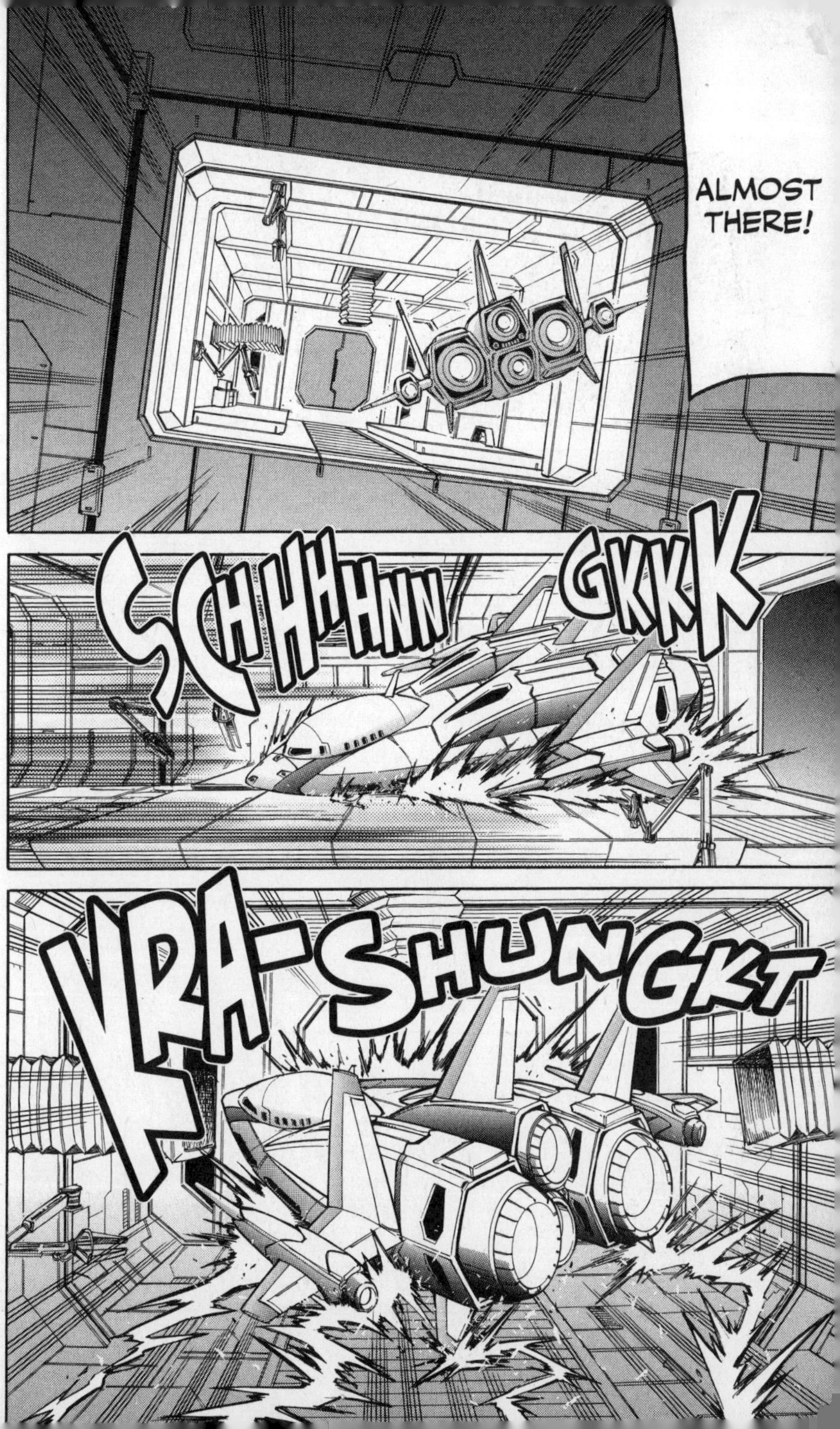
ALMOST THERE!
SCHHHHNN
GKKK
VRA-SHUNGKT

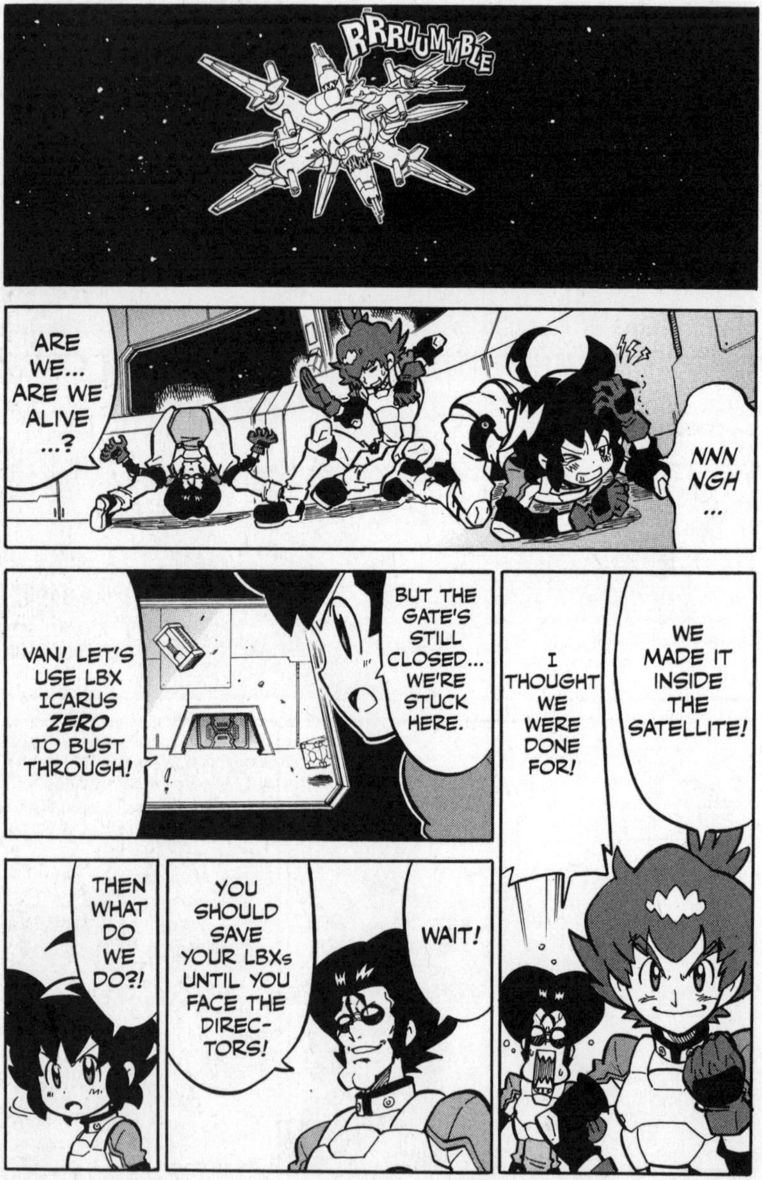

RRRUUMMBLE
NNNNGH...
ARE WE... ARE WE ALIVE...?
WE MADE IT INSIDE THE SATELLITE!
I THOUGHT WE WERE DONE FOR!
BUT THE GATE'S STILL CLOSED... WE'RE STUCK HERE.
VAN! LET'S USE LBX ICARUS ZERO TO BUST THROUGH!
WAIT!
YOU SHOULD SAVE YOUR LBXs UNTIL YOU FACE THE DIREC-TORS!
THEN WHAT DO WE DO?!

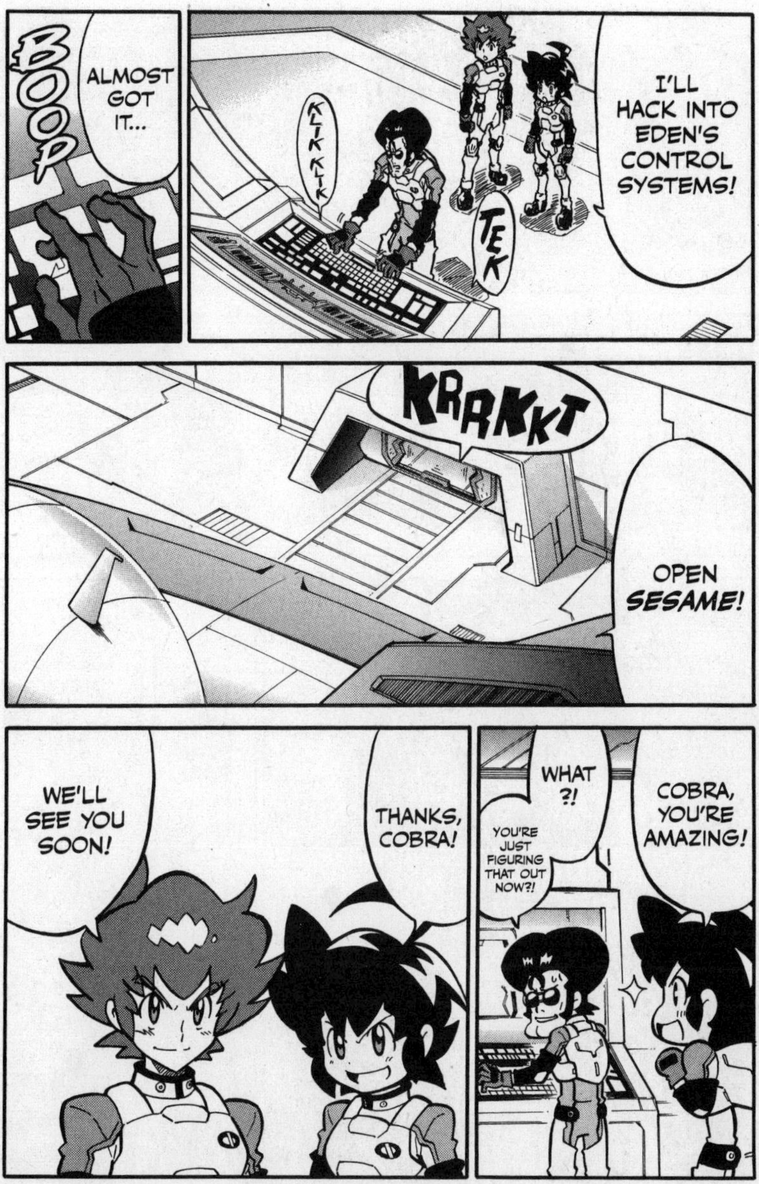
I'LL HACK INTO EDEN'S CONTROL SYSTEMS!
KLIK KLIK
TEK
ALMOST GOT IT...
BOOP
KRRKKT
OPEN SESAME!
COBRA, YOU'RE AMAZING!
WHAT?!
YOU'RE JUST FIGURING THAT OUT NOW?!
THANKS, COBRA!
WE'LL SEE YOU SOON!

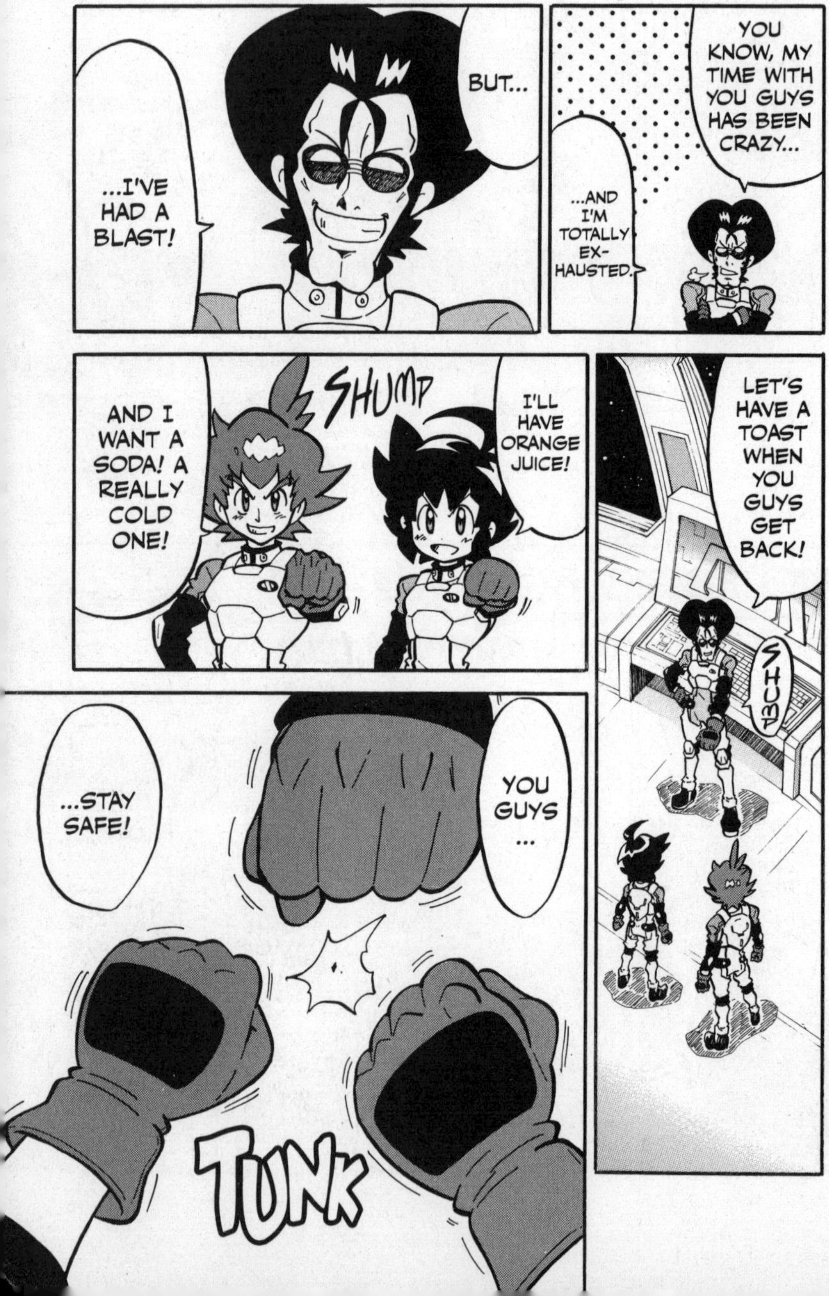
YOU KNOW, MY TIME WITH YOU GUYS HAS BEEN CRAZY...
...AND I'M TOTALLY EX-HAUSTED.
BUT...
...I'VE HAD A BLAST!
LET'S HAVE A TOAST WHEN YOU GUYS GET BACK!
SHUMP
I'LL HAVE ORANGE JUICE!
SHUMP
AND I WANT A SODA! A REALLY COLD ONE!
YOU GUYS ...
...STAY SAFE!
TUNK

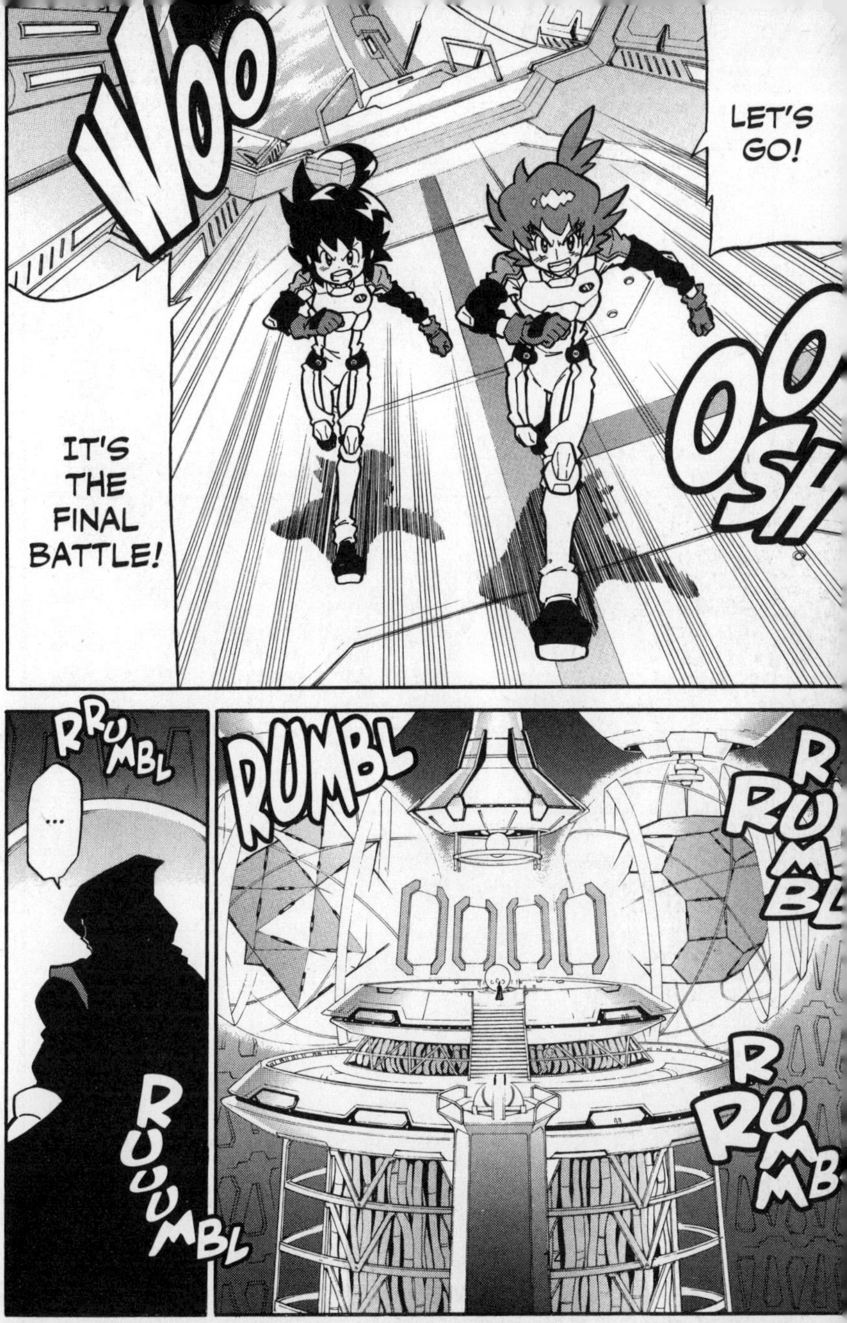
LET'S GO!
OOOSH
WOO
IT'S THE FINAL BATTLE!
RRUMBL
RRUMB
RUMBL
RRUMBL
...
RUUUMBL

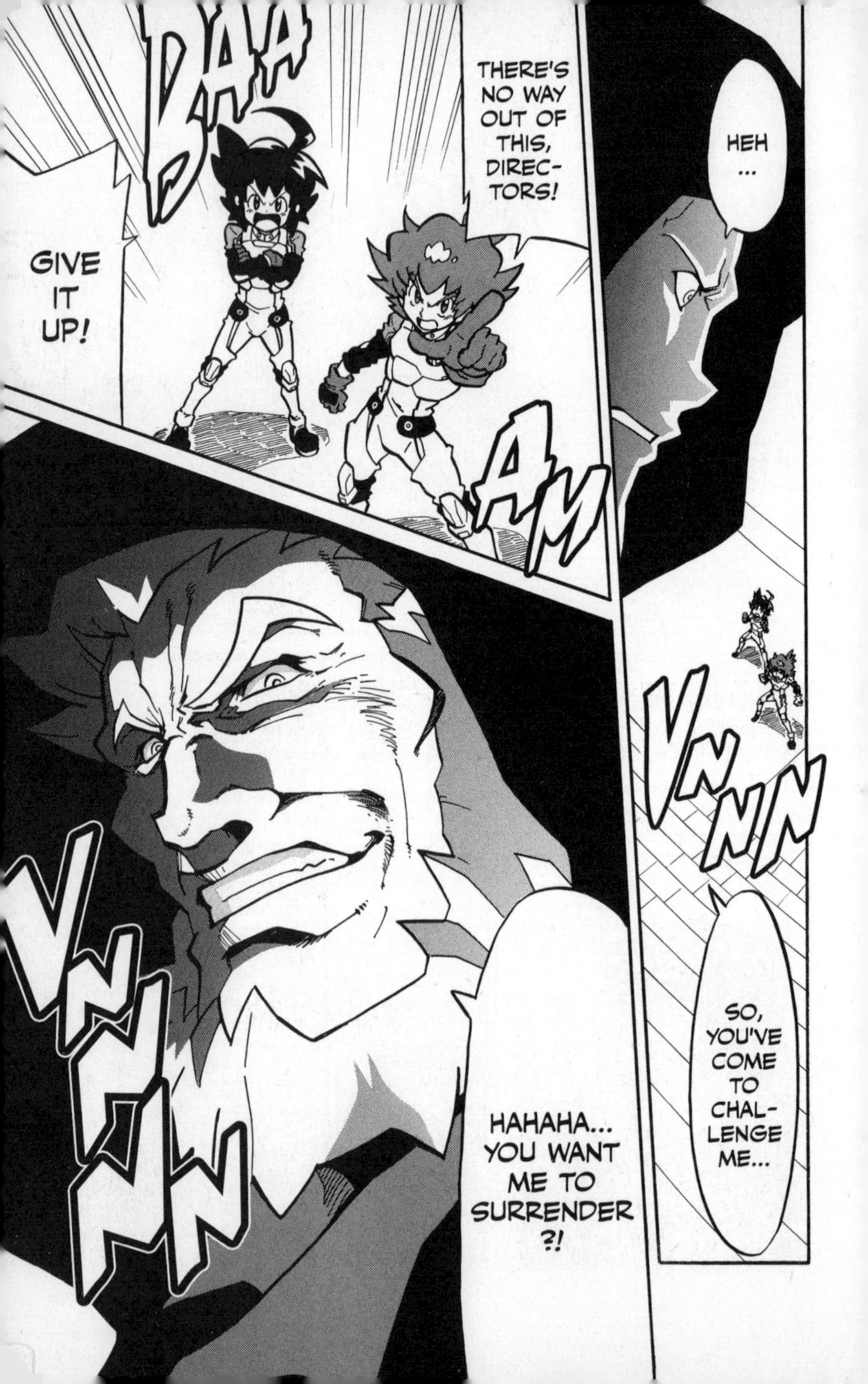
HEH ...
THERE'S NO WAY OUT OF THIS, DIREC-TORS!
DAA
GIVE IT UP!
AM
SO, YOU'VE COME TO CHAL-LENGE ME...
VNNNN
HAHAHA... YOU WANT ME TO SURRENDER ?!
VNNNN

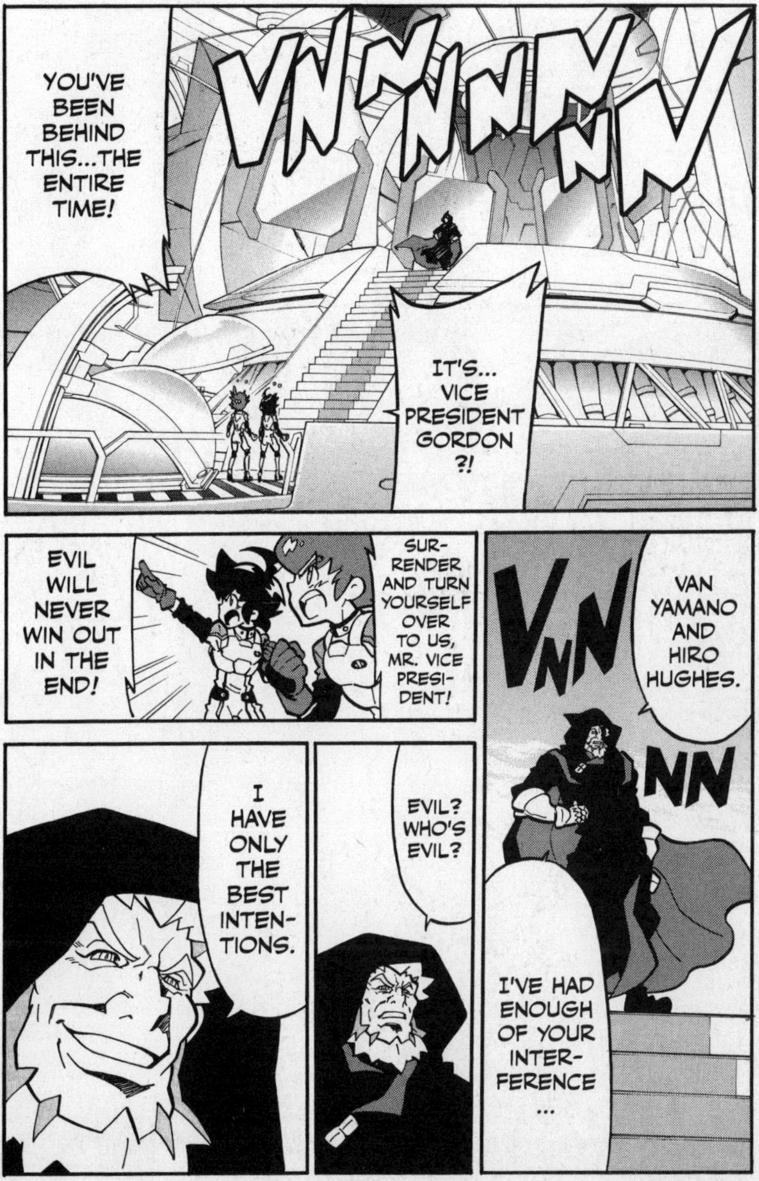
VNNNNNNNNNNN
IT'S... VICE PRESIDENT GORDON ?!
YOU'VE BEEN BEHIND THIS...THE ENTIRE TIME!
VNN
VAN YAMANO AND HIRO HUGHES.
NN
I'VE HAD ENOUGH OF YOUR INTER-FERENCE ...
SUR-RENDER AND TURN YOURSELF OVER TO US, MR. VICE PRESI-DENT!
EVIL WILL NEVER WIN OUT IN THE END!
EVIL? WHO'S EVIL?
I HAVE ONLY THE BEST INTEN-TIONS.

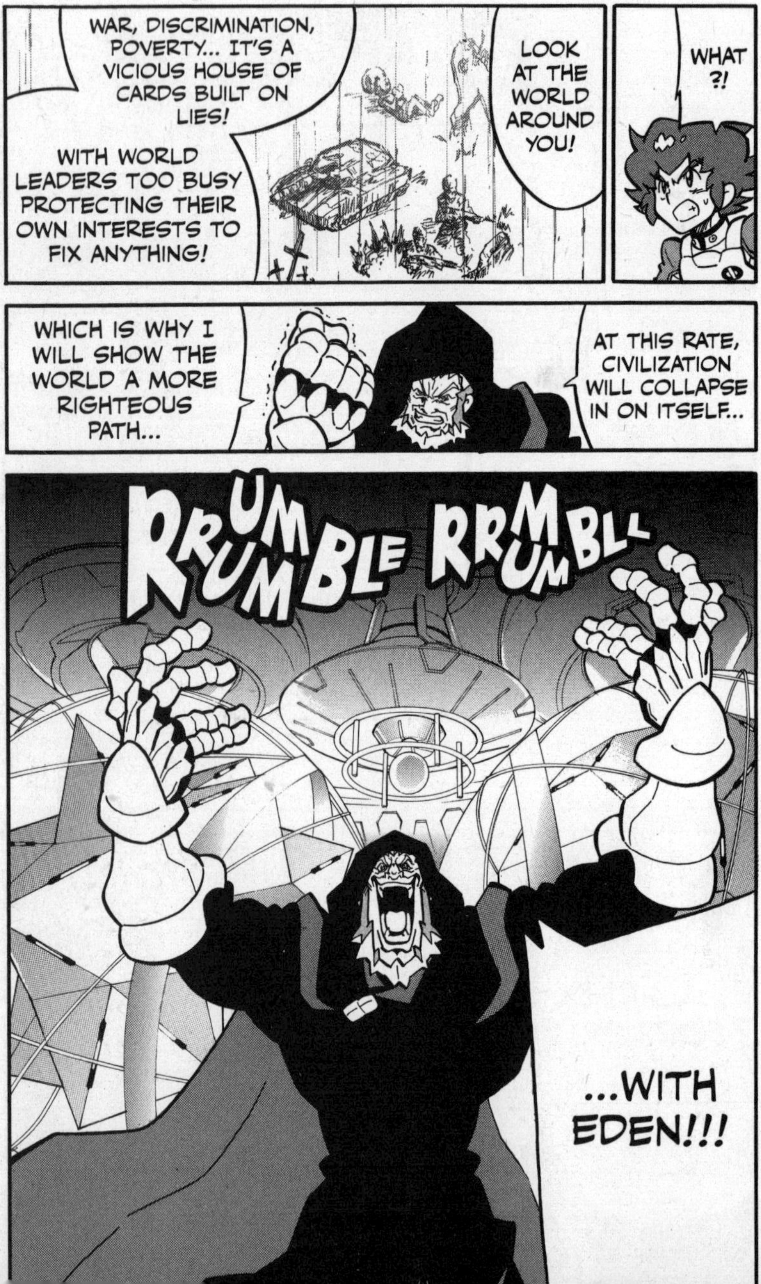
WHAT ?!
LOOK AT THE WORLD AROUND YOU!
WAR, DISCRIMINATION, POVERTY... IT'S A VICIOUS HOUSE OF CARDS BUILT ON LIES!
WITH WORLD LEADERS TOO BUSY PROTECTING THEIR OWN INTERESTS TO FIX ANYTHING!
AT THIS RATE, CIVILIZATION WILL COLLAPSE IN ON ITSELF...
WHICH IS WHY I WILL SHOW THE WORLD A MORE RIGHTEOUS PATH...
RRUMBLE RRUMBLL
...WITH EDEN!!!

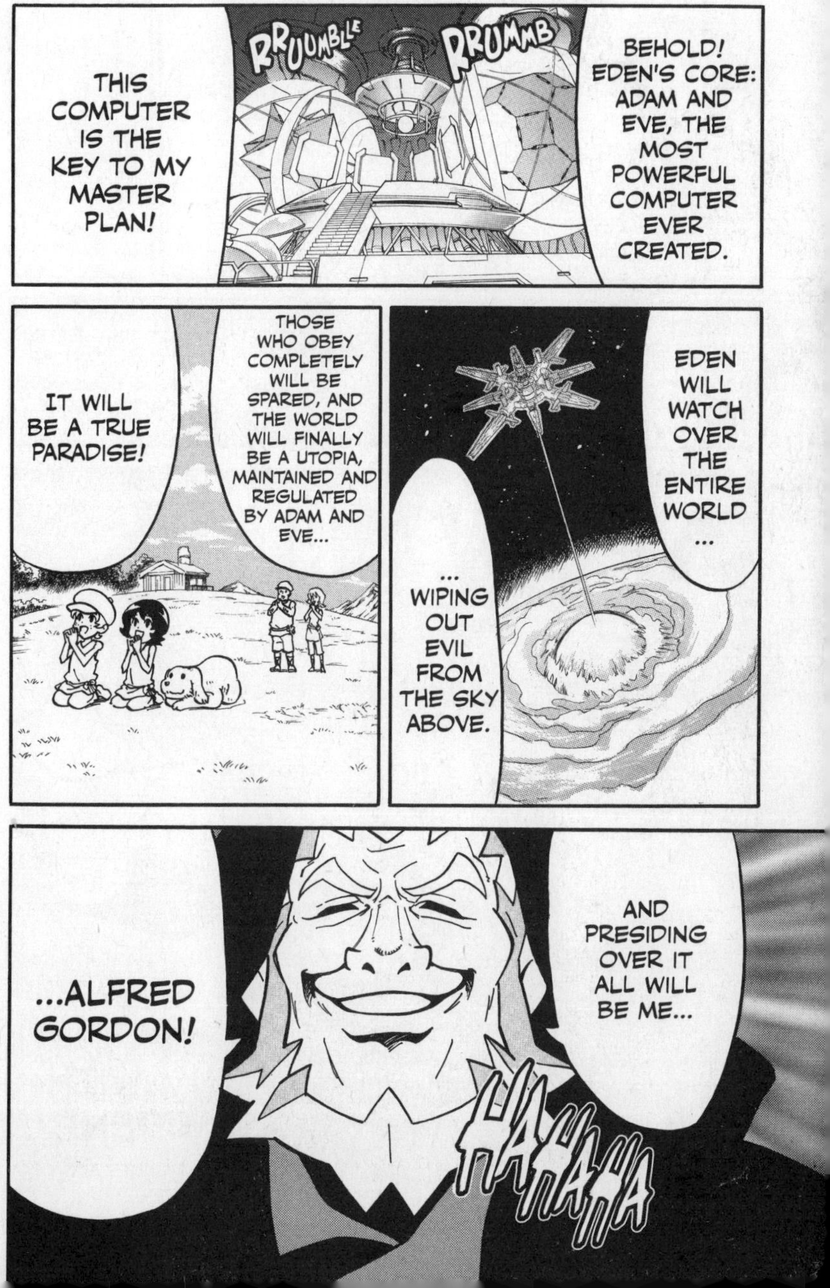
BEHOLD! EDEN'S CORE: ADAM AND EVE, THE MOST POWERFUL COMPUTER EVER CREATED.
RRUMMB
RRUUMBLLE
THIS COMPUTER IS THE KEY TO MY MASTER PLAN!
EDEN WILL WATCH OVER THE ENTIRE WORLD ...
... WIPING OUT EVIL FROM THE SKY ABOVE.
THOSE WHO OBEY COMPLETELY WILL BE SPARED, AND THE WORLD WILL FINALLY BE A UTOPIA, MAINTAINED AND REGULATED BY ADAM AND EVE...
IT WILL BE A TRUE PARADISE!
AND PRESIDING OVER IT ALL WILL BE ME...
...ALFRED GORDON!
HAHAHA

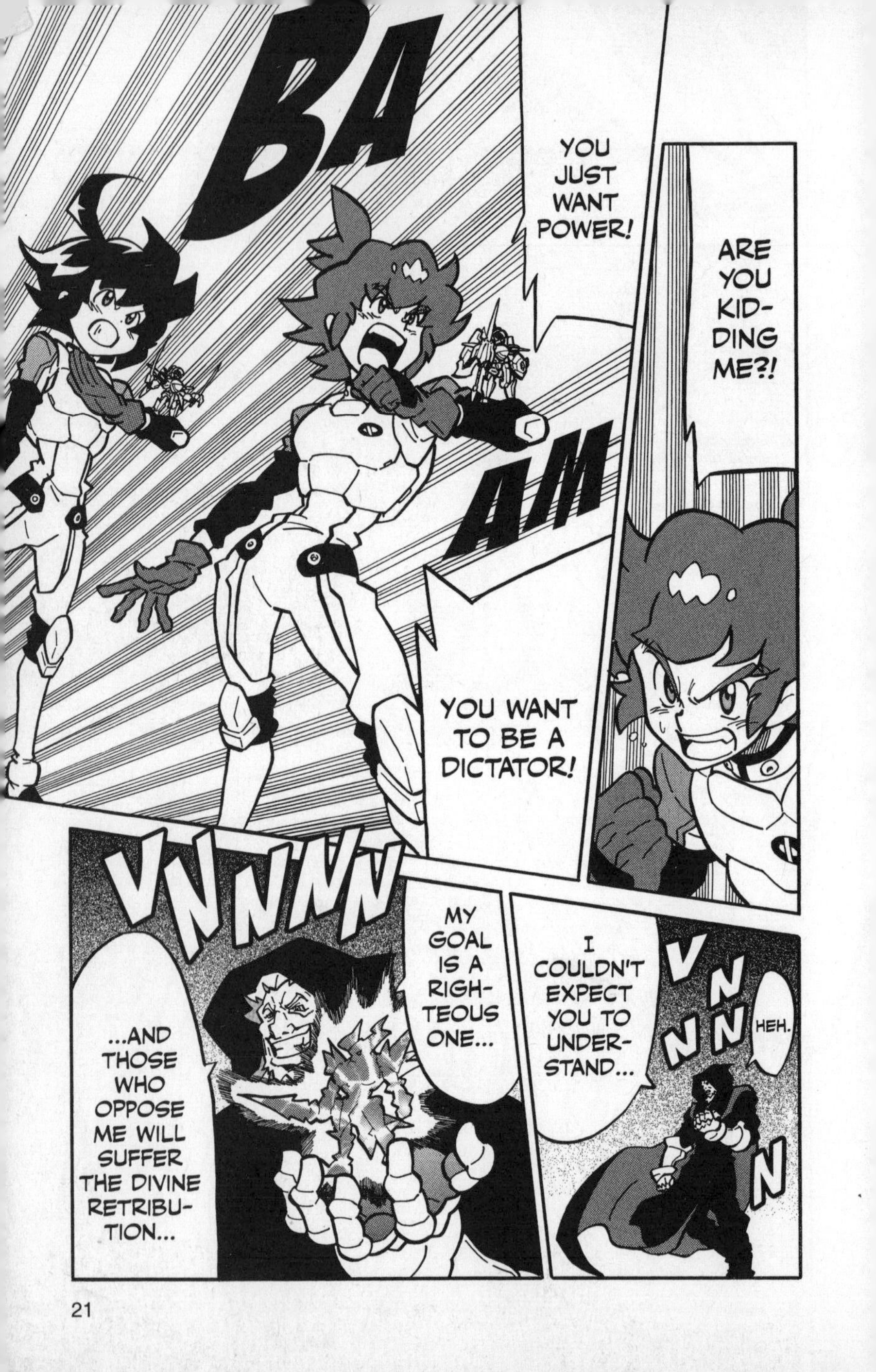
ARE YOU KID-DING ME?!
BA
AM
YOU JUST WANT POWER!
YOU WANT TO BE A DICTATOR!
VNNNN
HEH.
I COULDN'T EXPECT YOU TO UNDER-STAND...
VNNNNN
MY GOAL IS A RIGH-TEOUS ONE...
...AND THOSE WHO OPPOSE ME WILL SUFFER THE DIVINE RETRIBU-TION...

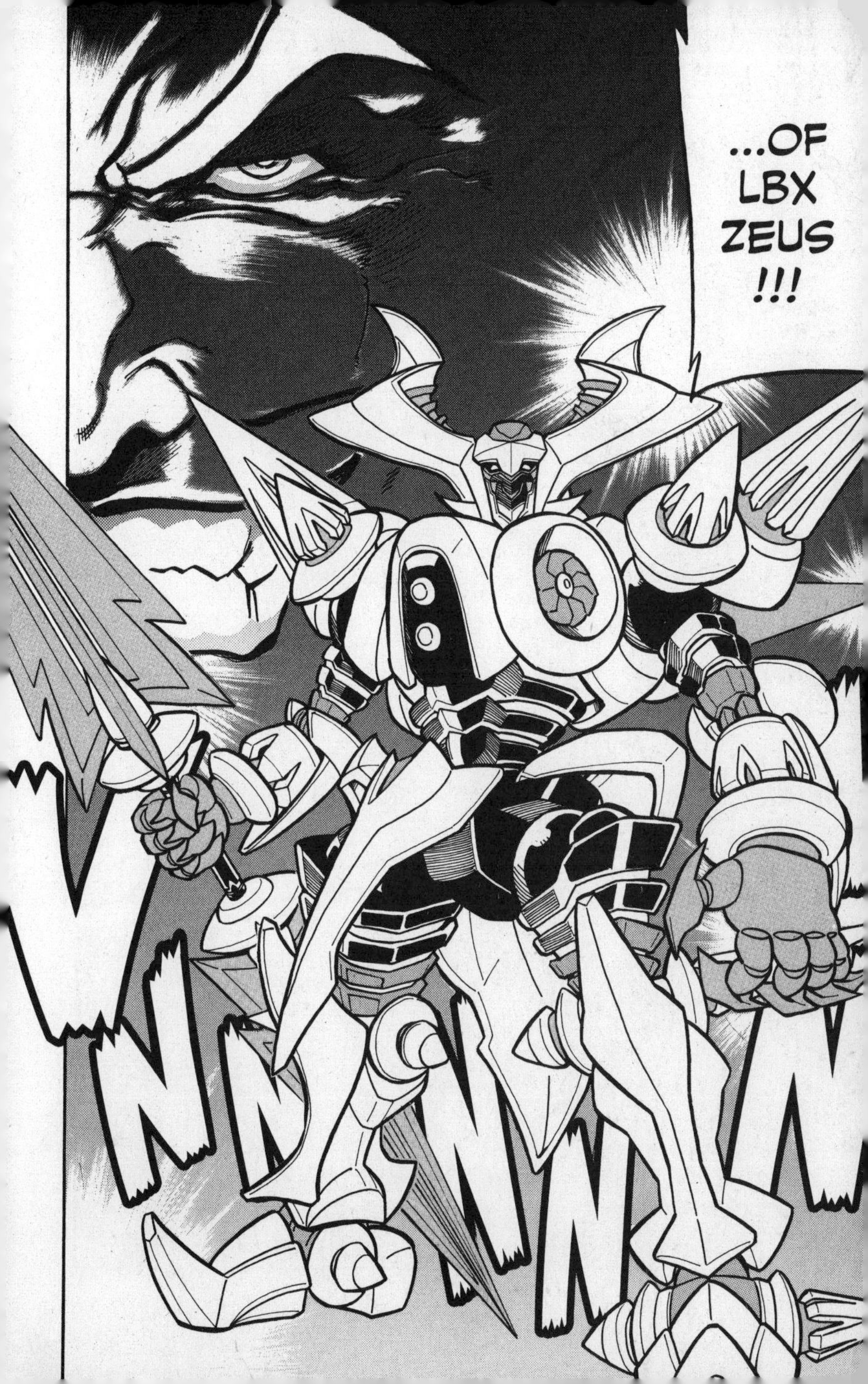
...OF LBX ZEUS !!!
VNNNNNNNNM

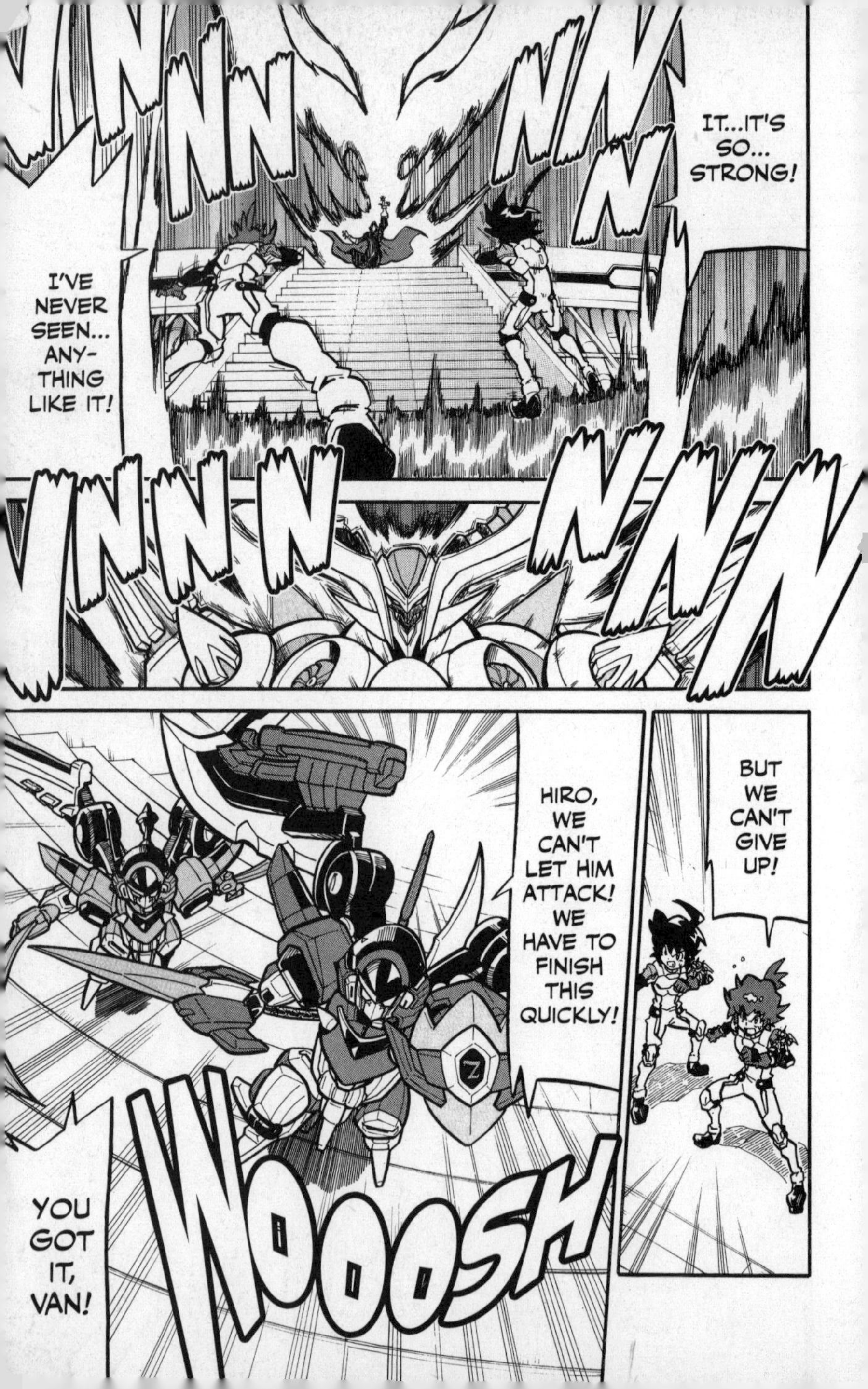
IT...IT'S SO... STRONG!
I'VE NEVER SEEN... ANY-THING LIKE IT!
BUT WE CAN'T GIVE UP!
HIRO, WE CAN'T LET HIM ATTACK! WE HAVE TO FINISH THIS QUICKLY!
YOU GOT IT, VAN!
WOOOSH

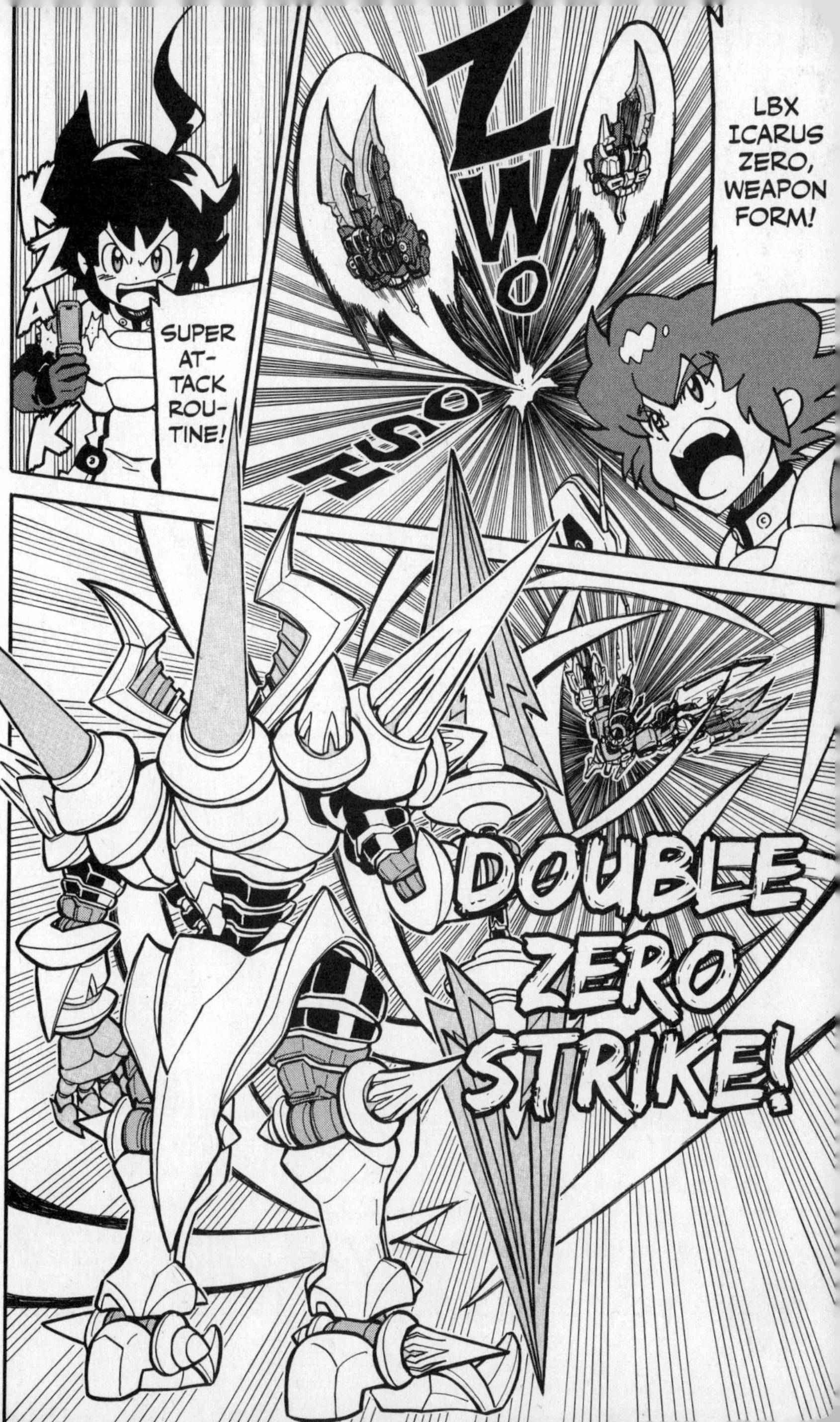
LBX ICARUS ZERO, WEAPON FORM!
ZWOOSH
KZAK
SUPER AT-TACK ROU-TINE!
DOUBLE ZERO STRIKE!

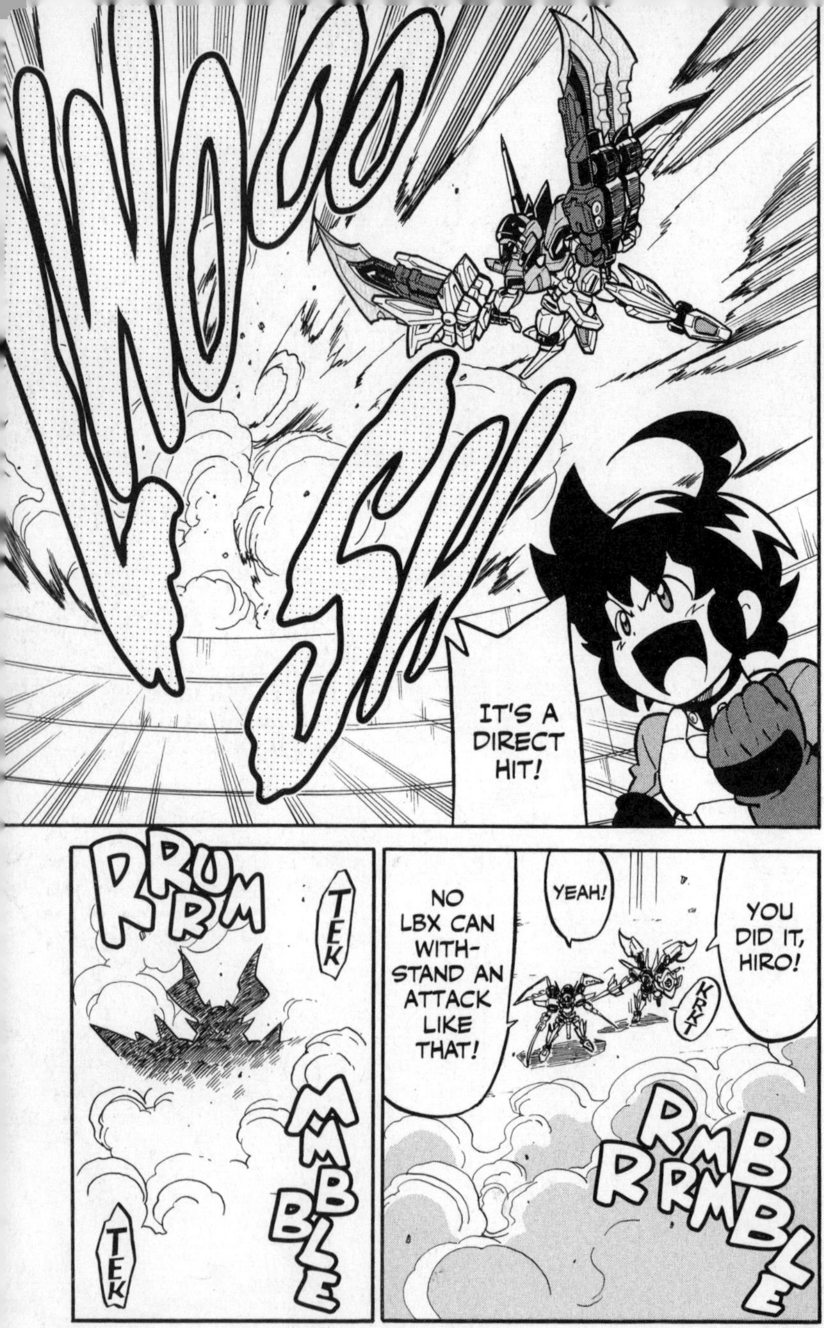
WOOOSH
IT'S A DIRECT HIT!
YOU DID IT, HIRO!
KRKT
YEAH!
NO LBX CAN WITH-STAND AN ATTACK LIKE THAT!
RMB RRMBLE
TEK
RRUM RM
MMBBLE
TEK

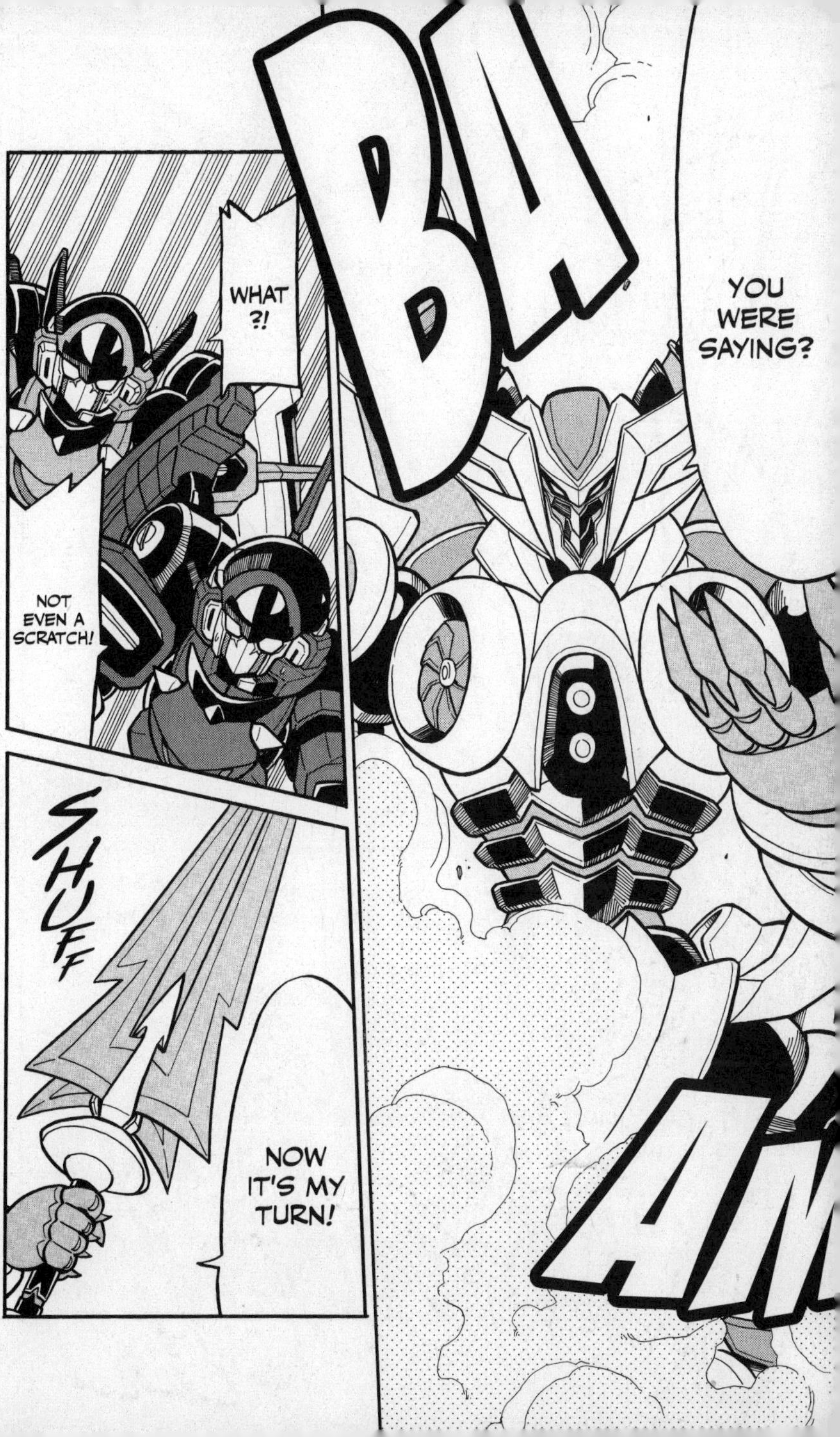
BA
YOU WERE SAYING?
AM
WHAT ?!
NOT EVEN A SCRATCH!
SHUFF
NOW IT'S MY TURN!

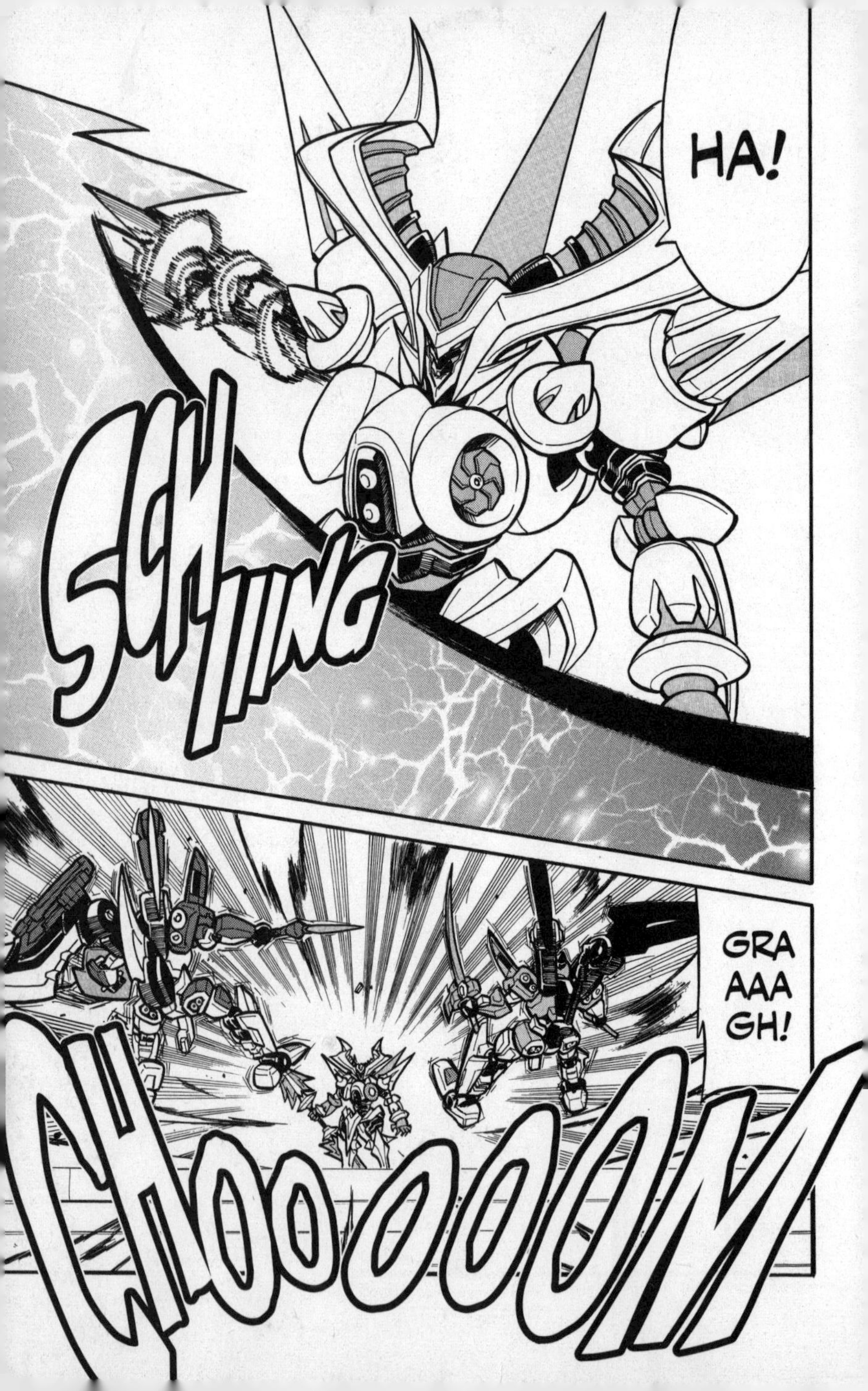
HA!
SCHIIING
GRAAAAGH!
CHOOOOM

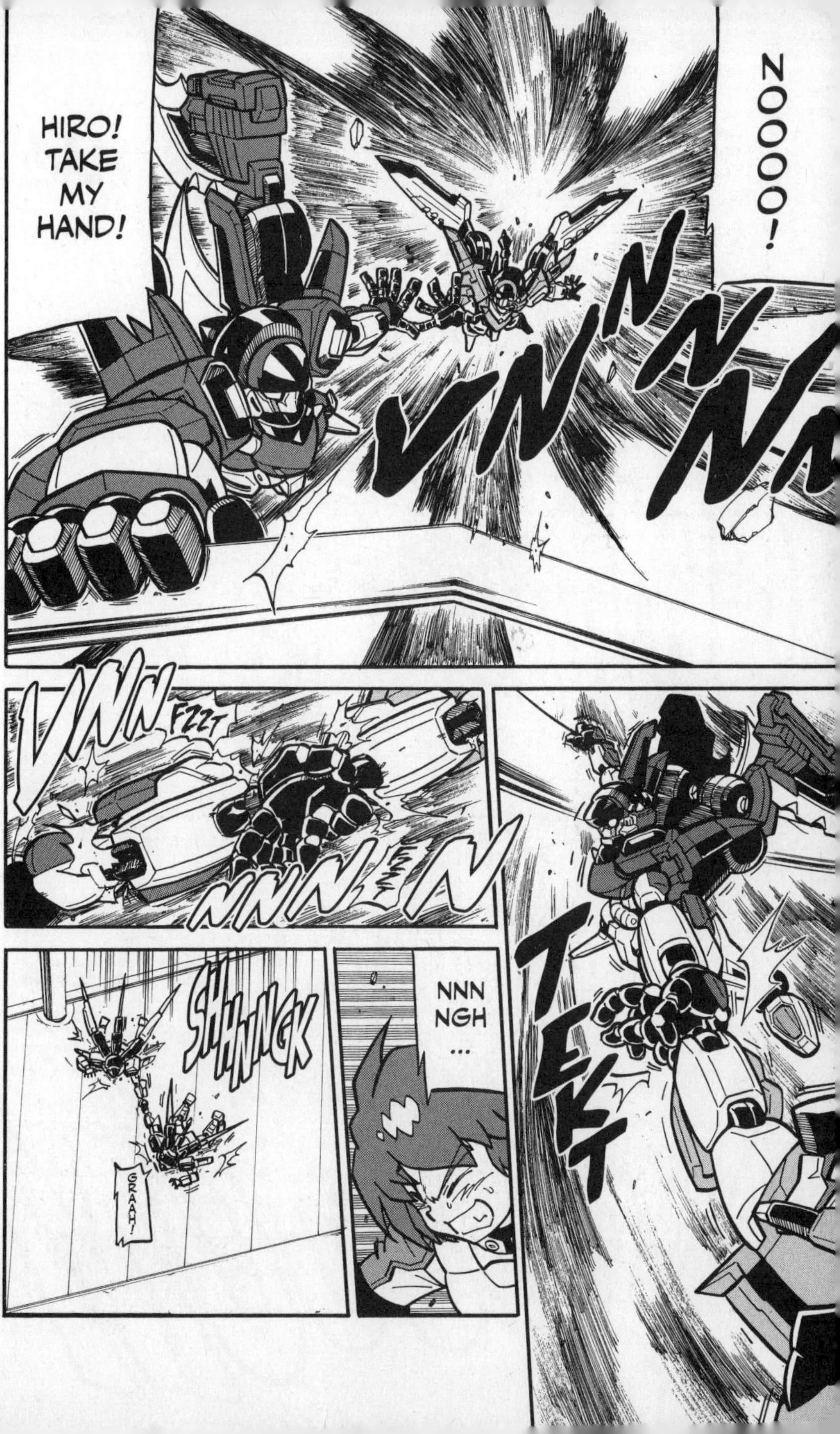
NOOOOO!
VNNNN
HIRO! TAKE MY HAND!
TEKT
VNN
FZZT
NNNN N
NNN NGH ...
SHHNNGK
GRAAH!

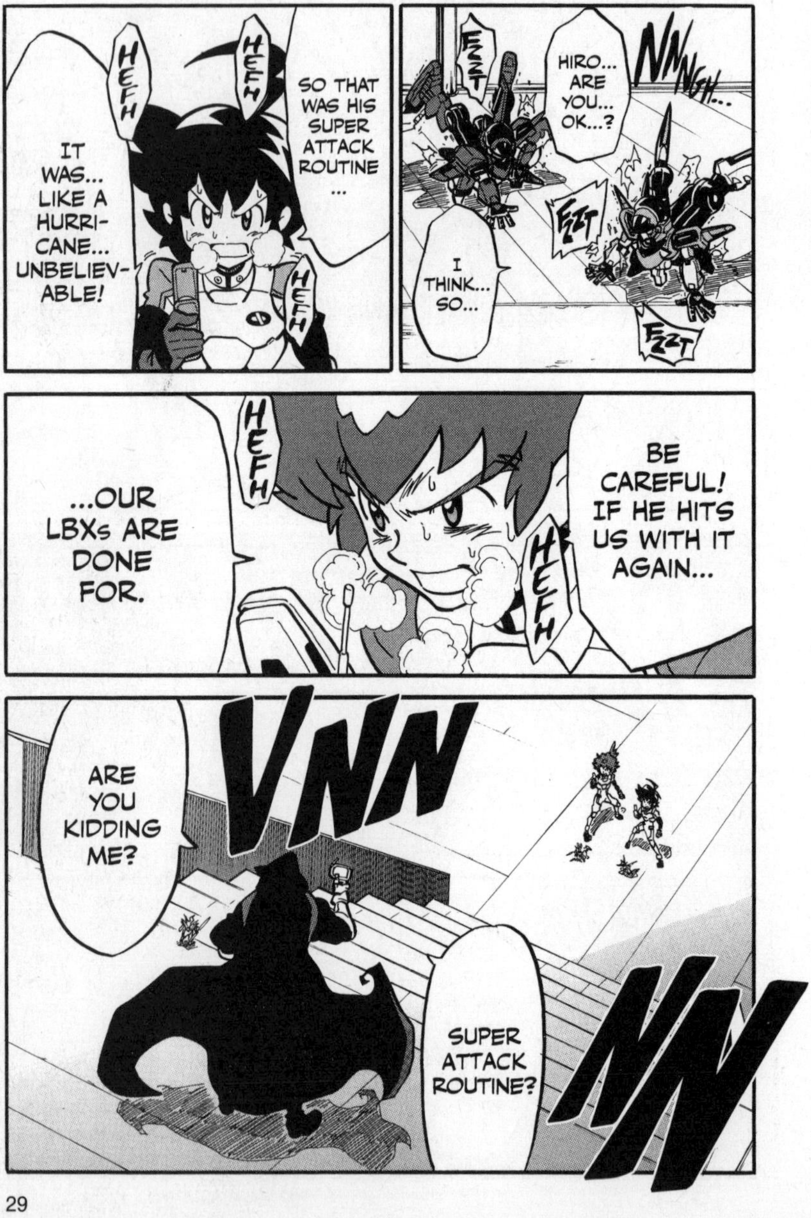
HIRO... ARE YOU... OK...?
NNNGH...
FZZT
I THINK... SO...
FZZT
FZZT
SO THAT WAS HIS SUPER ATTACK ROUTINE ...
HEFH
HEFH
IT WAS... LIKE A HURRI- CANE... UNBELIEV- ABLE!
HEFH
BE CAREFUL! IF HE HITS US WITH IT AGAIN...
HEFH
HEFH
...OUR LBXs ARE DONE FOR.
VNN
ARE YOU KIDDING ME?
MN
SUPER ATTACK ROUTINE?

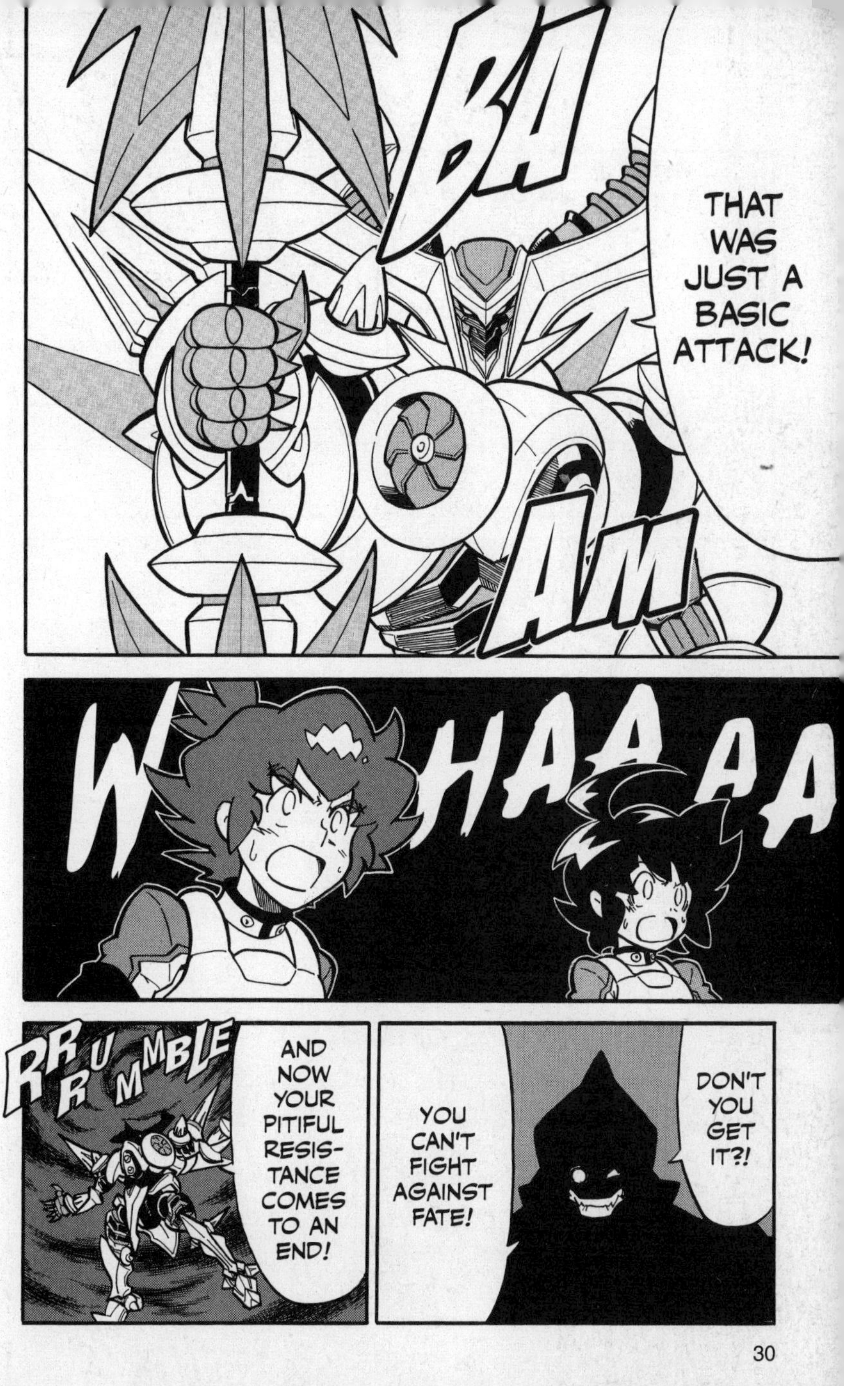
BAAM
THAT WAS JUST A BASIC ATTACK!
WHAAAA
DON'T YOU GET IT?!
YOU CAN'T FIGHT AGAINST FATE!
RRRUMMBLE
AND NOW YOUR PITIFUL RESIS-TANCE COMES TO AN END!

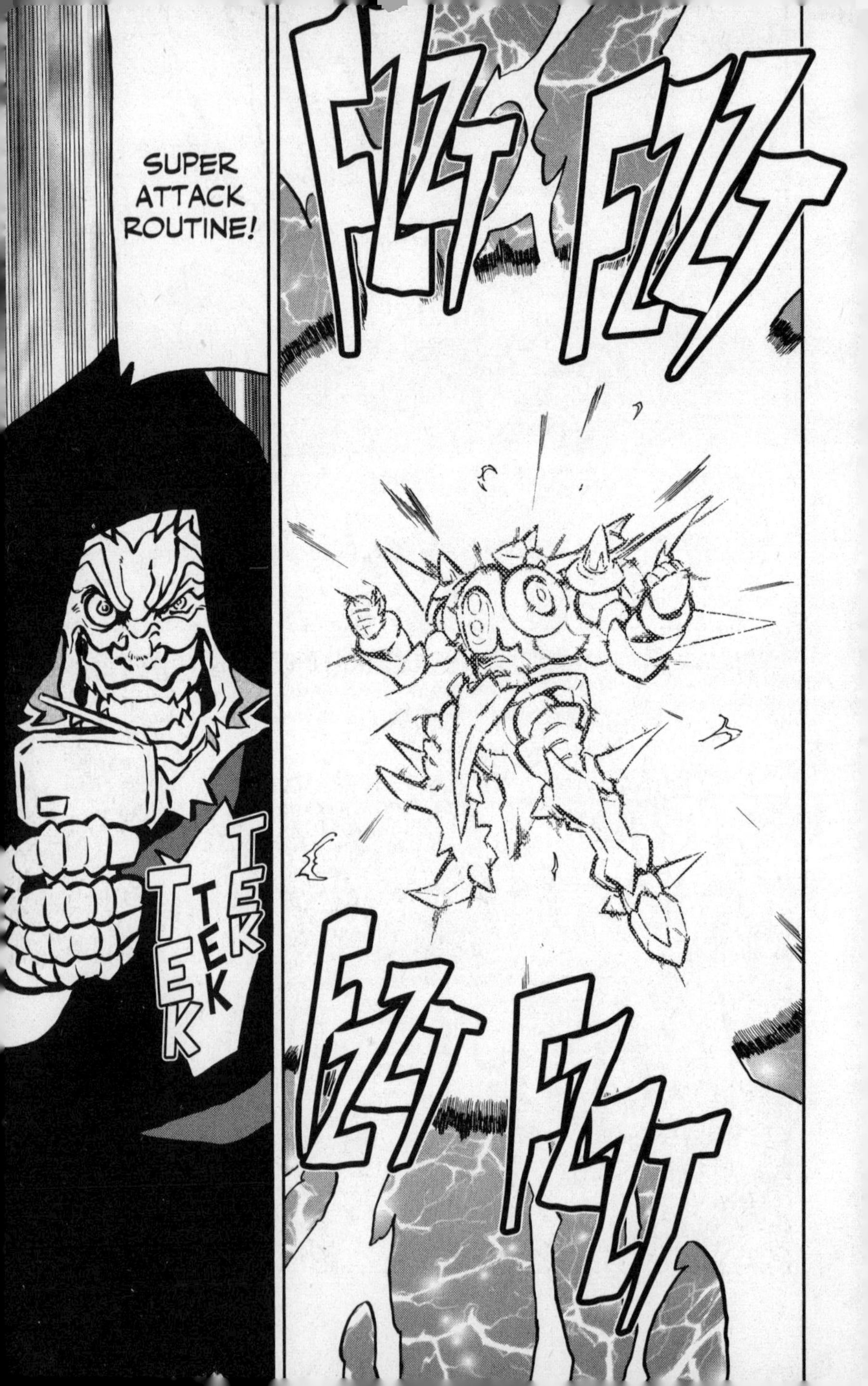
FZZT FZZT
FZZT FZZT
SUPER ATTACK ROUTINE!
TEEK TEEK TEEK

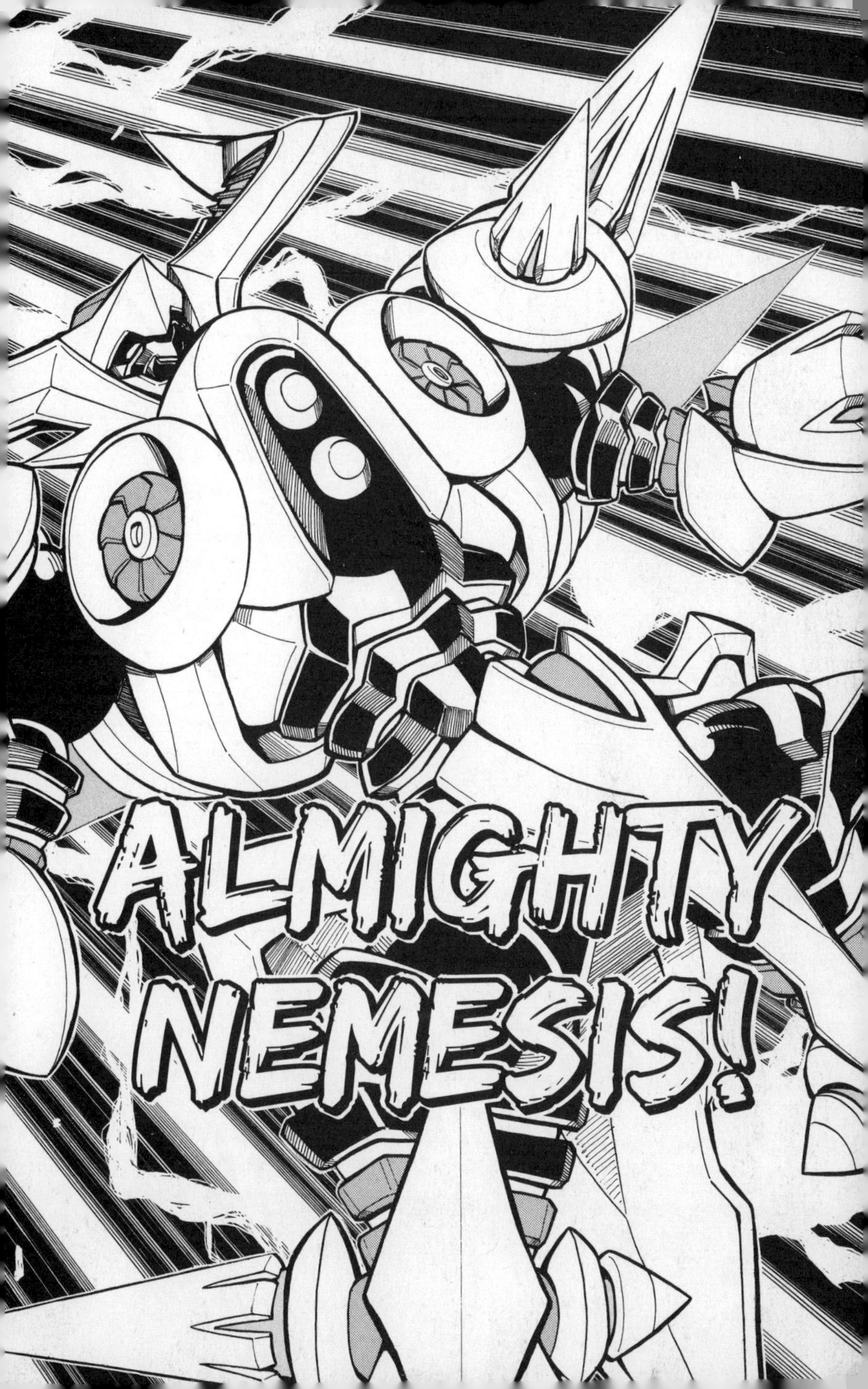
ALMIGHTY NEMESIS!

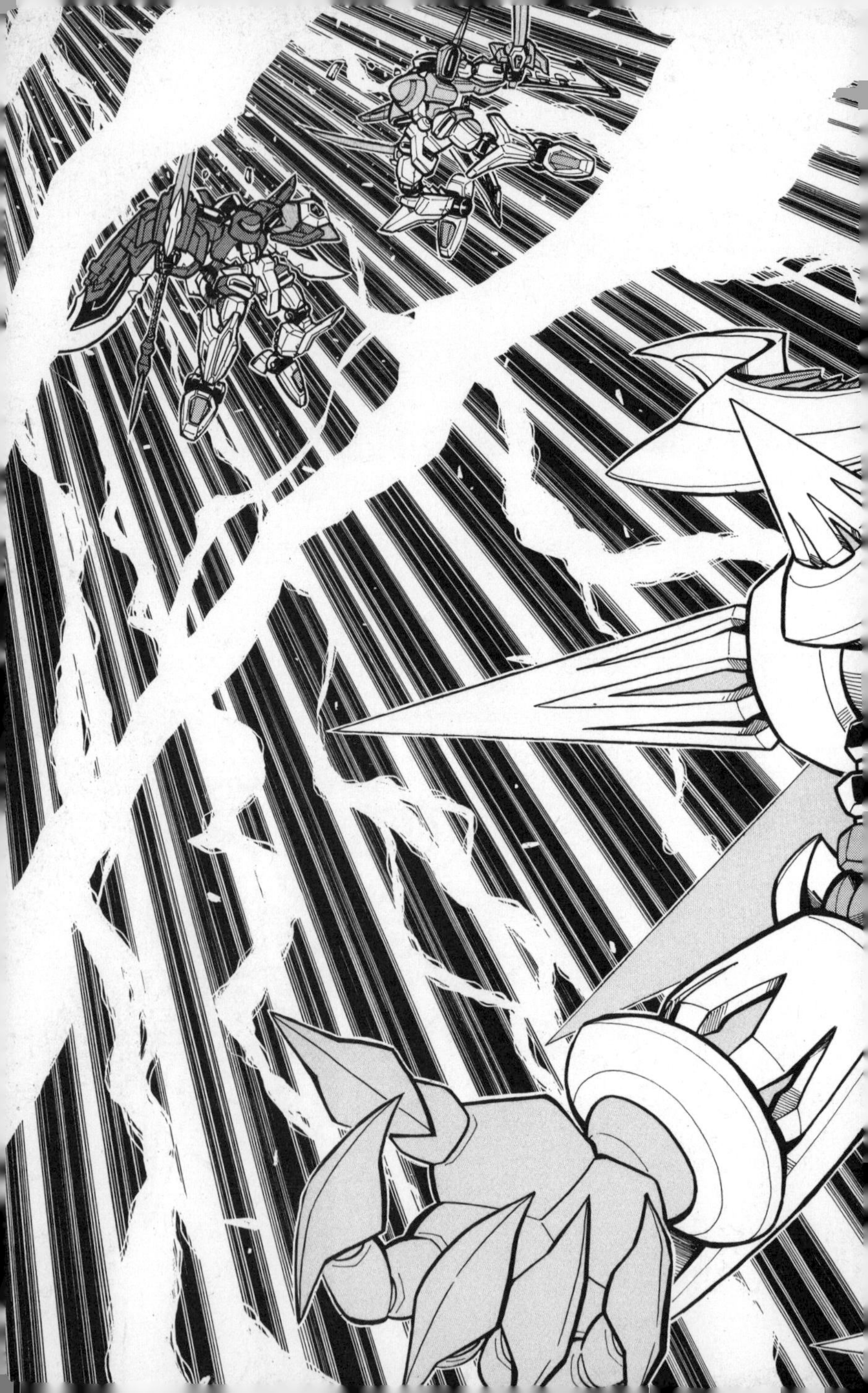

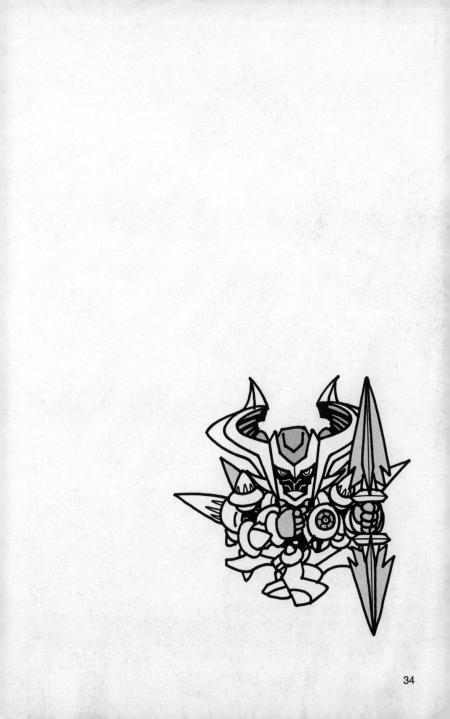

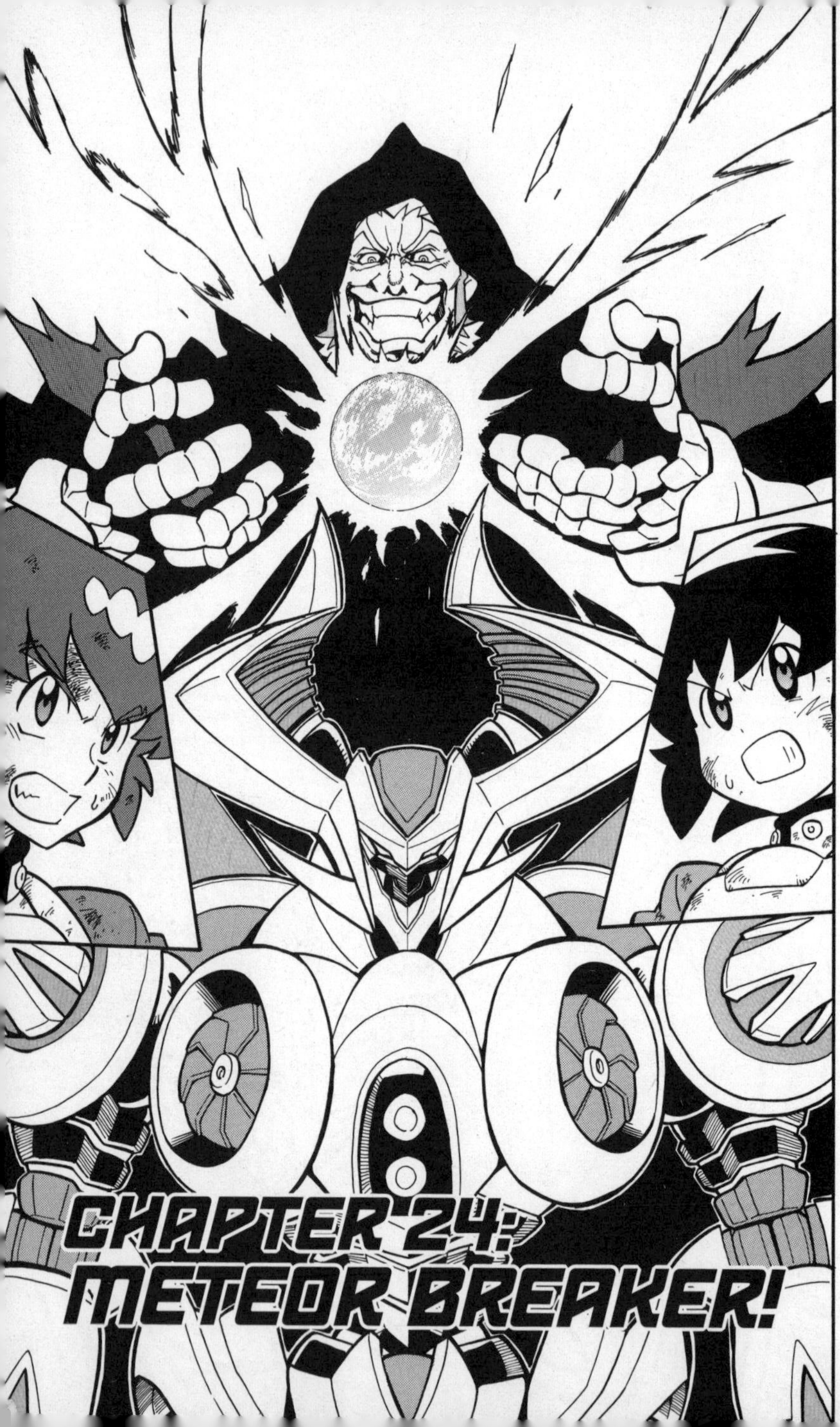
CHAPTER 24:
METEOR BREAKER!

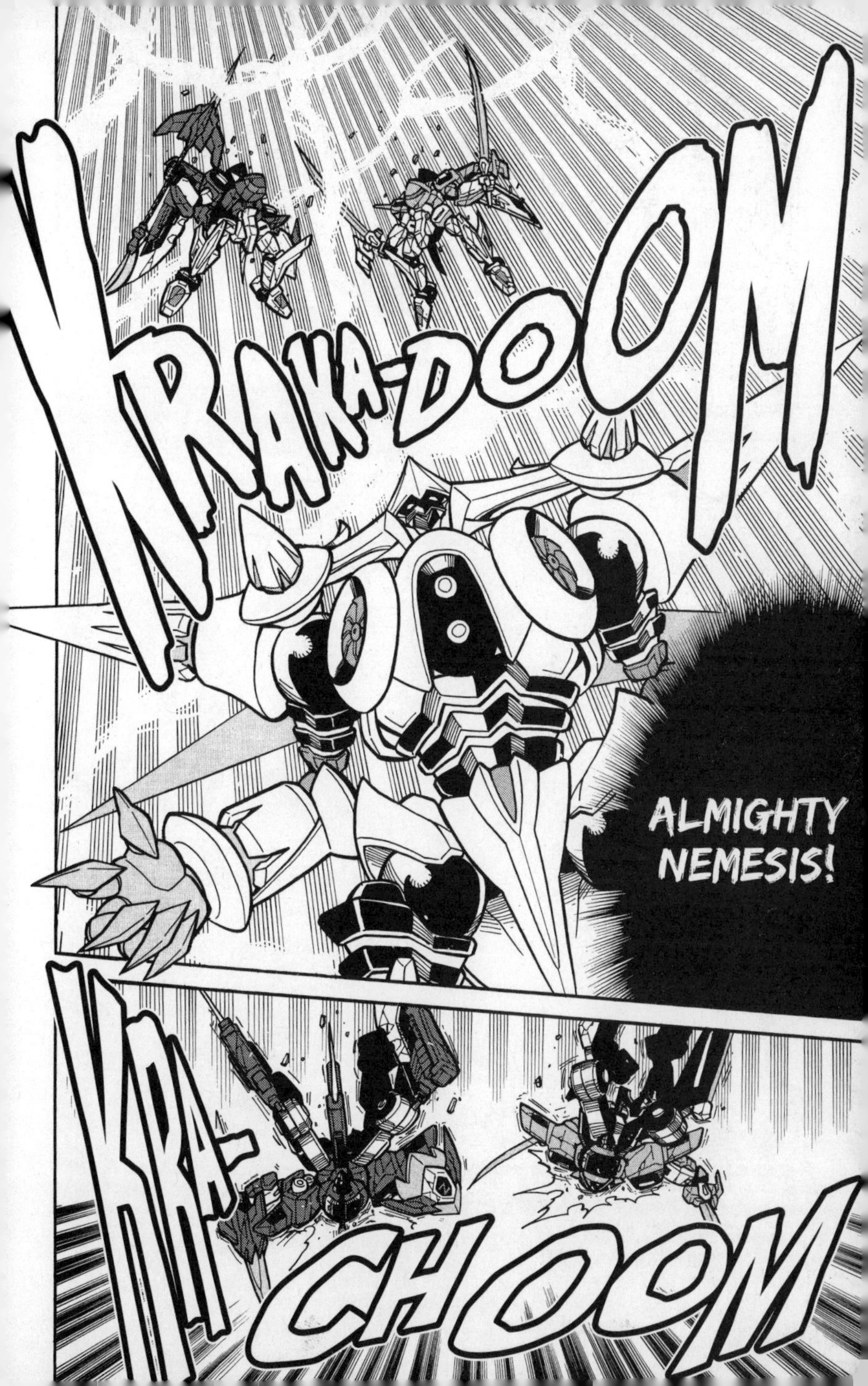
KRAKA-DOOM
ALMIGHTY NEMESIS!
KRA-CHOOM

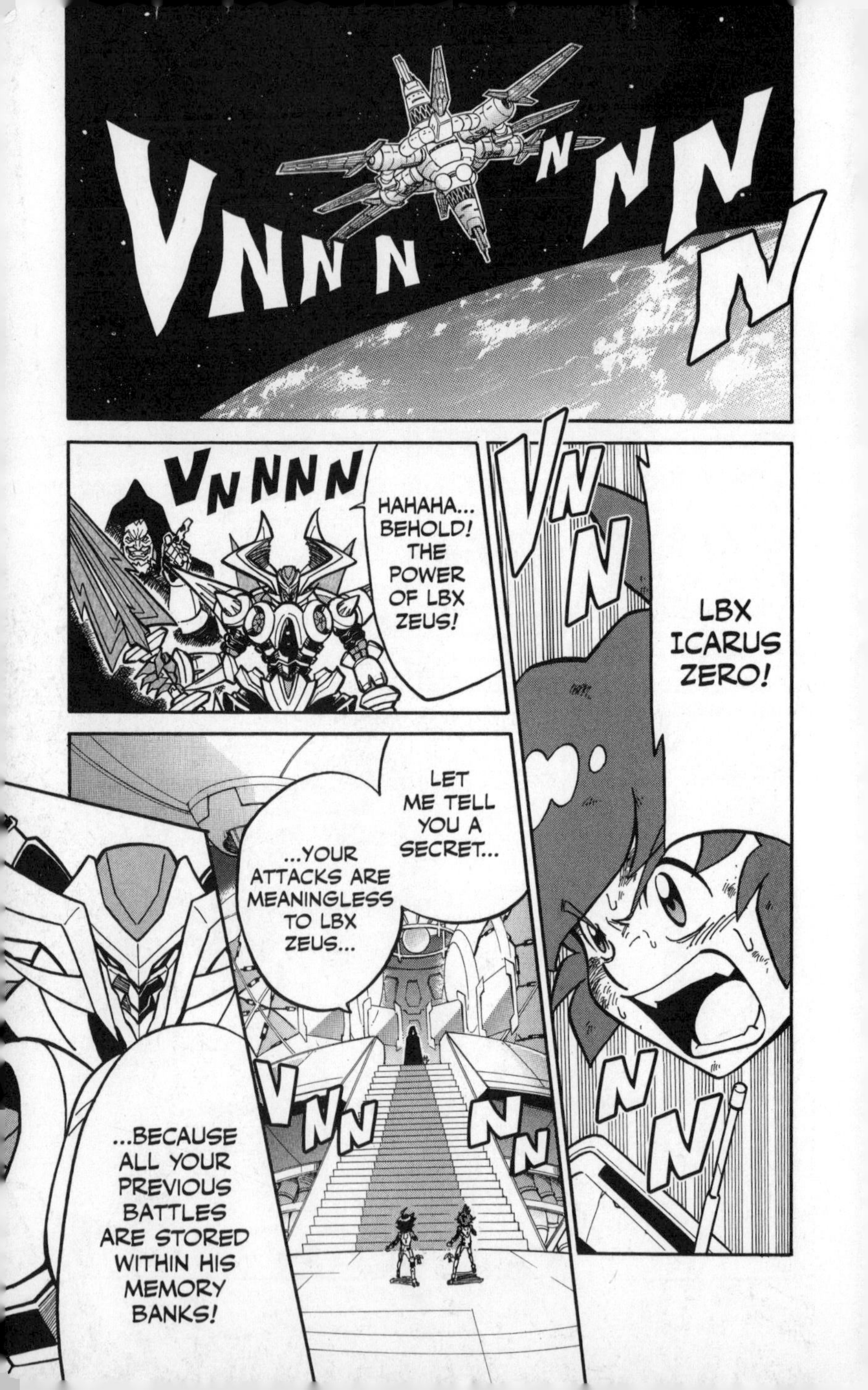
VNNNNNNNNN
VNN
LBX ICARUS ZERO!
NNNN
VNNNN
HAHAHA... BEHOLD! THE POWER OF LBX ZEUS!
LET ME TELL YOU A SECRET...
...YOUR ATTACKS ARE MEANINGLESS TO LBX ZEUS...
VNN
NN
...BECAUSE ALL YOUR PREVIOUS BATTLES ARE STORED WITHIN HIS MEMORY BANKS!

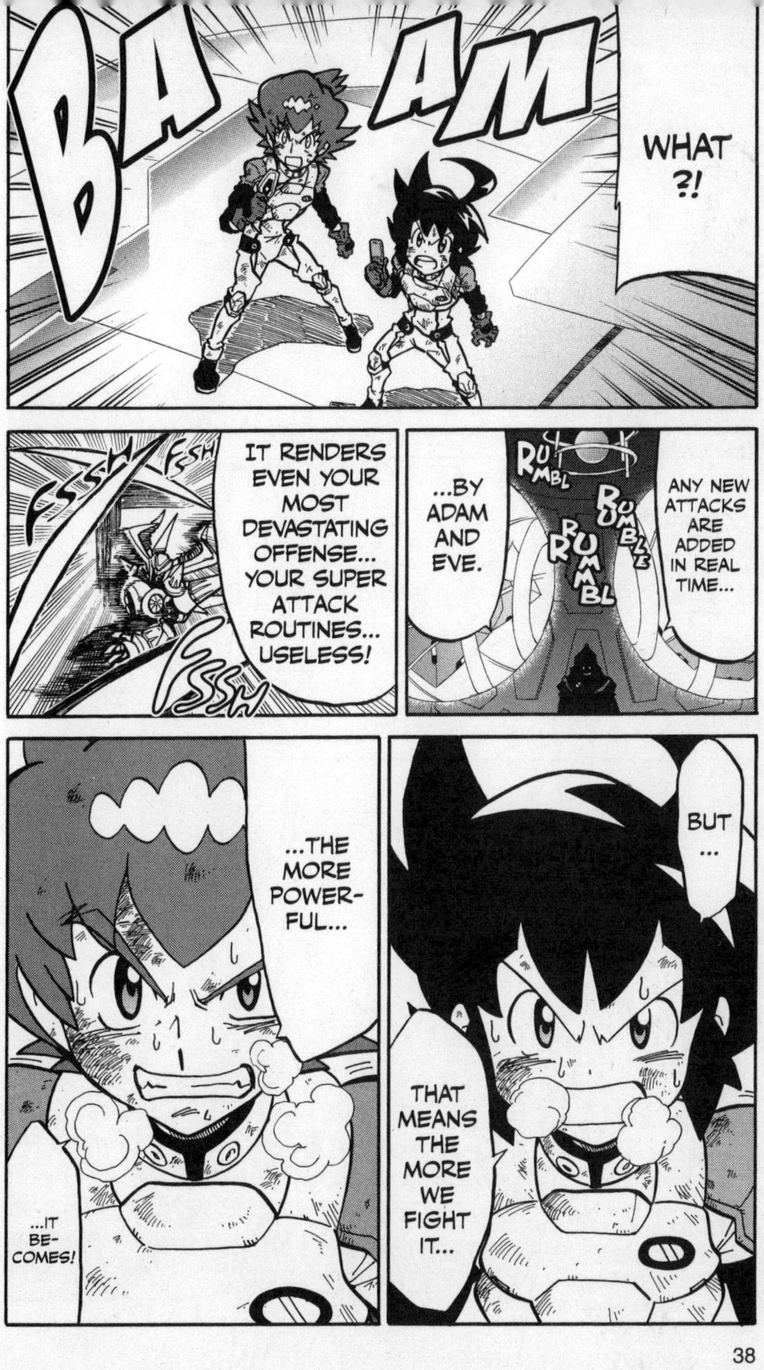
BA
AM
WHAT ?!
RUMBL
RUMBLE
RUMMBL
ANY NEW ATTACKS ARE ADDED IN REAL TIME...
...BY ADAM AND EVE.
FSSH
FSSH
IT RENDERS EVEN YOUR MOST DEVASTATING OFFENSE... YOUR SUPER ATTACK ROUTINES... USELESS!
FSSH
BUT...
THAT MEANS THE MORE WE FIGHT IT...
...THE MORE POWER-FUL...
...IT BE-COMES!

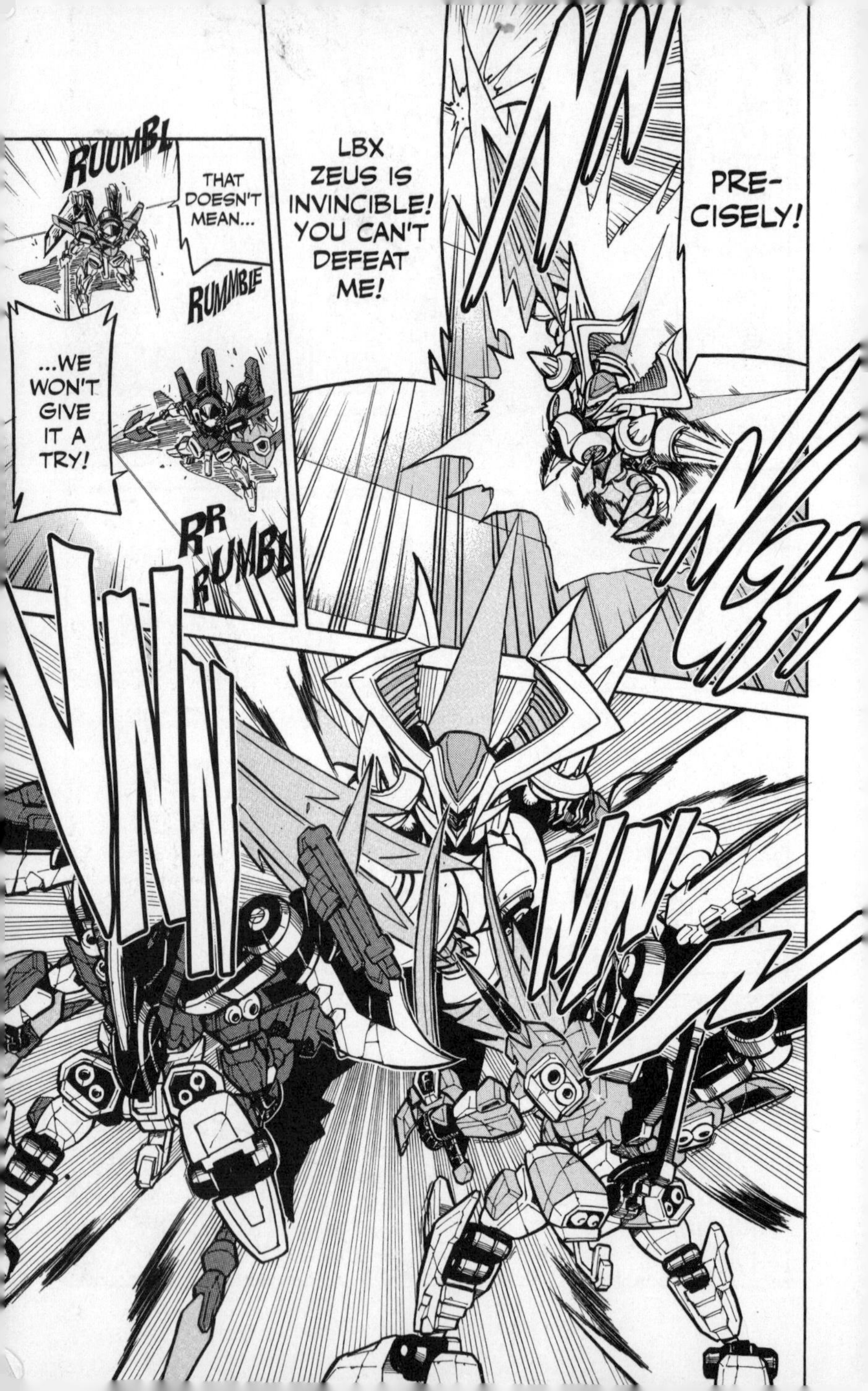
PRE-CISELY!
LBX ZEUS IS INVINCIBLE! YOU CAN'T DEFEAT ME!
RUUMBL
THAT DOESN'T MEAN...
RUMMBLE
...WE WON'T GIVE IT A TRY!
RR RUMBL

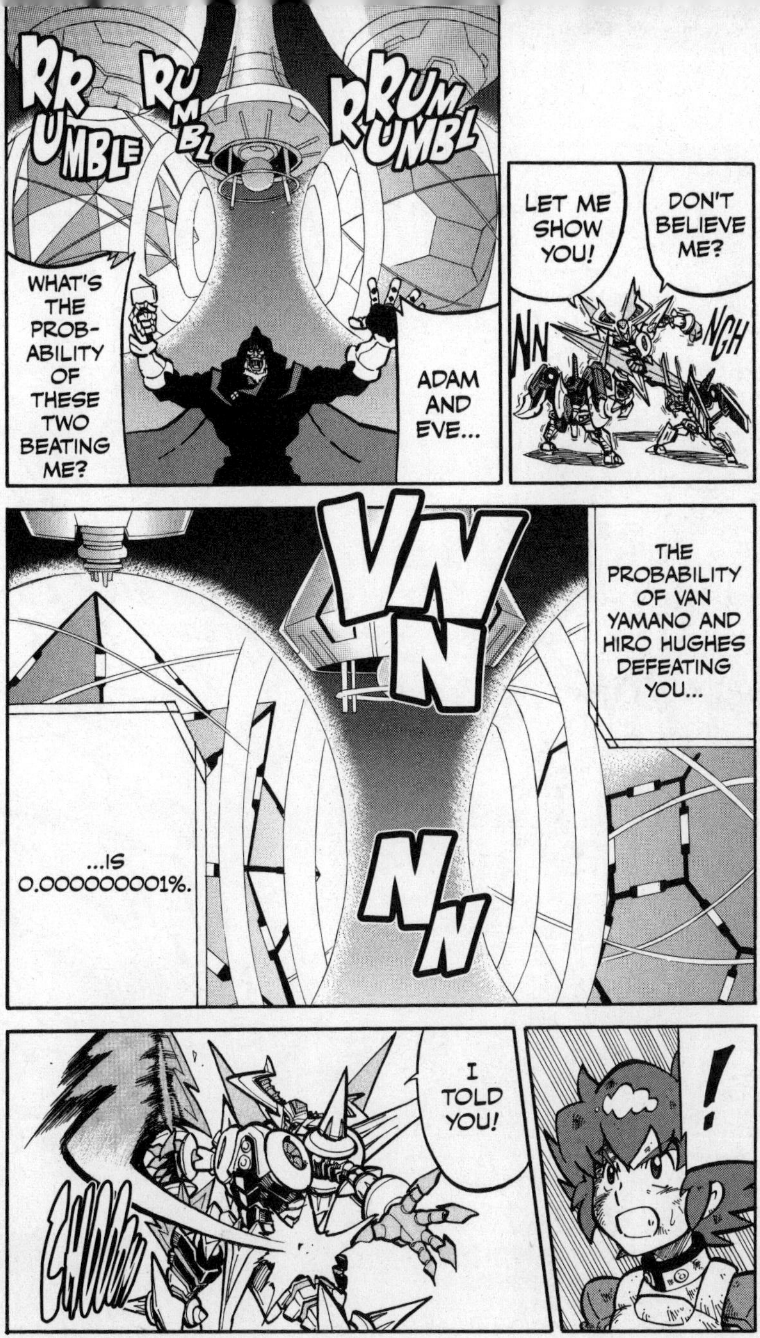
DON'T BELIEVE ME?
LET ME SHOW YOU!
NGH
NN
RRUM RUMBL
RUMBL
RRUMBLE
ADAM AND EVE...
WHAT'S THE PROBABILITY OF THESE TWO BEATING ME?
THE PROBABILITY OF VAN YAMANO AND HIRO HUGHES DEFEATING YOU...
VNN
NNN
...IS 0.000000001%.
!
I TOLD YOU!

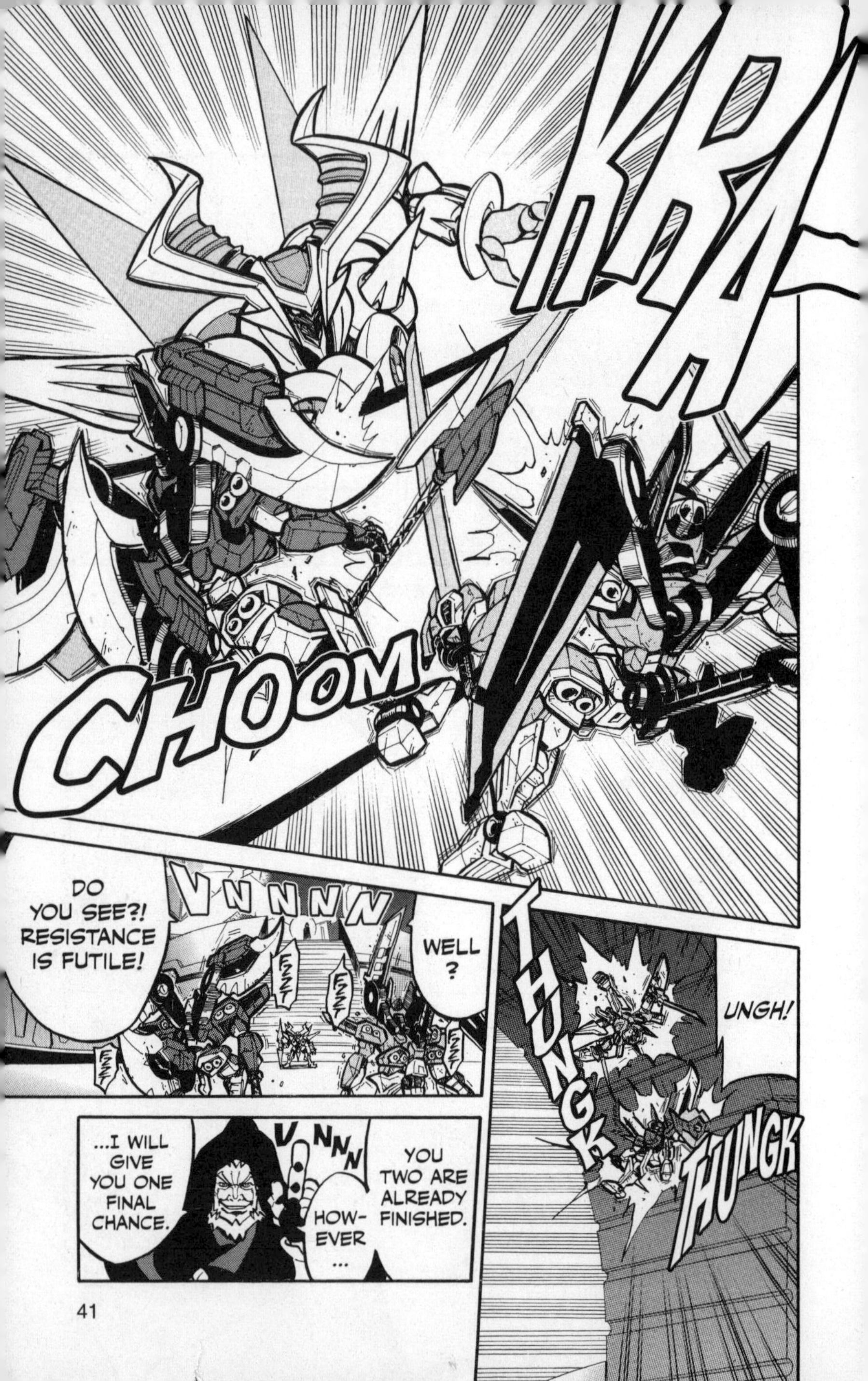
KRA
CHOOM
THUNK
UNGH!
THUNGK
WELL?
VNNNN
DO YOU SEE?! RESISTANCE IS FUTILE!
FZZT
FZZT
FZZT
FZZT
YOU TWO ARE ALREADY FINISHED.
HOW-EVER ...
VNNN
...I WILL GIVE YOU ONE FINAL CHANCE.

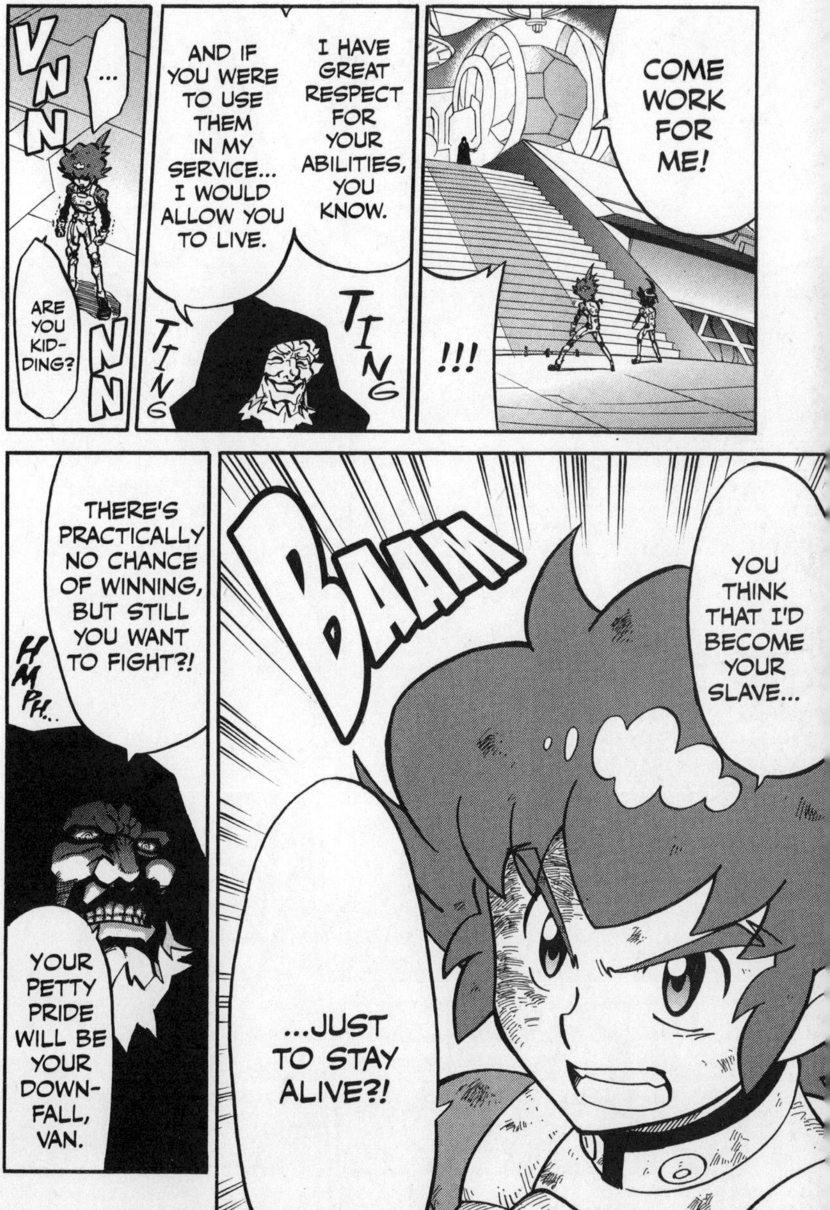
COME WORK FOR ME!
!!!
I HAVE GREAT RESPECT FOR YOUR ABILITIES, YOU KNOW.
AND IF YOU WERE TO USE THEM IN MY SERVICE... I WOULD ALLOW YOU TO LIVE.
TING
TING
...
VNN
NNN
ARE YOU KID-DING?
BAAM
YOU THINK THAT I'D BECOME YOUR SLAVE...
...JUST TO STAY ALIVE?!
THERE'S PRACTICALLY NO CHANCE OF WINNING, BUT STILL YOU WANT TO FIGHT?!
HMPH...
YOUR PETTY PRIDE WILL BE YOUR DOWN-FALL, VAN.

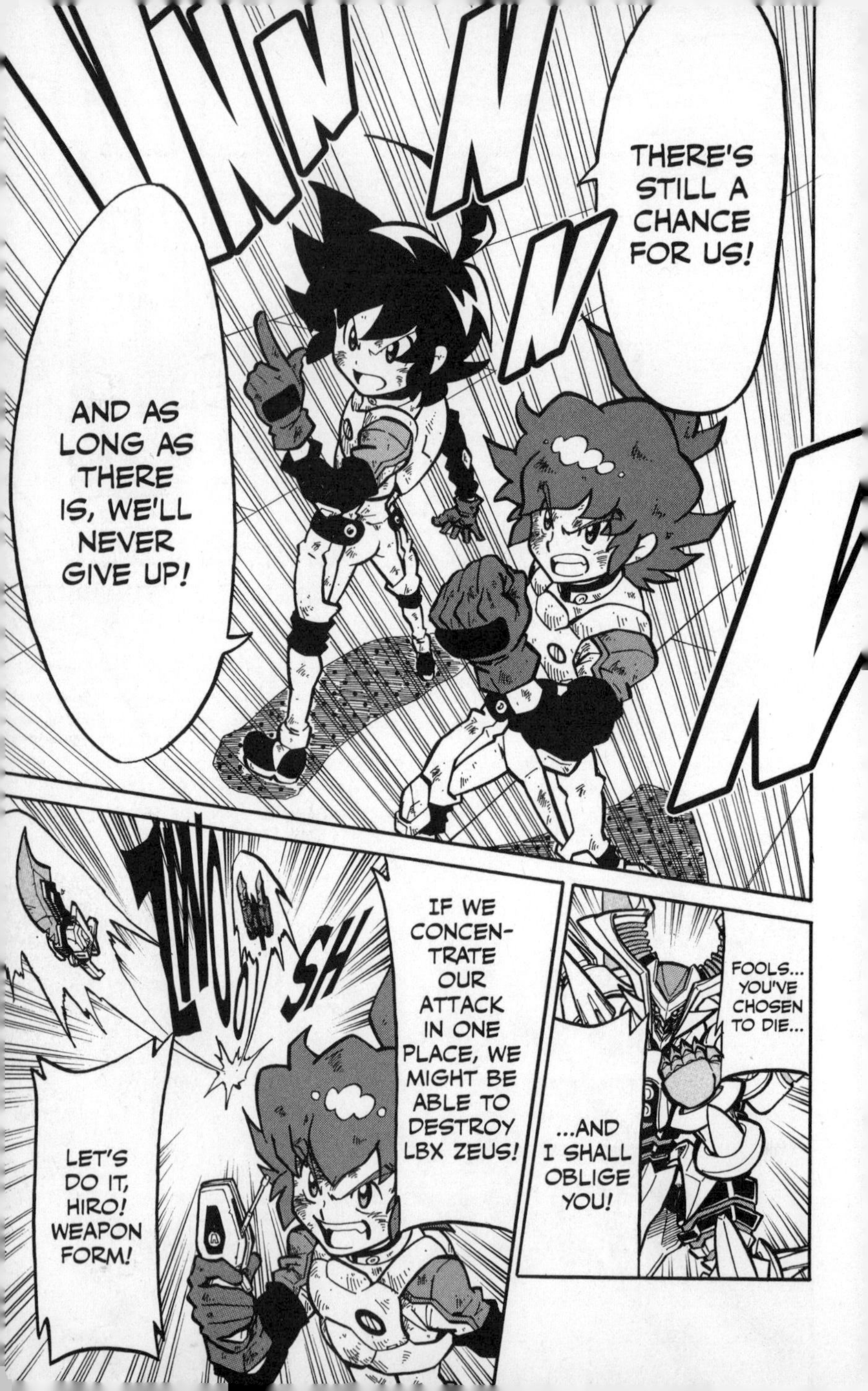
THERE'S STILL A CHANCE FOR US!
AND AS LONG AS THERE IS, WE'LL NEVER GIVE UP!
FOOLS... YOU'VE CHOSEN TO DIE...
...AND I SHALL OBLIGE YOU!
IF WE CONCENTRATE OUR ATTACK IN ONE PLACE, WE MIGHT BE ABLE TO DESTROY LBX ZEUS!
LET'S DO IT, HIRO! WEAPON FORM!

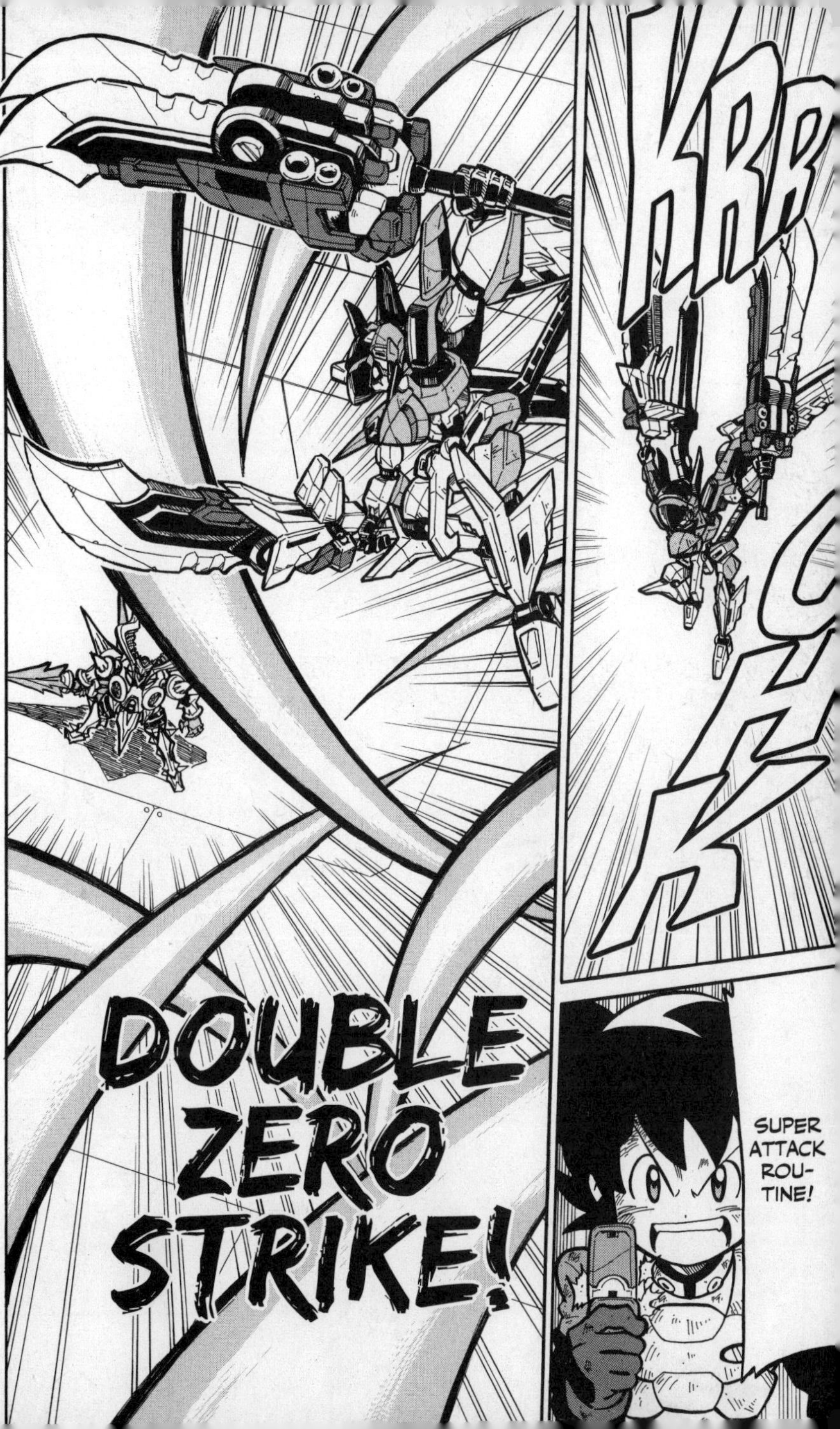
SUPER ATTACK ROU-TINE!
DOUBLE ZERO STRIKE!

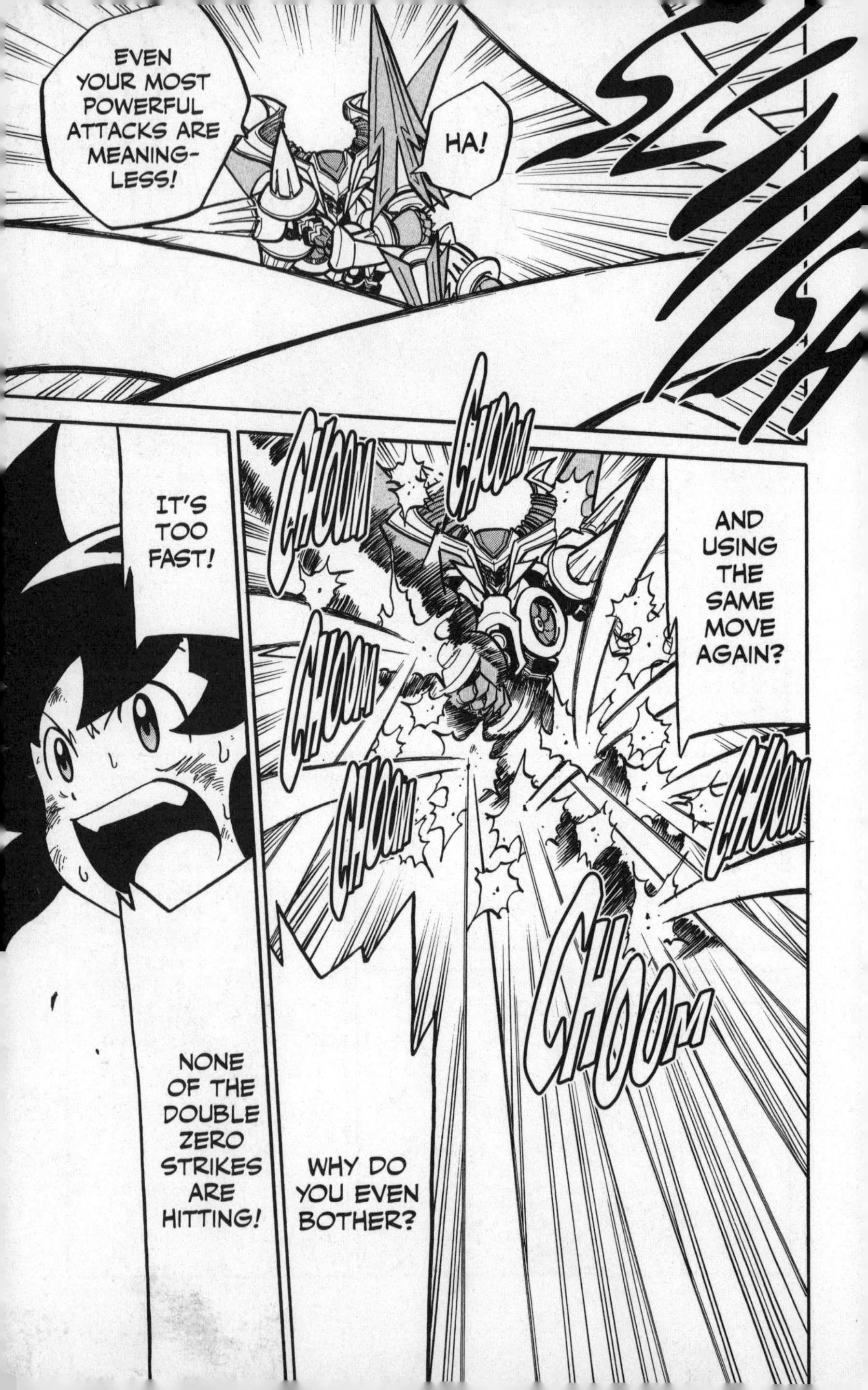
HA!
EVEN YOUR MOST POWERFUL ATTACKS ARE MEANING-LESS!
AND USING THE SAME MOVE AGAIN?
CHOOM
CHOOM
CHOOM
WHY DO YOU EVEN BOTHER?
IT'S TOO FAST!
NONE OF THE DOUBLE ZERO STRIKES ARE HITTING!

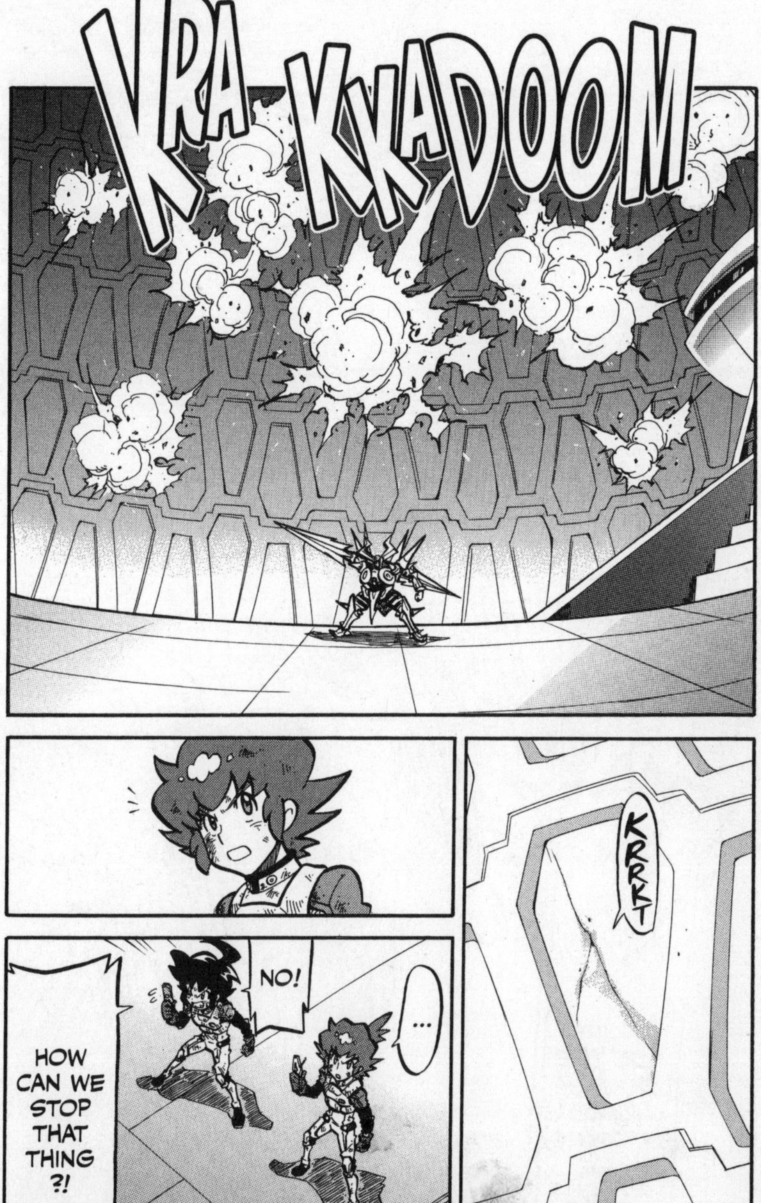
KRA-KKADOOM
KRRKT
...
NO!
HOW CAN WE STOP THAT THING?!

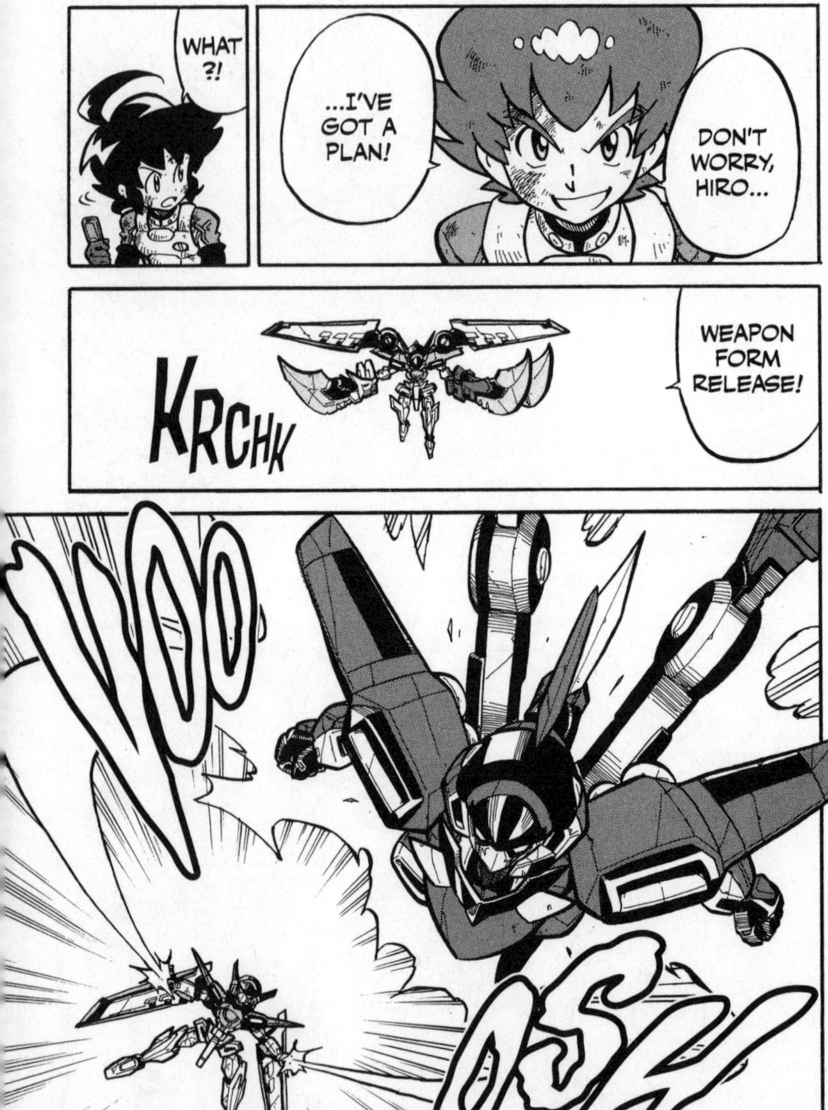
DON'T WORRY, HIRO...
...I'VE GOT A PLAN!
WHAT ?!
WEAPON FORM RELEASE!
KRCHK
VOOOSH

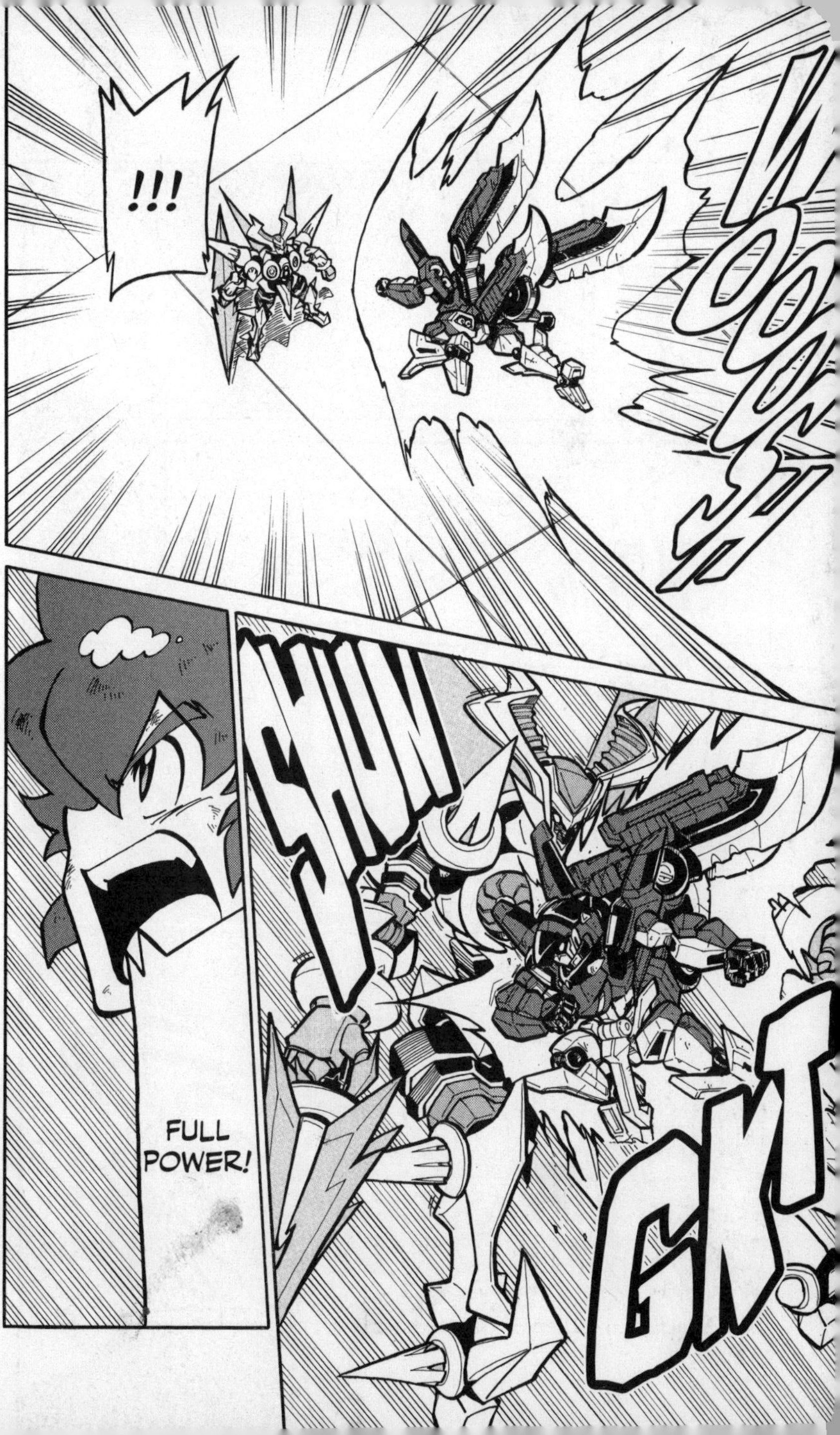
WOOOSH
!!!
SHUN
FULL POWER!

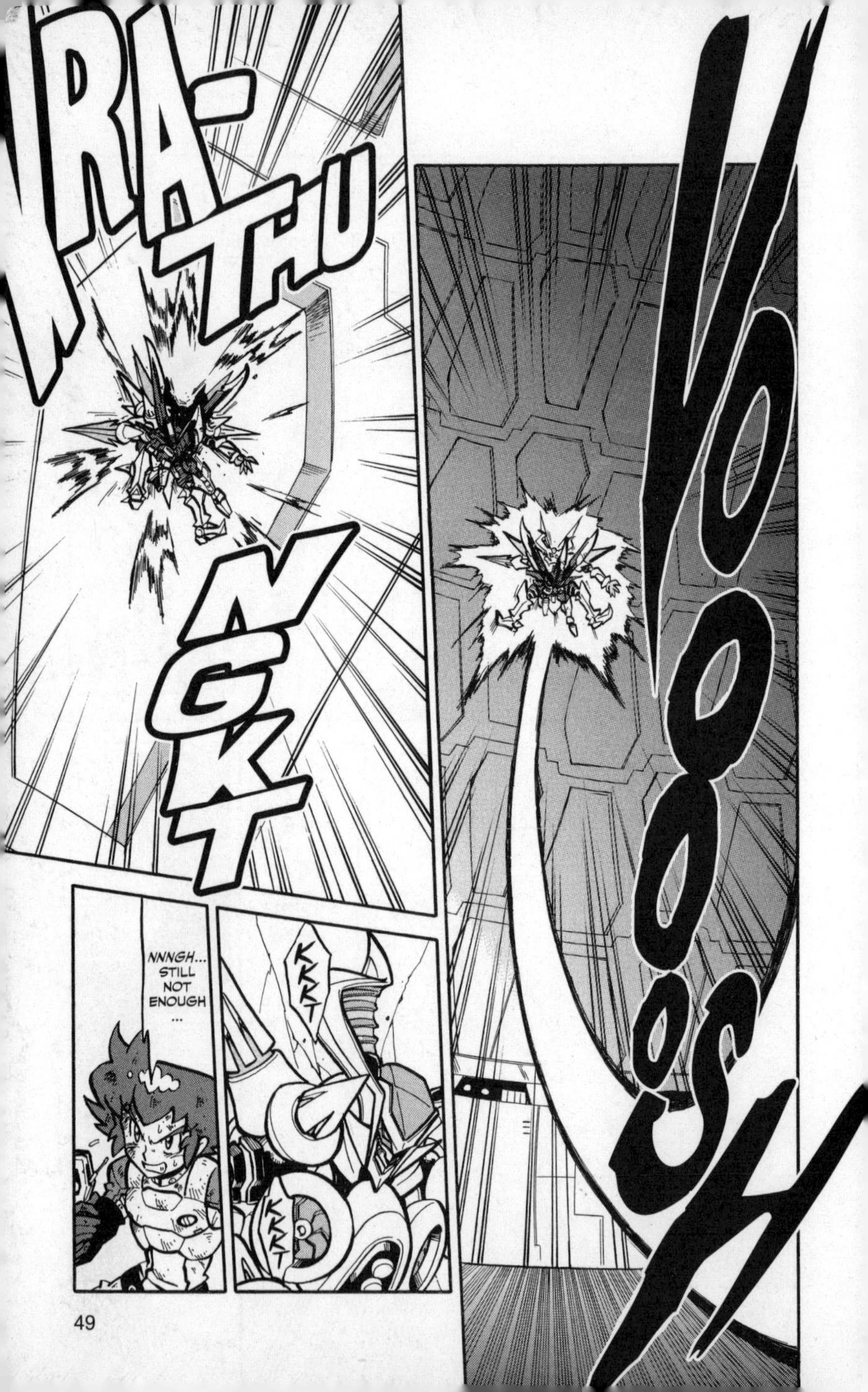
WOOOOOSH
WRA-
THU
NGKT
KKKT
KKKT
NNNGH... STILL NOT ENOUGH ...

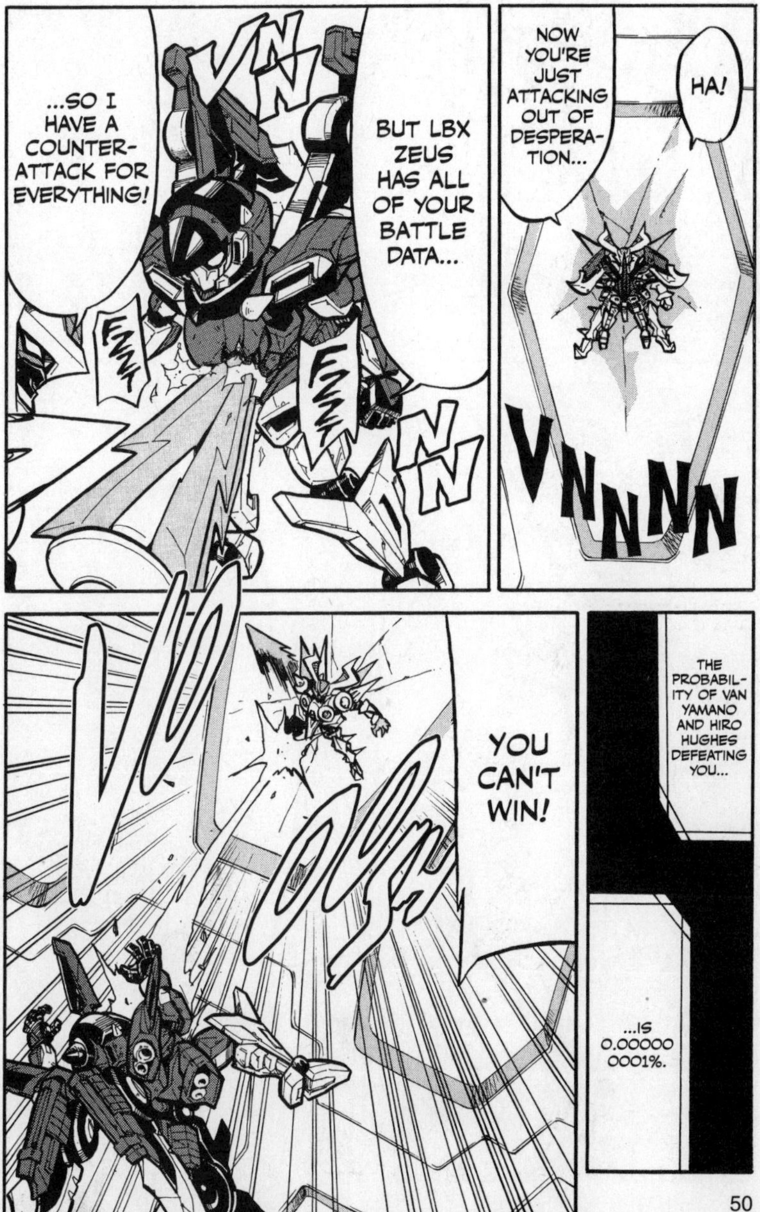
HA!
NOW YOU'RE JUST ATTACKING OUT OF DESPERA-TION...
VNNNNN
BUT LBX ZEUS HAS ALL OF YOUR BATTLE DATA...
...SO I HAVE A COUNTER-ATTACK FOR EVERYTHING!
VN
FZZZ
FZZZ
VN
THE PROBABIL-ITY OF VAN YAMANO AND HIRO HUGHES DEFEATING YOU...
...IS 0.00000 0001%.
YOU CAN'T WIN!

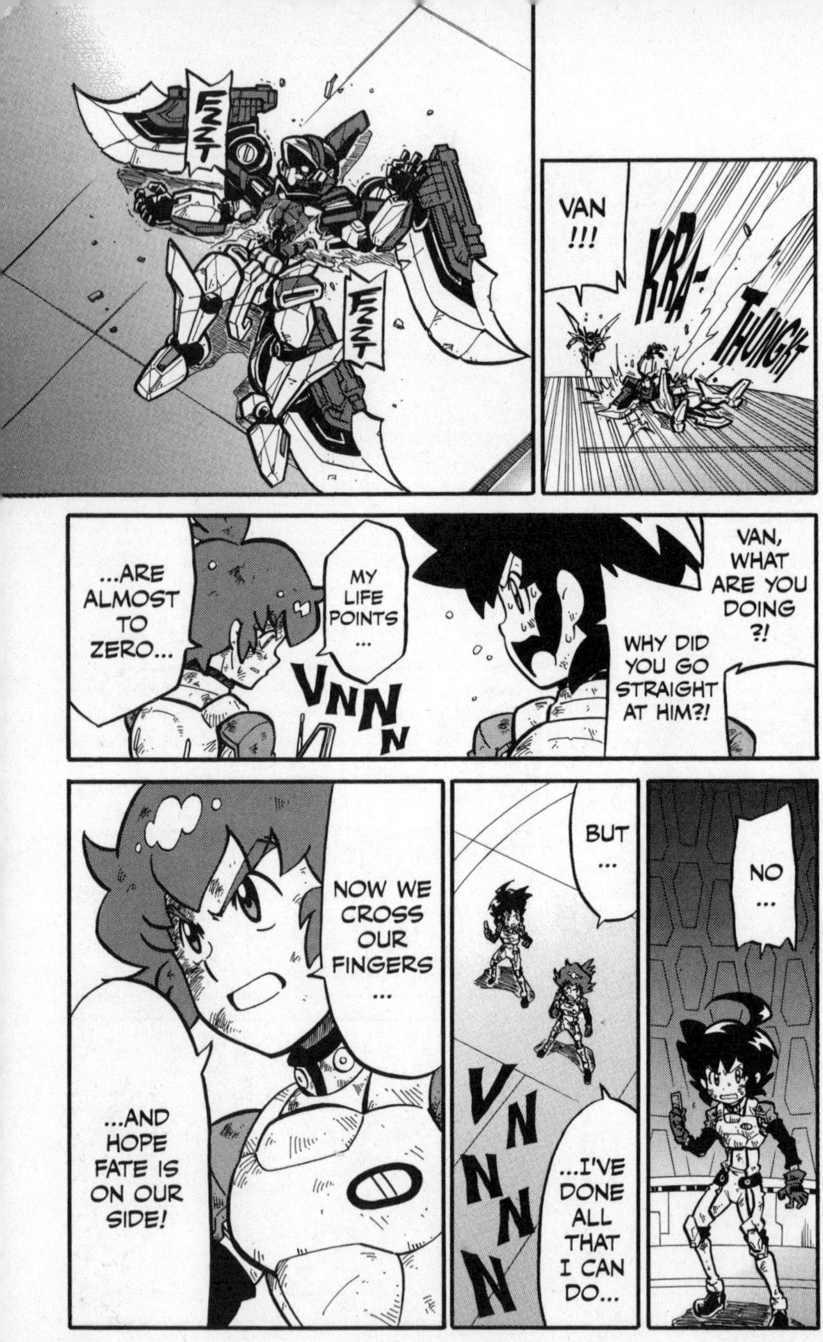
VAN !!!
KRA-THUNGK
FZZT
FZZT
VAN, WHAT ARE YOU DOING ?!
WHY DID YOU GO STRAIGHT AT HIM?!
MY LIFE POINTS ...
VNNN
...ARE ALMOST TO ZERO...
NO ...
BUT ...
VNNN
...I'VE DONE ALL THAT I CAN DO...
NOW WE CROSS OUR FINGERS ...
...AND HOPE FATE IS ON OUR SIDE!

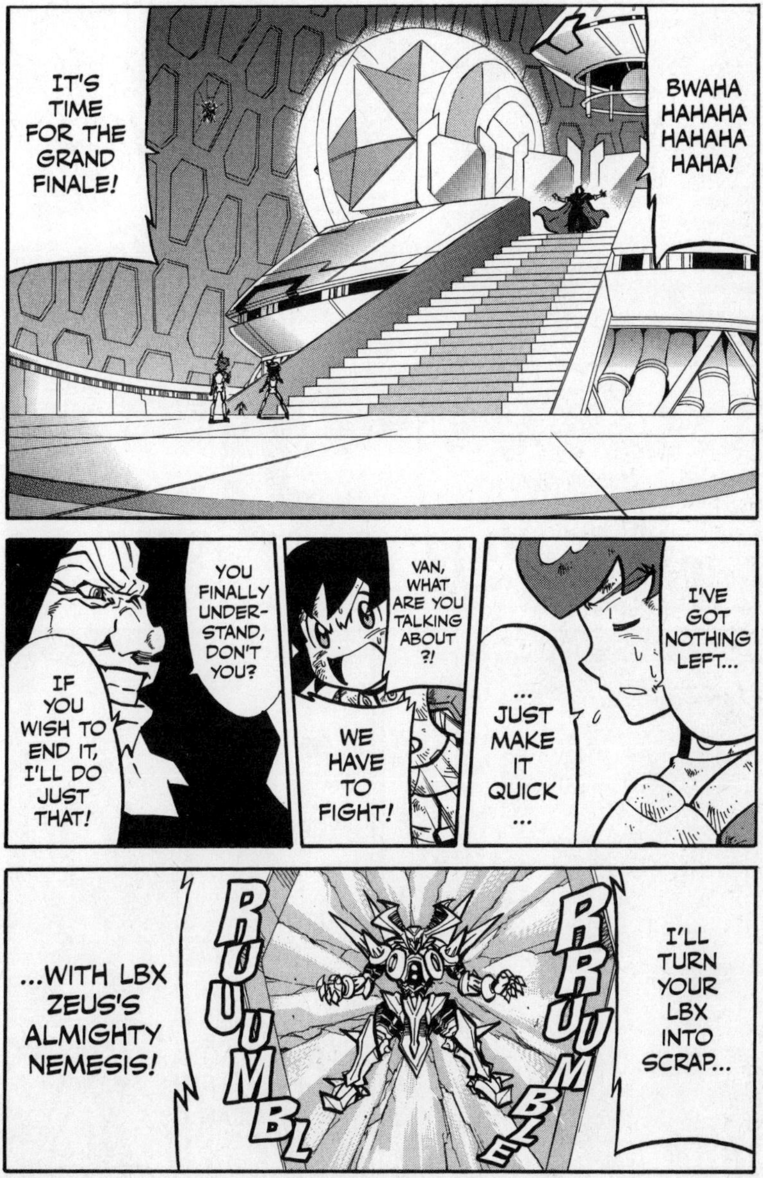
BWAHA HAHAHA HAHAHA HAHA!
IT'S TIME FOR THE GRAND FINALE!
I'VE GOT NOTHING LEFT...
... JUST MAKE IT QUICK ...
VAN, WHAT ARE YOU TALKING ABOUT ?!
WE HAVE TO FIGHT!
YOU FINALLY UNDER-STAND, DON'T YOU?
IF YOU WISH TO END IT, I'LL DO JUST THAT!
I'LL TURN YOUR LBX INTO SCRAP...
RRUUMBLE
...WITH LBX ZEUS'S ALMIGHTY NEMESIS!
RUUMBL

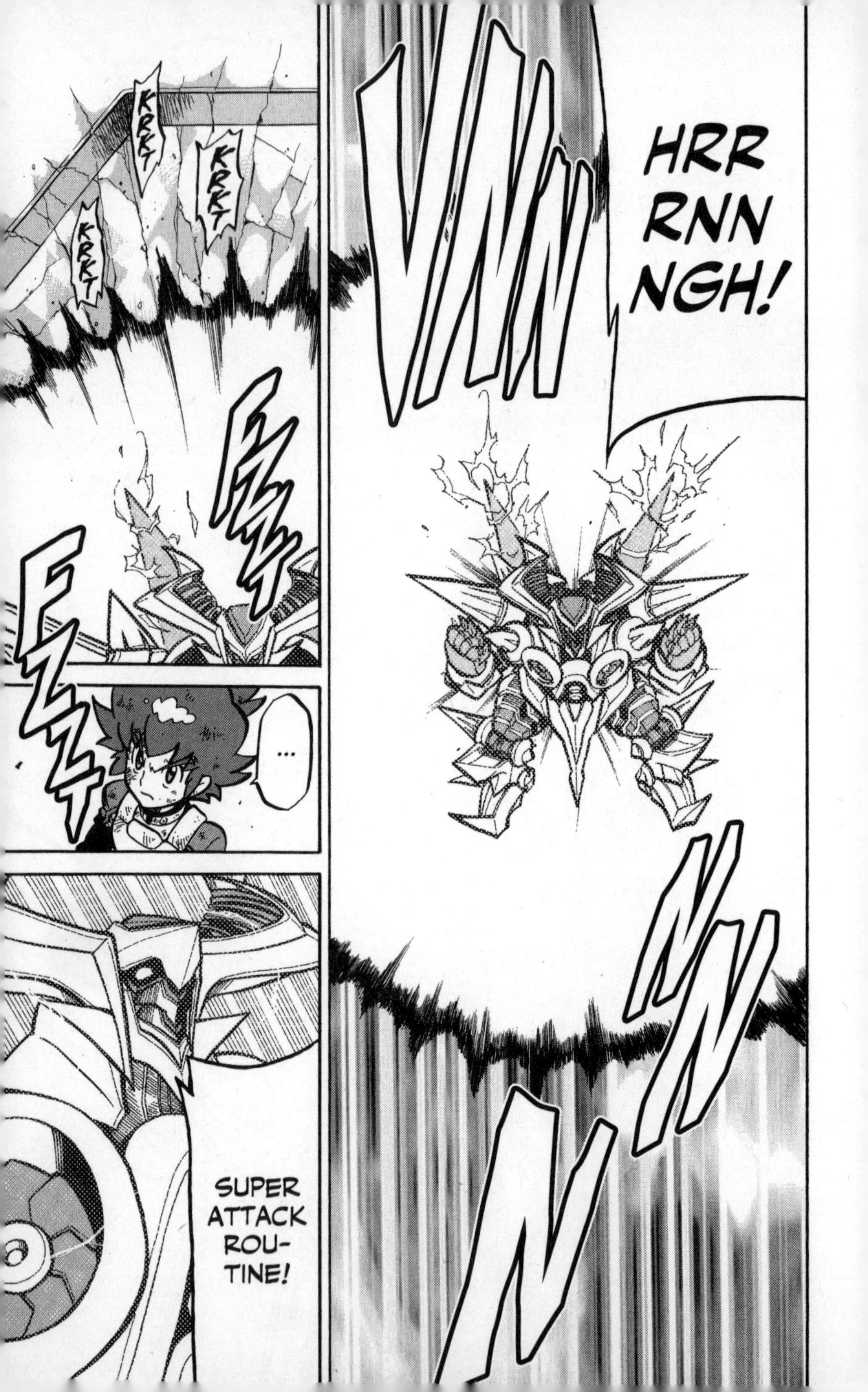

HRR RNN NGH!
KRKT
KRKT
KRKT
FZZZT
...
SUPER ATTACK ROU-TINE!

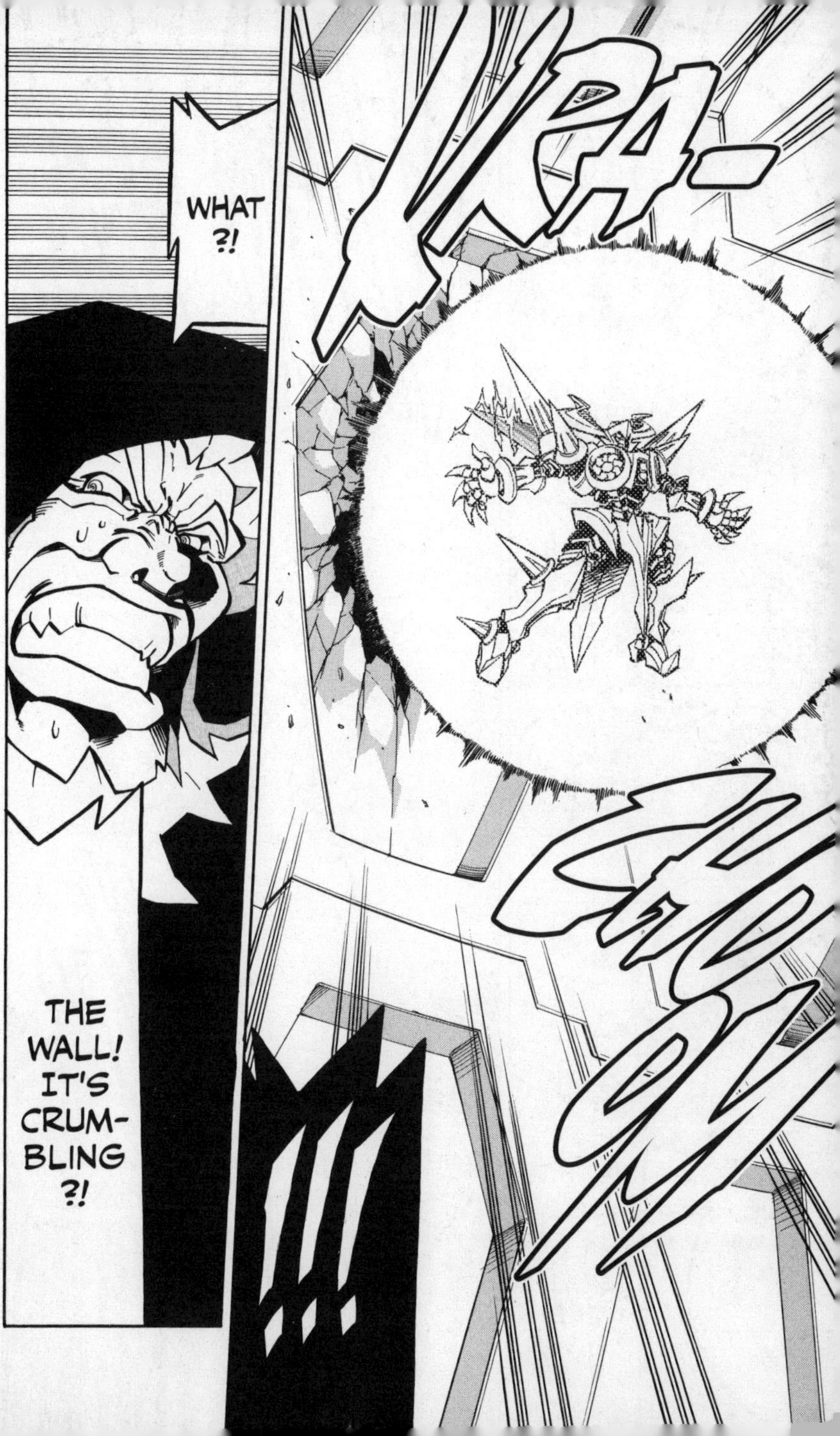
PA-
WHAT?!
THE WALL! IT'S CRUM-BLING?!
!!!

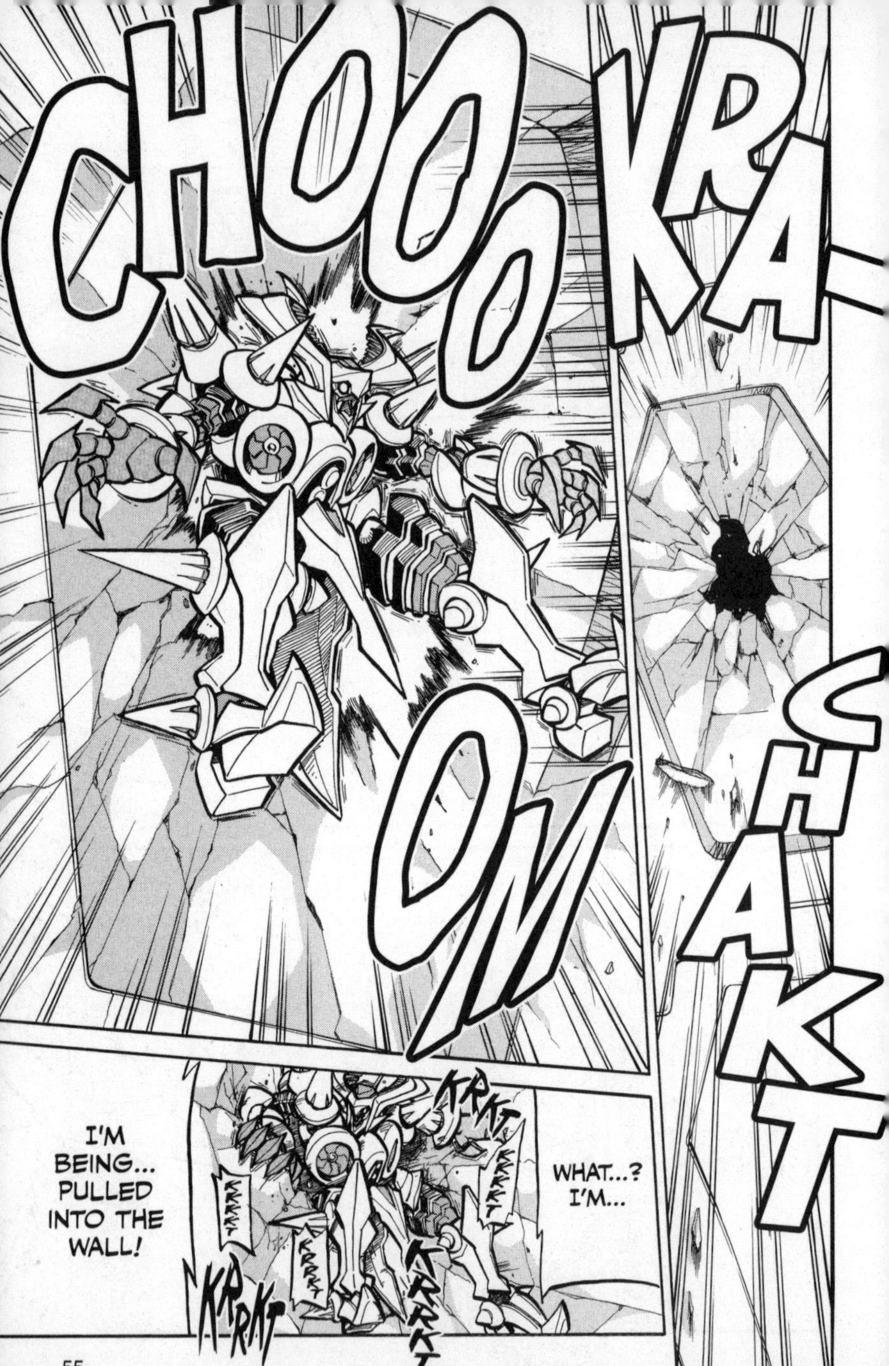

KRA-
CHAKT
CHOOOOOM
KRRKT
KRRRKT
WHAT...? I'M...
KRRRKT
KRRKT
KRRRKT
KRRRKT
KRRKT
I'M BEING... PULLED INTO THE WALL!

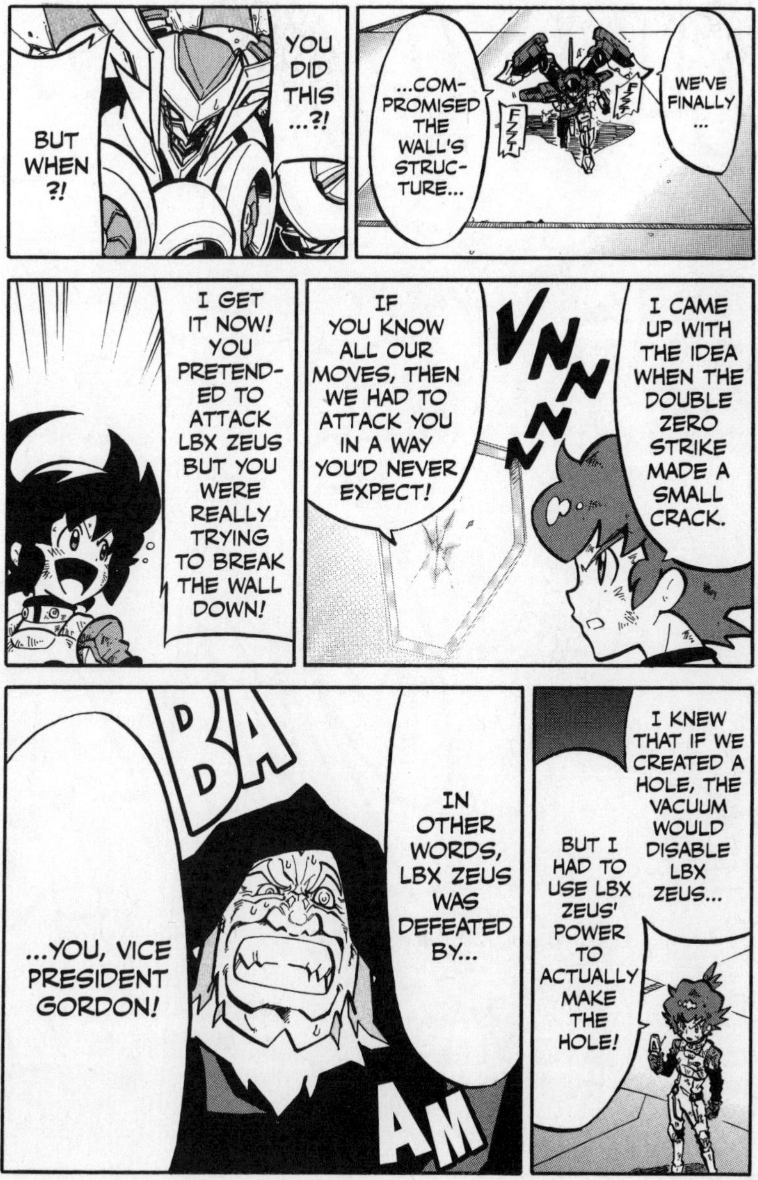
WE'VE FINALLY ...
...COM-PROMISED THE WALL'S STRUC-TURE...
FZZT
FZZT
YOU DID THIS ...?!
BUT WHEN ?!
I CAME UP WITH THE IDEA WHEN THE DOUBLE ZERO STRIKE MADE A SMALL CRACK.
VNNNN
IF YOU KNOW ALL OUR MOVES, THEN WE HAD TO ATTACK YOU IN A WAY YOU'D NEVER EXPECT!
I GET IT NOW! YOU PRETEND-ED TO ATTACK LBX ZEUS BUT YOU WERE REALLY TRYING TO BREAK THE WALL DOWN!
I KNEW THAT IF WE CREATED A HOLE, THE VACUUM WOULD DISABLE LBX ZEUS...
BUT I HAD TO USE LBX ZEUS' POWER TO ACTUALLY MAKE THE HOLE!
IN OTHER WORDS, LBX ZEUS WAS DEFEATED BY...
BADABAM
...YOU, VICE PRESIDENT GORDON!

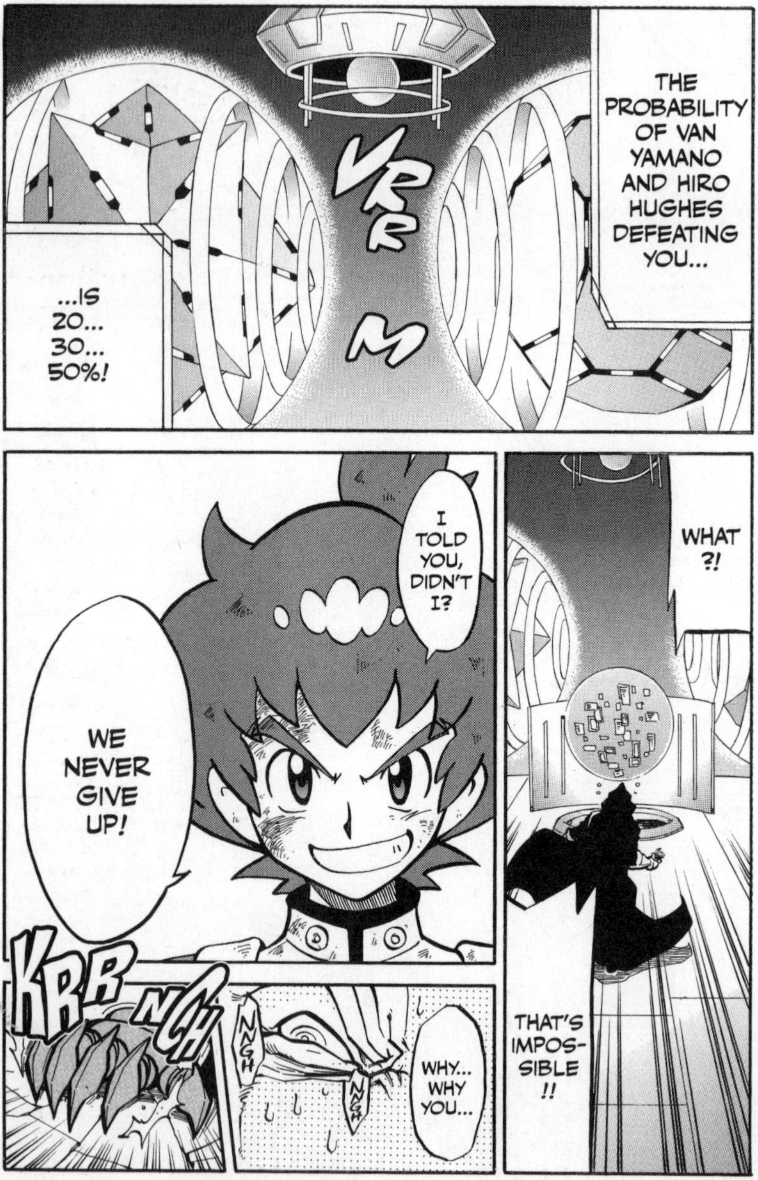
THE PROBABILITY OF VAN YAMANO AND HIRO HUGHES DEFEATING YOU...
VRRM
...IS 20... 30... 50%!
WHAT?!
THAT'S IMPOSSIBLE!!
I TOLD YOU, DIDN'T I?
WE NEVER GIVE UP!
NNGH
WHY... WHY YOU...
NNGH
KRRNCH

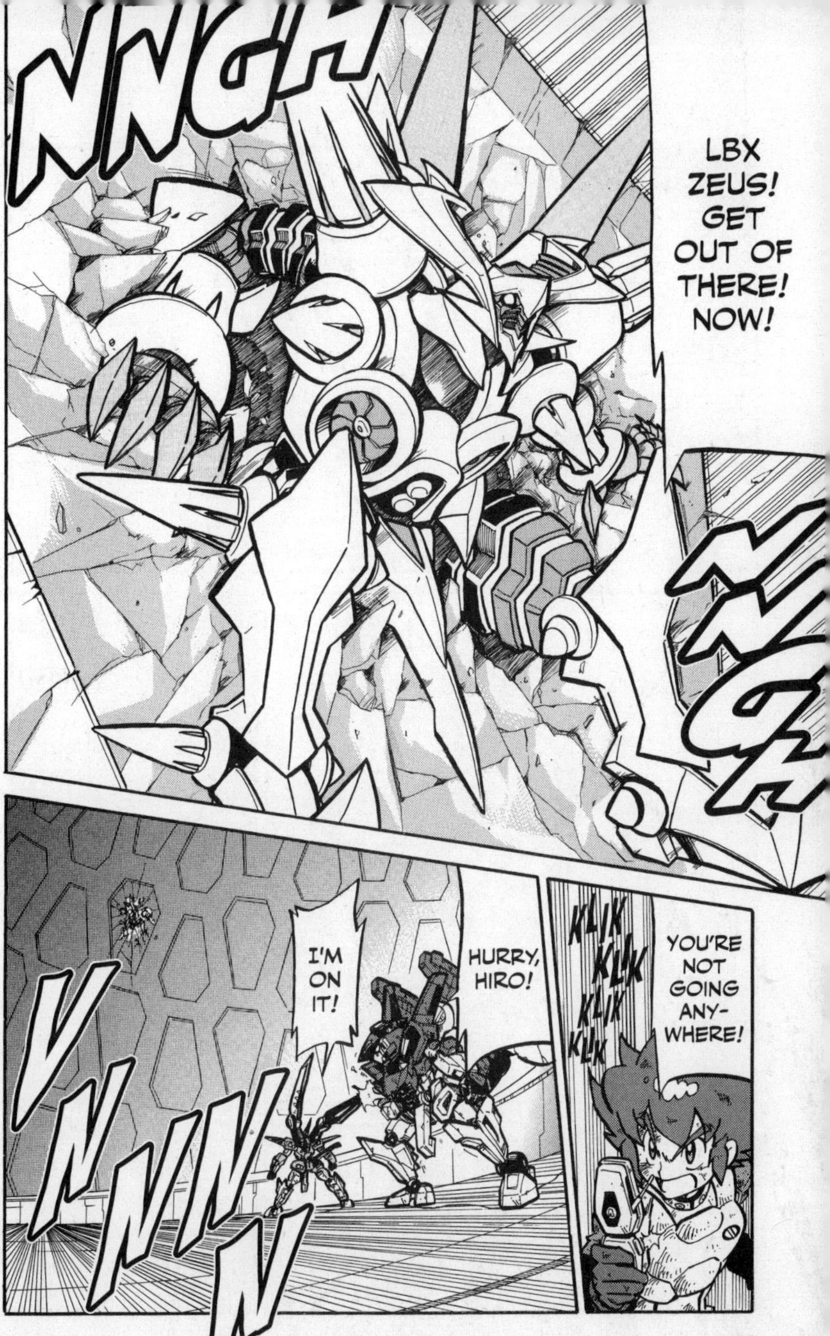
NNGH
LBX ZEUS! GET OUT OF THERE! NOW!
NNGH
YOU'RE NOT GOING ANY-WHERE!
KLIK KLIK KLIK KLIK
HURRY, HIRO!
I'M ON IT!
VNNNN

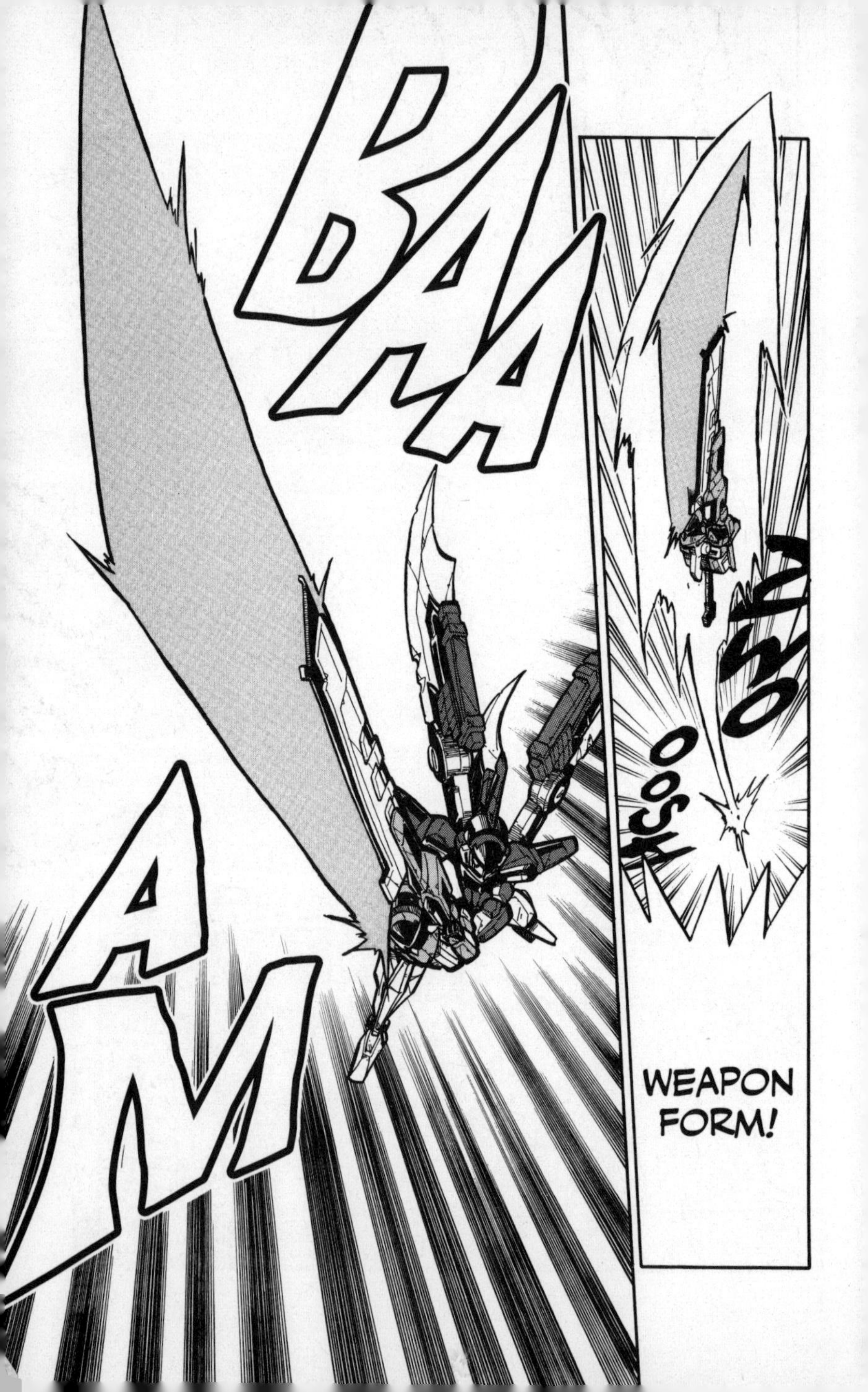

OOSH
WEAPON FORM!
BADAA
AM

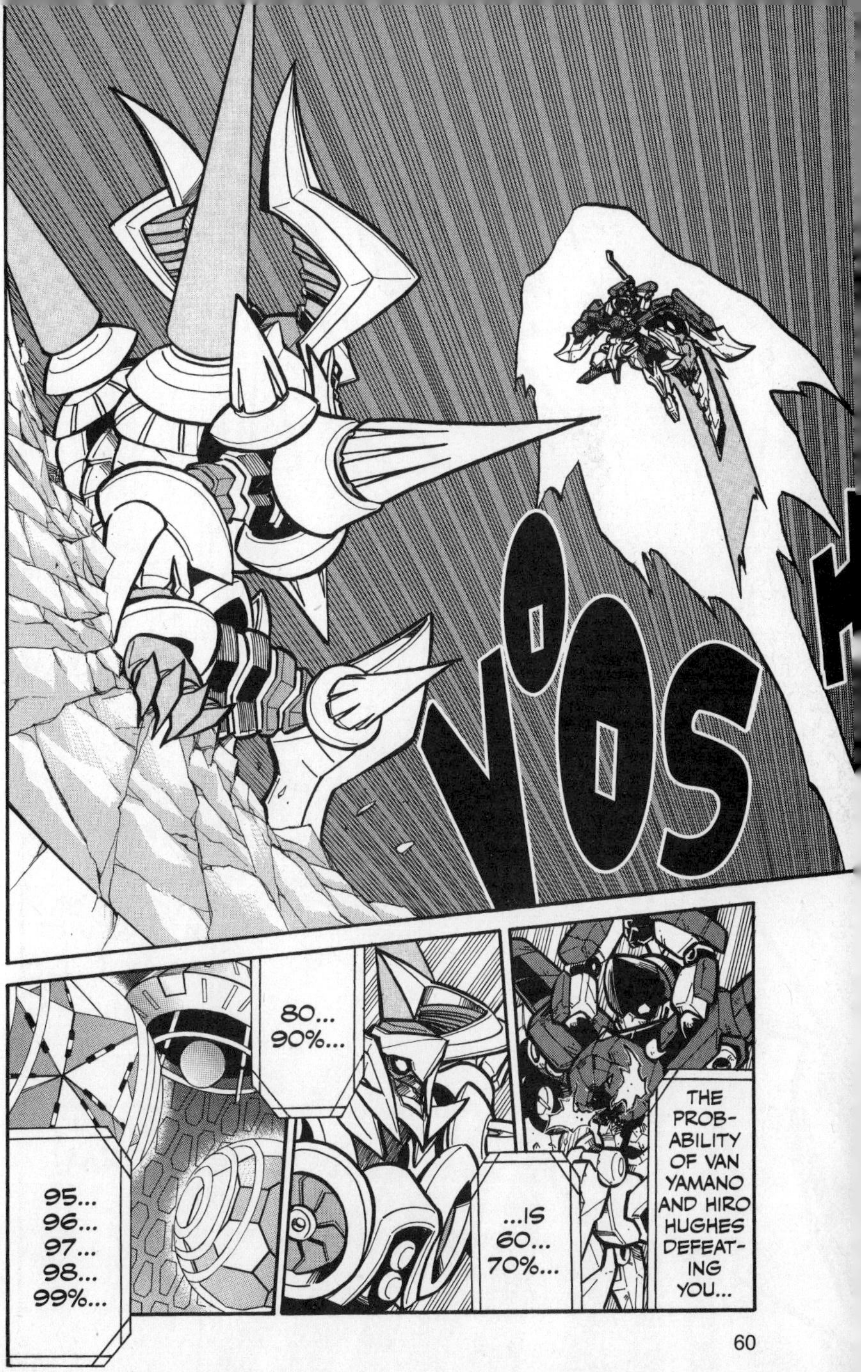
VOOSH
THE PROB-ABILITY OF VAN YAMANO AND HIRO HUGHES DEFEAT-ING YOU...
...IS 60... 70%...
80... 90%...
95... 96... 97... 98... 99%...

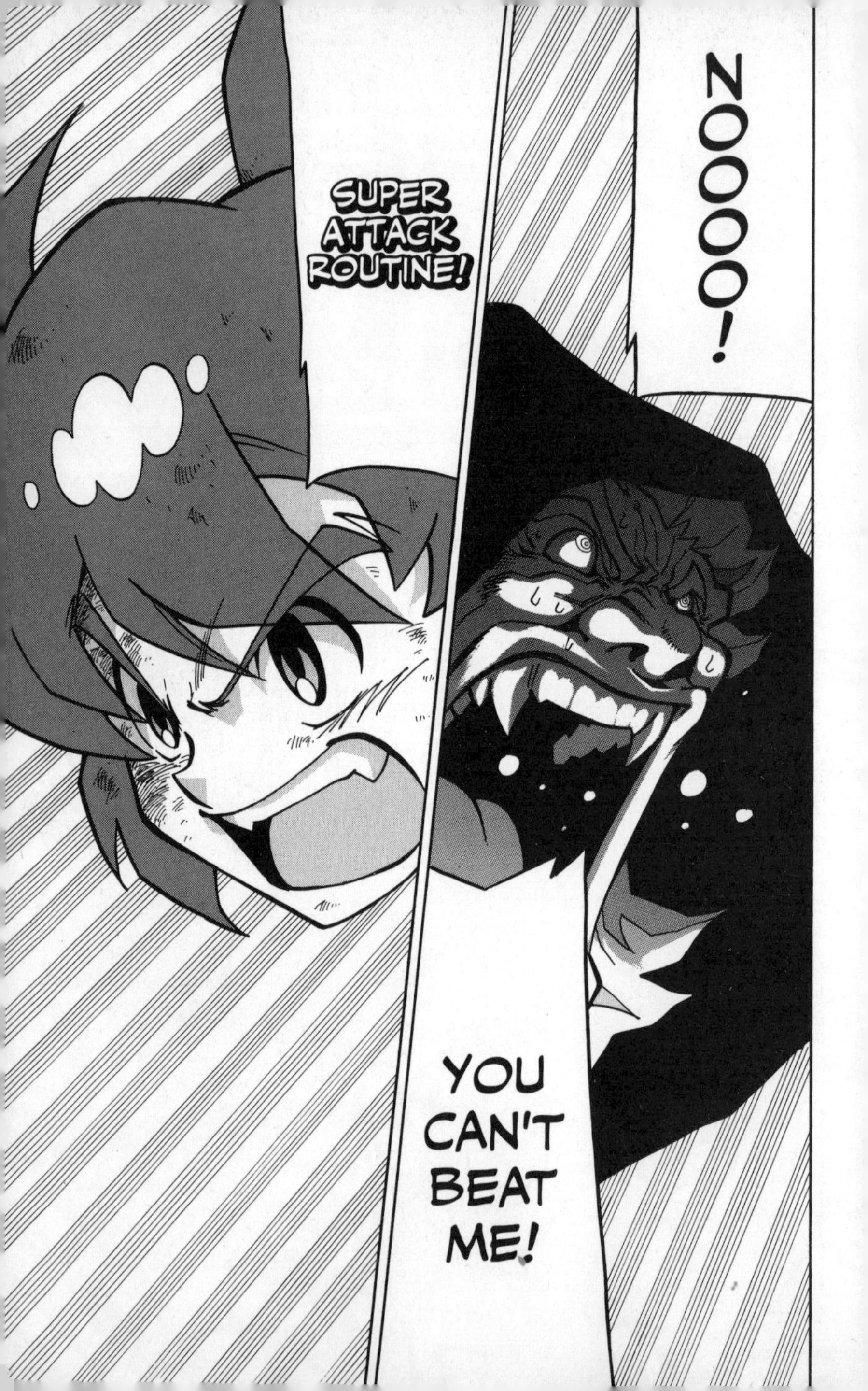
NOOOO!
YOU CAN'T BEAT ME!
SUPER ATTACK ROUTINE!

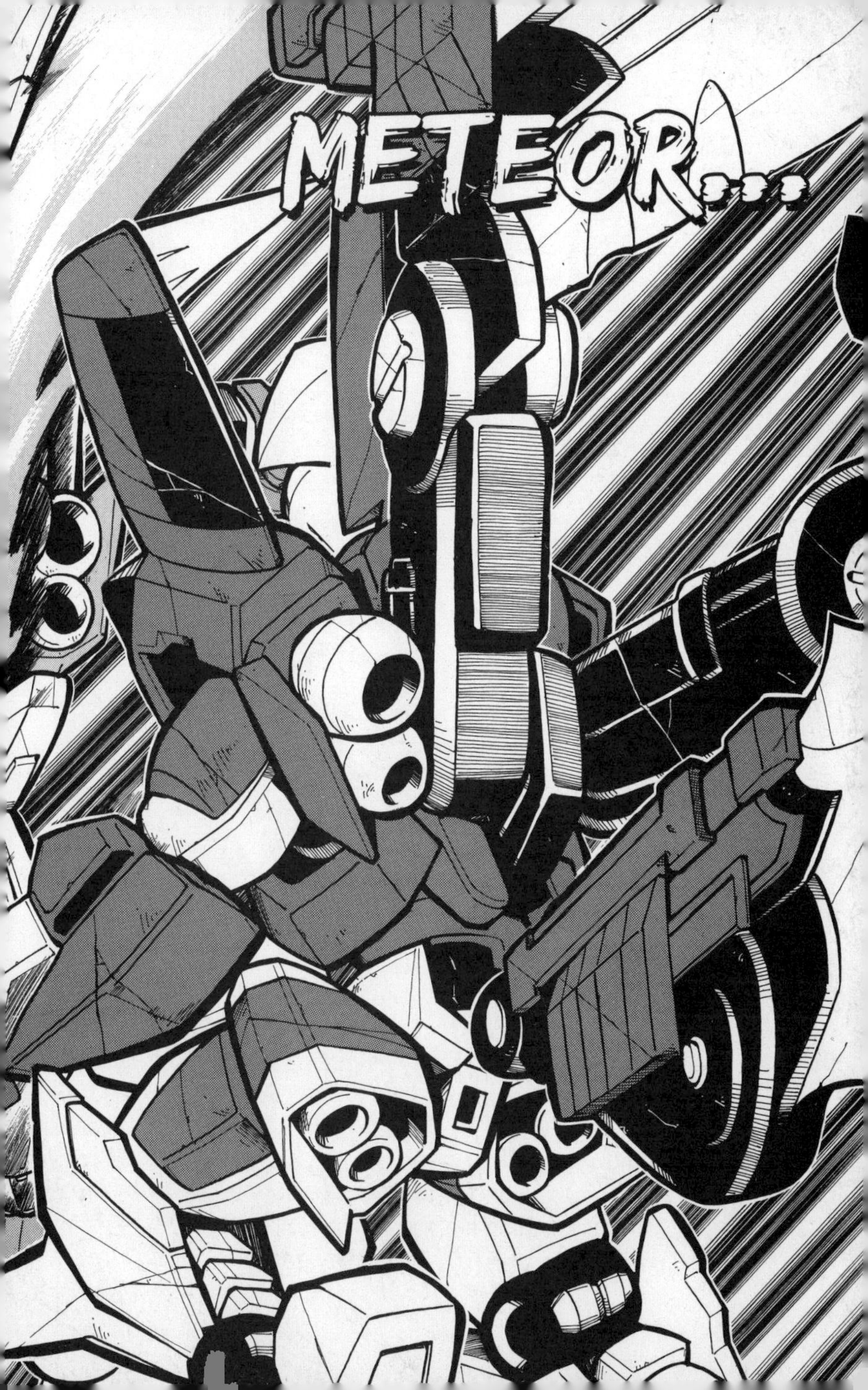
METEOR...

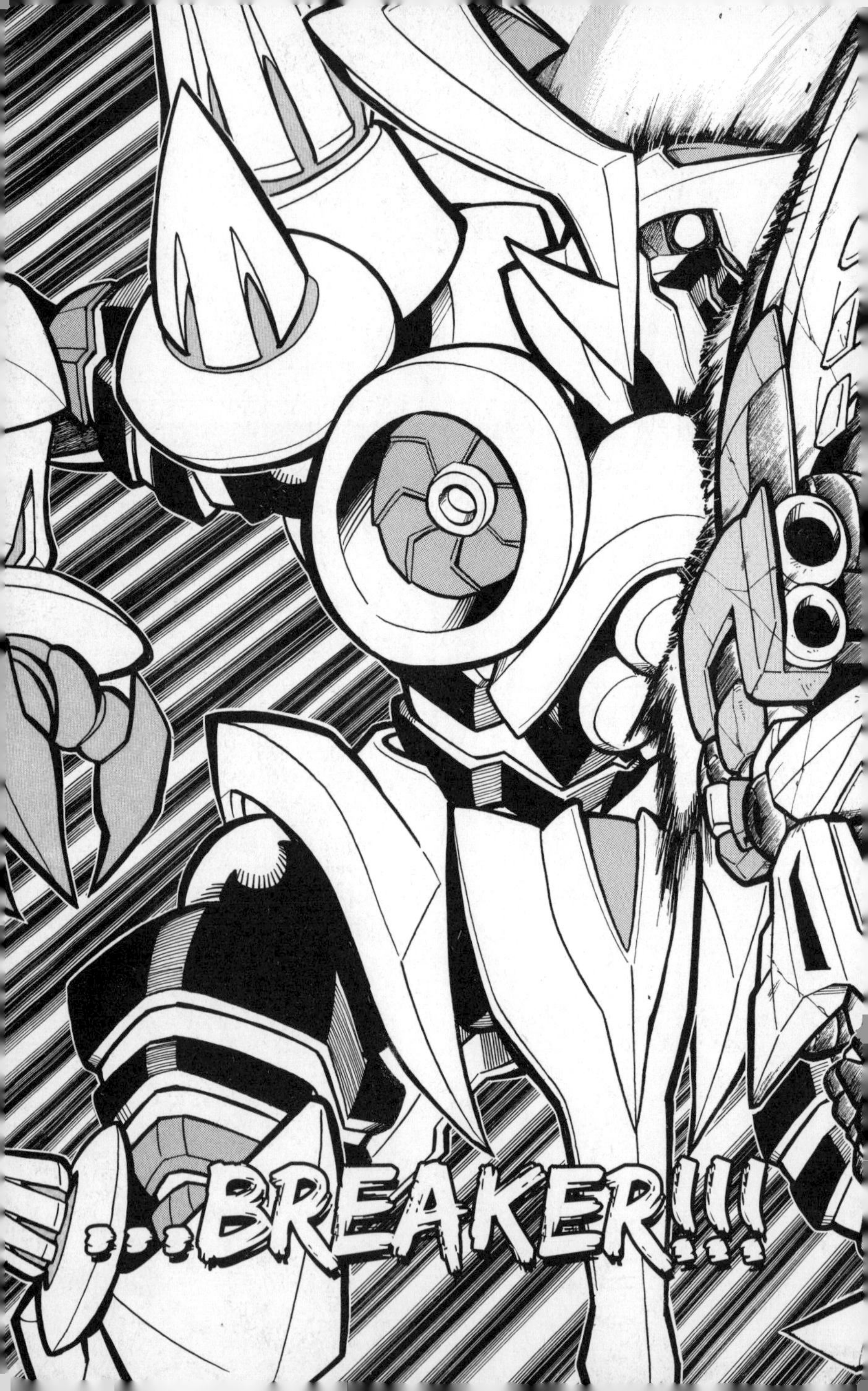
...BREAKER!!!

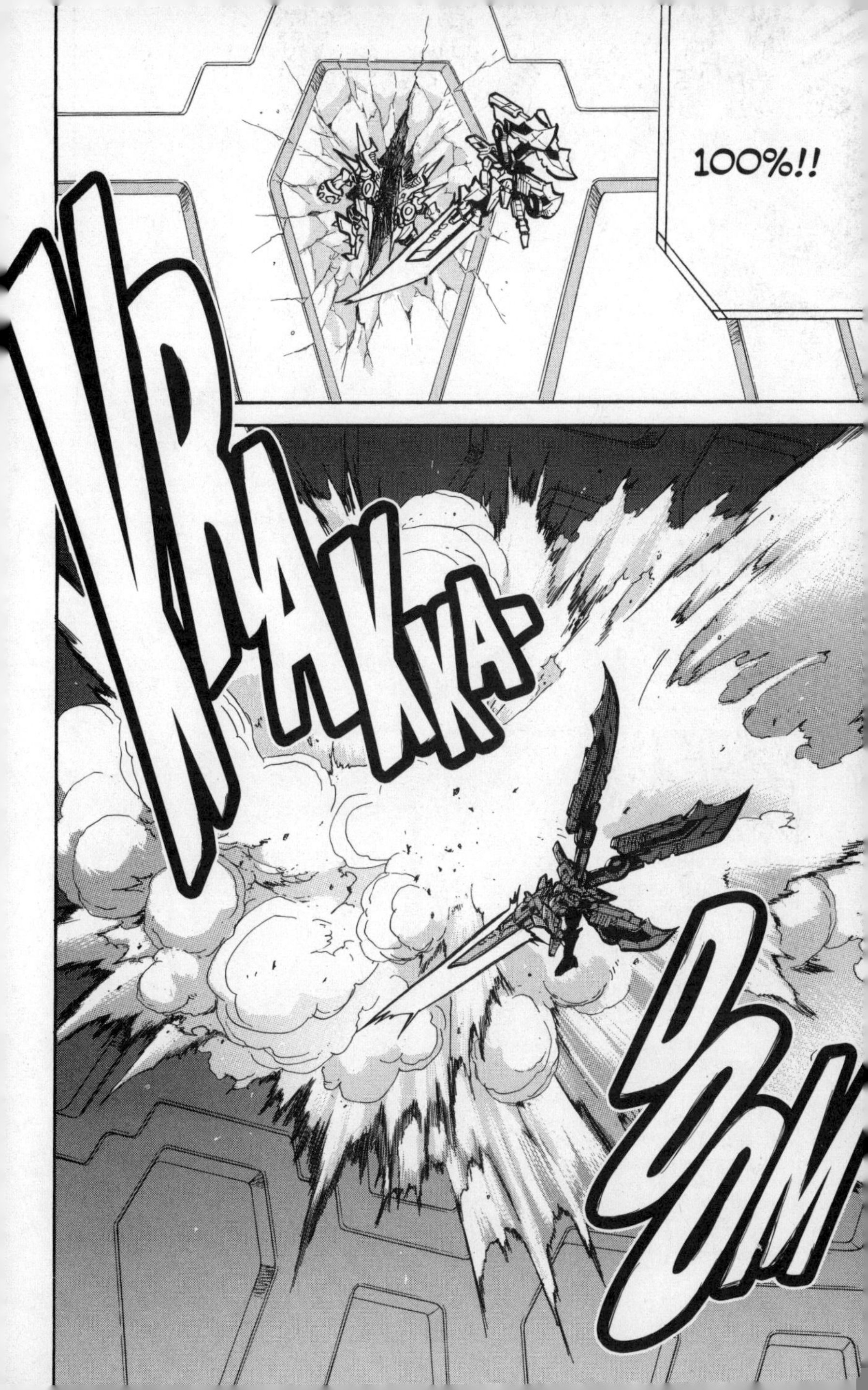
100%!!
VRAKKA-
DOOM

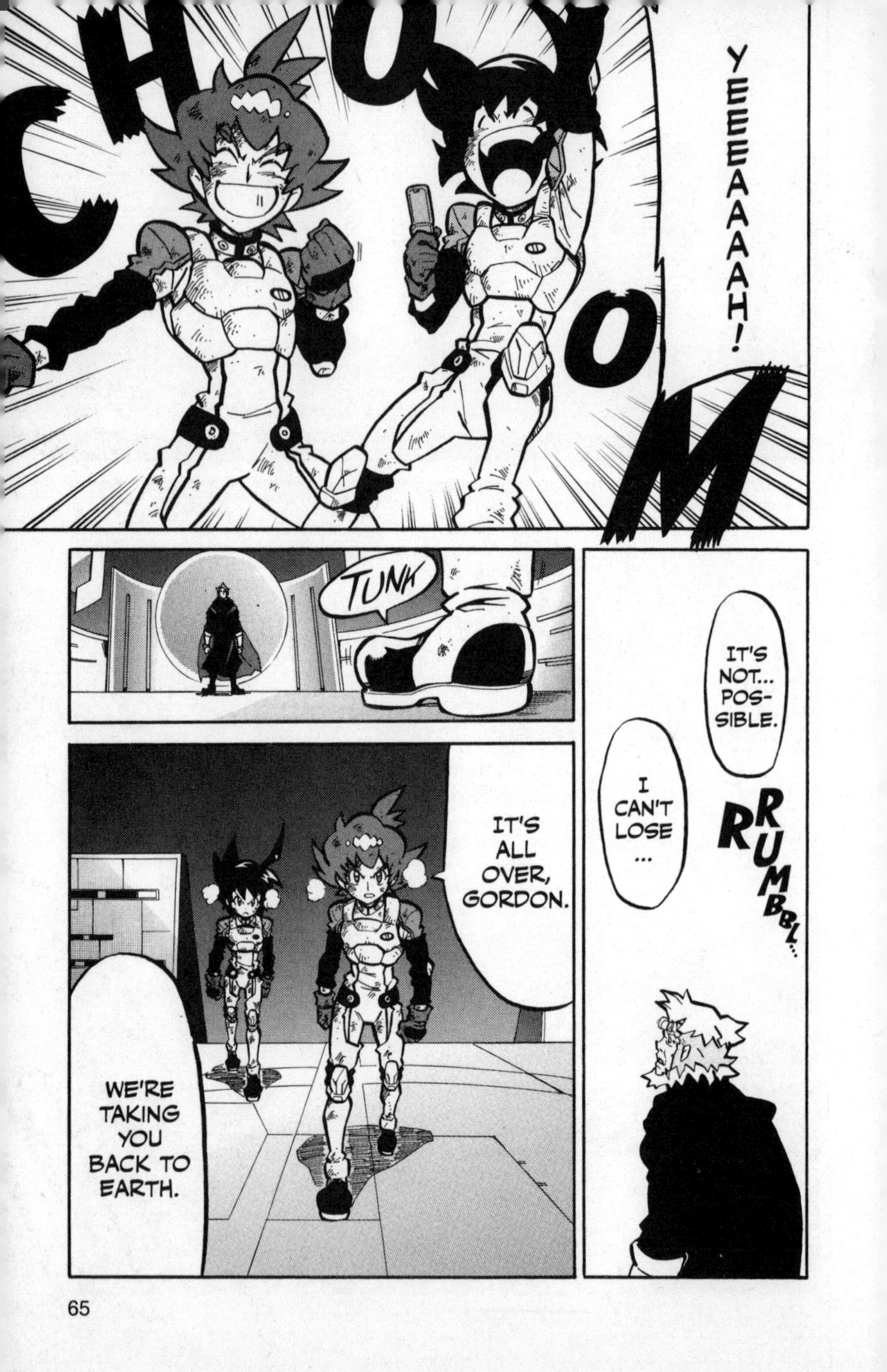
YEEEAAAAAH!
CHOOOM
IT'S NOT... POS-SIBLE.
I CAN'T LOSE ...
RRUMBBL...
TUNK
IT'S ALL OVER, GORDON.
WE'RE TAKING YOU BACK TO EARTH.

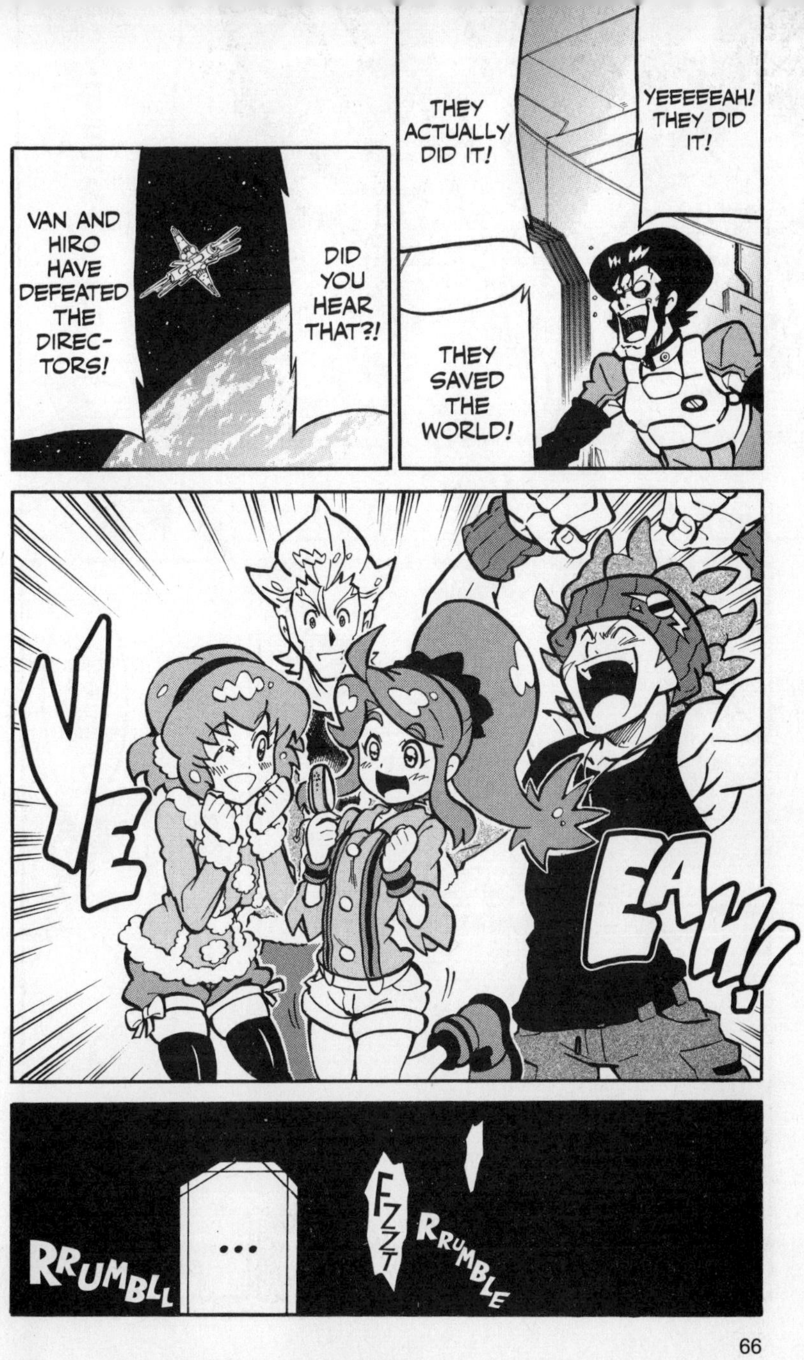
YEEEEEAH! THEY DID IT!
THEY ACTUALLY DID IT!
THEY SAVED THE WORLD!
DID YOU HEAR THAT?!
VAN AND HIRO HAVE DEFEATED THE DIREC- TORS!
YE
EAH!
RRUMBLE
FZZT
...
RRUMBLL

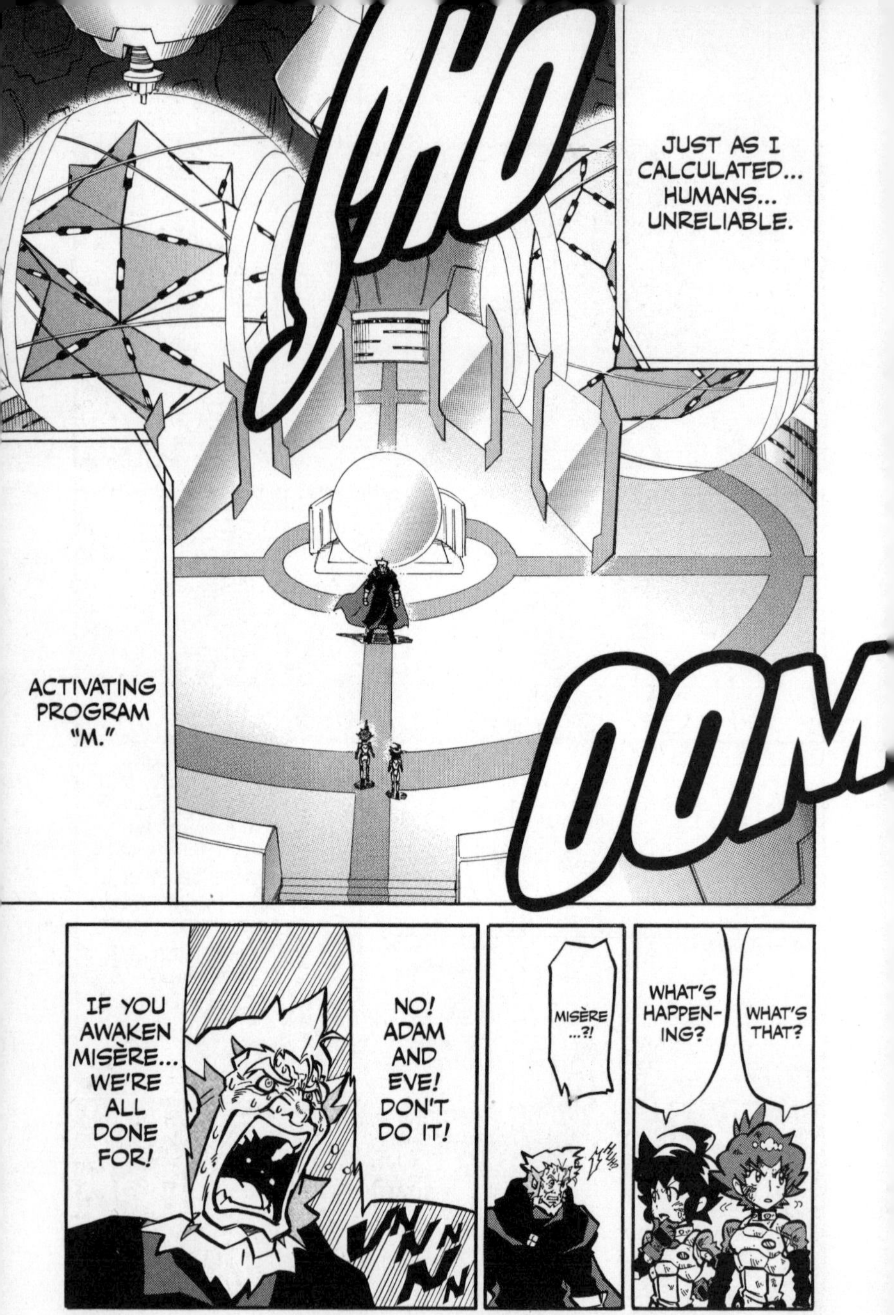
JUST AS I CALCULATED... HUMANS... UNRELIABLE.
OOM
ACTIVATING PROGRAM "M."
WHAT'S THAT?
WHAT'S HAPPEN-ING?
MISÈRE ...?!
NO! ADAM AND EVE! DON'T DO IT!
IF YOU AWAKEN MISÈRE... WE'RE ALL DONE FOR!

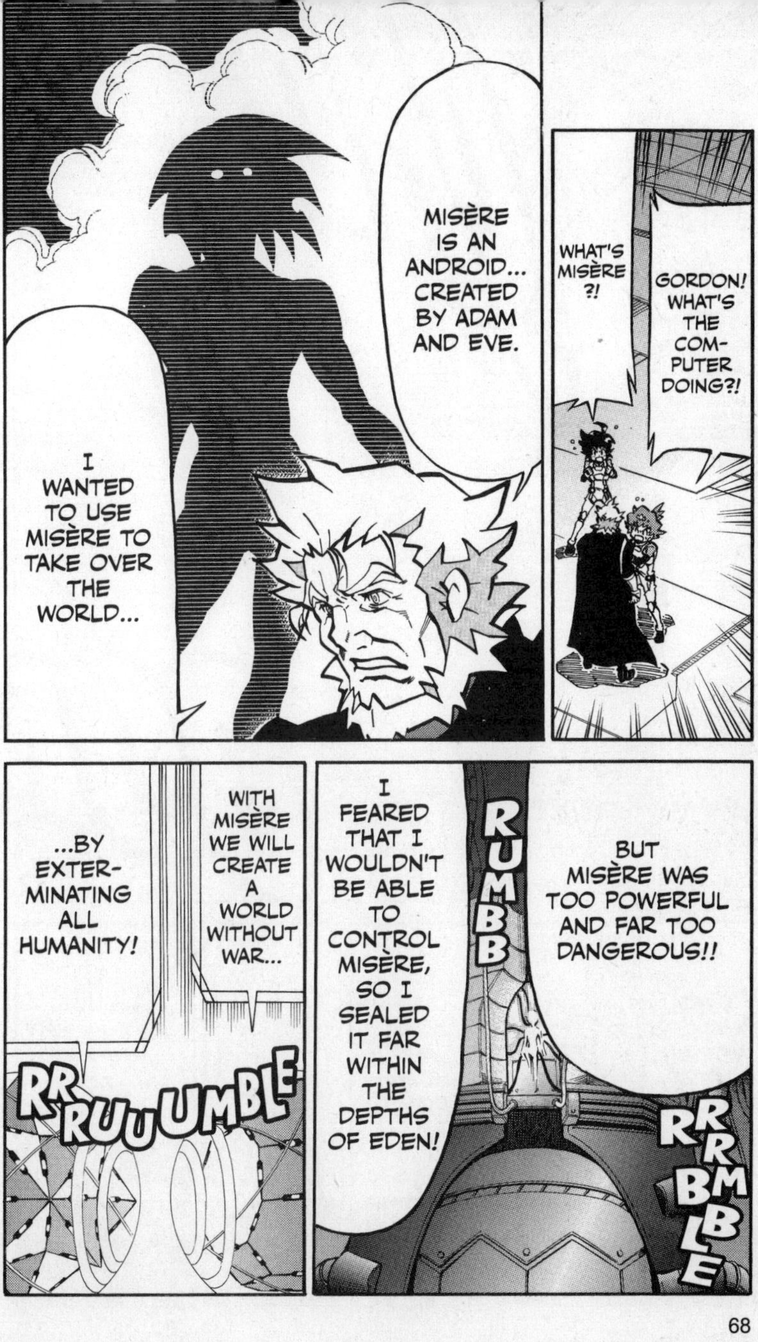
GORDON! WHAT'S THE COMPUTER DOING?!
WHAT'S MISÈRE ?!
MISÈRE IS AN ANDROID... CREATED BY ADAM AND EVE.
I WANTED TO USE MISÈRE TO TAKE OVER THE WORLD...
BUT MISÈRE WAS TOO POWERFUL AND FAR TOO DANGEROUS!!
RUMBB
RRRMBBLE
I FEARED THAT I WOULDN'T BE ABLE TO CONTROL MISÈRE, SO I SEALED IT FAR WITHIN THE DEPTHS OF EDEN!
WITH MISÈRE WE WILL CREATE A WORLD WITHOUT WAR...
...BY EXTERMINATING ALL HUMANITY!
RRRUUUMBLE

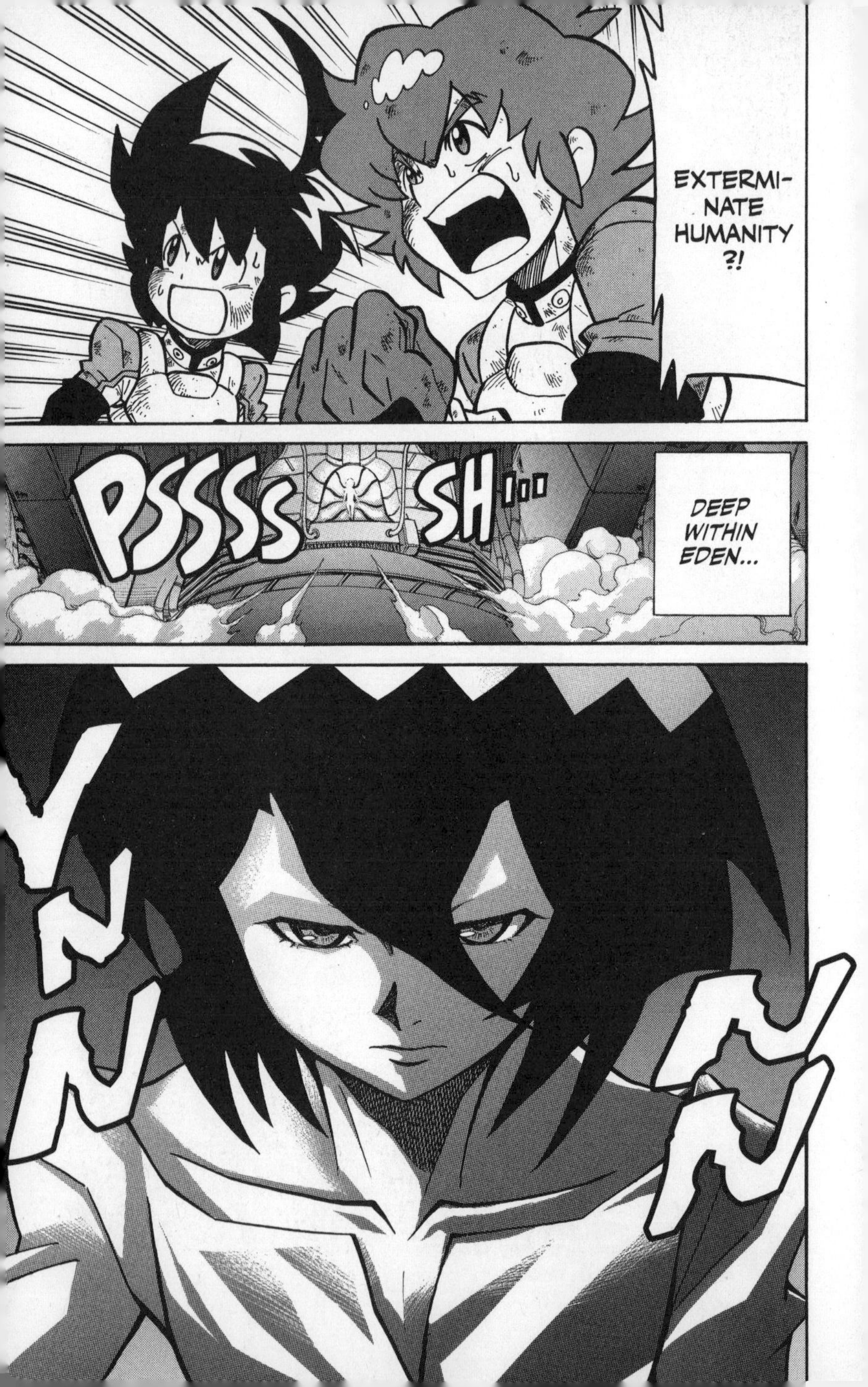
EXTERMINATE HUMANITY ?!
DEEP WITHIN EDEN...
PSSSSSH...

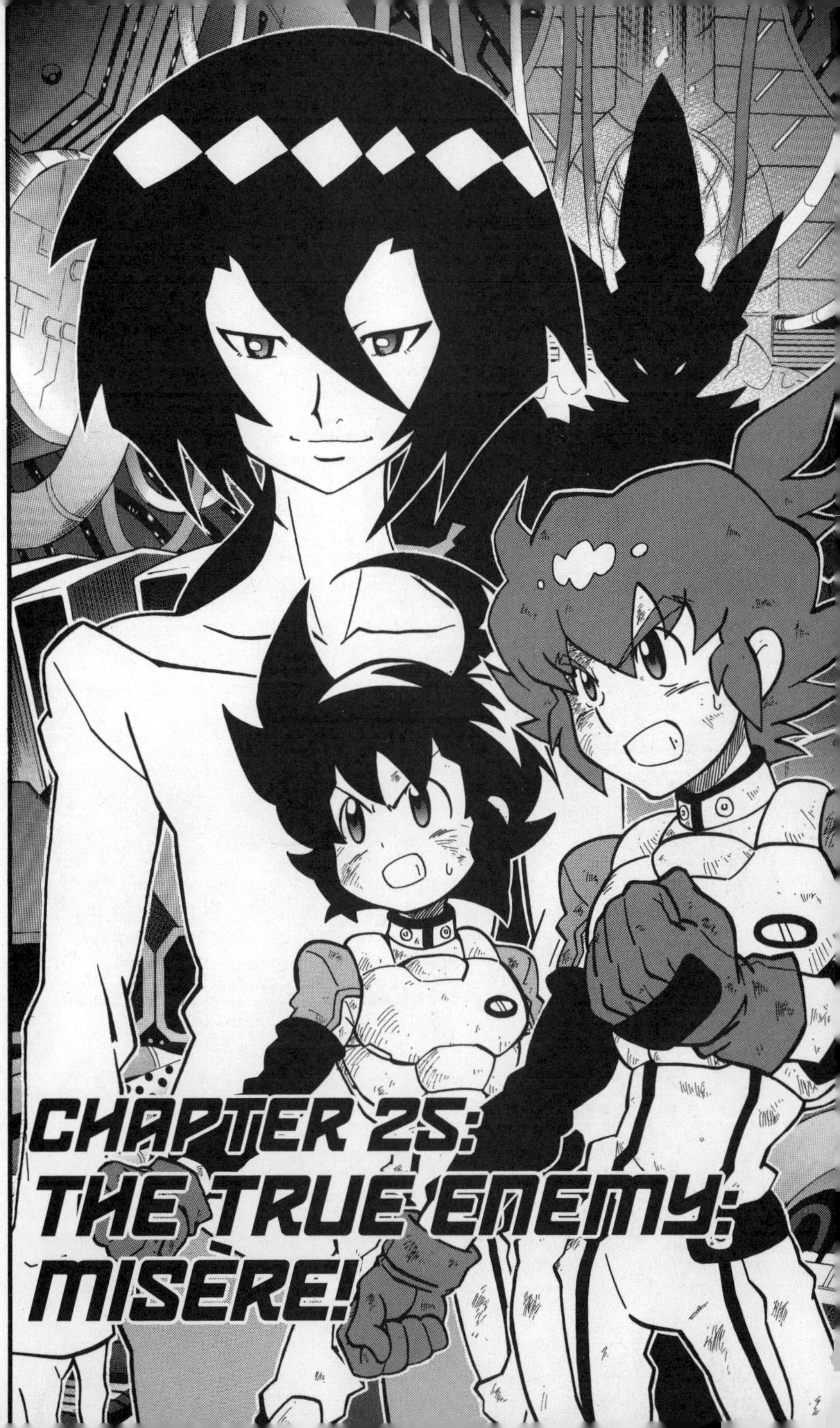
CHAPTER 25:
THE TRUE ENEMY:
MISÈRE!

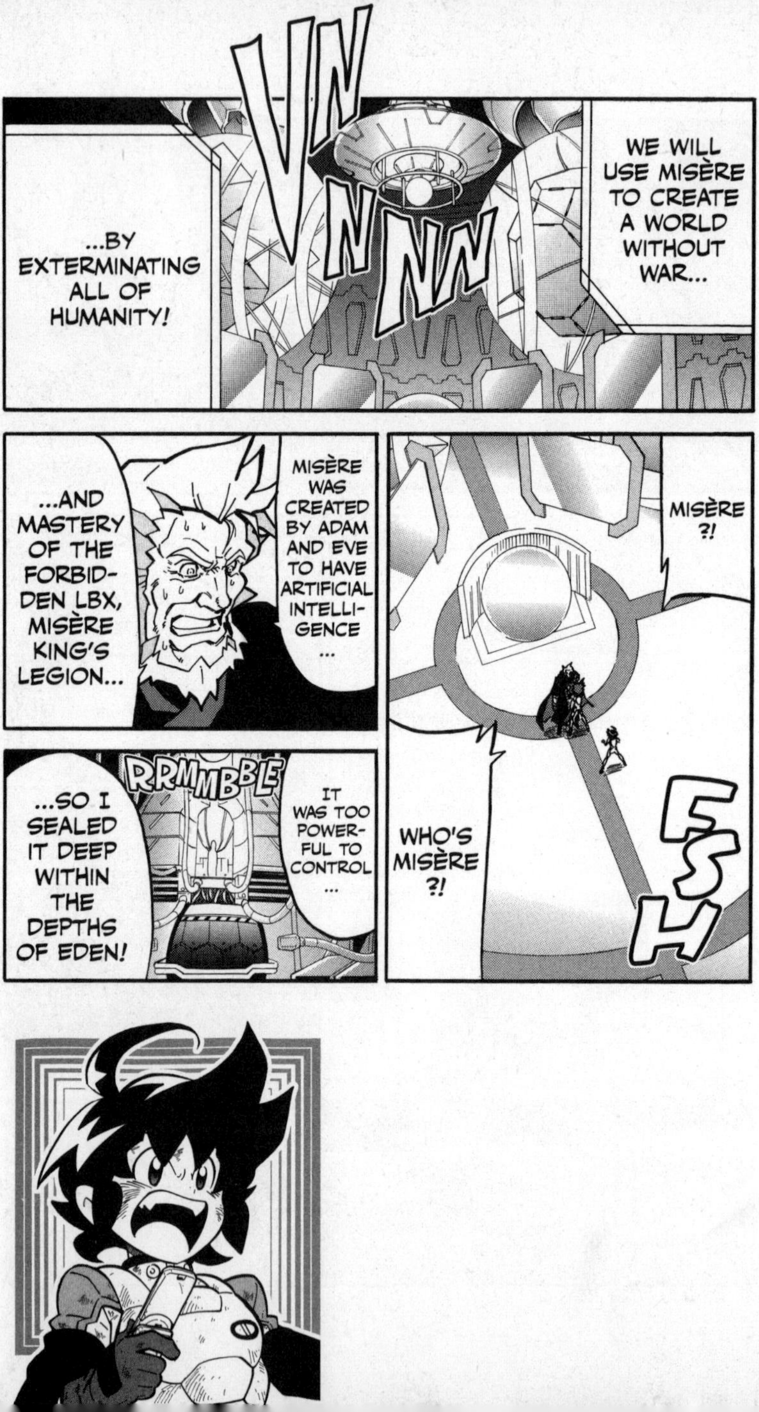
WE WILL USE MISÈRE TO CREATE A WORLD WITHOUT WAR...
VNNNN
...BY EXTERMINATING ALL OF HUMANITY!
MISÈRE ?!
WHO'S MISÈRE ?!
FSH
MISÈRE WAS CREATED BY ADAM AND EVE TO HAVE ARTIFICIAL INTELLIGENCE ...
...AND MASTERY OF THE FORBIDDEN LBX, MISÈRE KING'S LEGION...
IT WAS TOO POWERFUL TO CONTROL ...
RRMMBBLE
...SO I SEALED IT DEEP WITHIN THE DEPTHS OF EDEN!

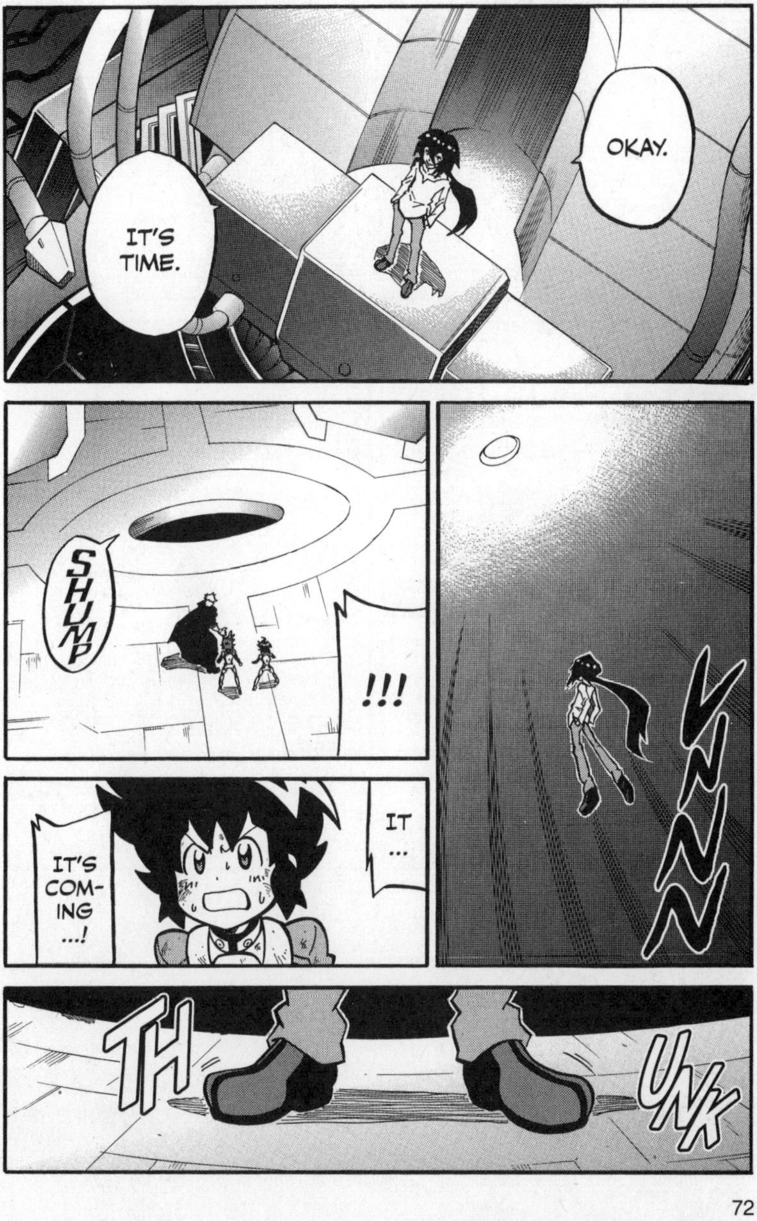
OKAY.
IT'S TIME.
VNNNN
SHUMP
!!!
IT...
IT'S COMING...!
THUNK

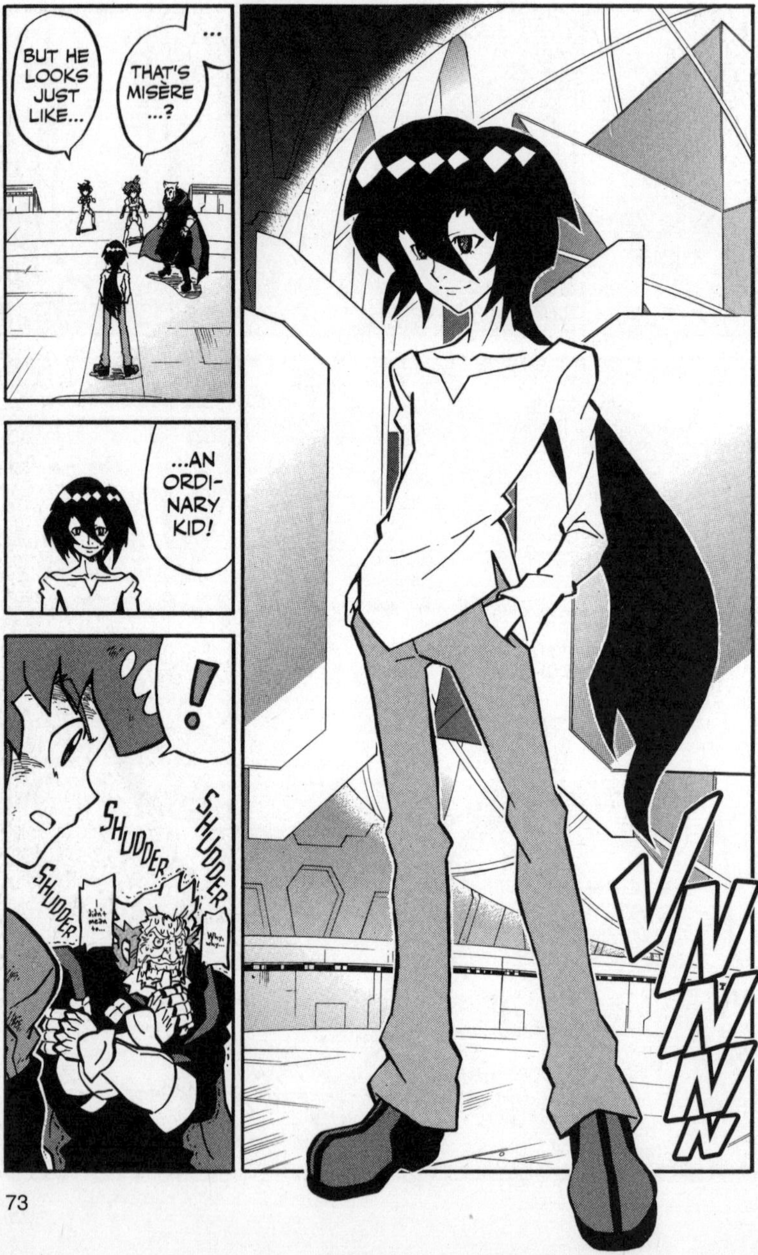
JNNNNN
... THAT'S MISÈRE ...?
BUT HE LOOKS JUST LIKE...
...AN ORDINARY KID!
!
SHUDDER
SHUDDER
SHUDDER
Why, why...
I didn't mean to...

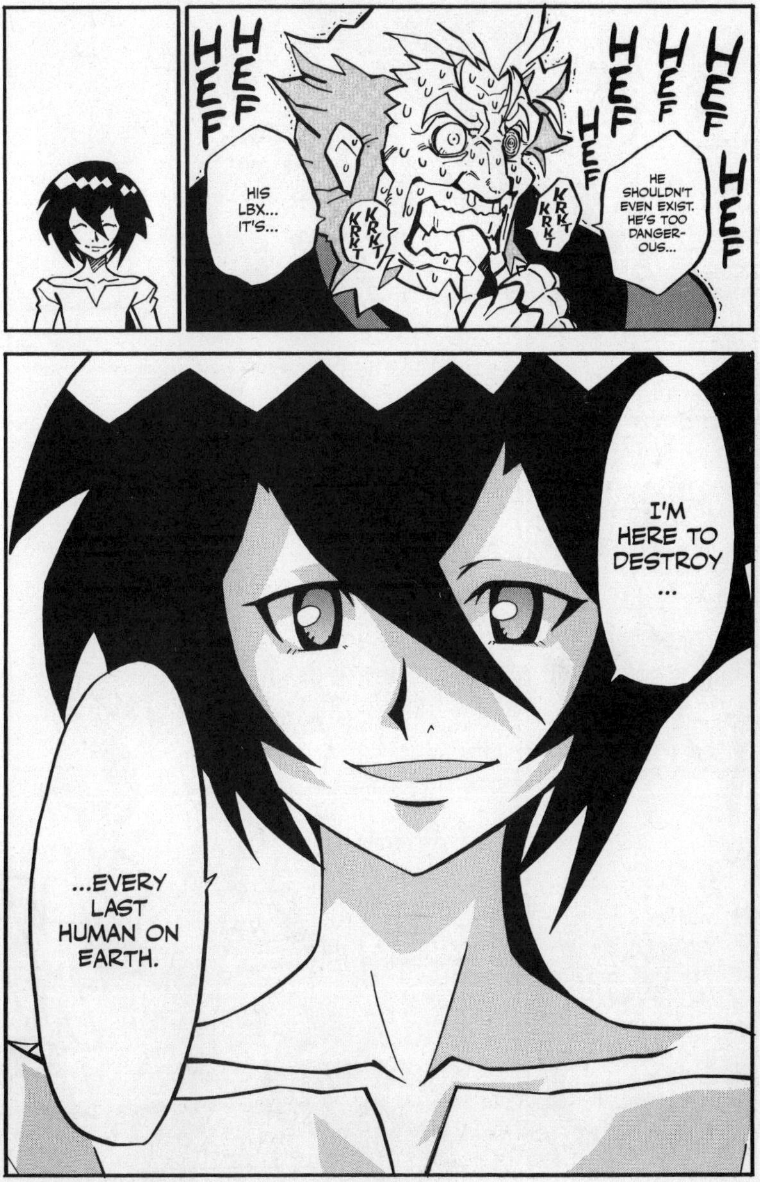
HEF HEF HEF HEF HEF
HE SHOULDN'T EVEN EXIST. HE'S TOO DANGER-OUS...
KRKT KRKT
KRKT KRKT
HIS LBX... IT'S...
HEF HEF
I'M HERE TO DESTROY ...
...EVERY LAST HUMAN ON EARTH.

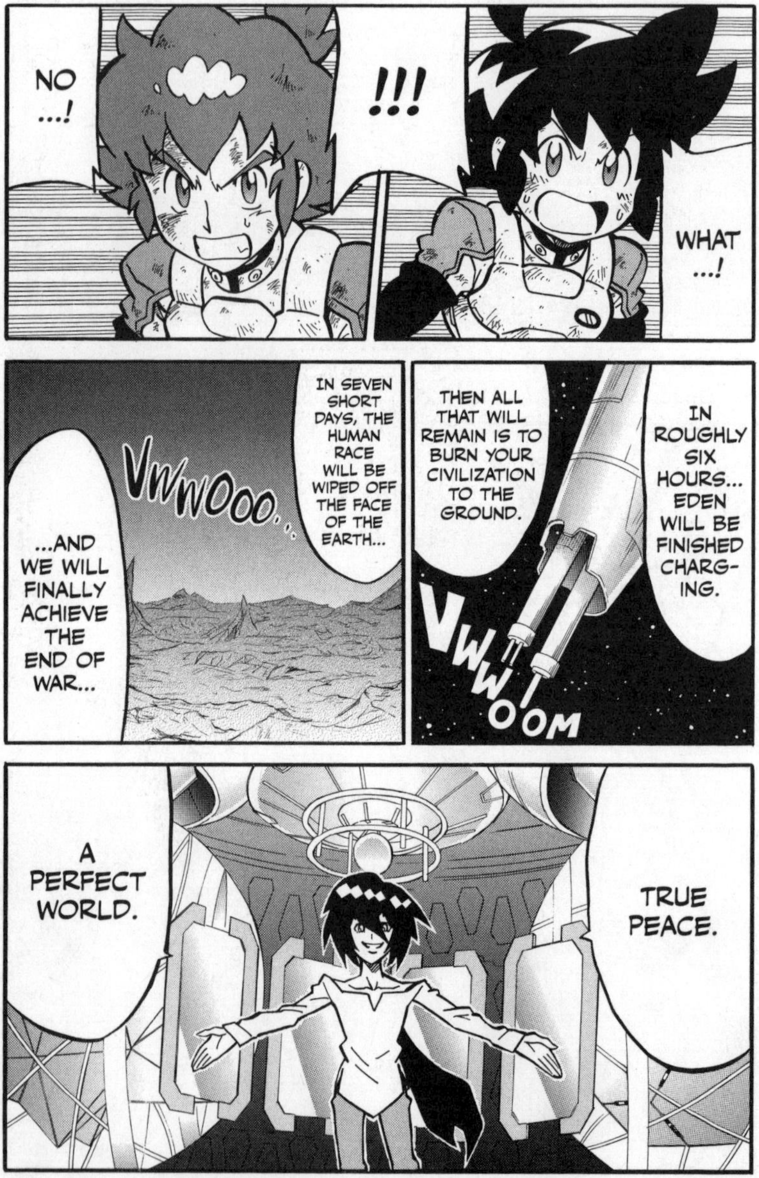
!!!
WHAT ...!
NO ...!
IN ROUGHLY SIX HOURS... EDEN WILL BE FINISHED CHARG-ING.
THEN ALL THAT WILL REMAIN IS TO BURN YOUR CIVILIZATION TO THE GROUND.
VWWWOOM
IN SEVEN SHORT DAYS, THE HUMAN RACE WILL BE WIPED OFF THE FACE OF THE EARTH...
VWWOOO...
...AND WE WILL FINALLY ACHIEVE THE END OF WAR...
TRUE PEACE.
A PERFECT WORLD.

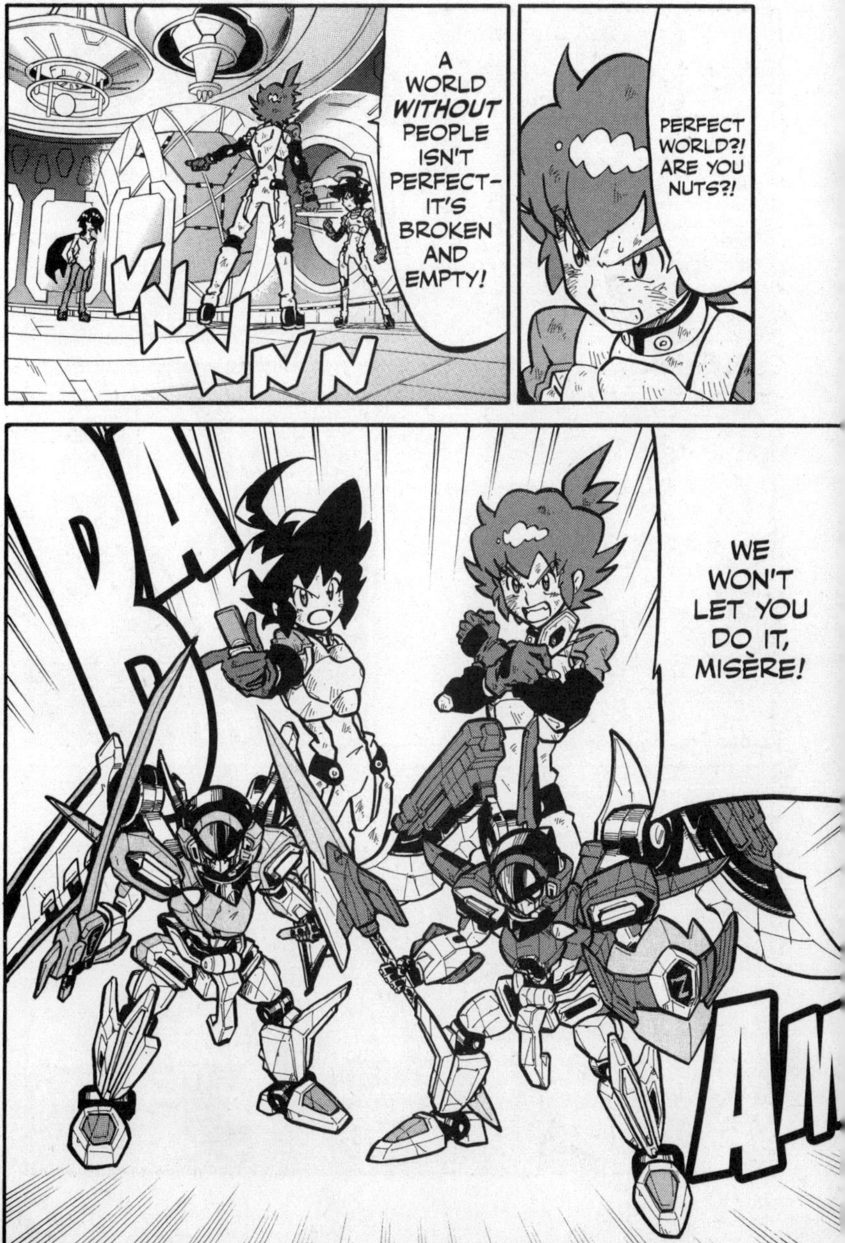
PERFECT WORLD?! ARE YOU NUTS?!
A WORLD *WITHOUT* PEOPLE ISN'T PERFECT–IT'S BROKEN AND EMPTY!
VNNNN
WE WON'T LET YOU DO IT, MISÈRE!

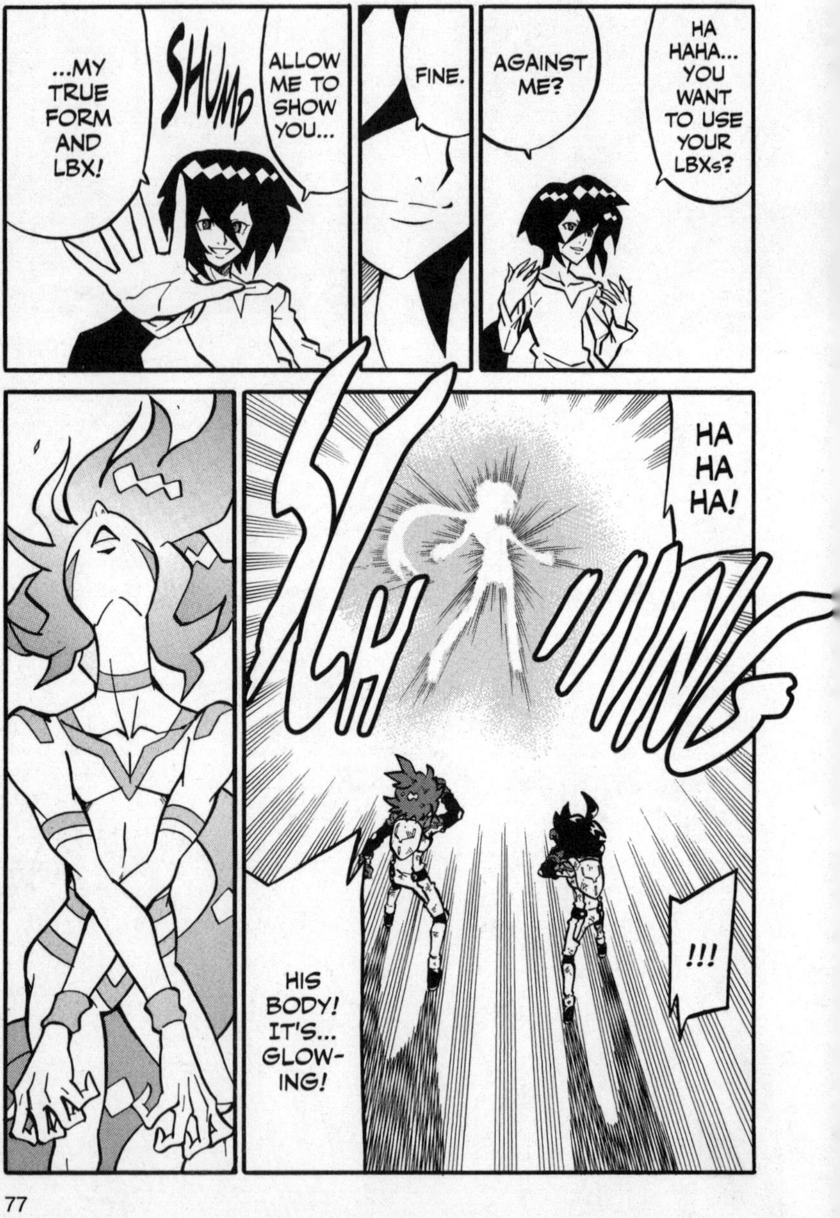
HA HAHA... YOU WANT TO USE YOUR LBXs?
AGAINST ME?
FINE.
ALLOW ME TO SHOW YOU...
SHUMP
...MY TRUE FORM AND LBX!
HA HA HA!
!!!
HIS BODY! IT'S... GLOW-ING!

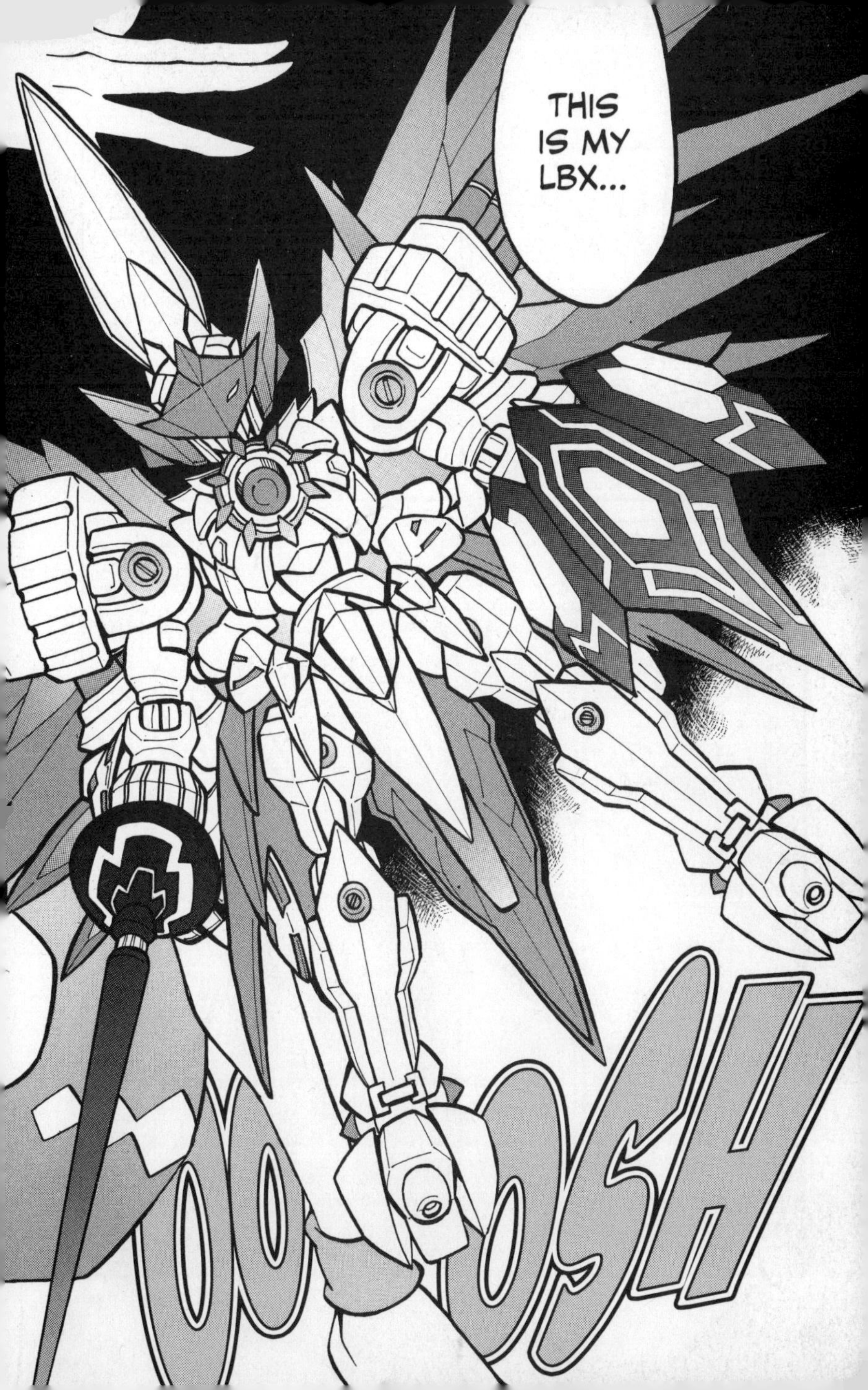
THIS IS MY LBX...
WHOOOOSH

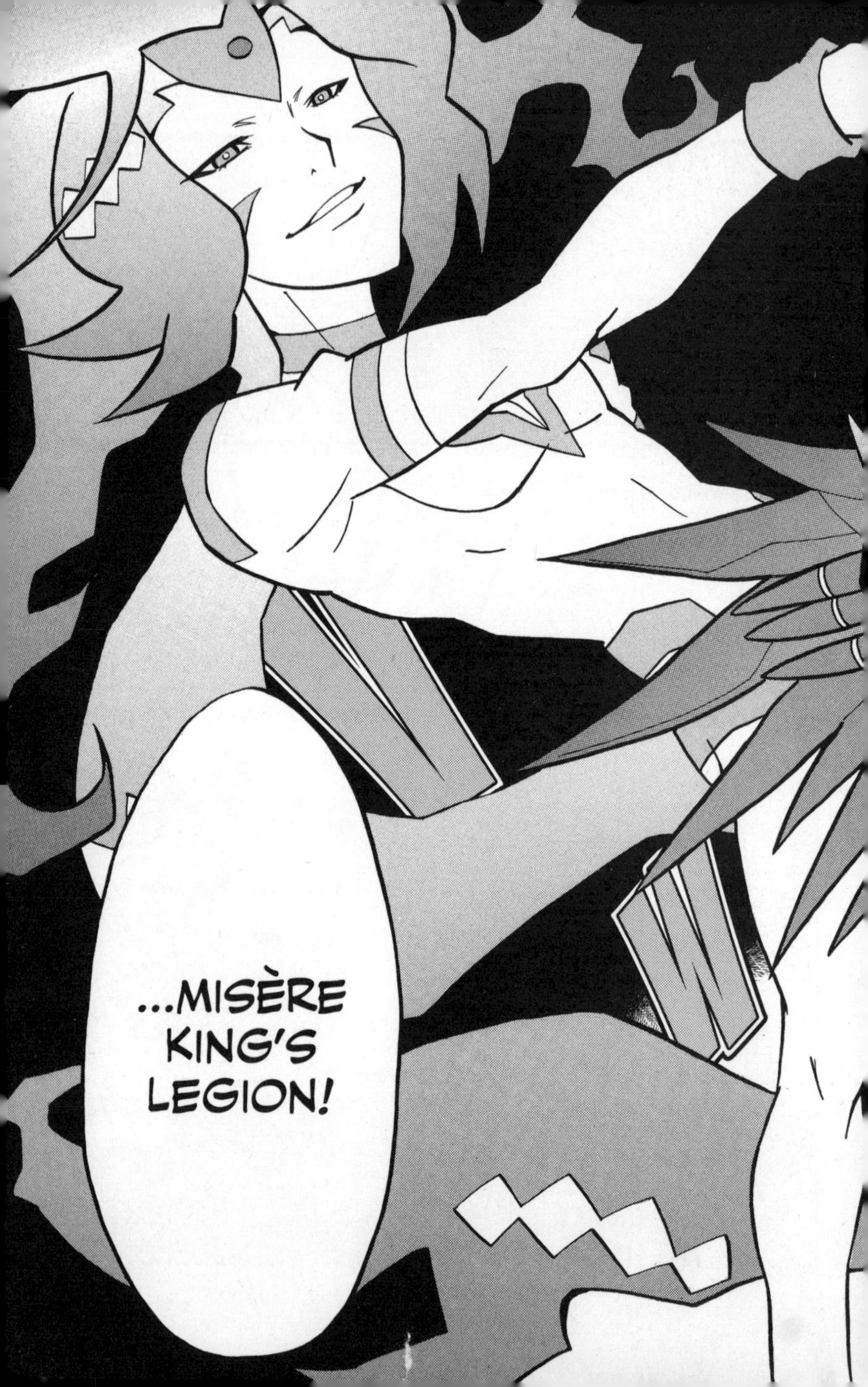
...MISÈRE KING'S LEGION!

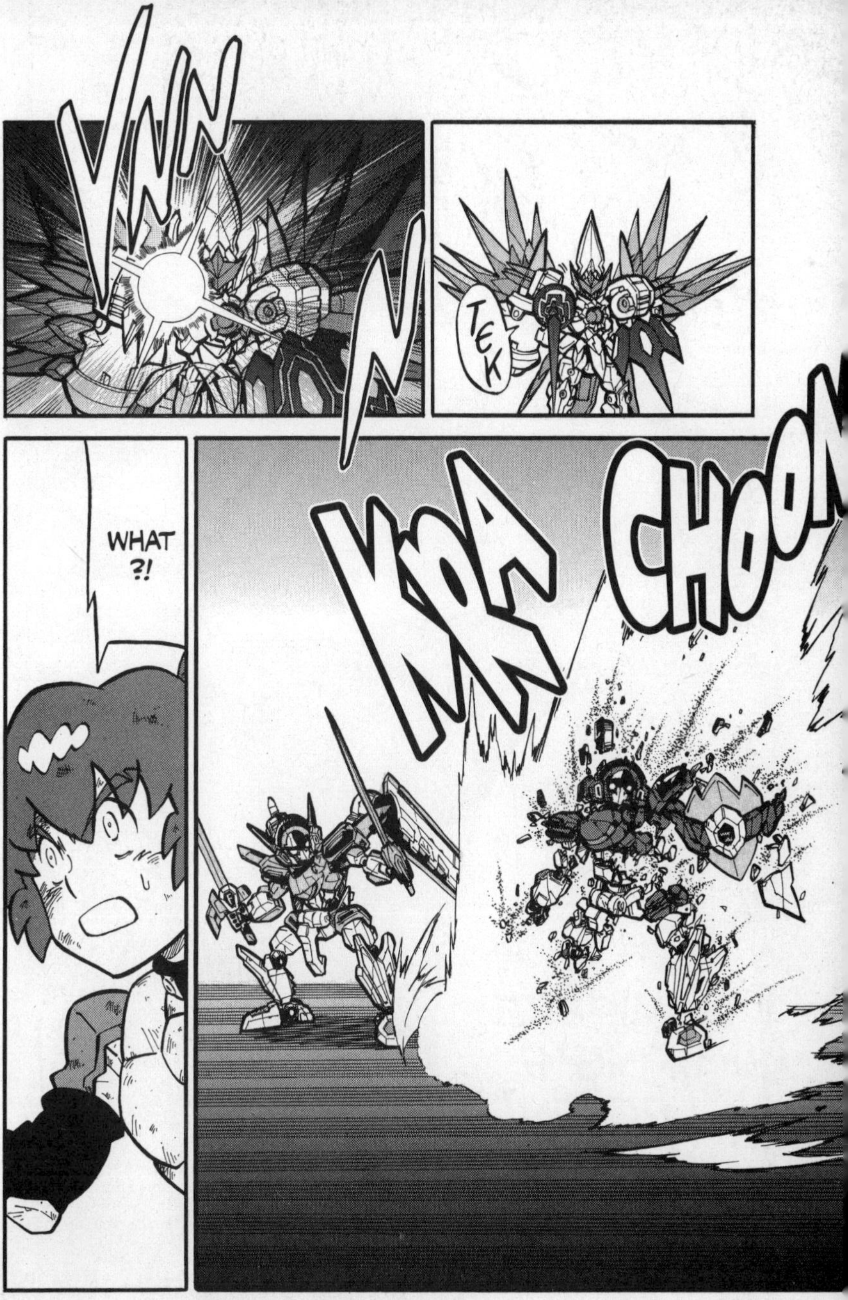
TEK
VWIN
KRA
CHOO
WHAT ?!

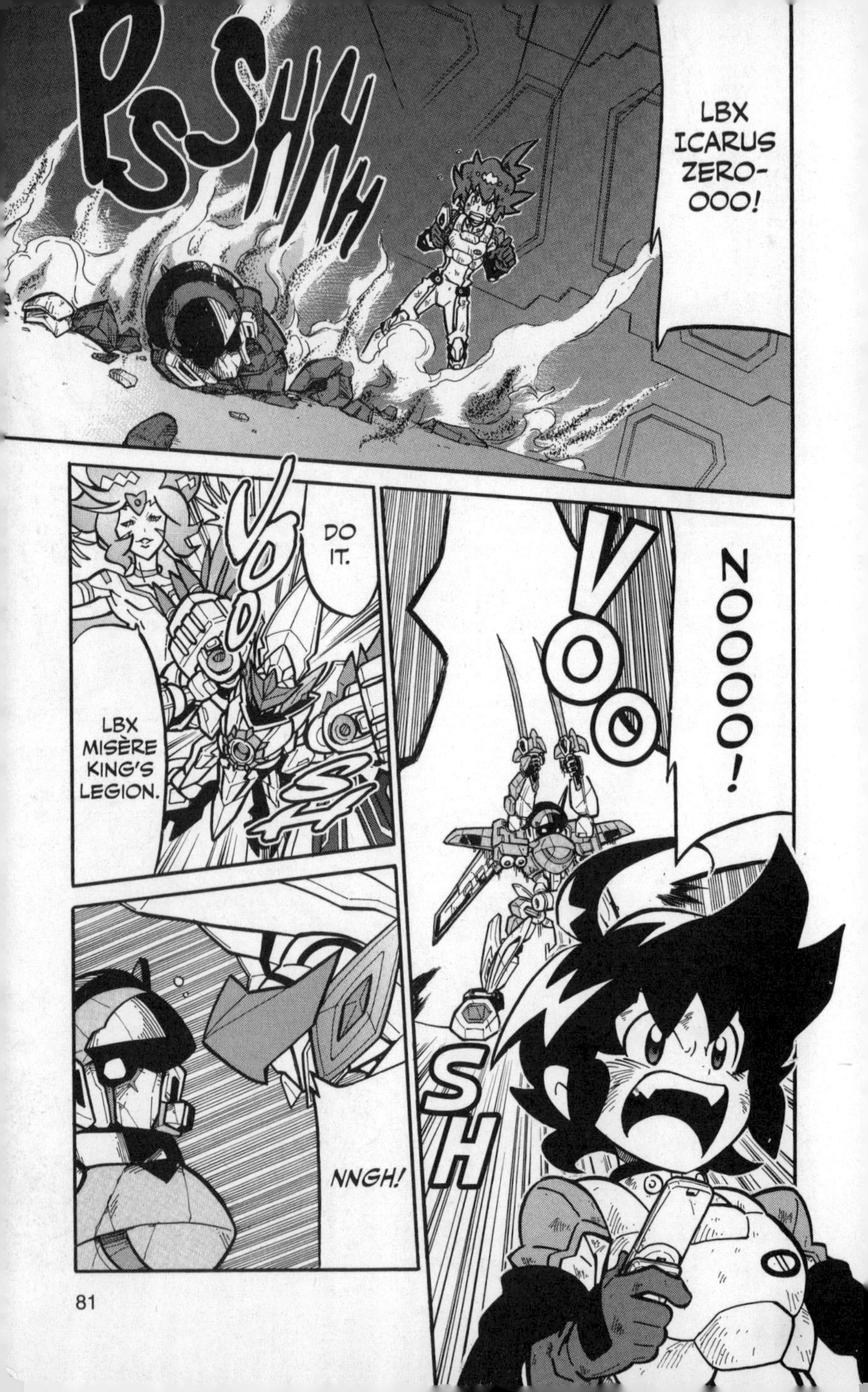
PSSHH
LBX ICARUS ZERO-OOO!
VOO
NOOOOO!
SH
DO IT.
VOOO
LBX MISÈRE KING'S LEGION.
NNGH!

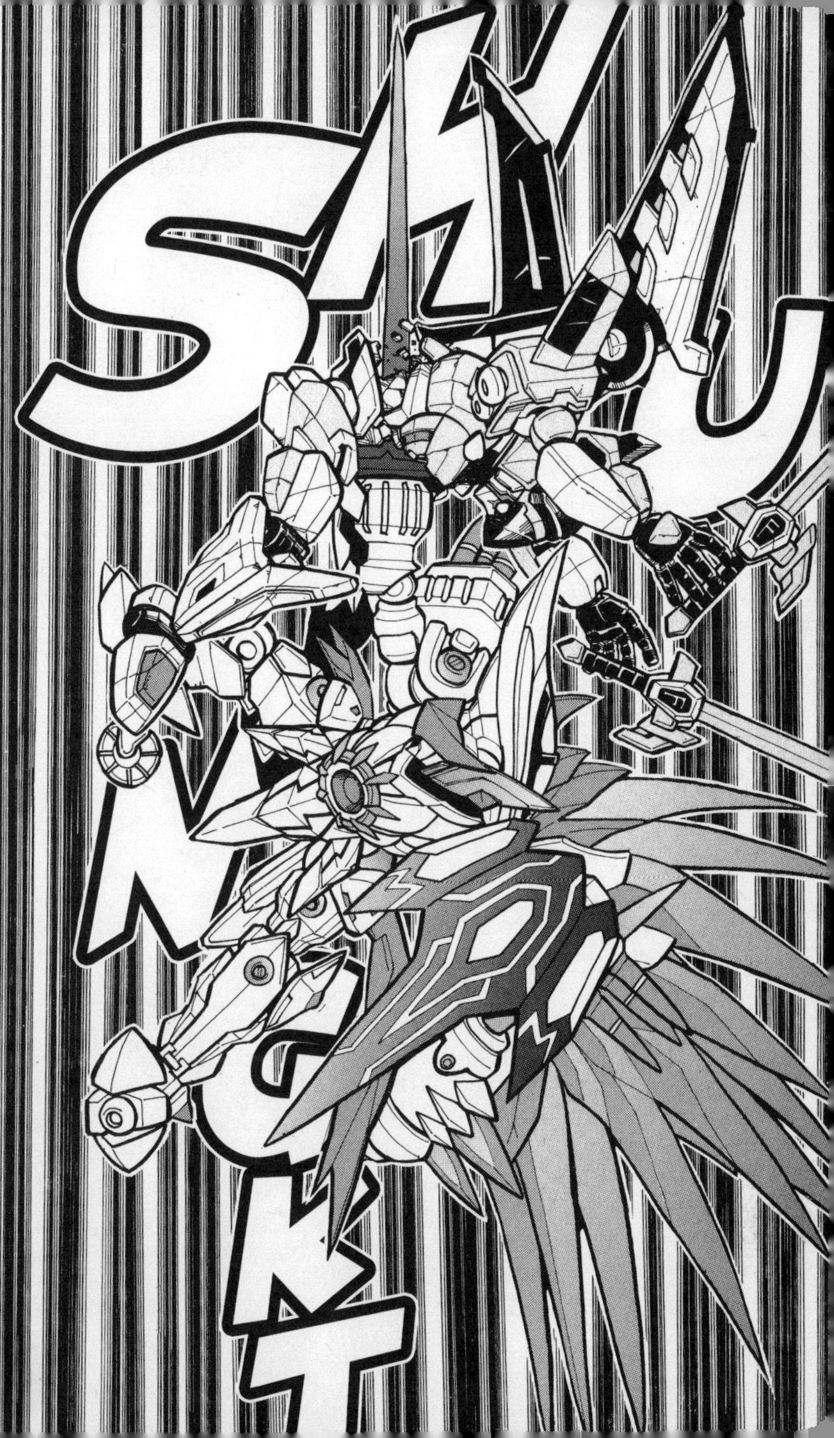
SHUNG

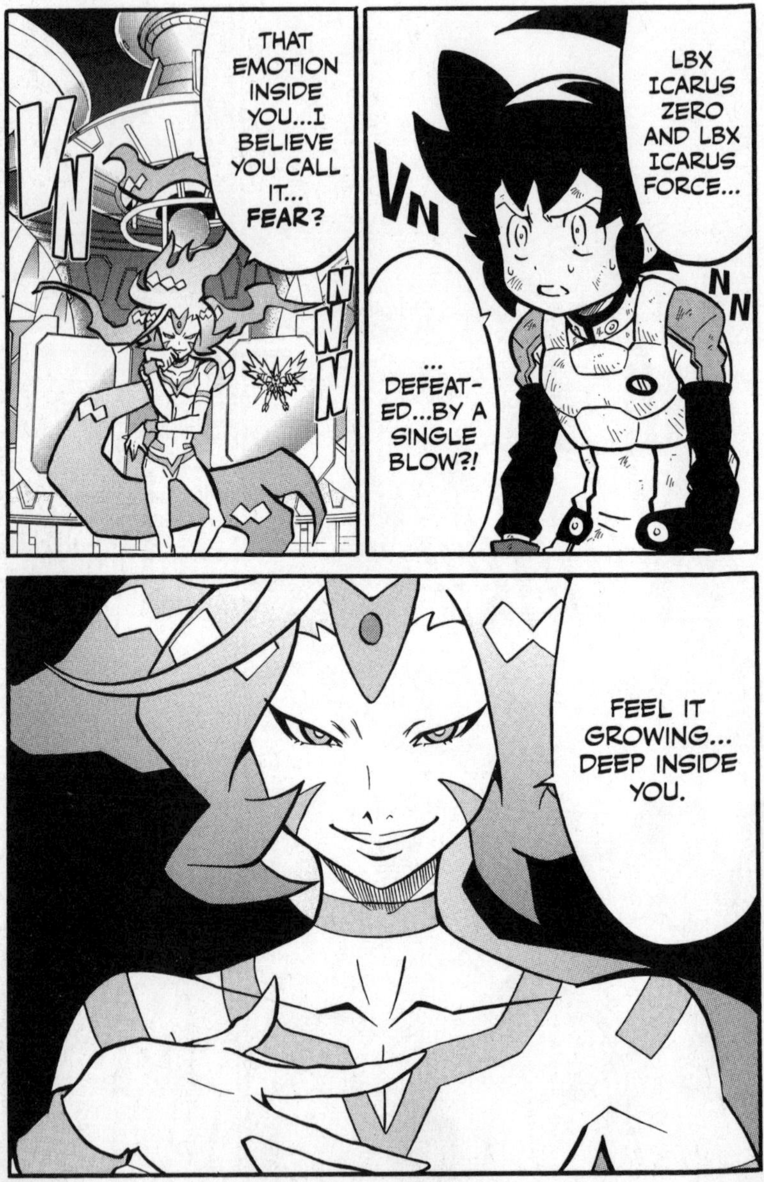
LBX ICARUS ZERO AND LBX ICARUS FORCE...
VN
NN
... DEFEAT-ED...BY A SINGLE BLOW?!
THAT EMOTION INSIDE YOU...I BELIEVE YOU CALL IT... **FEAR?**
VN
NNN
FEEL IT GROWING... DEEP INSIDE YOU.

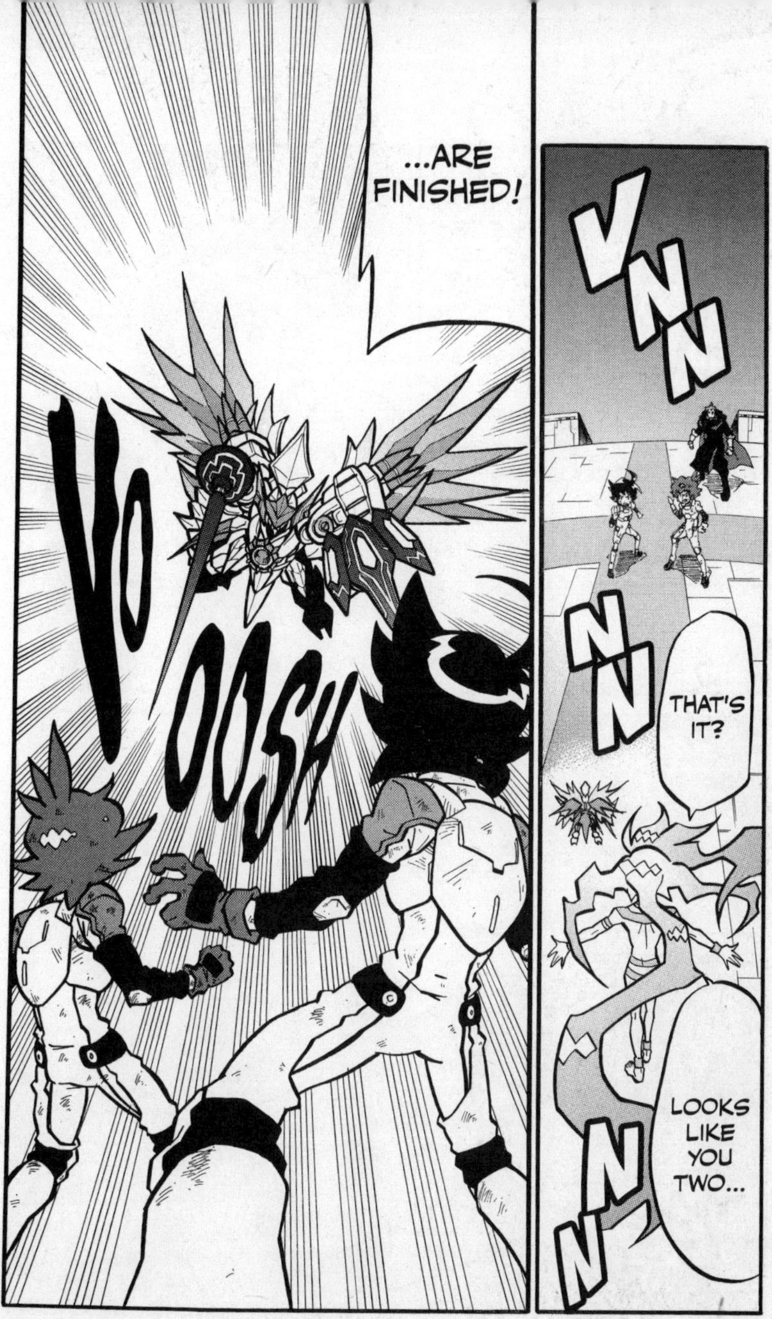
VNNNNNNN
THAT'S IT?
LOOKS LIKE YOU TWO...
...ARE FINISHED!
VOOOSH

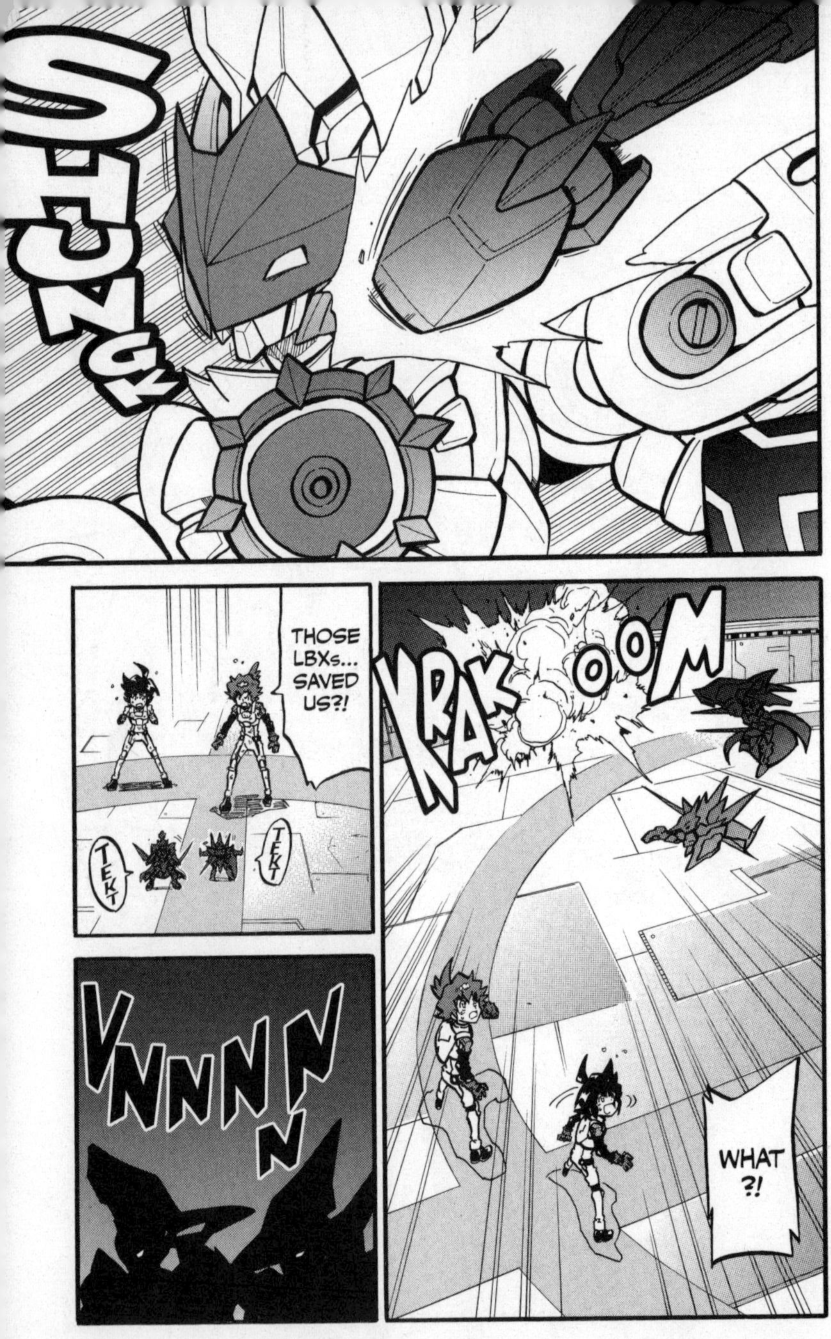
SHUNGK
KRAKOOM
WHAT?!
THOSE LBXs... SAVED US?!
TEKT
TEKT
VNNNNN

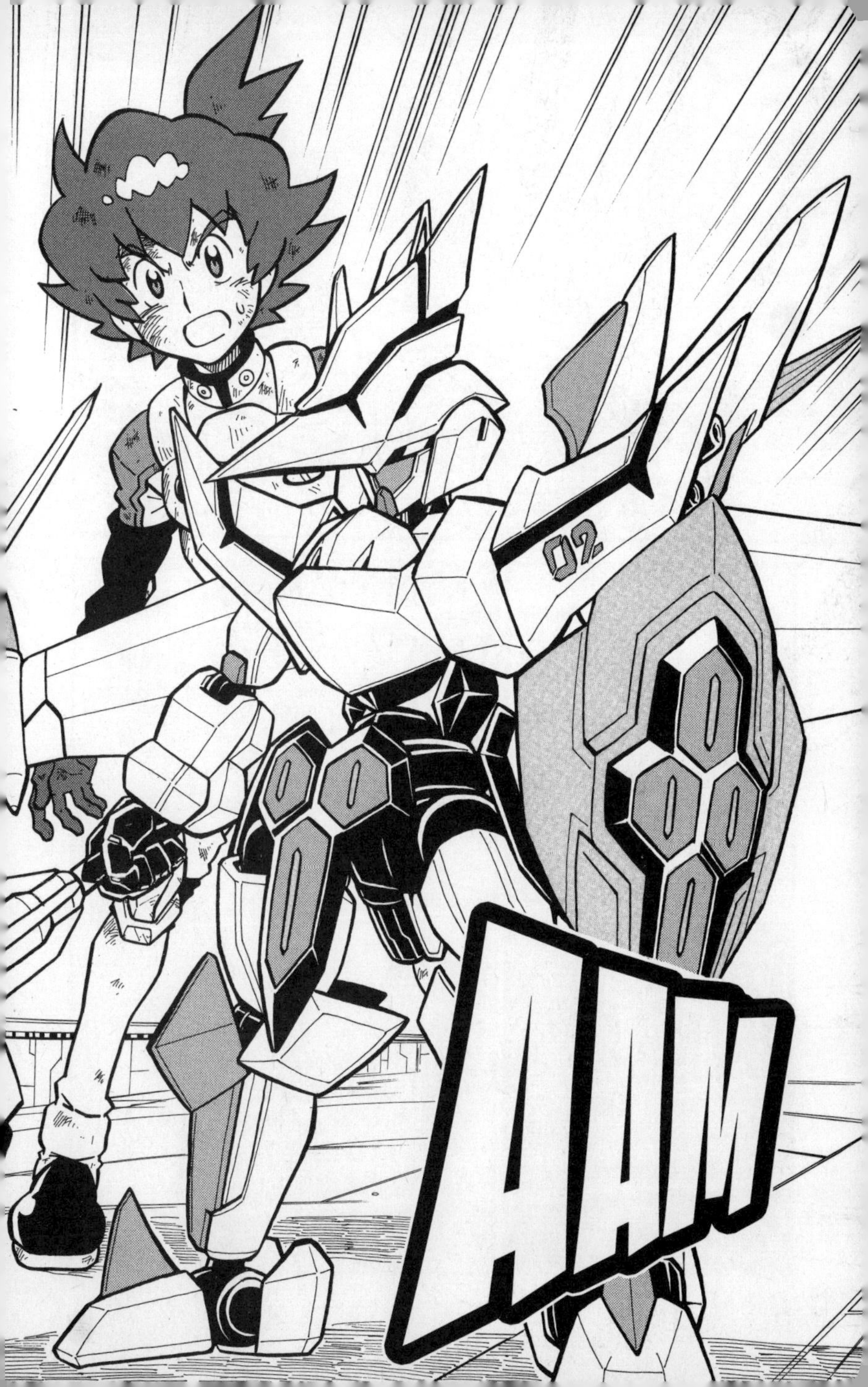
02
AAM

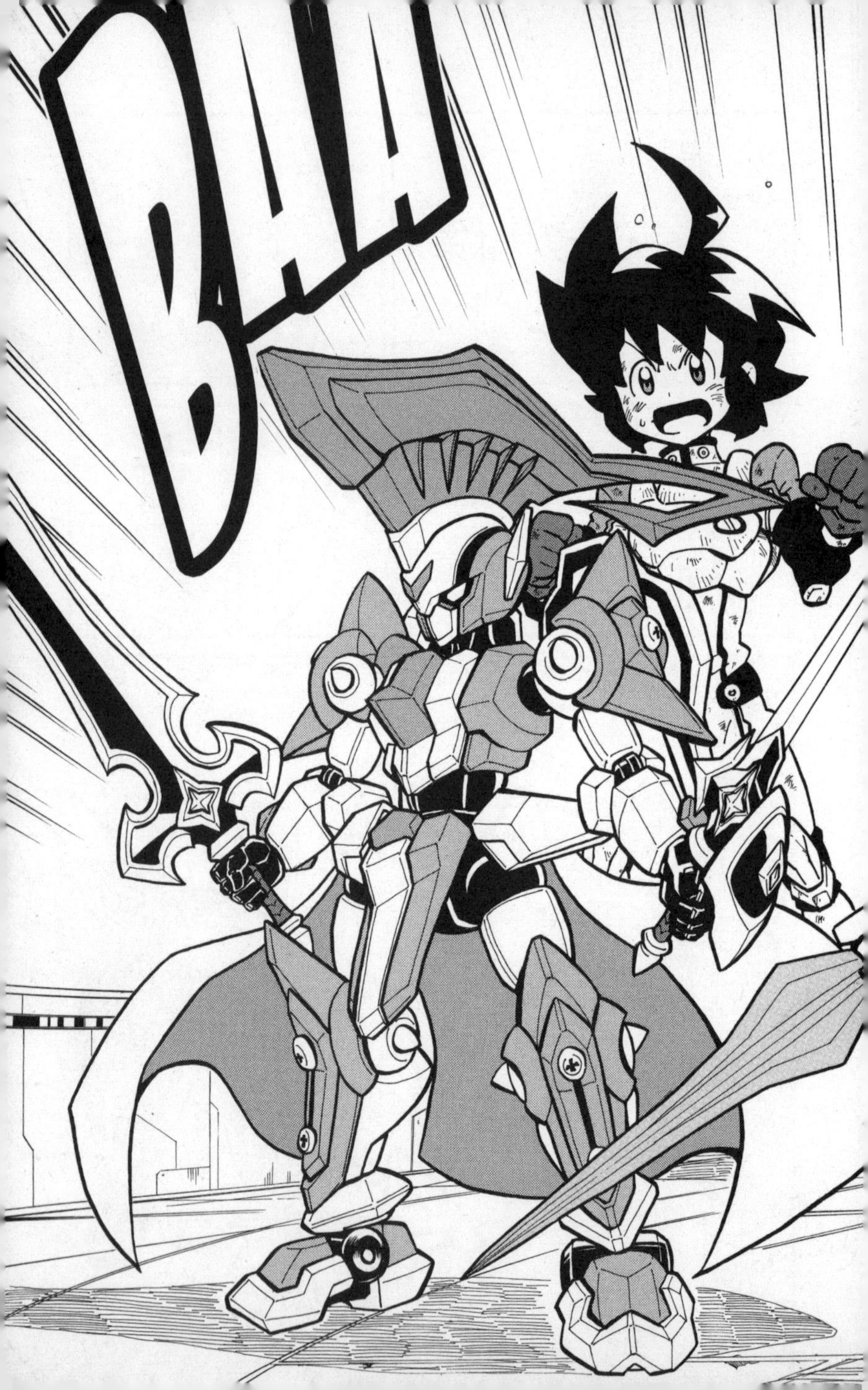
BAM

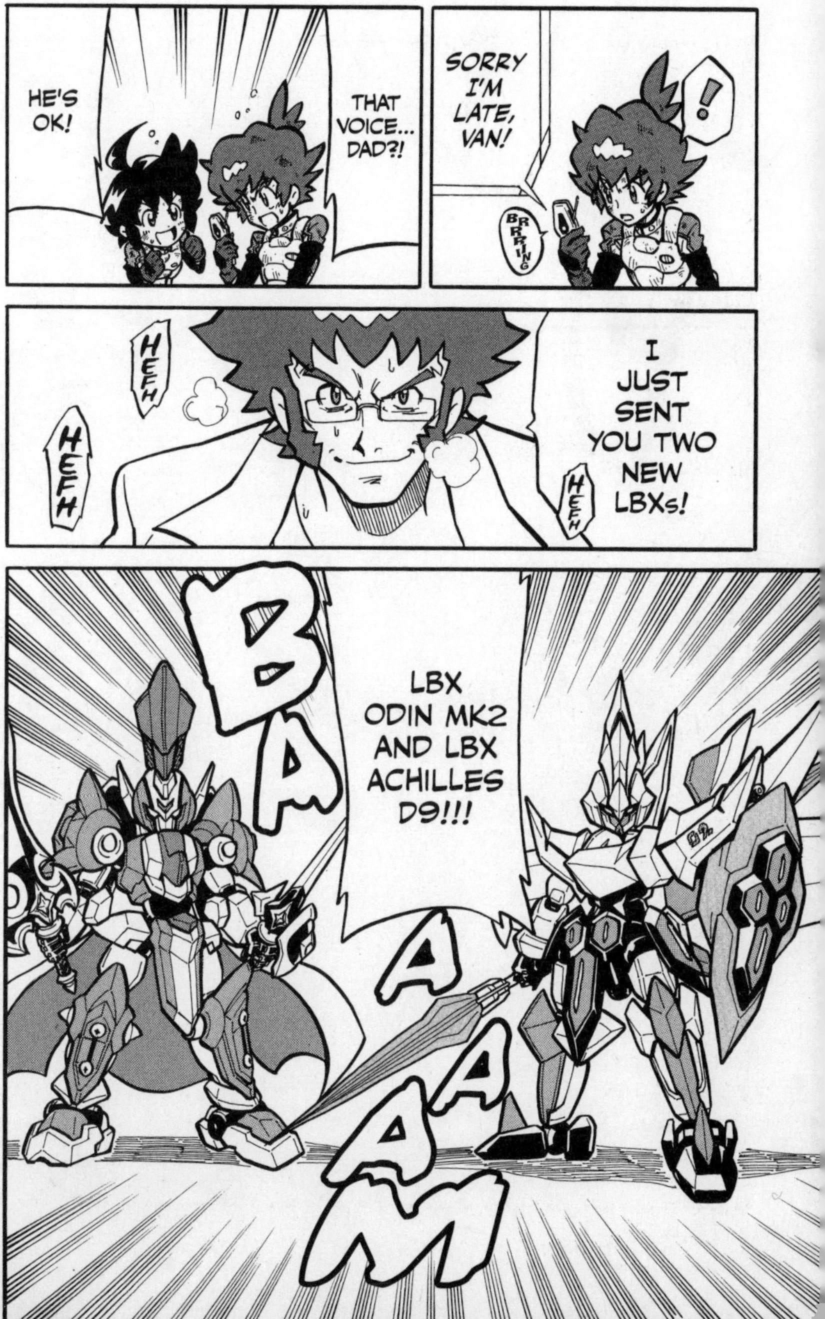
!
SORRY I'M LATE, VAN!
BRRRING
THAT VOICE... DAD?!
HE'S OK!
I JUST SENT YOU TWO NEW LBXs!
HEFH
HEFH
HEFH
LBX ODIN MK2 AND LBX ACHILLES D9!!!
BAAAAAM

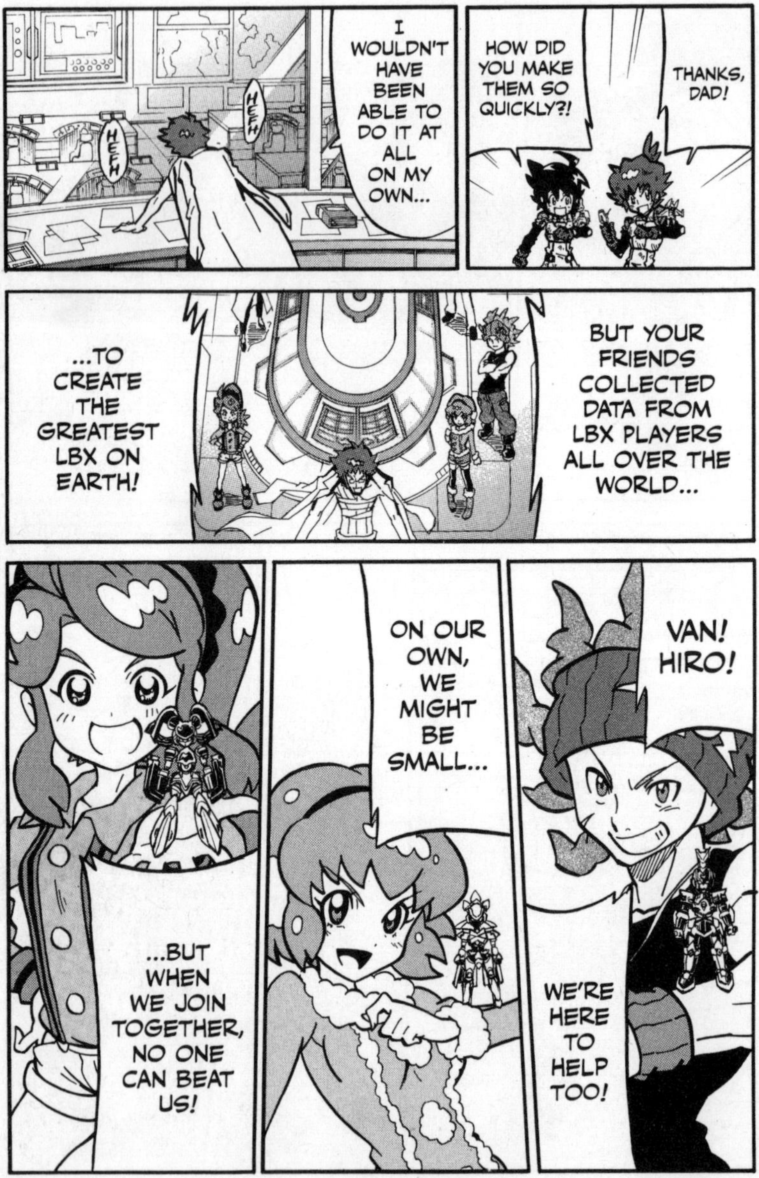
THANKS, DAD!
HOW DID YOU MAKE THEM SO QUICKLY?!
I WOULDN'T HAVE BEEN ABLE TO DO IT AT ALL ON MY OWN...
HEEH
HEEH
BUT YOUR FRIENDS COLLECTED DATA FROM LBX PLAYERS ALL OVER THE WORLD...
...TO CREATE THE GREATEST LBX ON EARTH!
VAN! HIRO!
WE'RE HERE TO HELP TOO!
ON OUR OWN, WE MIGHT BE SMALL...
...BUT WHEN WE JOIN TOGETHER, NO ONE CAN BEAT US!

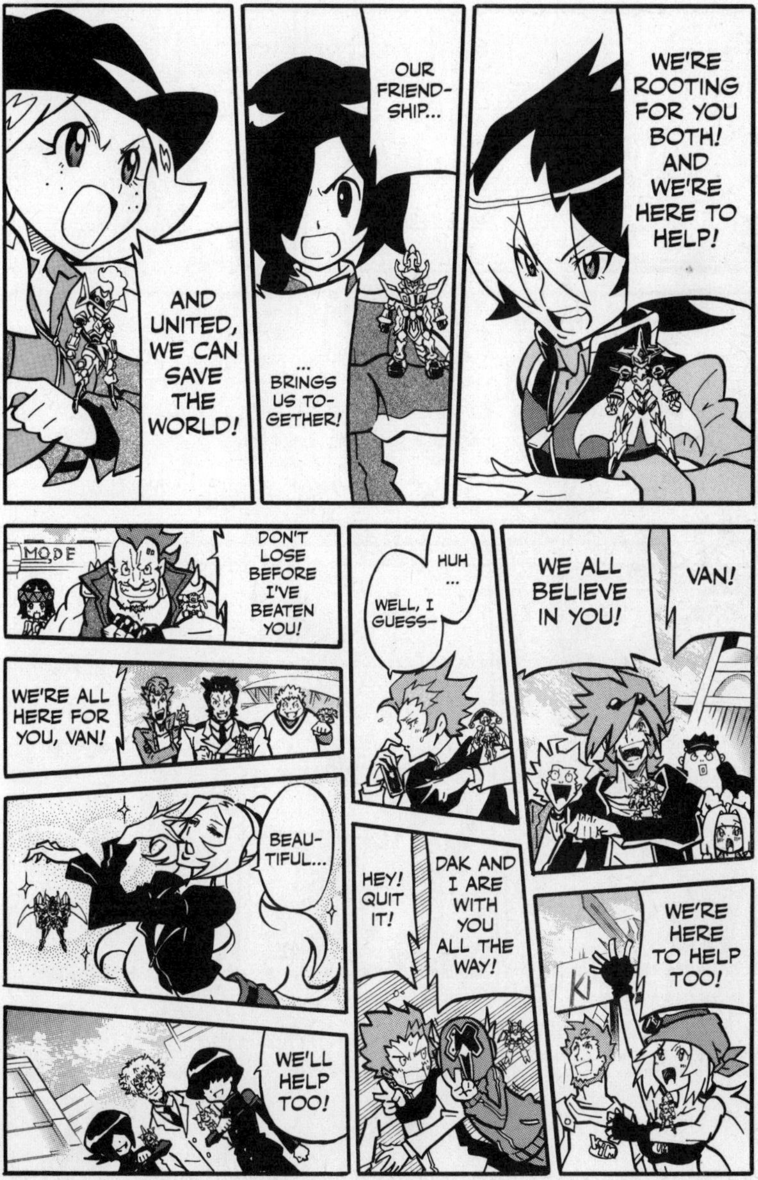
WE'RE ROOTING FOR YOU BOTH! AND WE'RE HERE TO HELP!
OUR FRIEND-SHIP...
...BRINGS US TO-GETHER!
AND UNITED, WE CAN SAVE THE WORLD!
VAN!
WE ALL BELIEVE IN YOU!
HUH...
WELL, I GUESS–
MODE
DON'T LOSE BEFORE I'VE BEATEN YOU!
WE'RE ALL HERE FOR YOU, VAN!
WE'RE HERE TO HELP TOO!
DAK AND I ARE WITH YOU ALL THE WAY!
HEY! QUIT IT!
BEAU-TIFUL...
WE'LL HELP TOO!

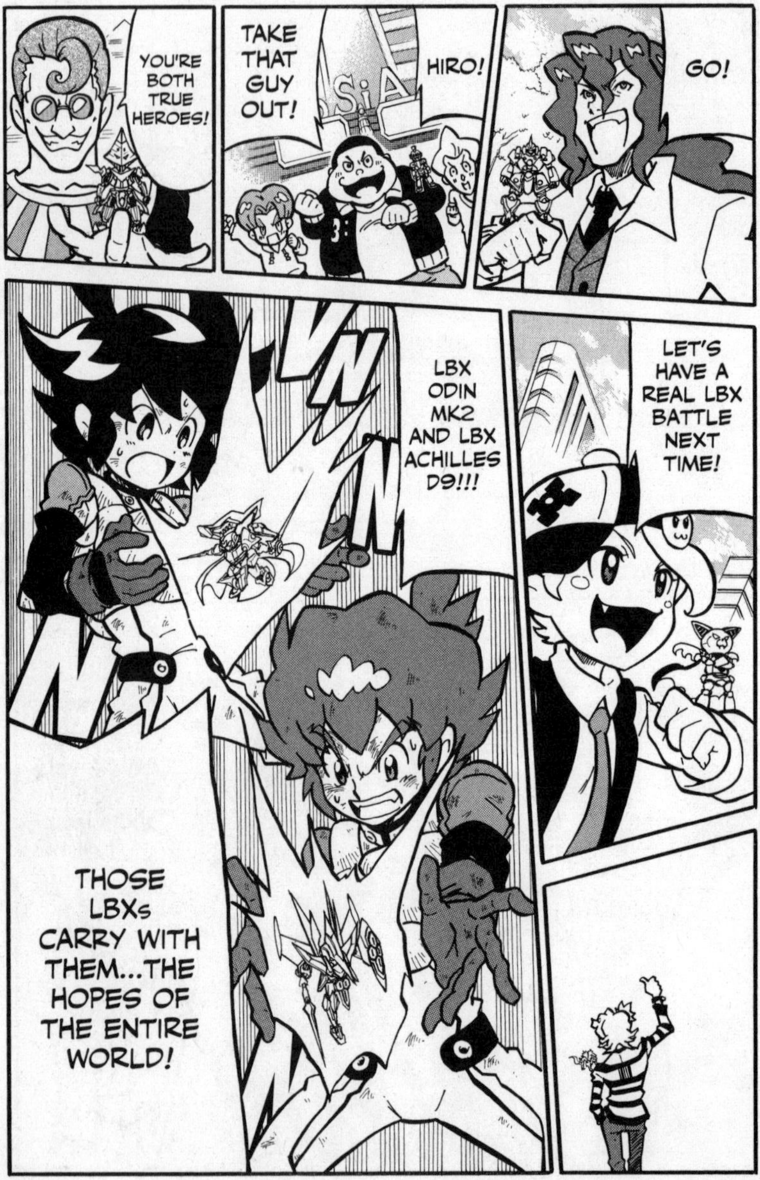
GO!
HIRO!
TAKE THAT GUY OUT!
YOU'RE BOTH TRUE HEROES!
LET'S HAVE A REAL LBX BATTLE NEXT TIME!
LBX ODIN MK2 AND LBX ACHILLES D9!!!
THOSE LBXs CARRY WITH THEM...THE HOPES OF THE ENTIRE WORLD!

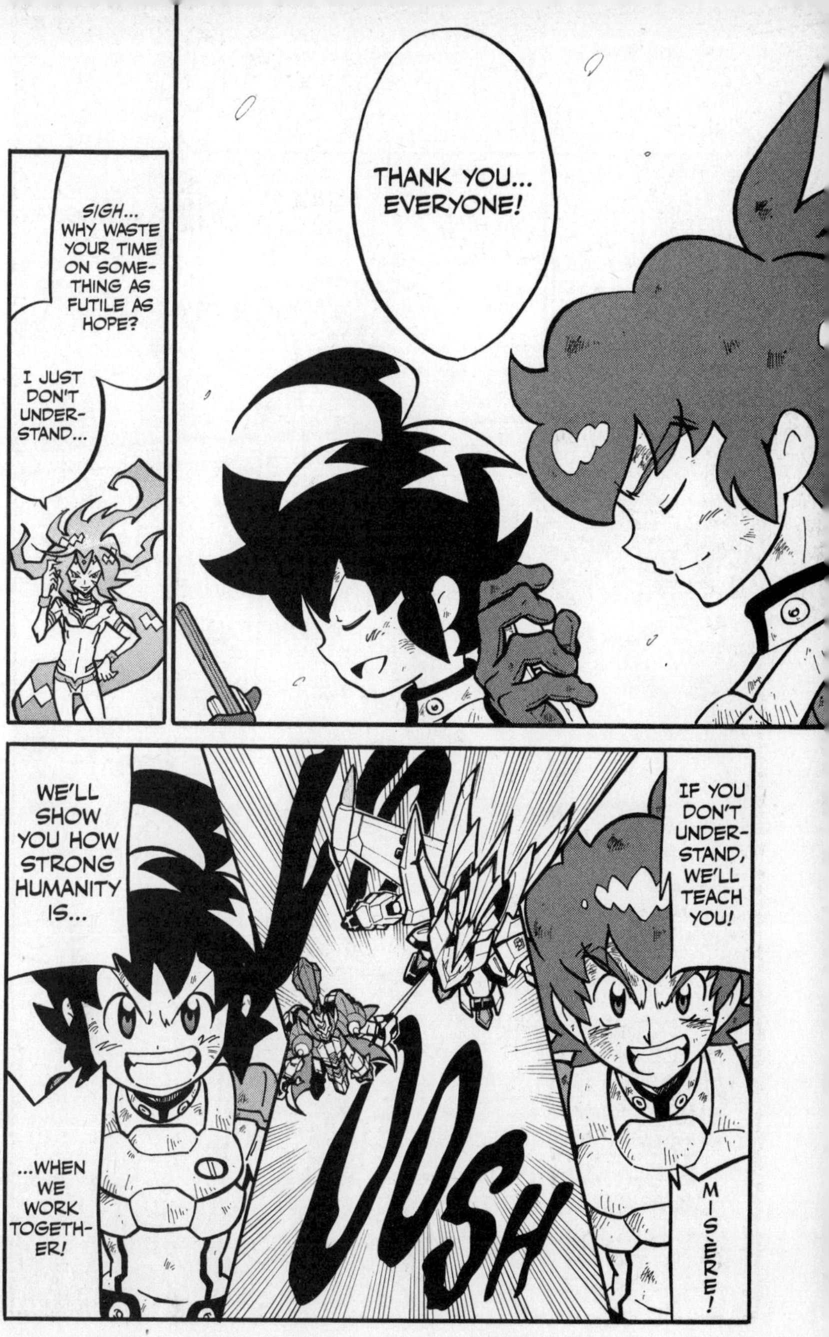
THANK YOU... EVERYONE!
SIGH... WHY WASTE YOUR TIME ON SOME-THING AS FUTILE AS HOPE?
I JUST DON'T UNDER-STAND...
IF YOU DON'T UNDER-STAND, WE'LL TEACH YOU!
WE'LL SHOW YOU HOW STRONG HUMANITY IS...
VOOSH
MI-S'ERE!
...WHEN WE WORK TOGETH-ER!

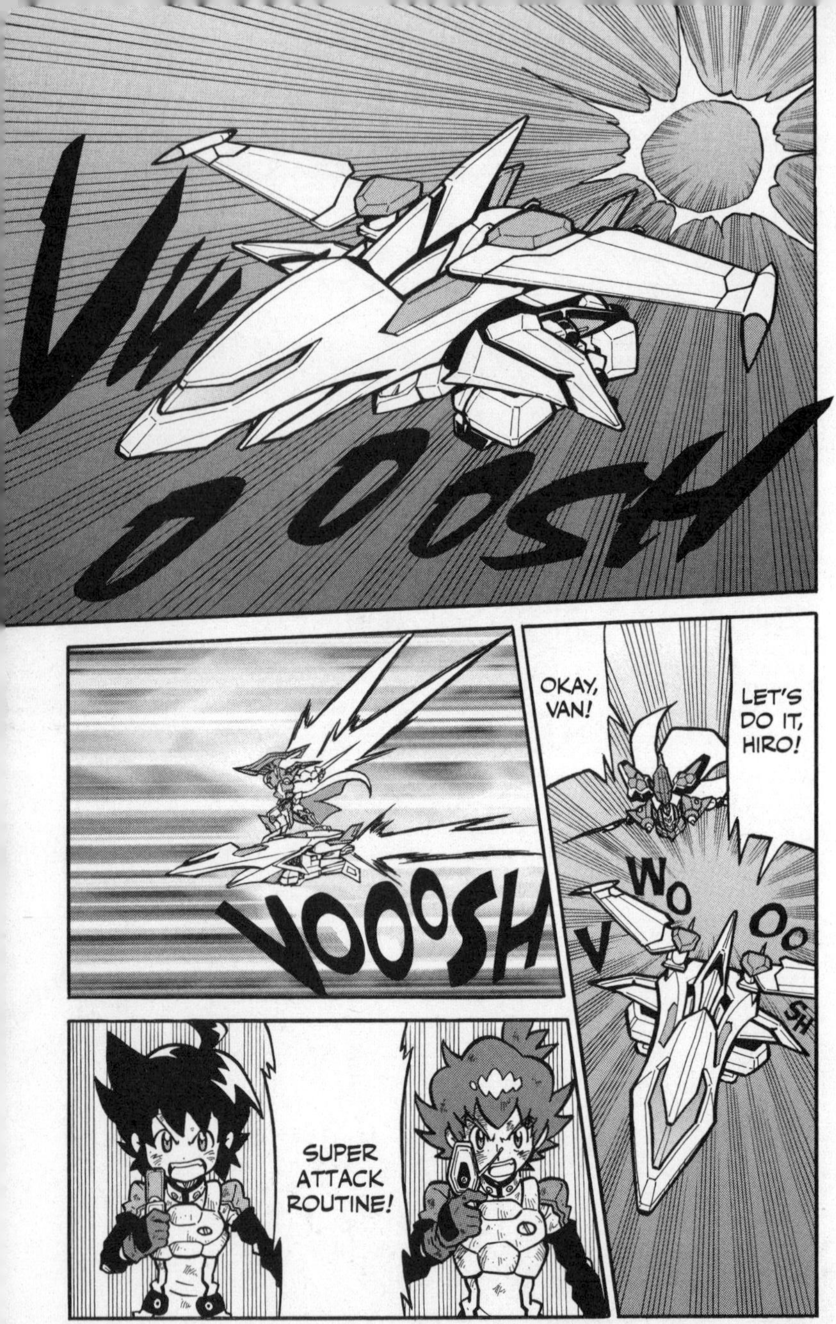
WHOOOSH
LET'S DO IT, HIRO!
OKAY, VAN!
VWOOOSH
VOOOSH
SUPER ATTACK ROUTINE!

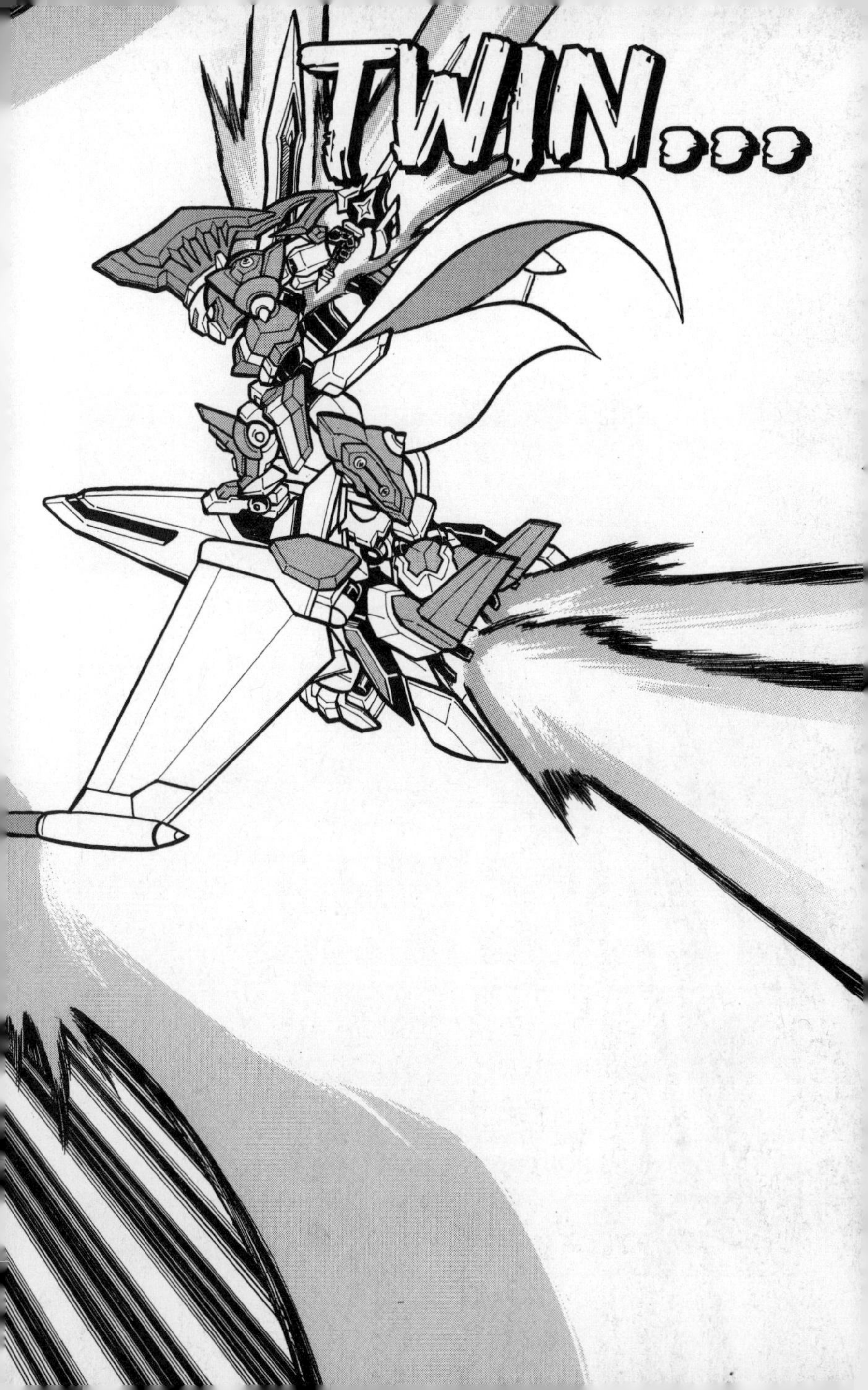
TWIN...

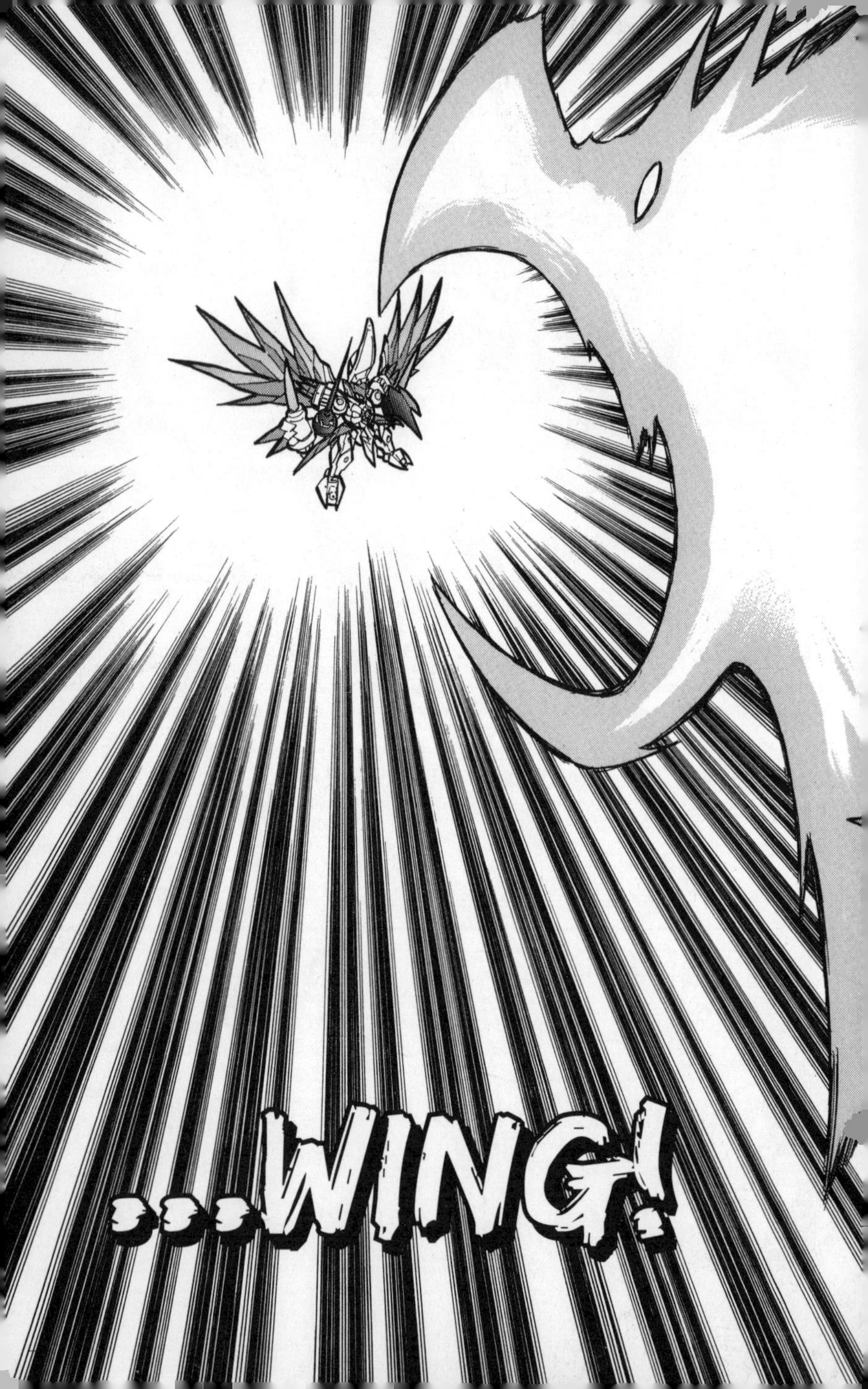
...WING!

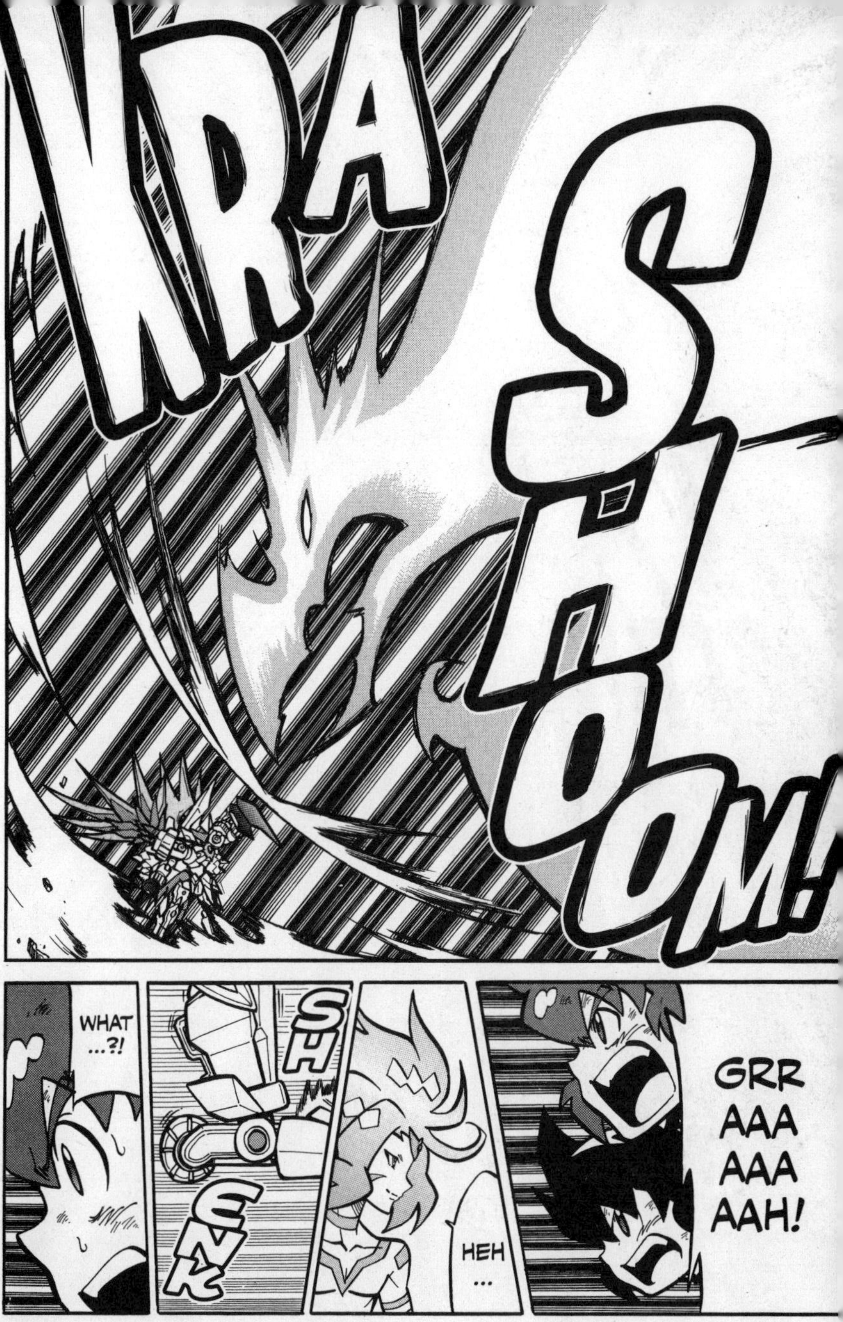
KRASHOOM!
GRR AAA AAA AAH!
HEH...
SHENK
WHAT...?!

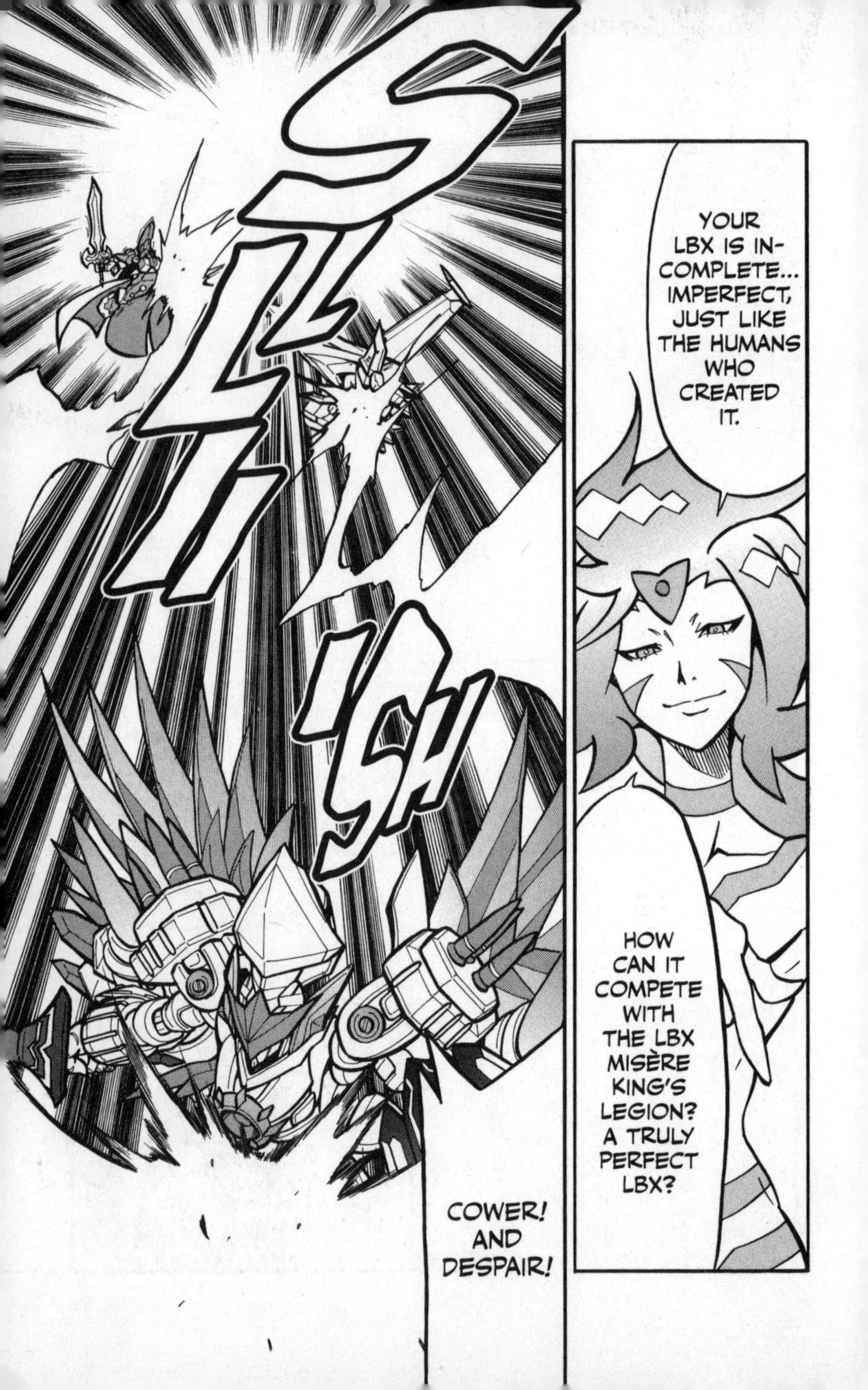
YOUR LBX IS IN-COMPLETE... IMPERFECT, JUST LIKE THE HUMANS WHO CREATED IT.
HOW CAN IT COMPETE WITH THE LBX MISÈRE KING'S LEGION? A TRULY PERFECT LBX?
COWER! AND DESPAIR!

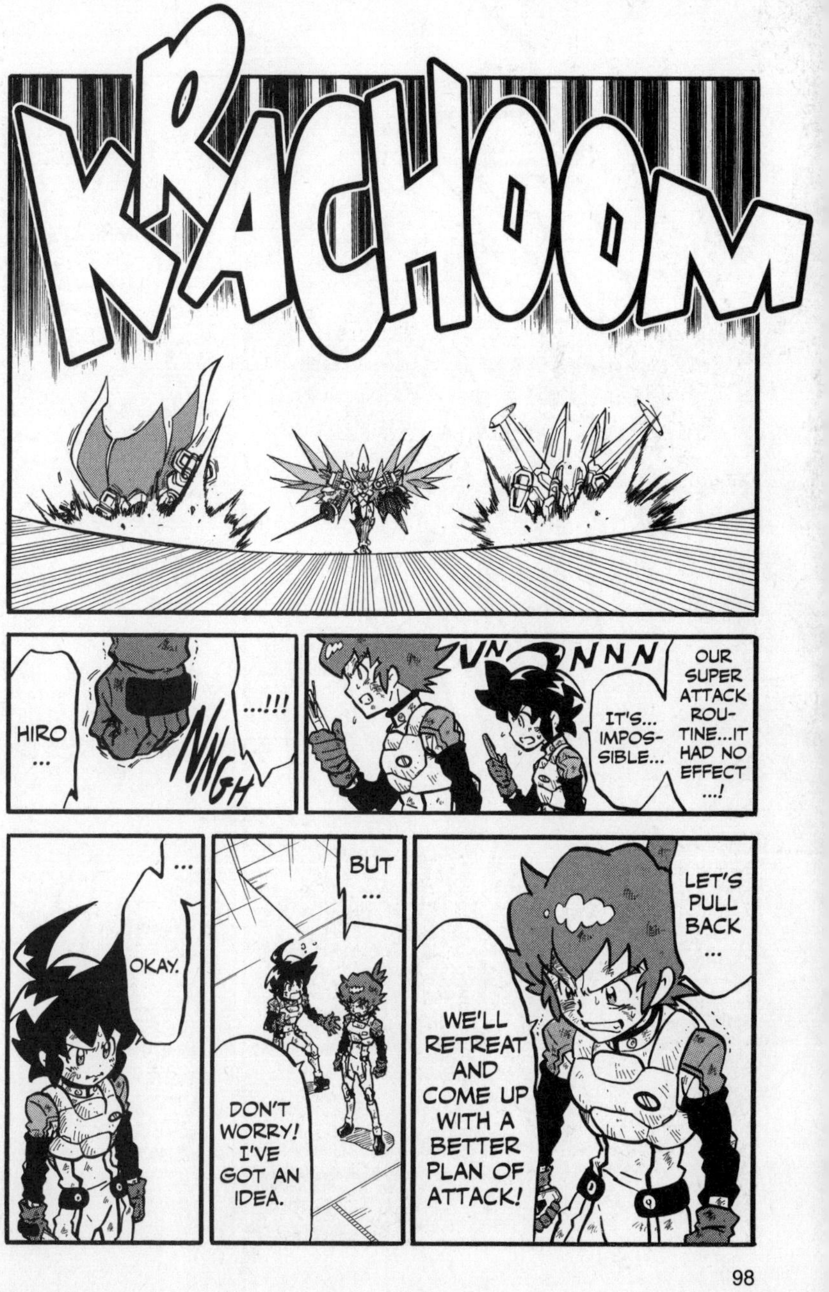
KRACHOOM
OUR SUPER ATTACK ROU-TINE...IT HAD NO EFFECT ...!
UNNNN
IT'S... IMPOS-SIBLE...
...!!!
NNGH
HIRO ...
LET'S PULL BACK ...
WE'LL RETREAT AND COME UP WITH A BETTER PLAN OF ATTACK!
BUT ...
DON'T WORRY! I'VE GOT AN IDEA.
...
OKAY.

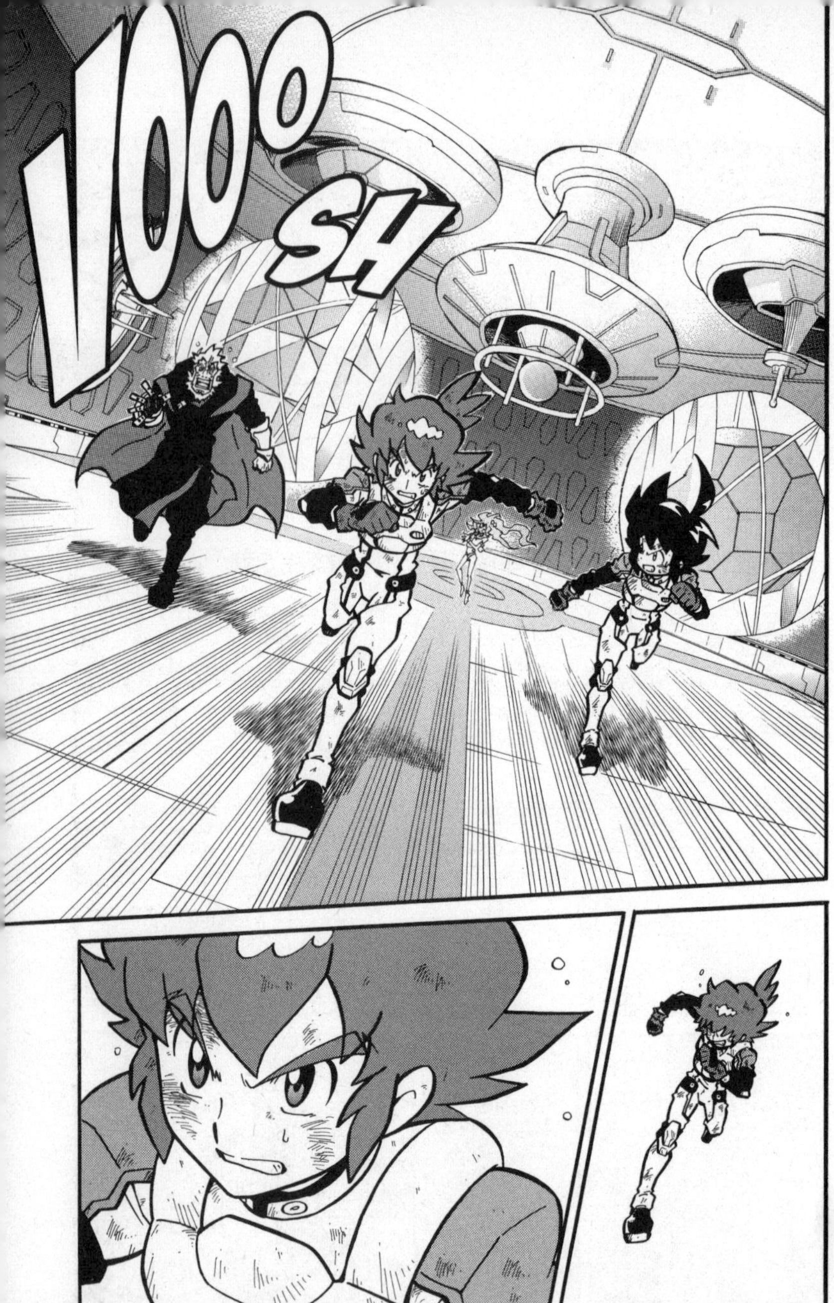
VOOOSH

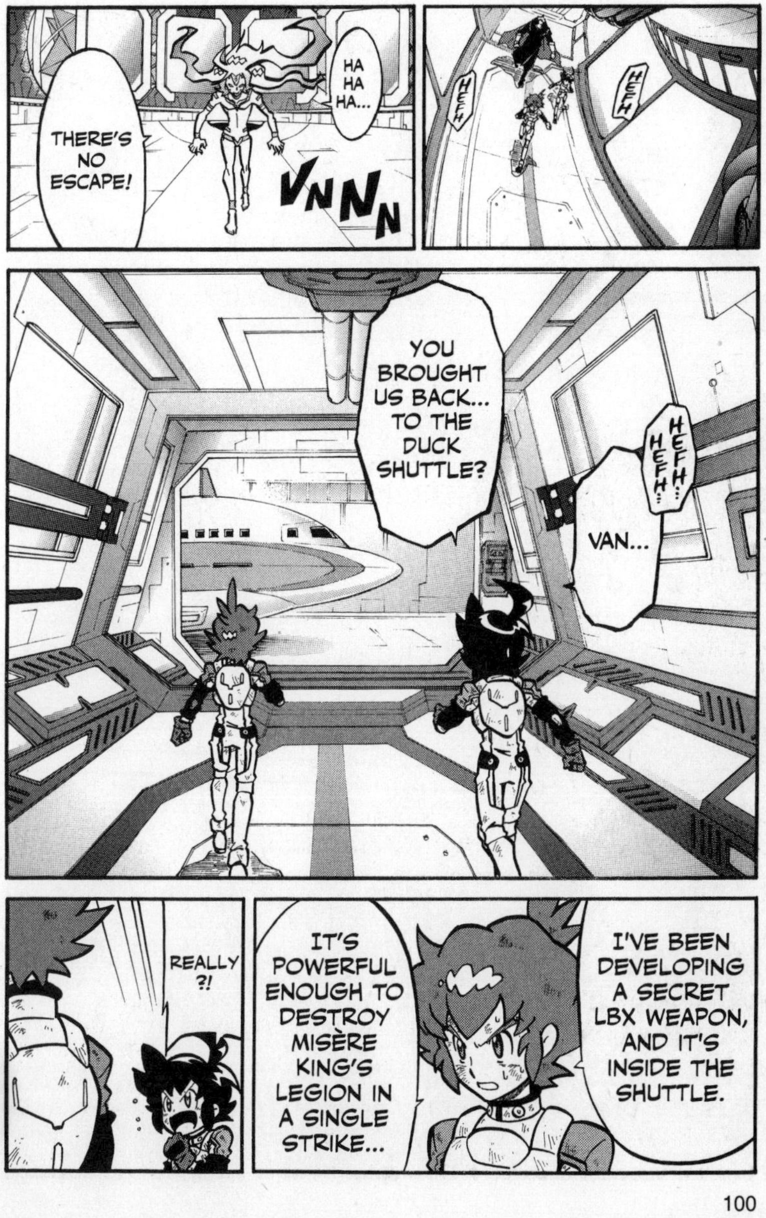
HEFH
HEFH
HA HA HA...
THERE'S NO ESCAPE!
VNNN
YOU BROUGHT US BACK... TO THE DUCK SHUTTLE?
HEFH... HEFH...
VAN...
I'VE BEEN DEVELOPING A SECRET LBX WEAPON, AND IT'S INSIDE THE SHUTTLE.
IT'S POWERFUL ENOUGH TO DESTROY MISÈRE KING'S LEGION IN A SINGLE STRIKE...
REALLY?!

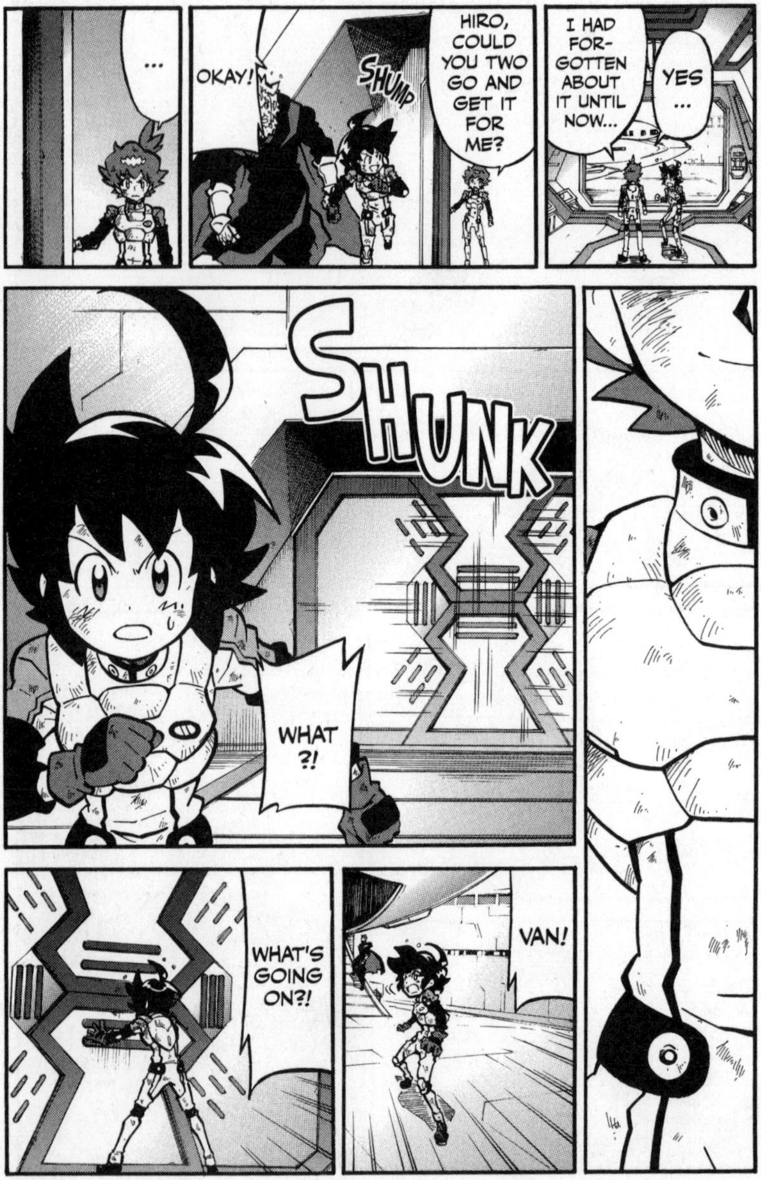
I HAD FOR-GOTTEN ABOUT IT UNTIL NOW...
YES ...
HIRO, COULD YOU TWO GO AND GET IT FOR ME?
SHUMP
OKAY!
...
SHUNK
WHAT ?!
VAN!
WHAT'S GOING ON?!

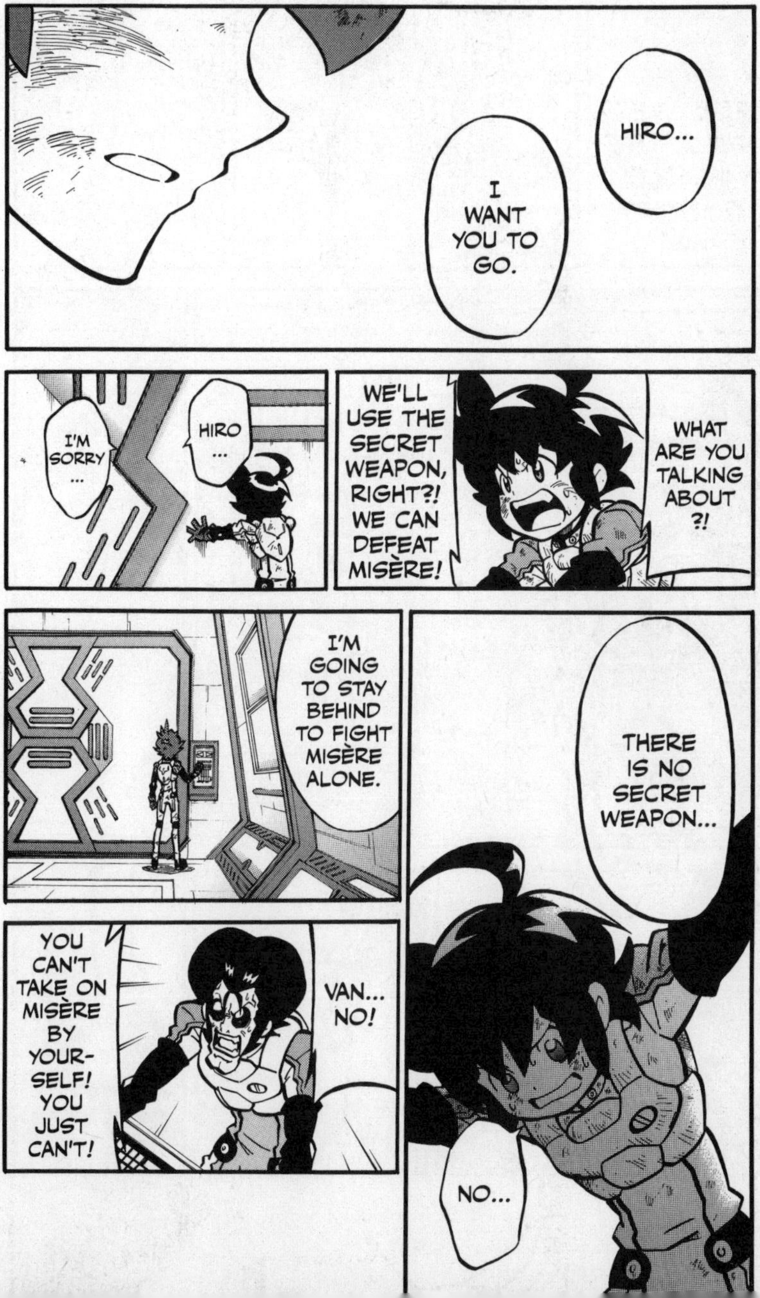
HIRO...
I WANT YOU TO GO.
WHAT ARE YOU TALKING ABOUT ?!
WE'LL USE THE SECRET WEAPON, RIGHT?! WE CAN DEFEAT MISÈRE!
HIRO ...
I'M SORRY ...
THERE IS NO SECRET WEAPON...
NO...
I'M GOING TO STAY BEHIND TO FIGHT MISÈRE ALONE.
VAN... NO!
YOU CAN'T TAKE ON MISÈRE BY YOURSELF! YOU JUST CAN'T!

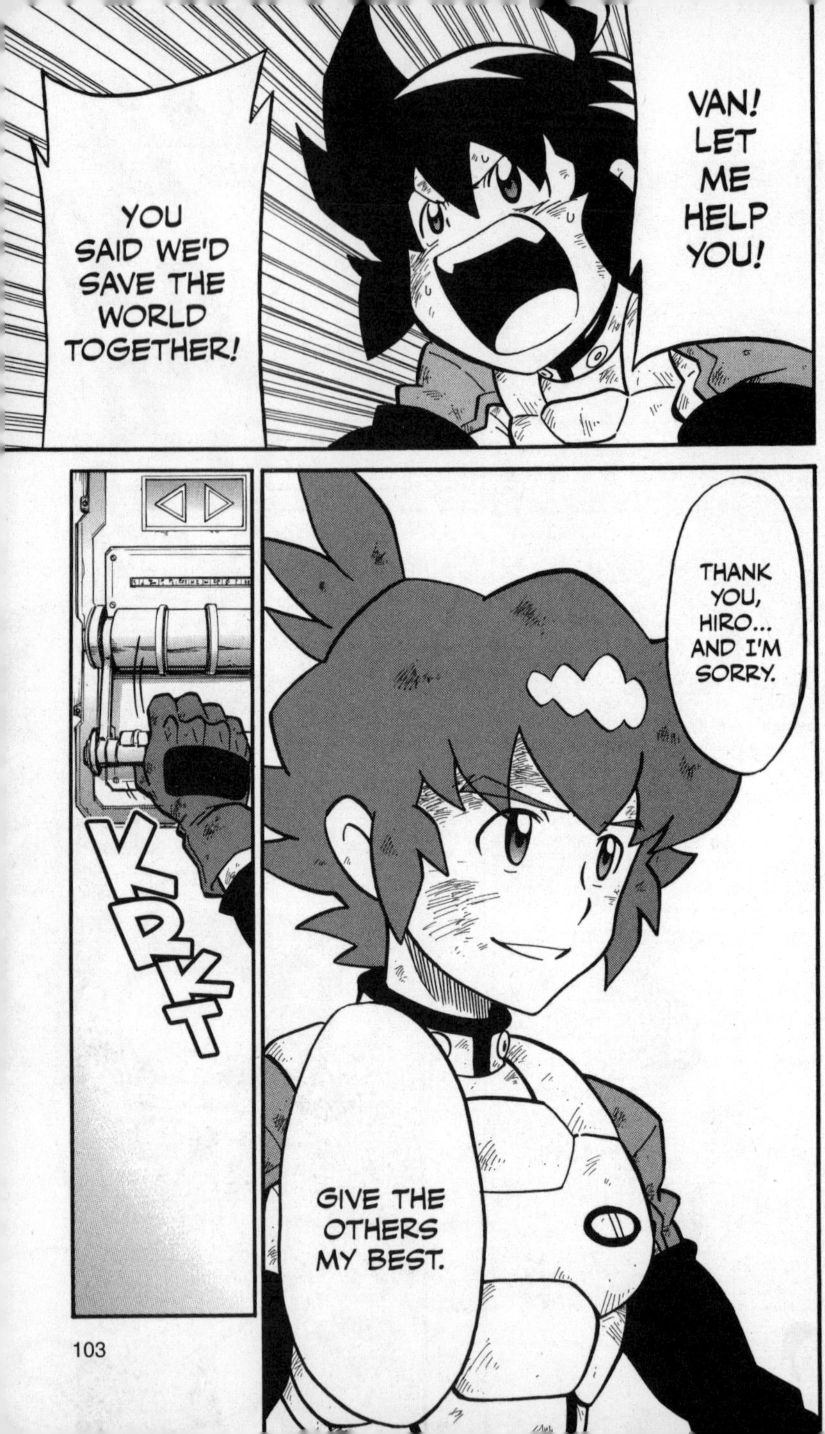
VAN! LET ME HELP YOU!
YOU SAID WE'D SAVE THE WORLD TOGETHER!
THANK YOU, HIRO... AND I'M SORRY.
GIVE THE OTHERS MY BEST.
VRKT

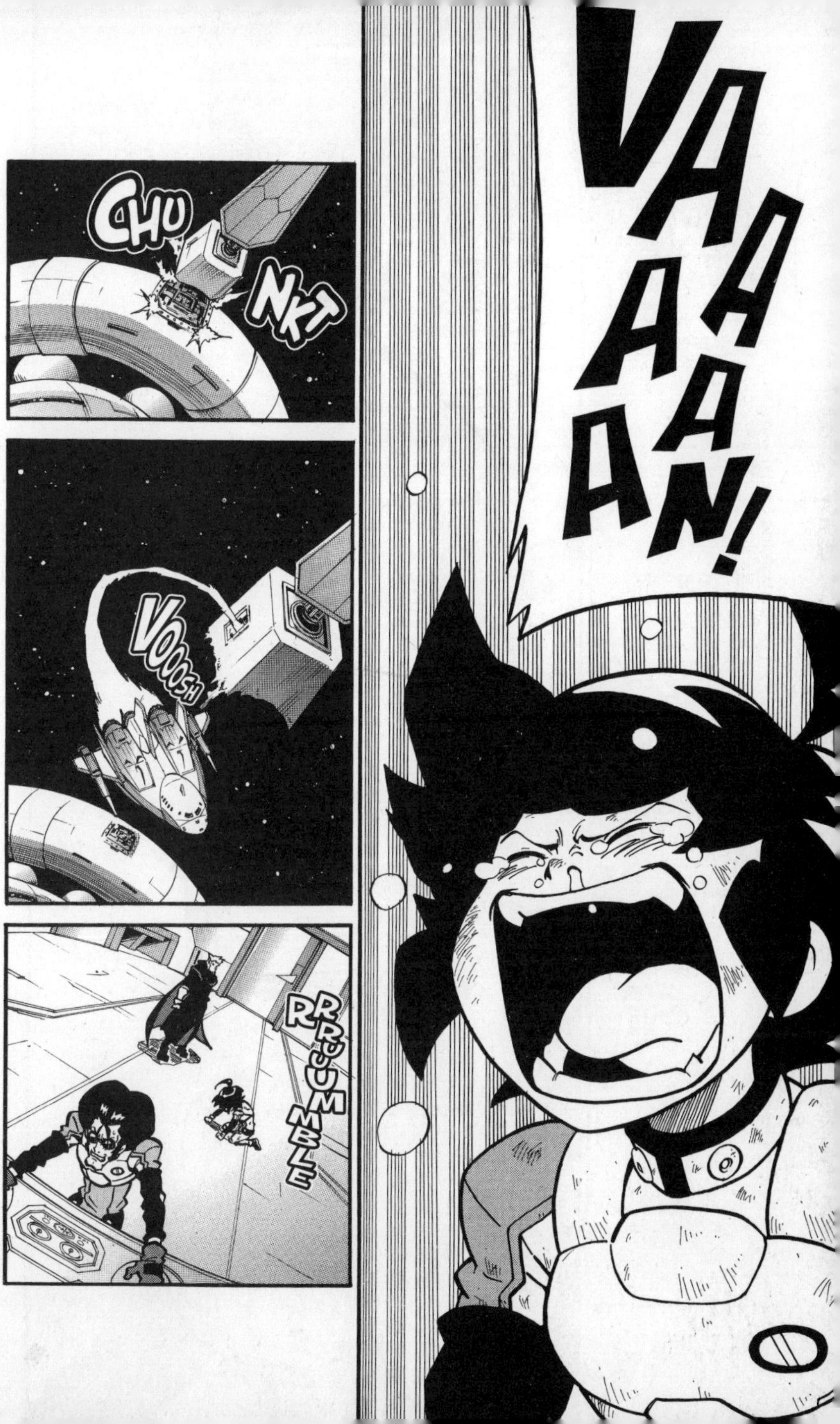
VAAAAAAN!
CHU NKT
VOOOOSH
RRRUUUMBLE

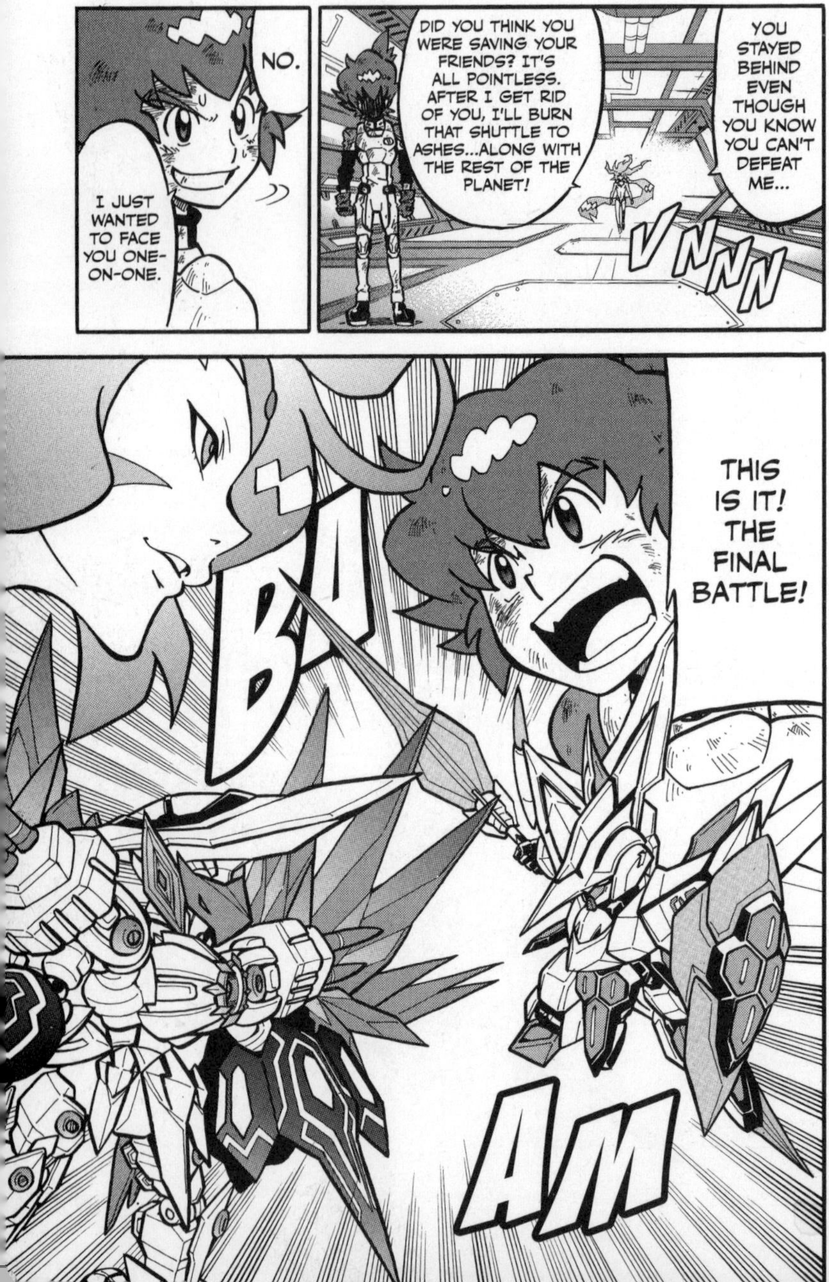
YOU STAYED BEHIND EVEN THOUGH YOU KNOW YOU CAN'T DEFEAT ME...
DID YOU THINK YOU WERE SAVING YOUR FRIENDS? IT'S ALL POINTLESS. AFTER I GET RID OF YOU, I'LL BURN THAT SHUTTLE TO ASHES...ALONG WITH THE REST OF THE PLANET!
VNNN
NO.
I JUST WANTED TO FACE YOU ONE-ON-ONE.
THIS IS IT! THE FINAL BATTLE!
BA
AM

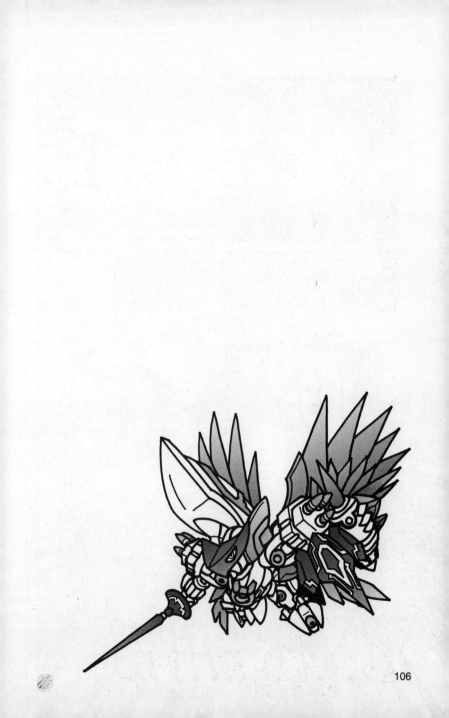

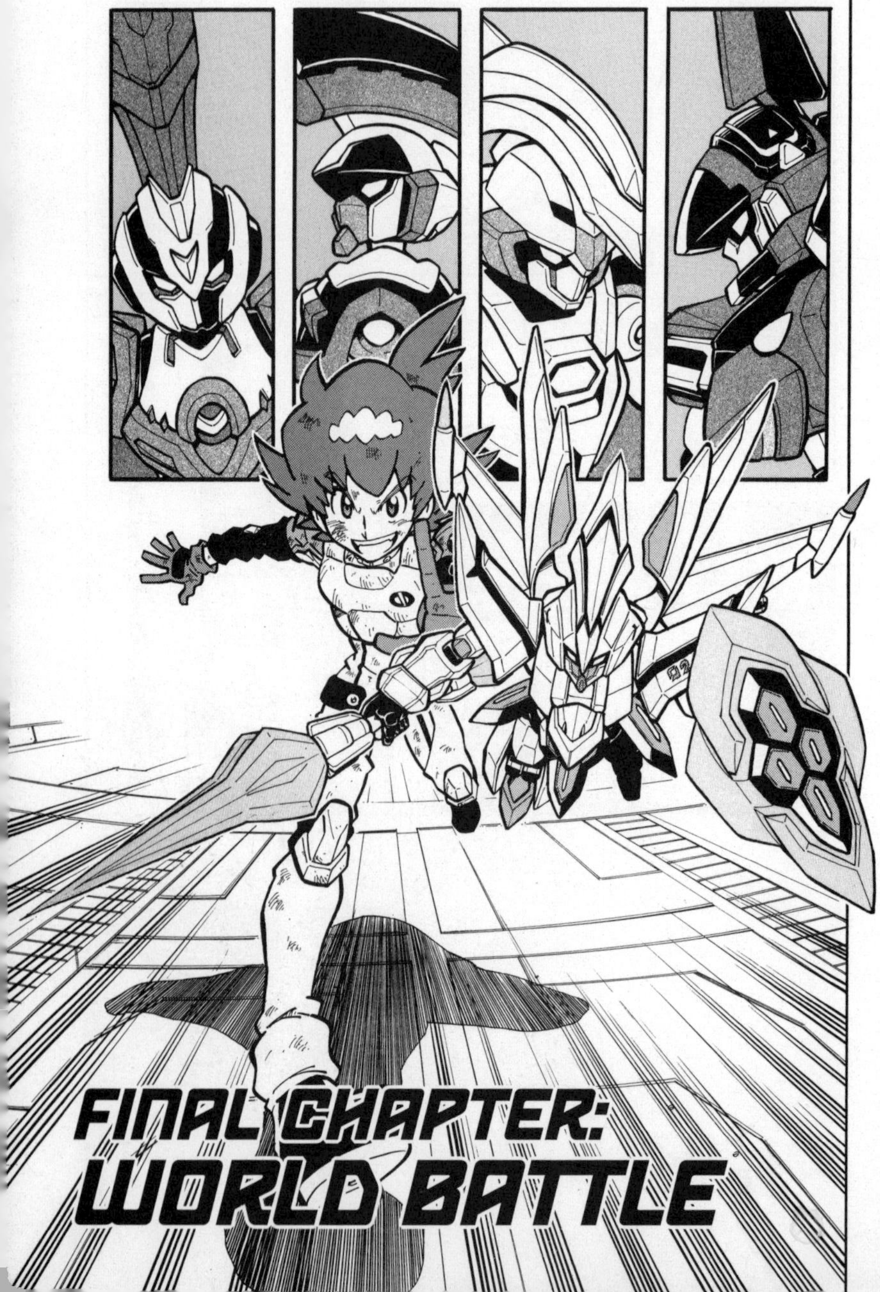
FINAL CHAPTER:
WORLD BATTLE

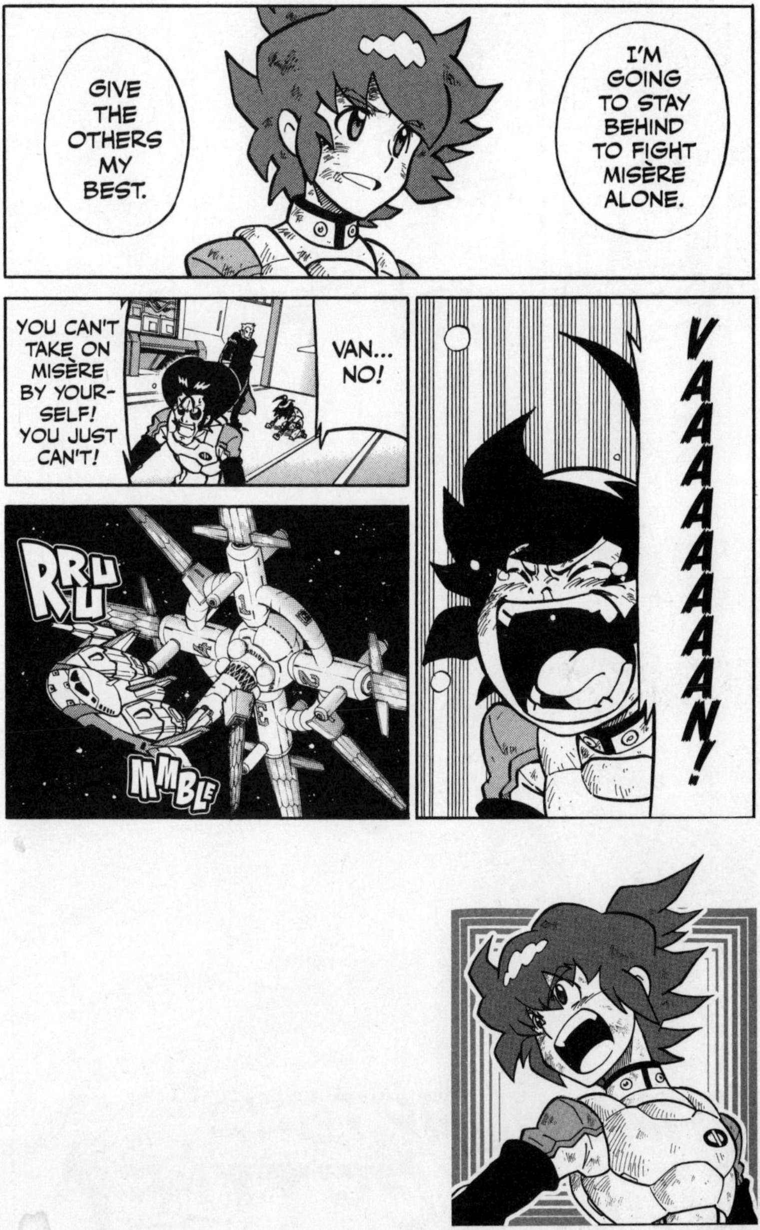
I'M GOING TO STAY BEHIND TO FIGHT MISÈRE ALONE.
GIVE THE OTHERS MY BEST.
VAAAAAAAAN!
VAN... NO!
YOU CAN'T TAKE ON MISÈRE BY YOUR-SELF! YOU JUST CAN'T!
RRUMMBLE

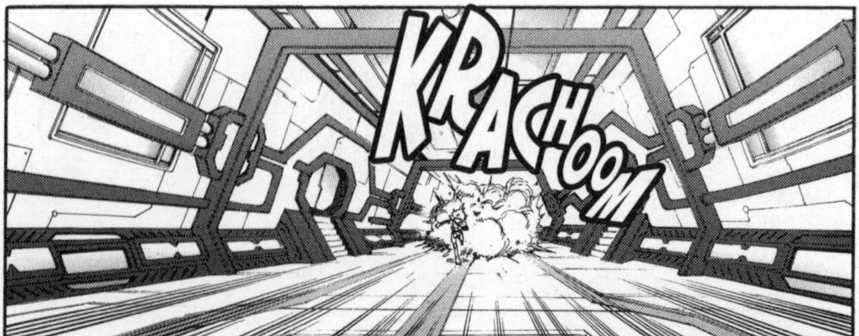
KRACHOOM
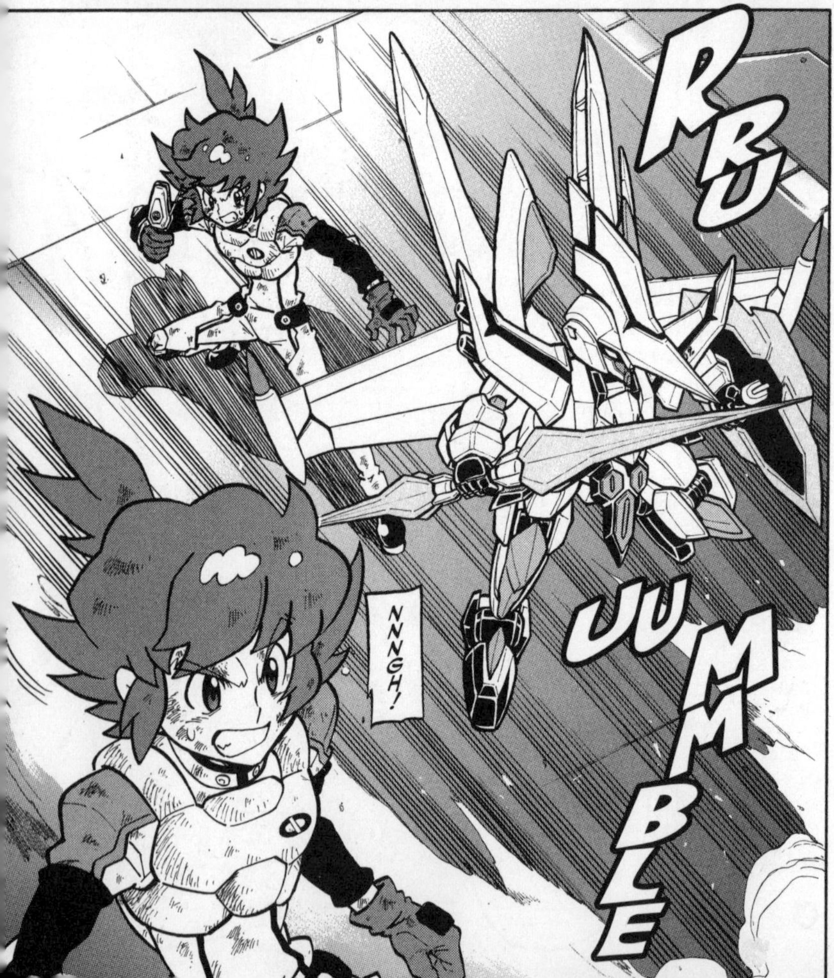
RRU
NNNGH!
UUMMMBLE

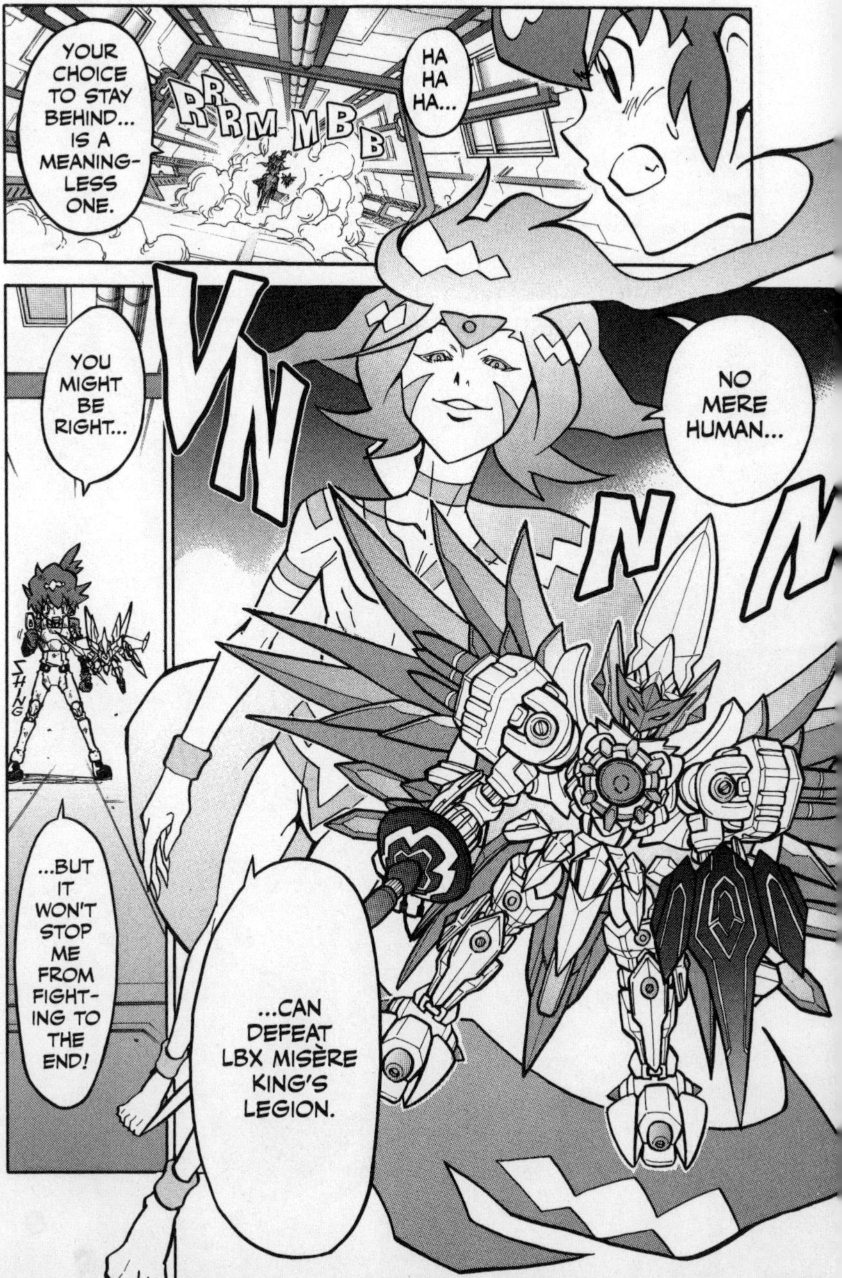
HA HA HA...
YOUR CHOICE TO STAY BEHIND... IS A MEANING-LESS ONE.
RRRMMBB
NO MERE HUMAN...
VNNN
...CAN DEFEAT LBX MISÈRE KING'S LEGION.
YOU MIGHT BE RIGHT...
SHING
...BUT IT WON'T STOP ME FROM FIGHT-ING TO THE END!

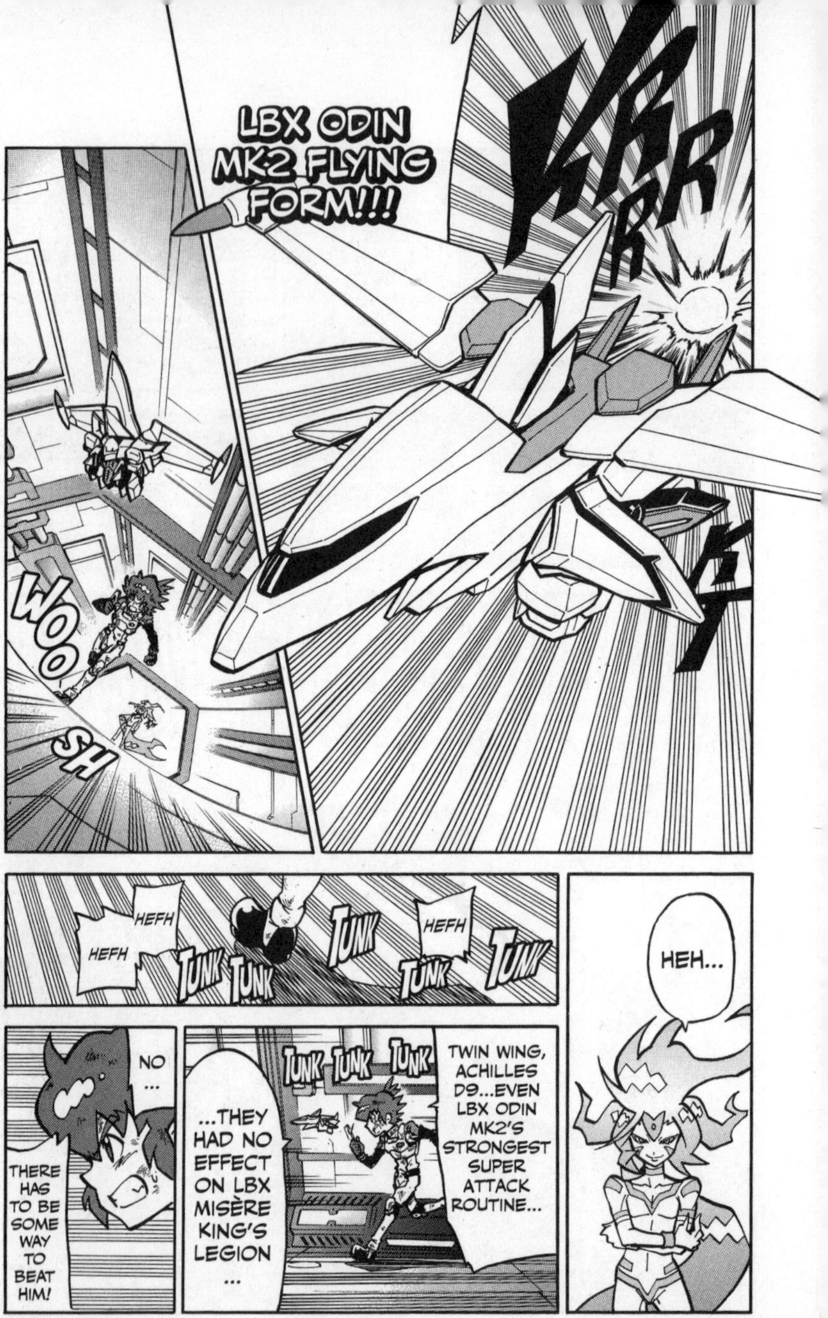
LBX ODIN MK2 FLYING FORM!!!
WOO
SH
HEH...
HEFH
HEFH
TUNK
TUNK
HEFH
TUNK
TUNK
TUNK
TUNK TUNK TUNK
TWIN WING, ACHILLES D9...EVEN LBX ODIN MK2'S STRONGEST SUPER ATTACK ROUTINE...
...THEY HAD NO EFFECT ON LBX MISÈRE KING'S LEGION ...
NO ...
THERE HAS TO BE SOME WAY TO BEAT HIM!

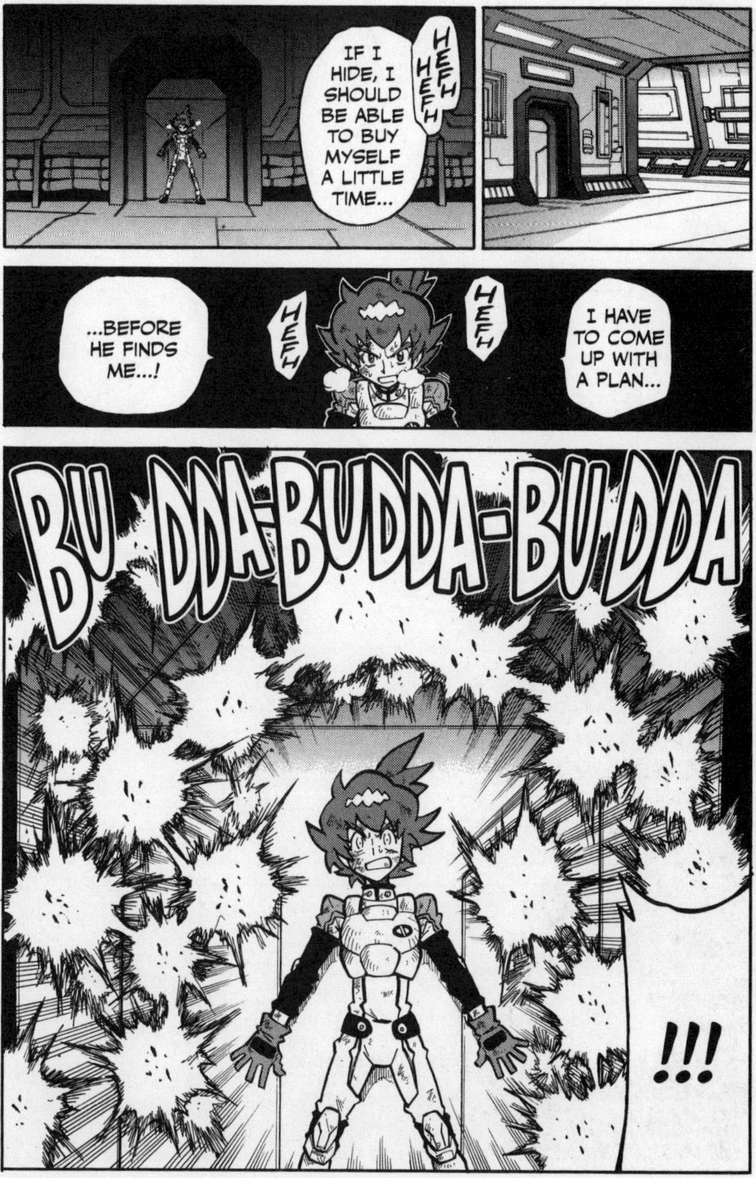
HEFH HEFH
IF I HIDE, I SHOULD BE ABLE TO BUY MYSELF A LITTLE TIME...
I HAVE TO COME UP WITH A PLAN...
HEFH
HEFH
...BEFORE HE FINDS ME...!
BUDDA-BUDDA-BUDDA
!!!

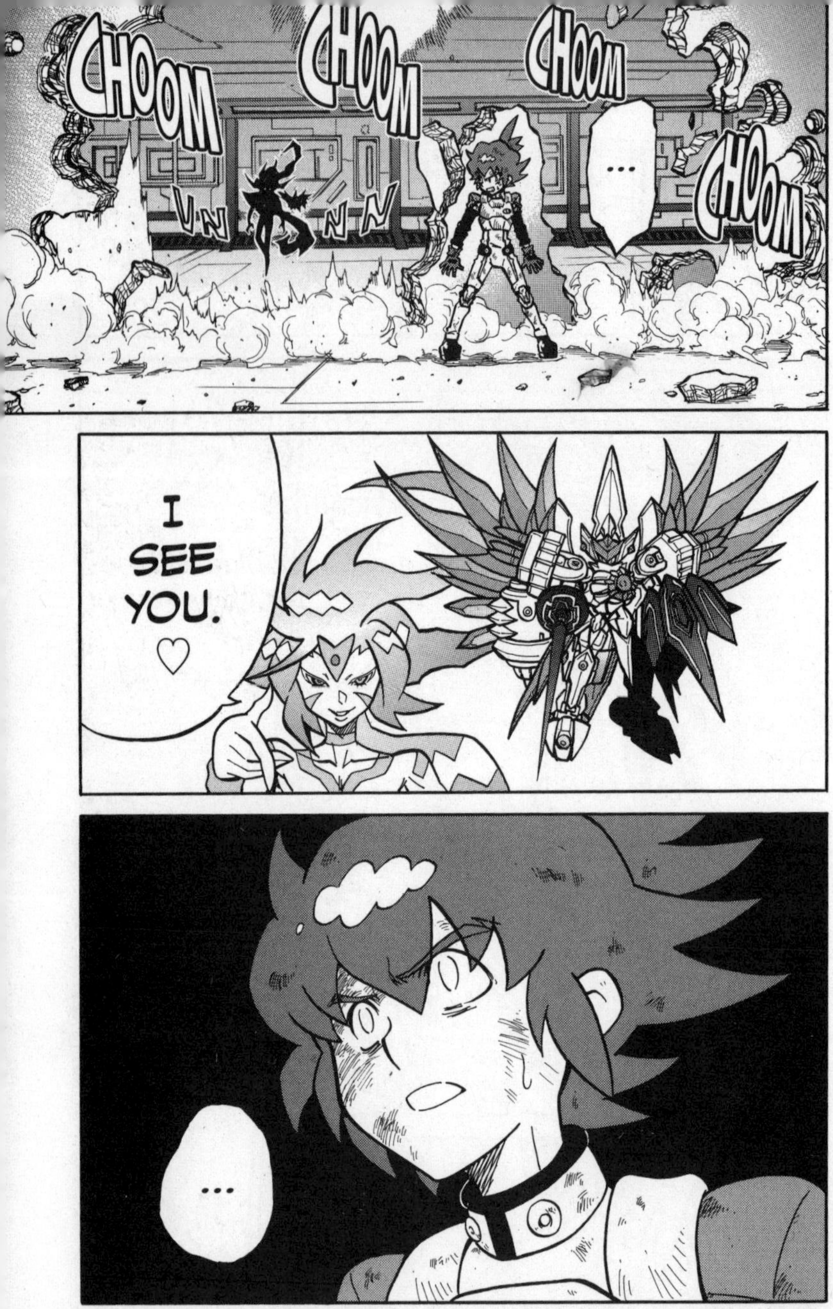
CHOOM
...
CHOOM
CHOOM
CHOOM
VNNN
I SEE YOU. ♡
...

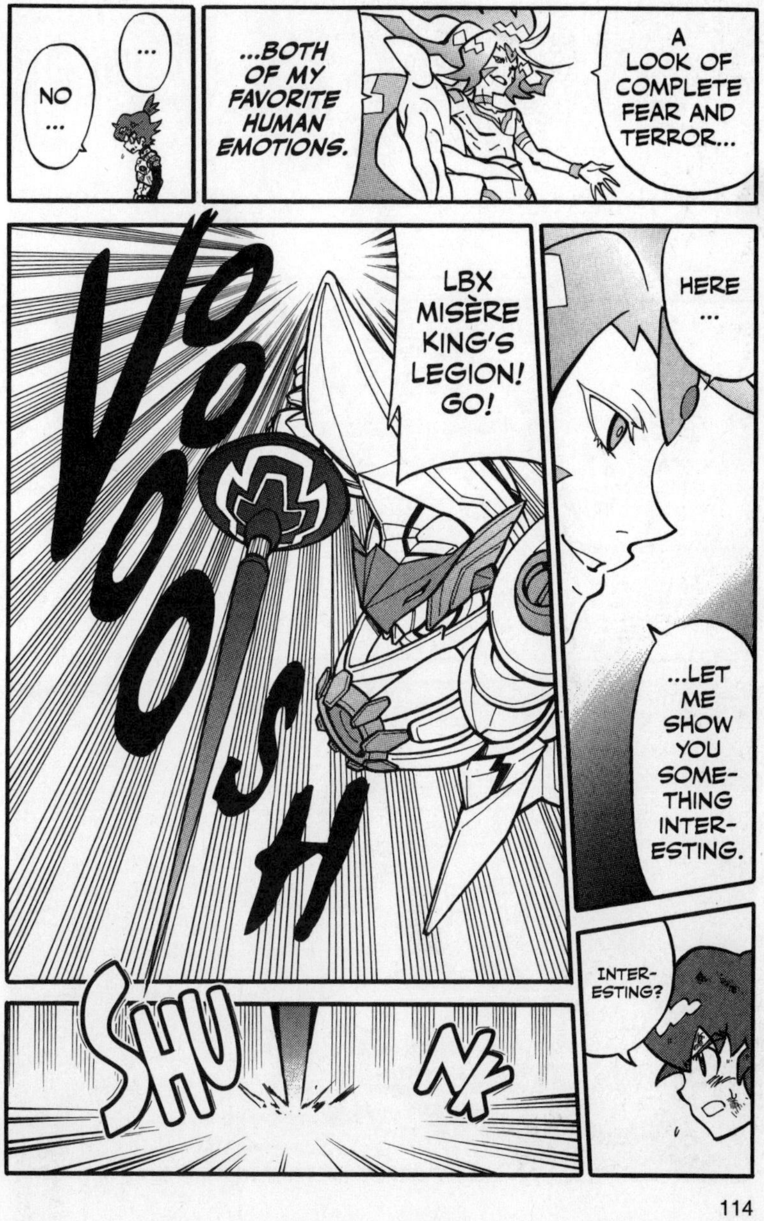
A LOOK OF COMPLETE FEAR AND TERROR...
...BOTH OF MY FAVORITE HUMAN EMOTIONS.
...
NO ...
HERE ...
...LET ME SHOW YOU SOME-THING INTER-ESTING.
INTER-ESTING?
LBX MISÈRE KING'S LEGION! GO!
VOOOOOSH
SHUNK

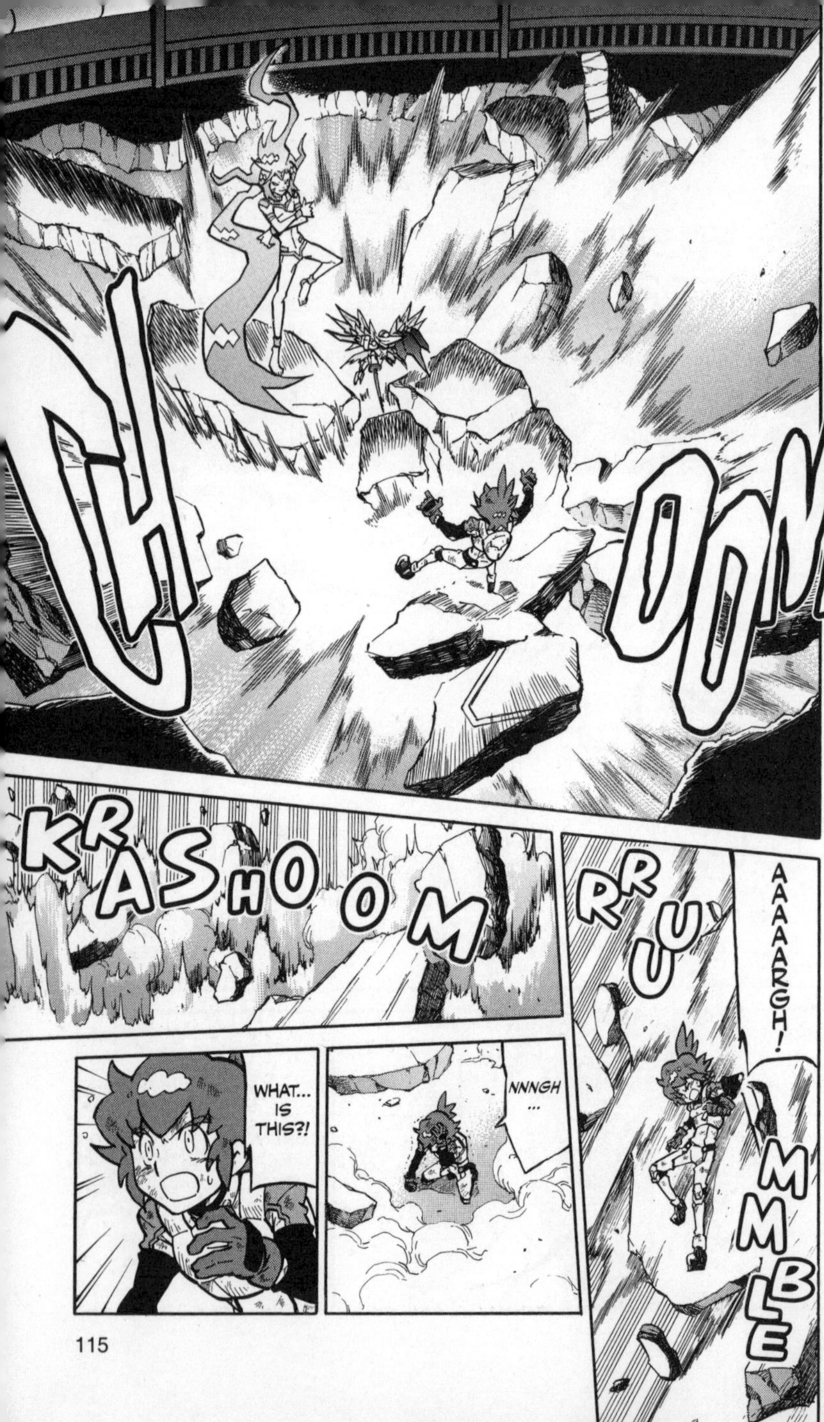
CHOOM
RRUUMMBLE
AAAAARGH!
KRASHOOM
NNNGH...
WHAT... IS THIS?!

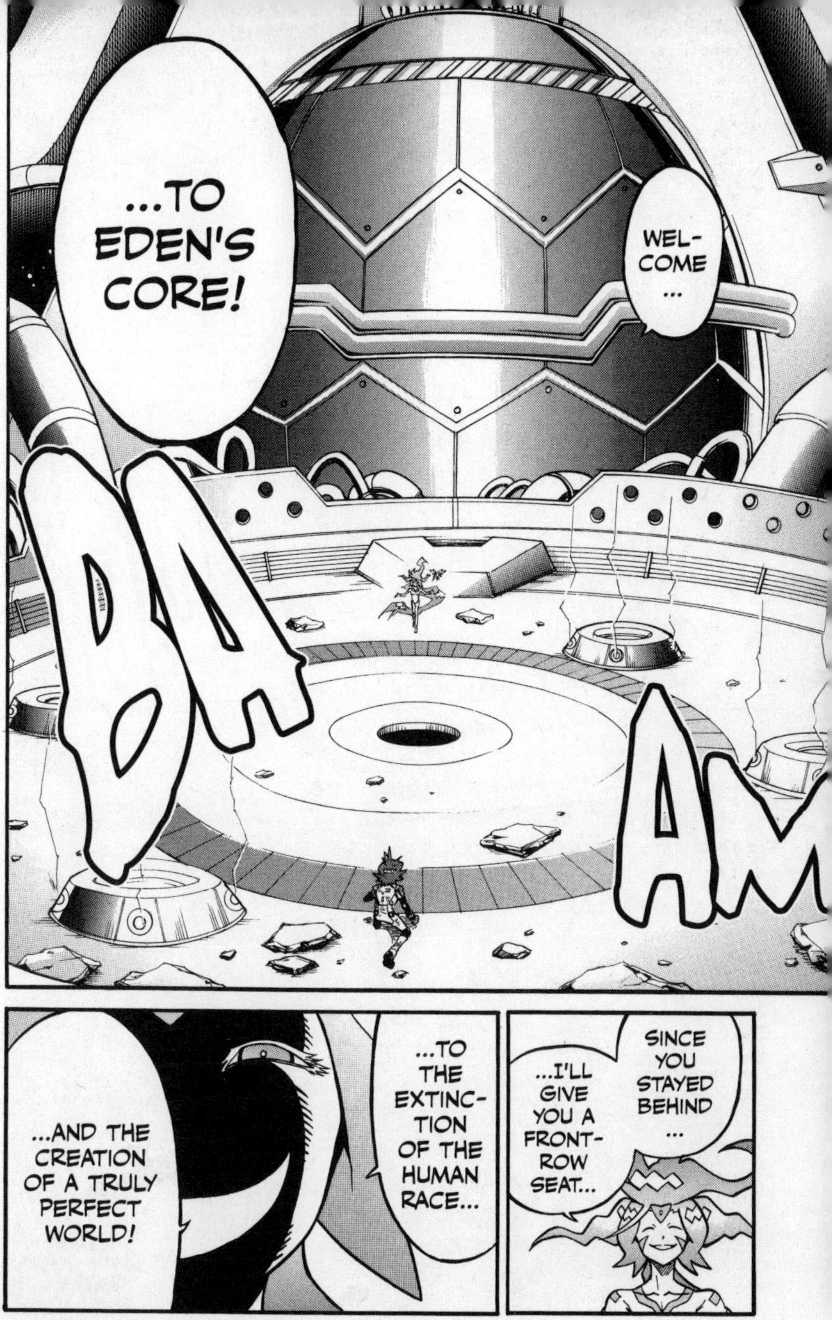
WEL-COME...
...TO EDEN'S CORE!
BA
AM
SINCE YOU STAYED BEHIND...
...I'LL GIVE YOU A FRONT-ROW SEAT...
...TO THE EXTINCTION OF THE HUMAN RACE...
...AND THE CREATION OF A TRULY PERFECT WORLD!

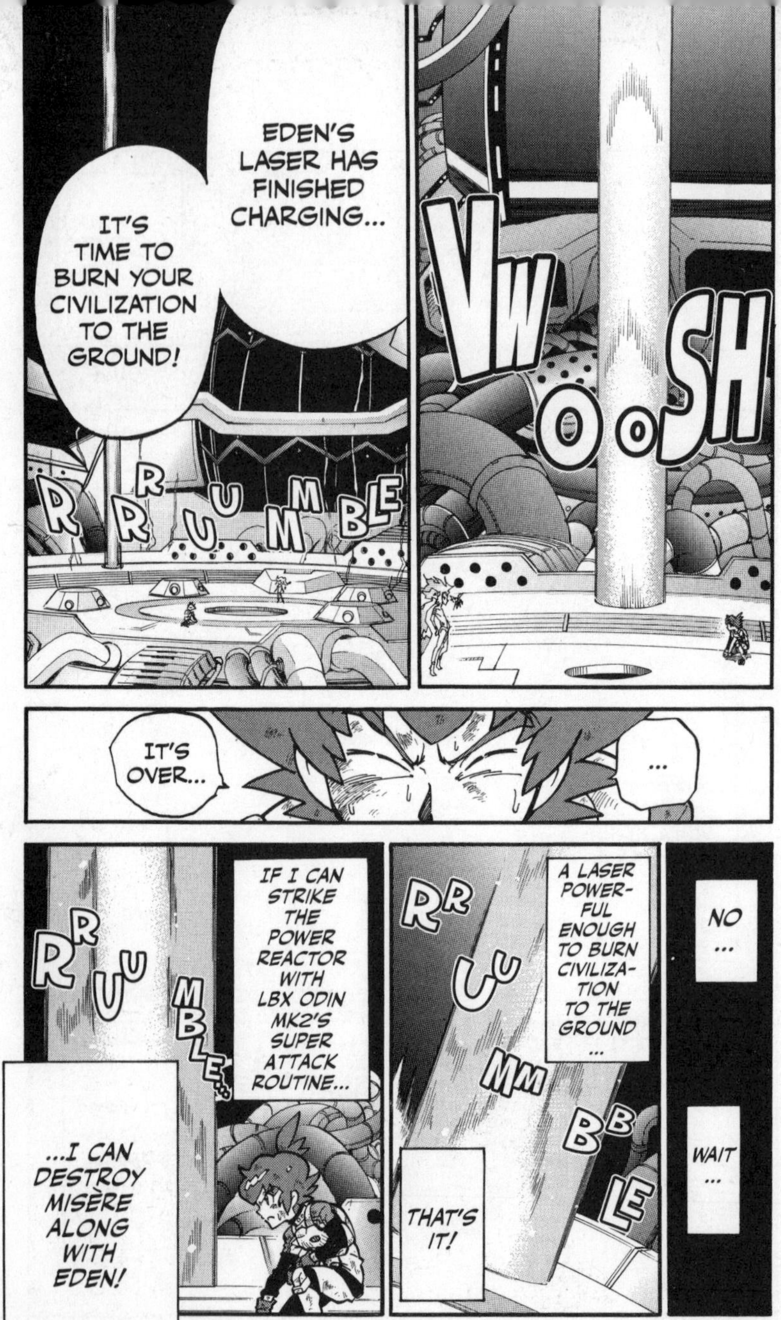
VWOOOSH
EDEN'S LASER HAS FINISHED CHARGING...
IT'S TIME TO BURN YOUR CIVILIZATION TO THE GROUND!
RRRUUMMBLE
...
IT'S OVER...
NO...
WAIT...
A LASER POWERFUL ENOUGH TO BURN CIVILIZATION TO THE GROUND...
RRUUMMBBLE
THAT'S IT!
IF I CAN STRIKE THE POWER REACTOR WITH LBX ODIN MK2'S SUPER ATTACK ROUTINE...
RRRUUMBLE...
...I CAN DESTROY MISÈRE ALONG WITH EDEN!

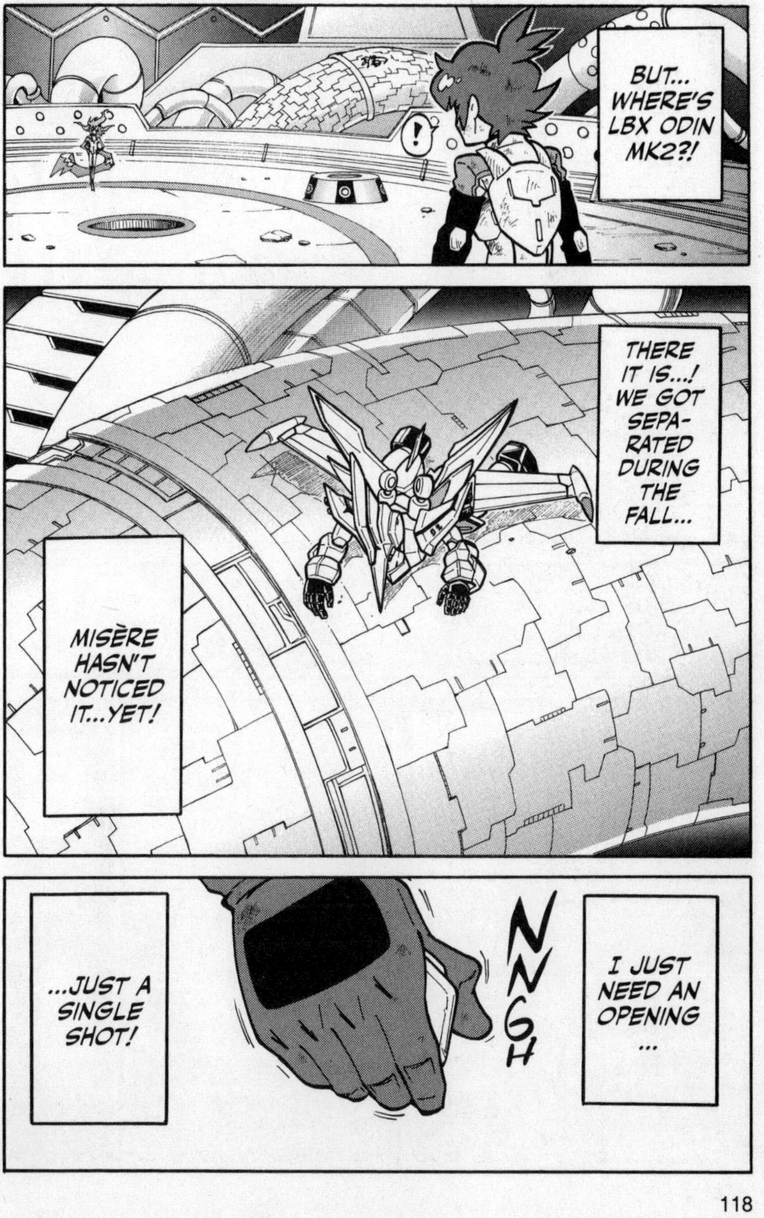
BUT... WHERE'S LBX ODIN MK2?!
!
THERE IT IS...! WE GOT SEPA-RATED DURING THE FALL...
MISÈRE HASN'T NOTICED IT...YET!
I JUST NEED AN OPENING ...
NNGH
...JUST A SINGLE SHOT!

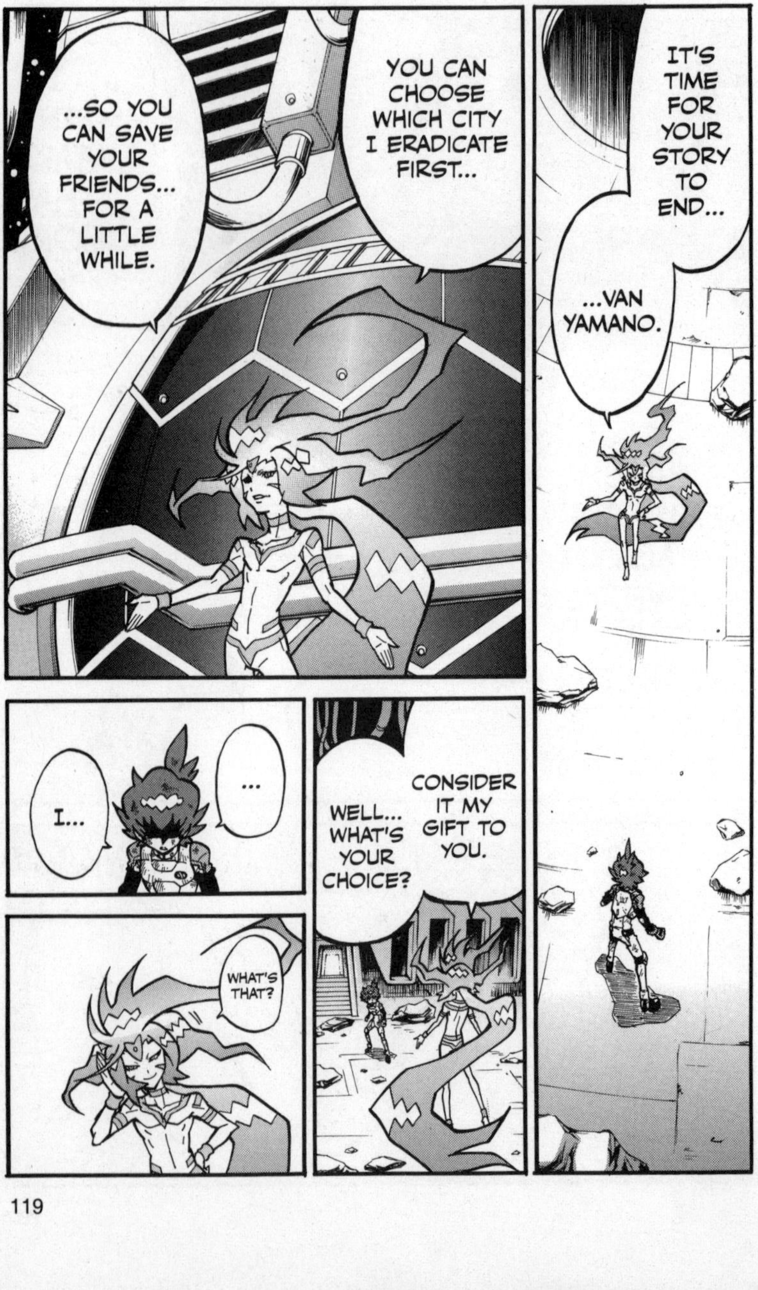
IT'S TIME FOR YOUR STORY TO END...
...VAN YAMANO.
YOU CAN CHOOSE WHICH CITY I ERADICATE FIRST...
...SO YOU CAN SAVE YOUR FRIENDS... FOR A LITTLE WHILE.
CONSIDER IT MY GIFT TO YOU.
WELL... WHAT'S YOUR CHOICE?
...
I...
WHAT'S THAT?

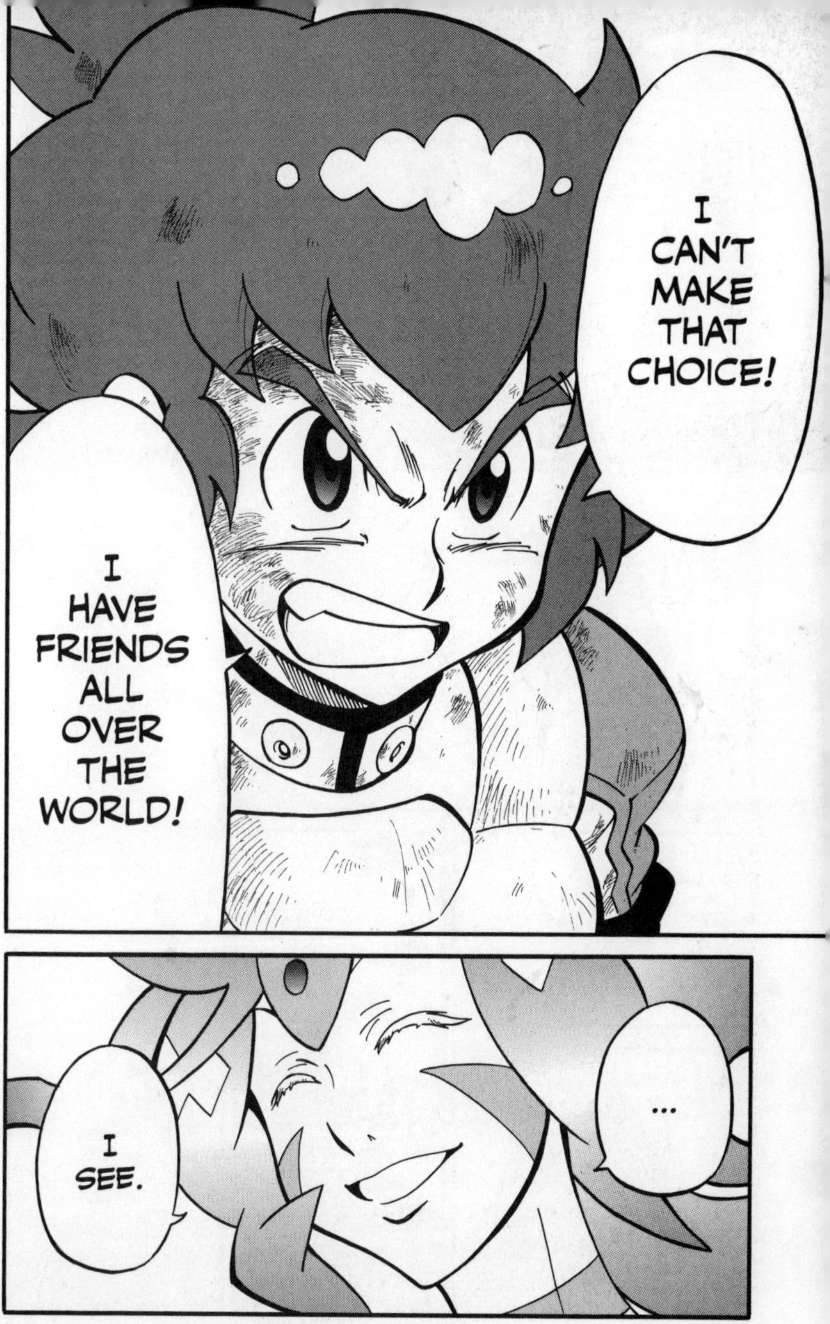
I CAN'T MAKE THAT CHOICE!
I HAVE FRIENDS ALL OVER THE WORLD!
...
I SEE.

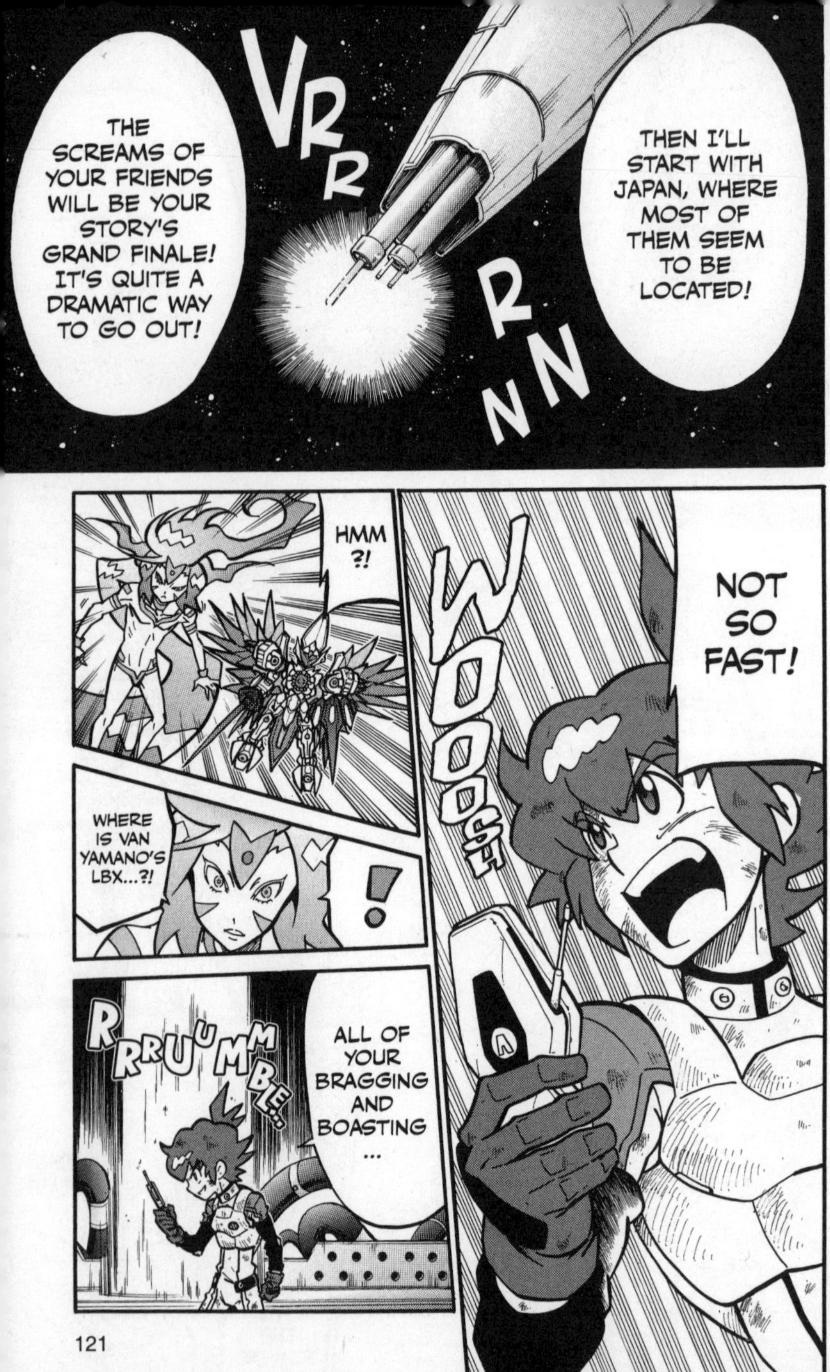
THEN I'LL START WITH JAPAN, WHERE MOST OF THEM SEEM TO BE LOCATED!
VRRRRNN
THE SCREAMS OF YOUR FRIENDS WILL BE YOUR STORY'S GRAND FINALE! IT'S QUITE A DRAMATIC WAY TO GO OUT!
NOT SO FAST!
WOOOOSH
HMM ?!
!
WHERE IS VAN YAMANO'S LBX...?!
ALL OF YOUR BRAGGING AND BOASTING ...
RRRUUMMBLE..

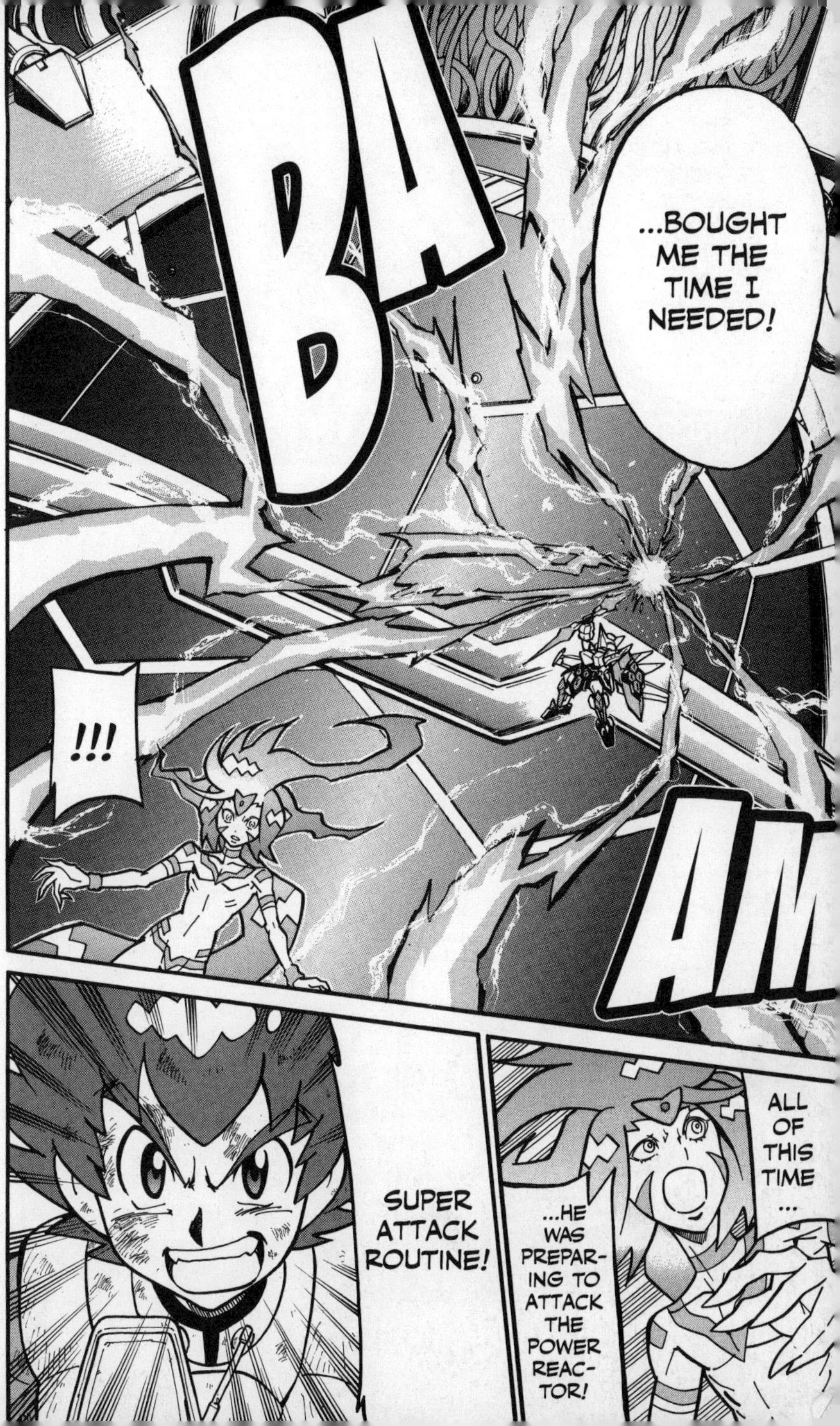
...BOUGHT ME THE TIME I NEEDED!
BA
!!!
AM
ALL OF THIS TIME ...
...HE WAS PREPAR-ING TO ATTACK THE POWER REAC-TOR!
SUPER ATTACK ROUTINE!

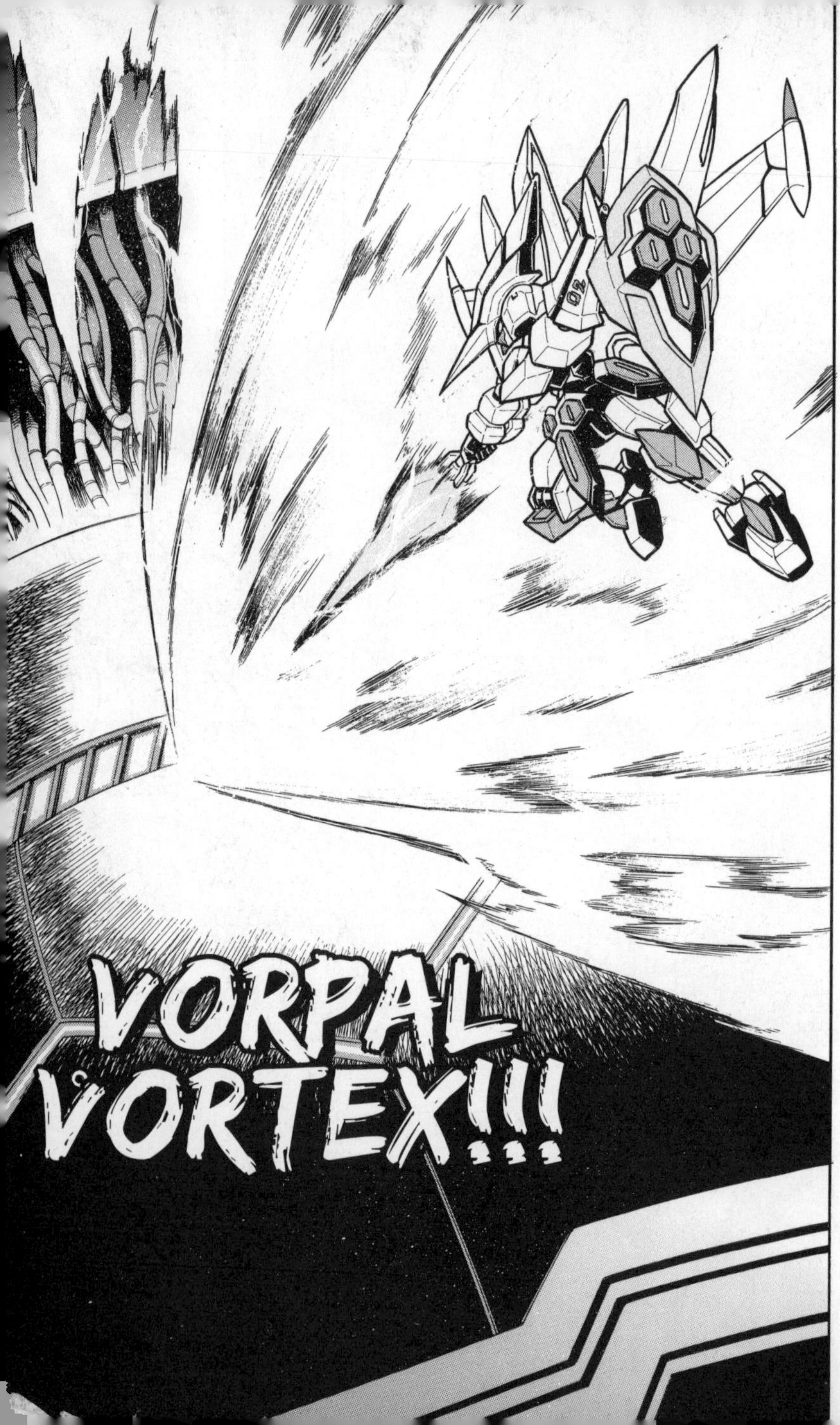
VORPAL VORTEX!!!

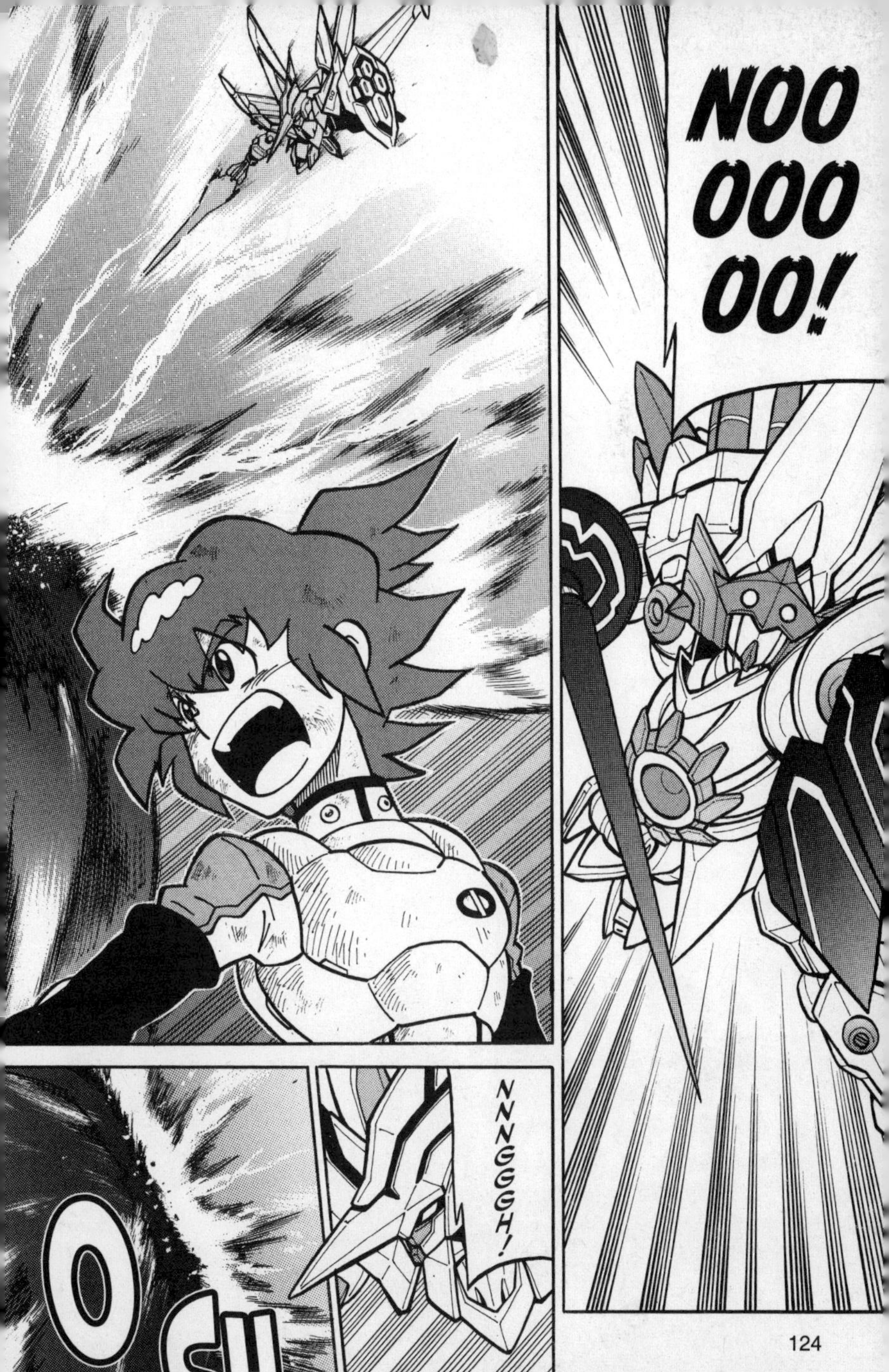
NOO
OOO
OO!
NNNGGGH!
OSH

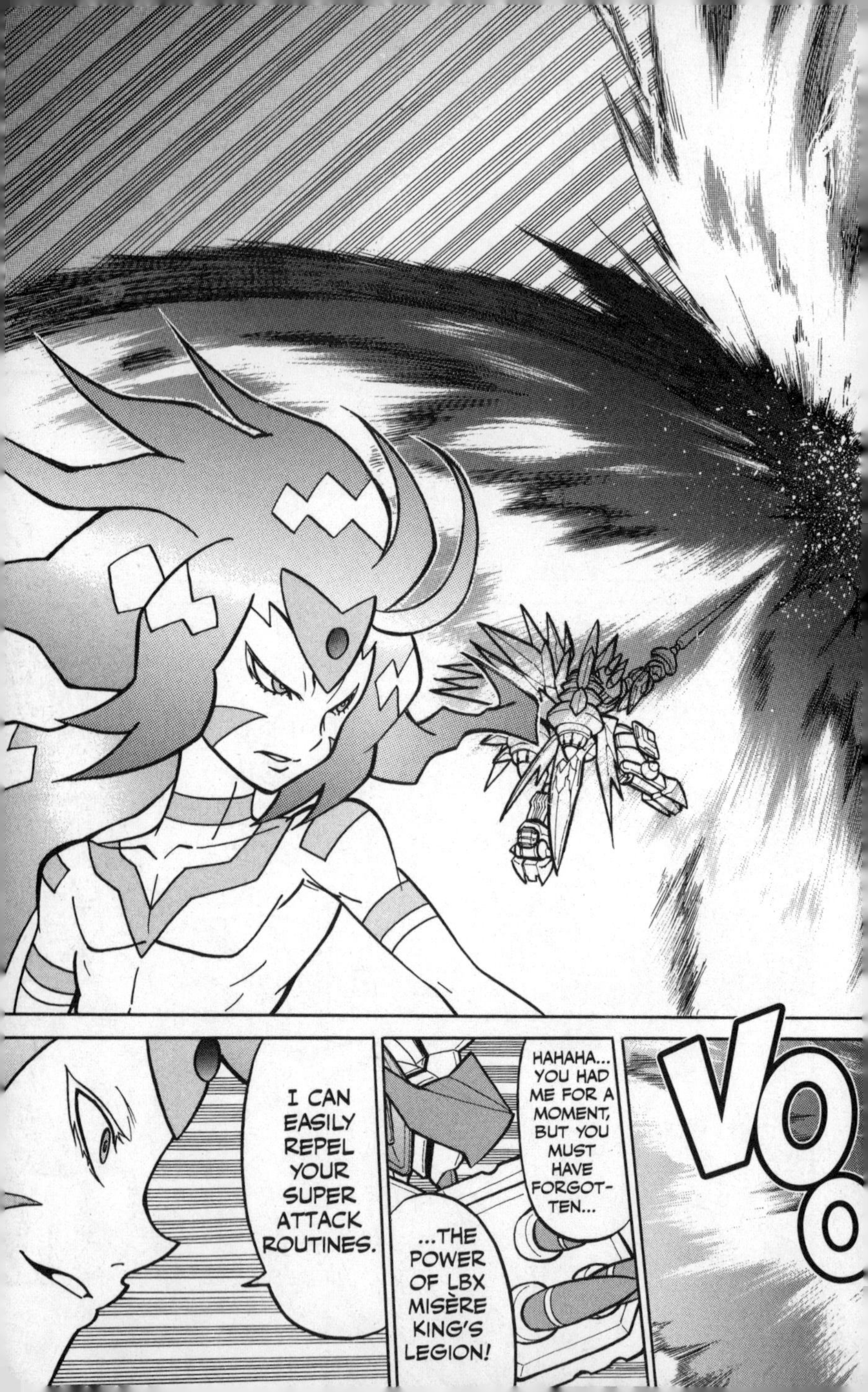
VOO
HAHAHA... YOU HAD ME FOR A MOMENT, BUT YOU MUST HAVE FORGOT-TEN...
...THE POWER OF LBX MISÈRE KING'S LEGION!
I CAN EASILY REPEL YOUR SUPER ATTACK ROUTINES.

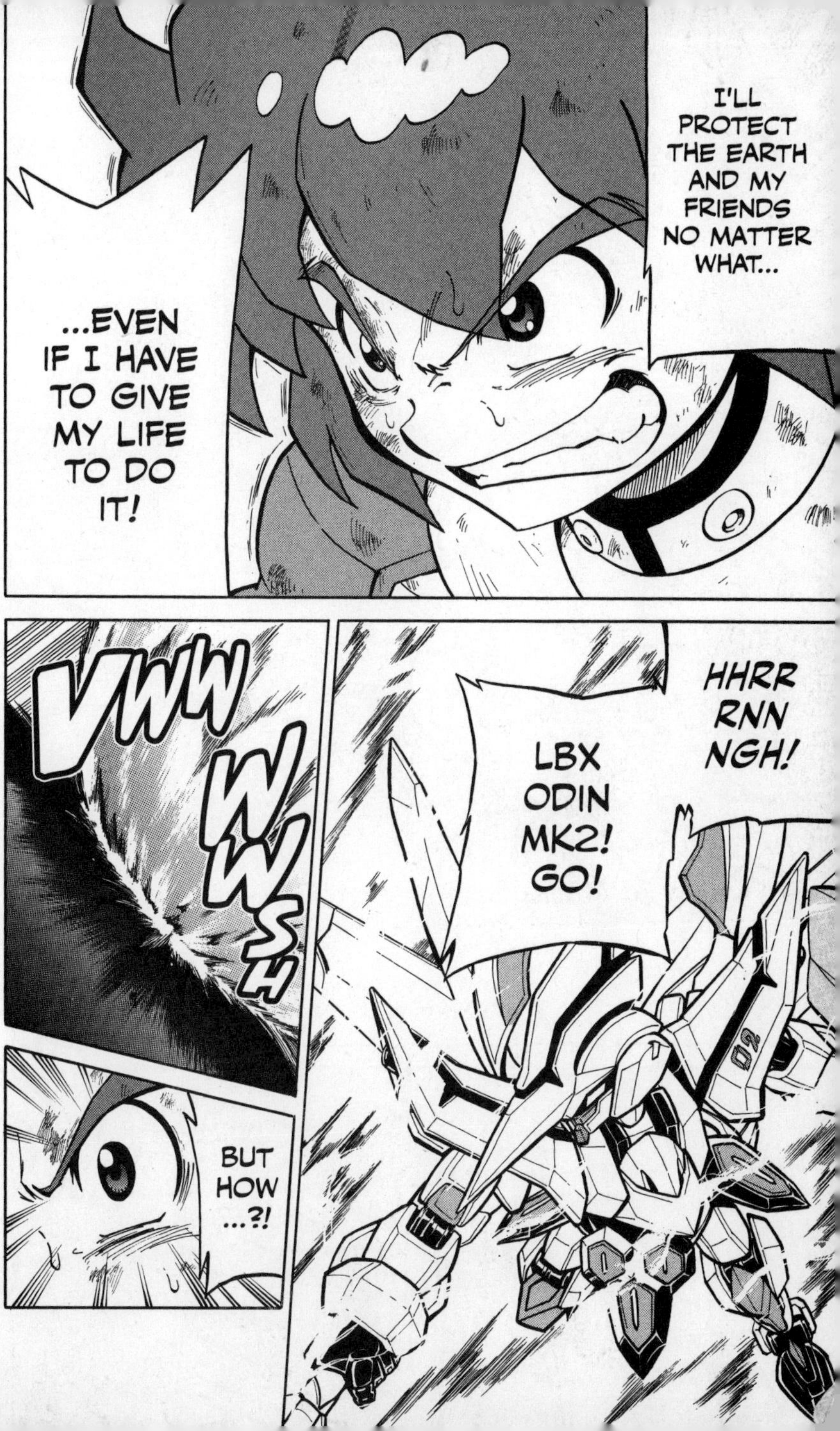
I'LL PROTECT THE EARTH AND MY FRIENDS NO MATTER WHAT...
...EVEN IF I HAVE TO GIVE MY LIFE TO DO IT!
HHRR RNN NGH!
LBX ODIN MK2! GO!
VWWWWSH
BUT HOW ...?!

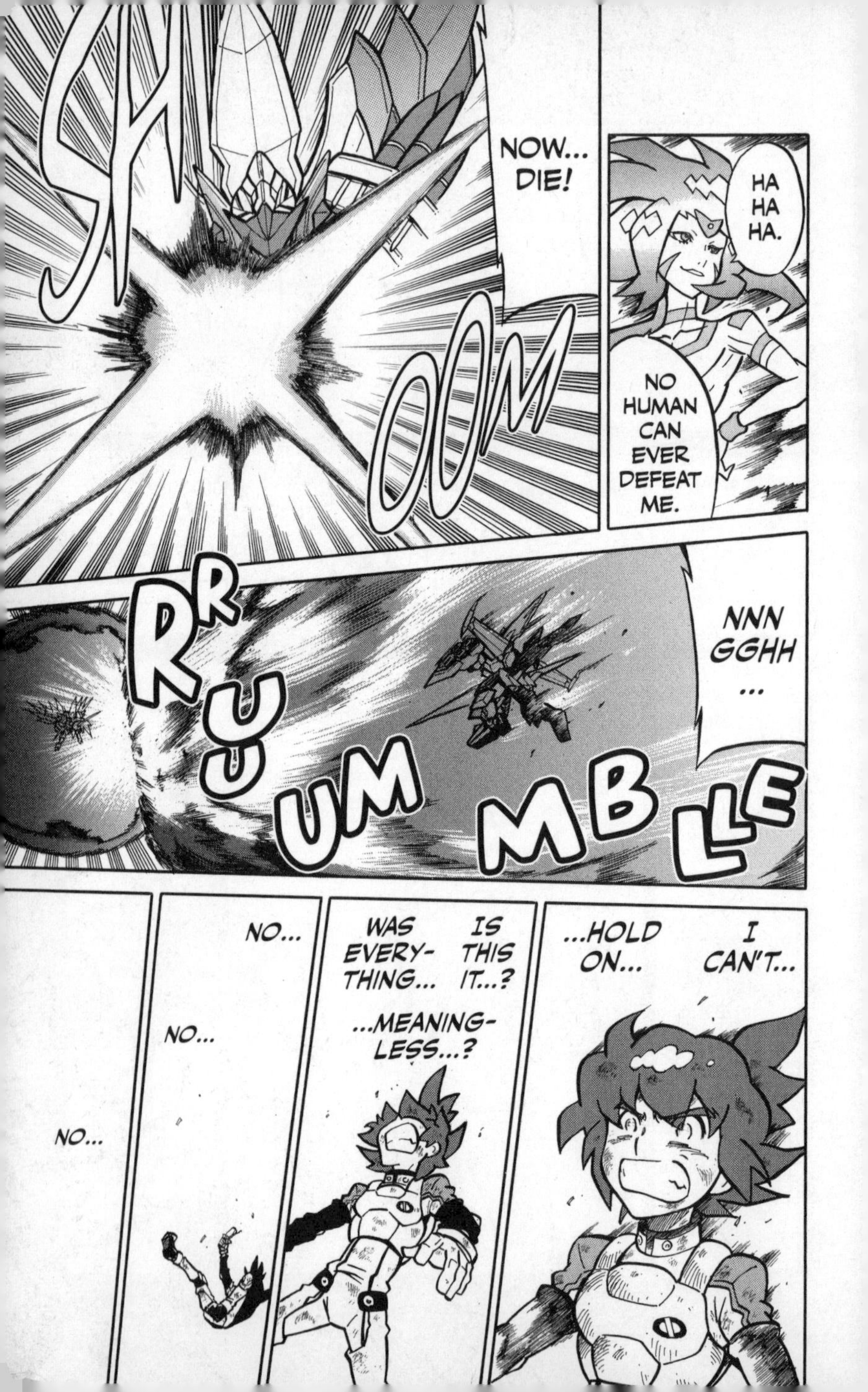
HA HA HA.
NO HUMAN CAN EVER DEFEAT ME.
NOW... DIE!
OOOM
NNN GGHH ...
RRUUUMMBLLE
I CAN'T...
...HOLD ON...
IS THIS IT...?
WAS EVERY-THING...
...MEANING-LESS...?
NO...
NO...
NO...

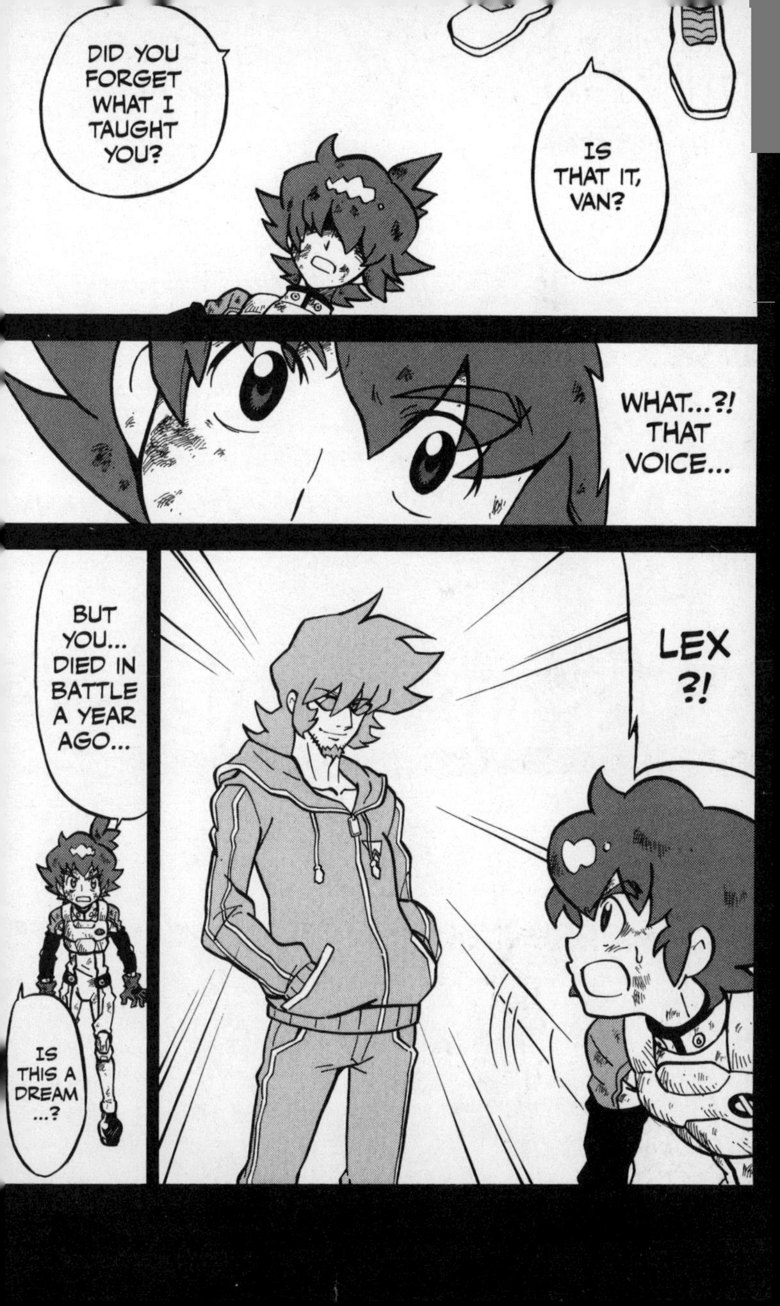

IS THAT IT, VAN?
DID YOU FORGET WHAT I TAUGHT YOU?
WHAT...?! THAT VOICE...
LEX ?!
BUT YOU... DIED IN BATTLE A YEAR AGO...
IS THIS A DREAM ...?

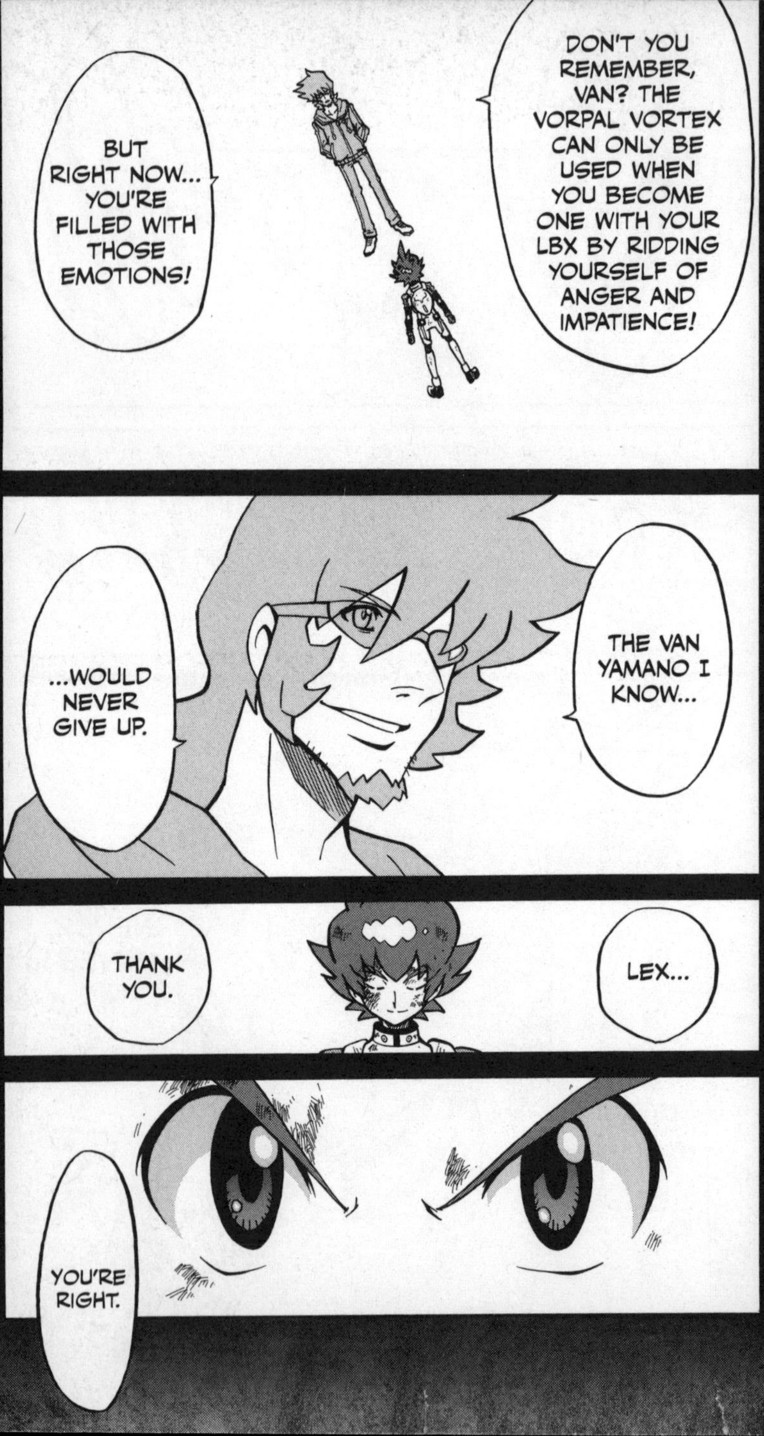
DON'T YOU REMEMBER, VAN? THE VORPAL VORTEX CAN ONLY BE USED WHEN YOU BECOME ONE WITH YOUR LBX BY RIDDING YOURSELF OF ANGER AND IMPATIENCE!
BUT RIGHT NOW... YOU'RE FILLED WITH THOSE EMOTIONS!
THE VAN YAMANO I KNOW...
...WOULD NEVER GIVE UP.
LEX...
THANK YOU.
YOU'RE RIGHT.

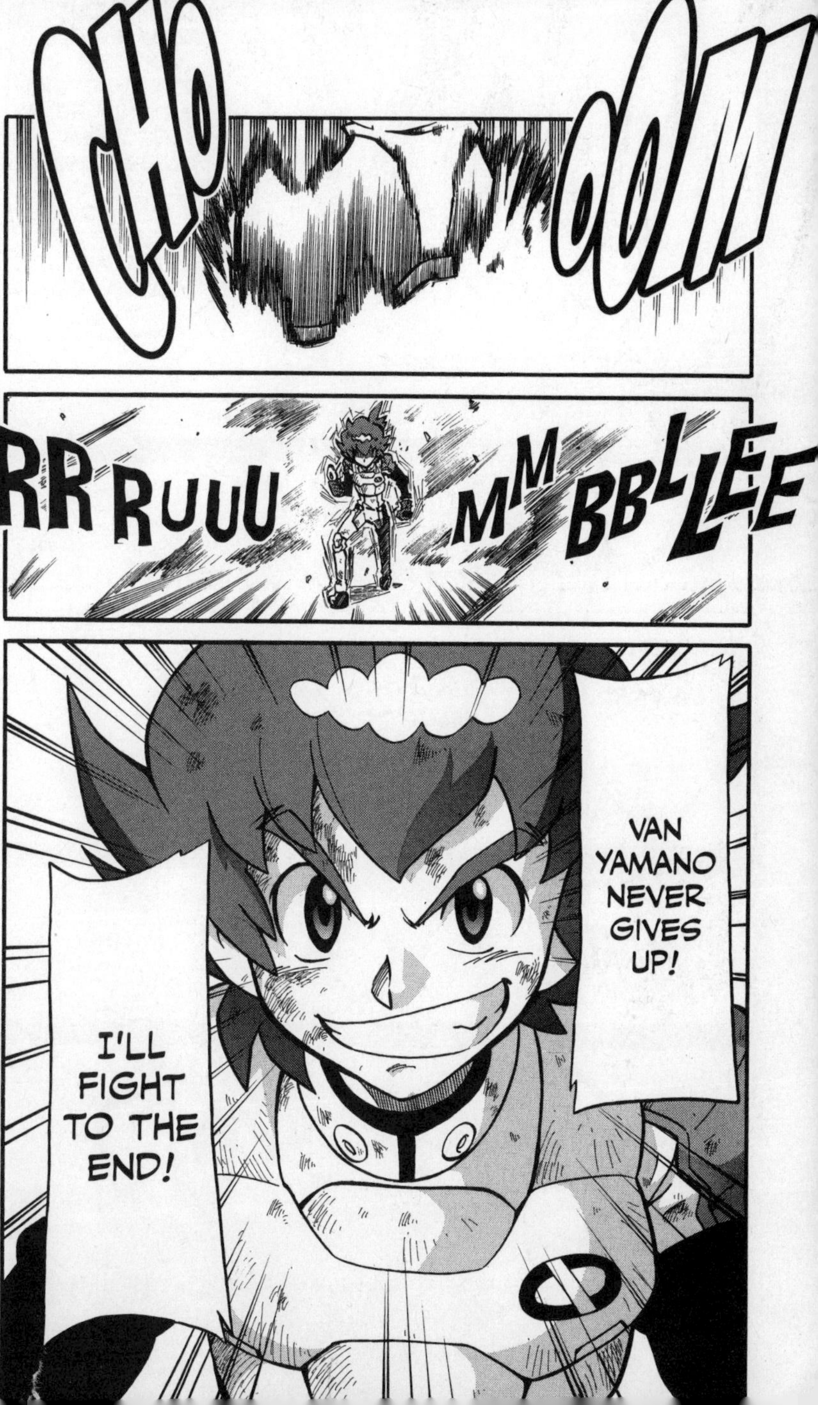
CHO
OOM
RR RUUU MM BBLLEE
VAN YAMANO NEVER GIVES UP!
I'LL FIGHT TO THE END!

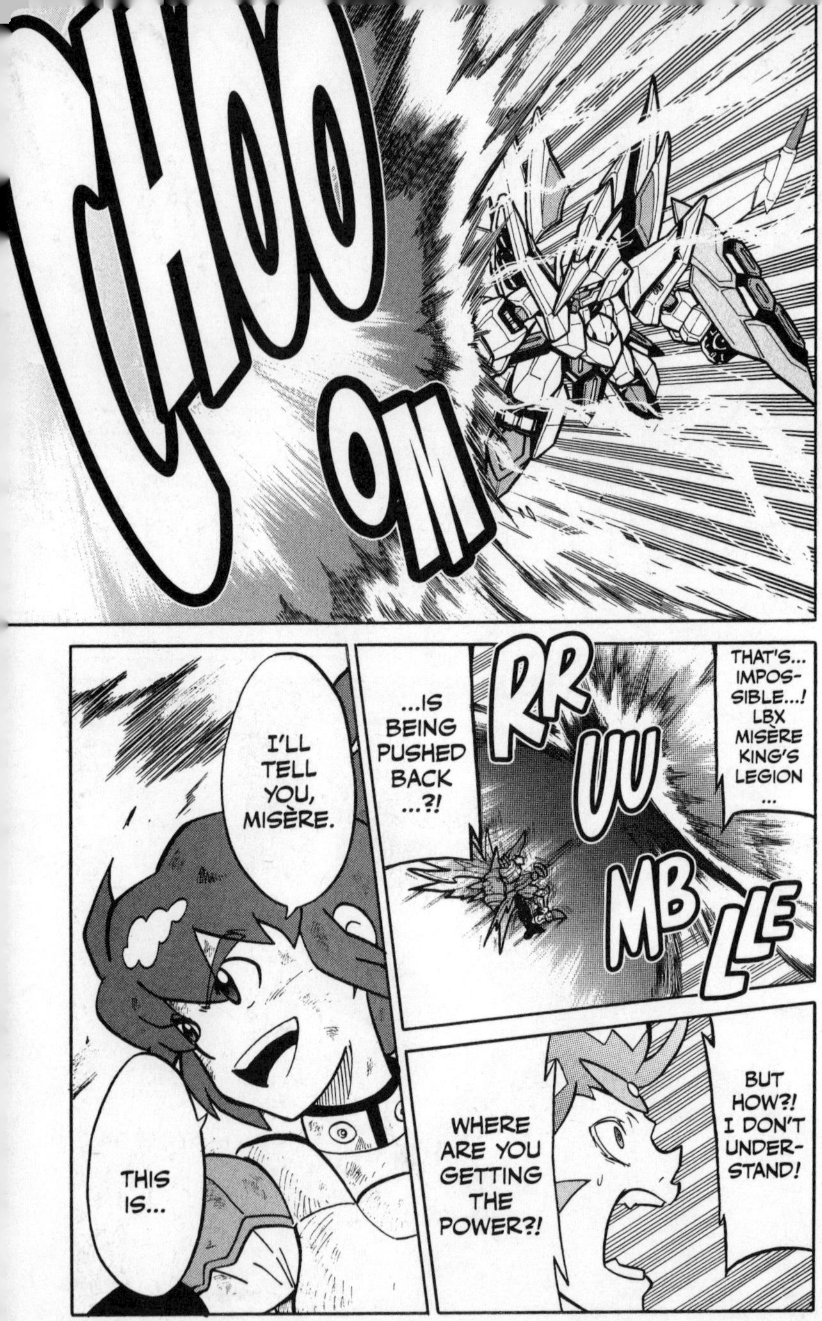
CHOOOM
THAT'S... IMPOSSIBLE...! LBX MISÈRE KING'S LEGION ...
RRUUMBLLE
...IS BEING PUSHED BACK ...?!
BUT HOW?! I DON'T UNDERSTAND!
WHERE ARE YOU GETTING THE POWER?!
I'LL TELL YOU, MISÈRE.
THIS IS...

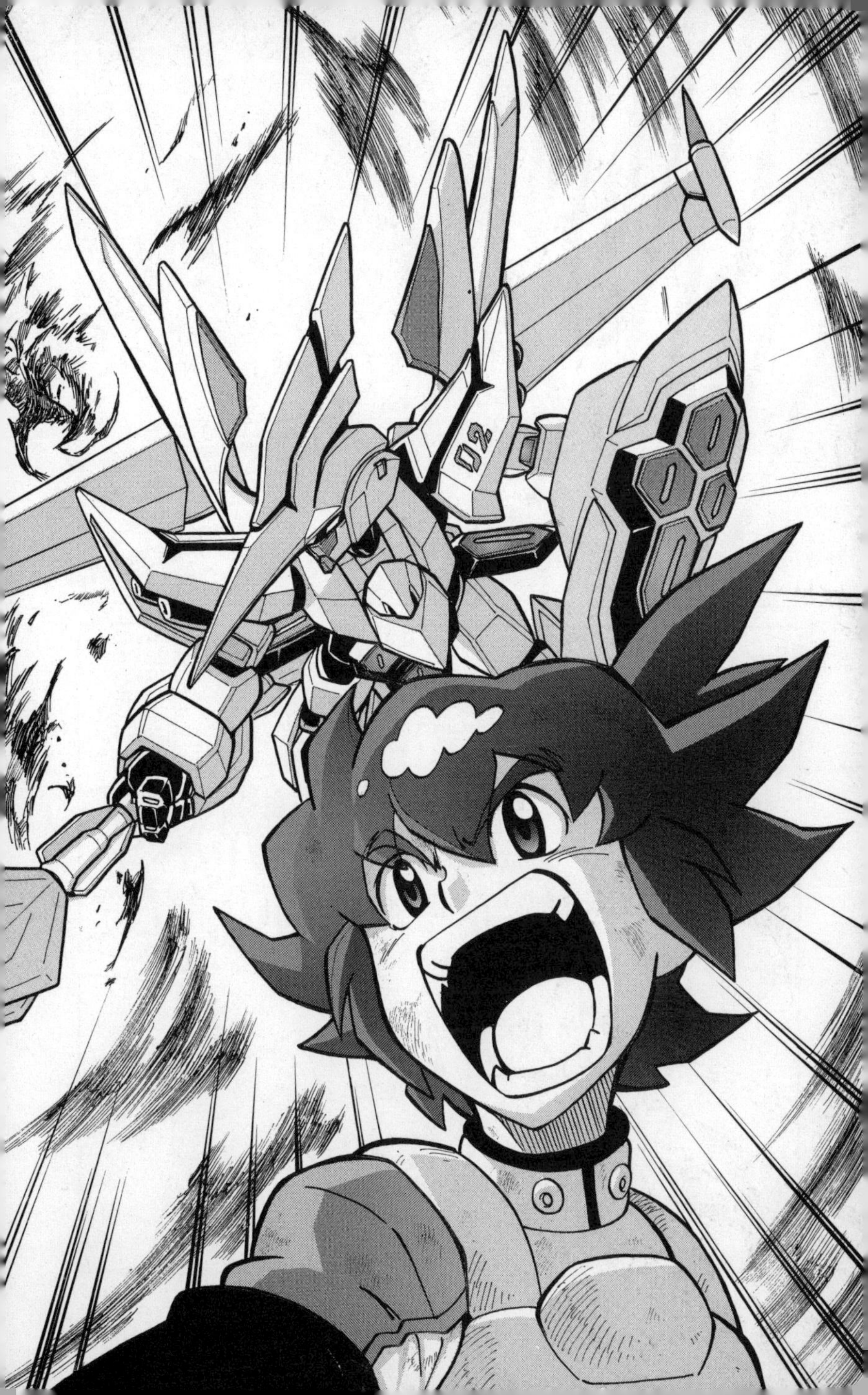
02

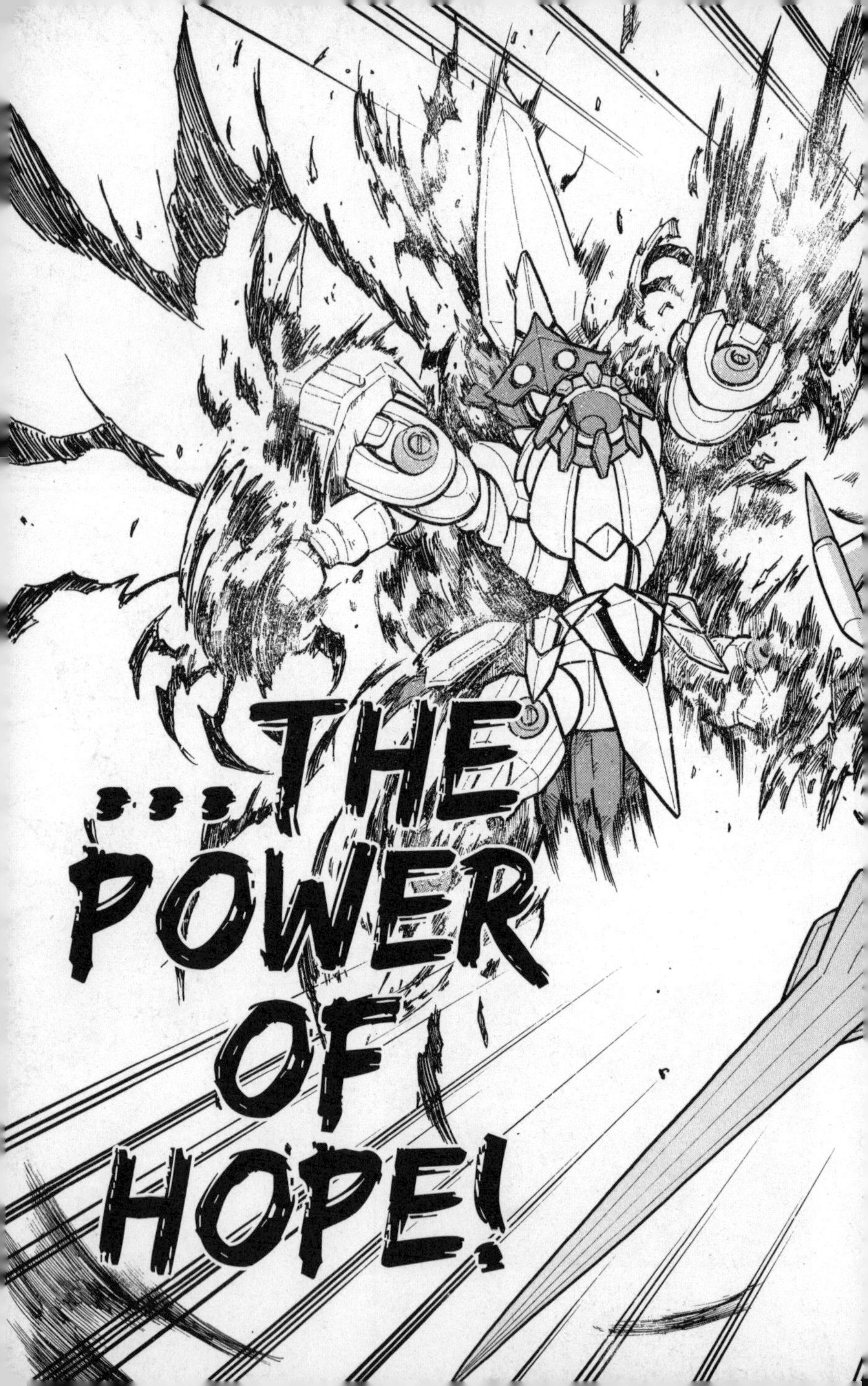
...THE POWER OF HOPE!

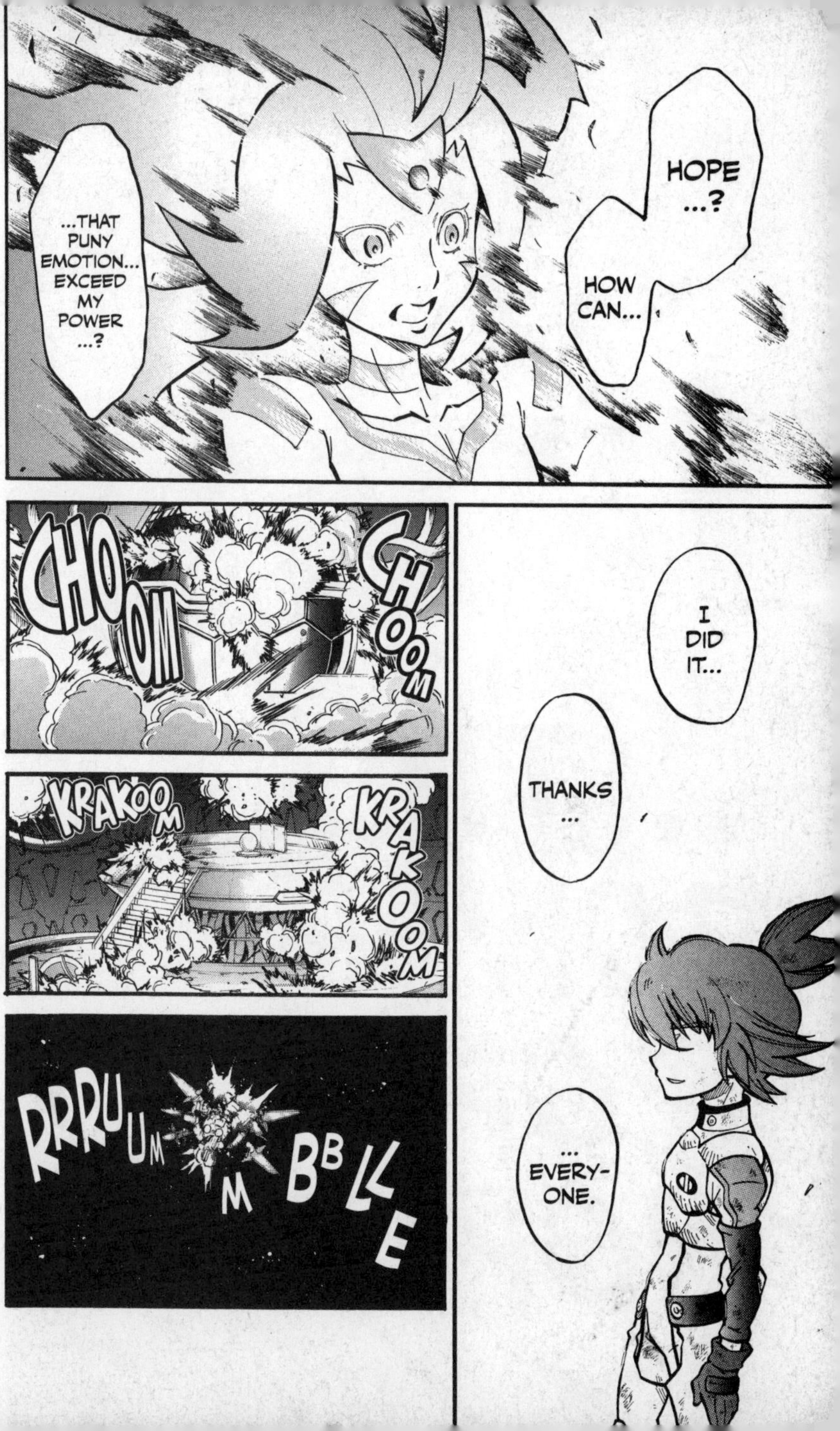
HOPE ...?
HOW CAN...
...THAT PUNY EMOTION... EXCEED MY POWER ...?
I DID IT...
THANKS ...
... EVERY-ONE.
CHOOM
CHOOM
KRAKOOM
KRAKOOM
RRRUUMMBBLLE

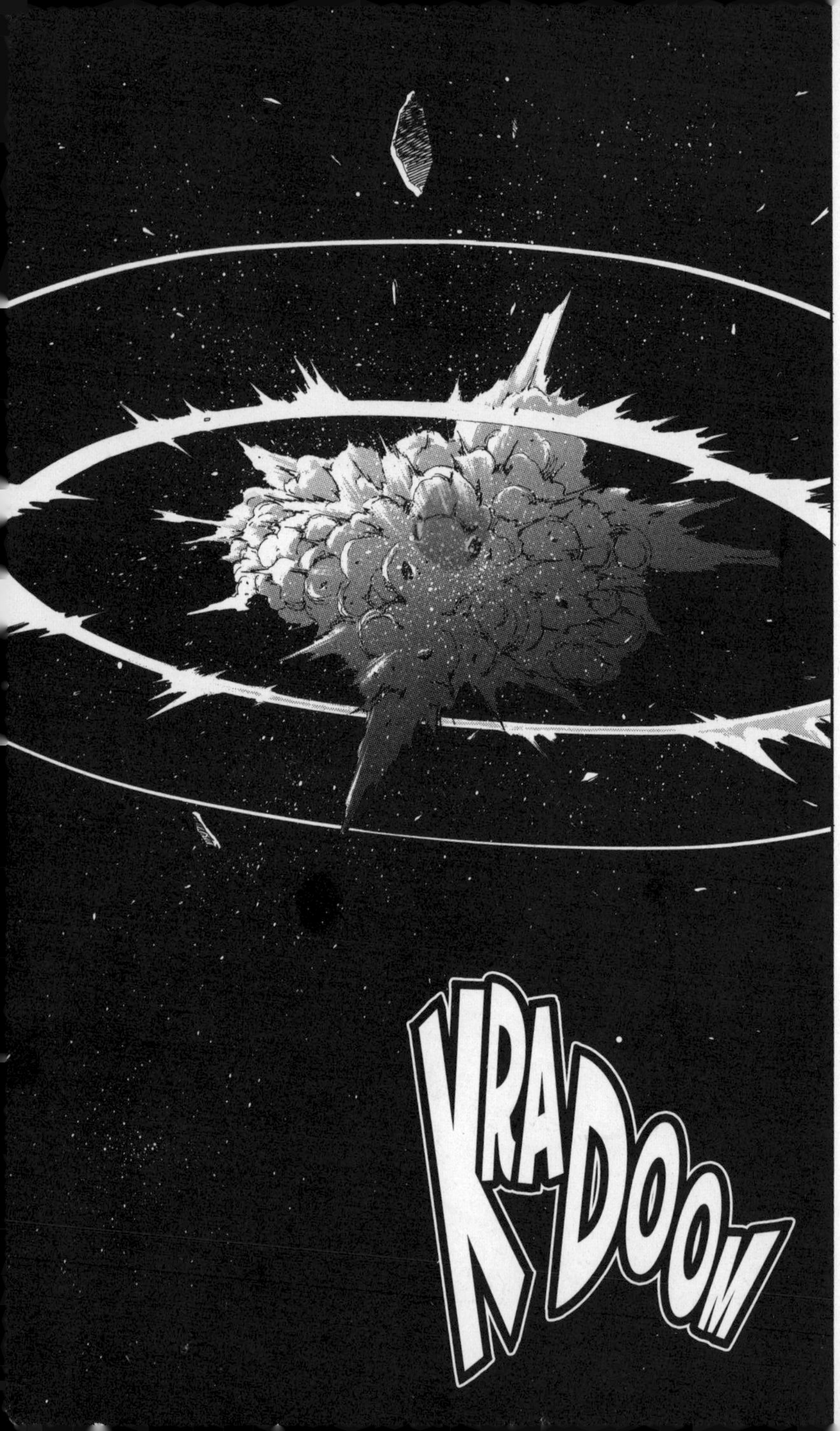
KRADOOM

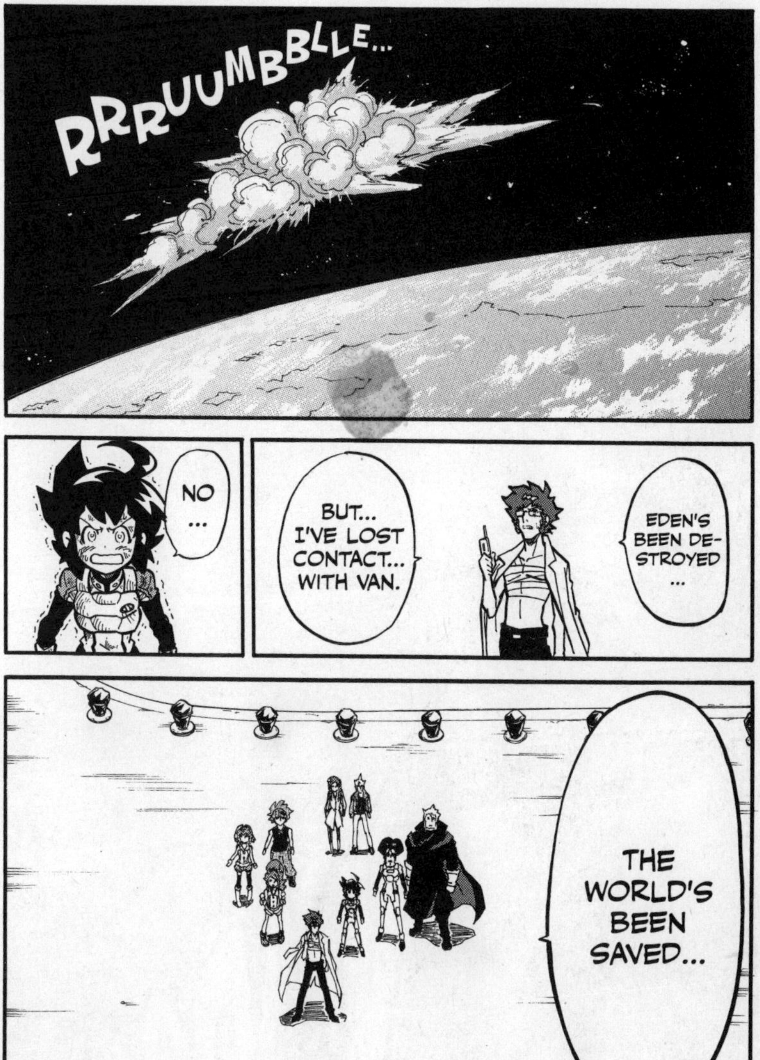
RRRUUMBBLLE...
EDEN'S BEEN DE-STROYED ...
BUT... I'VE LOST CONTACT... WITH VAN.
NO ...
THE WORLD'S BEEN SAVED...

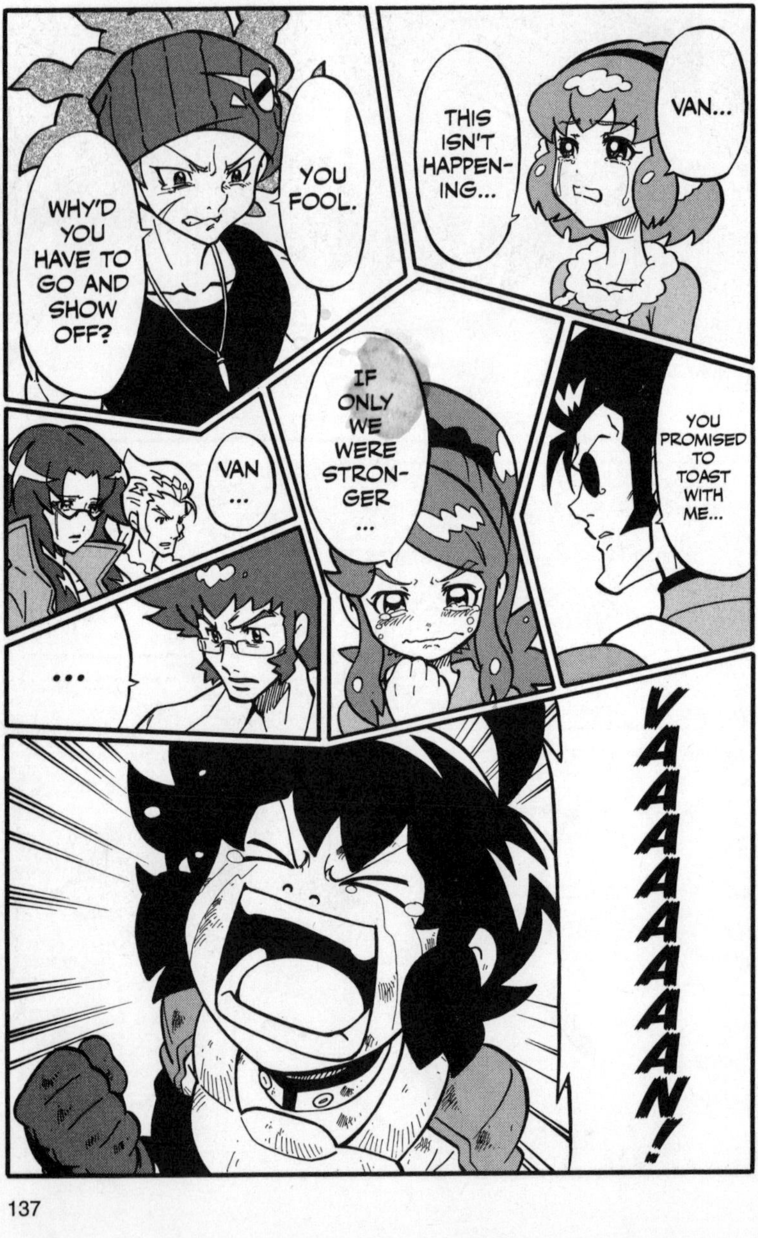
VAN...
THIS ISN'T HAPPEN-ING...
YOU FOOL.
WHY'D YOU HAVE TO GO AND SHOW OFF?
YOU PROMISED TO TOAST WITH ME...
IF ONLY WE WERE STRON-GER ...
VAN ...
...
VAAAAAAAAN!

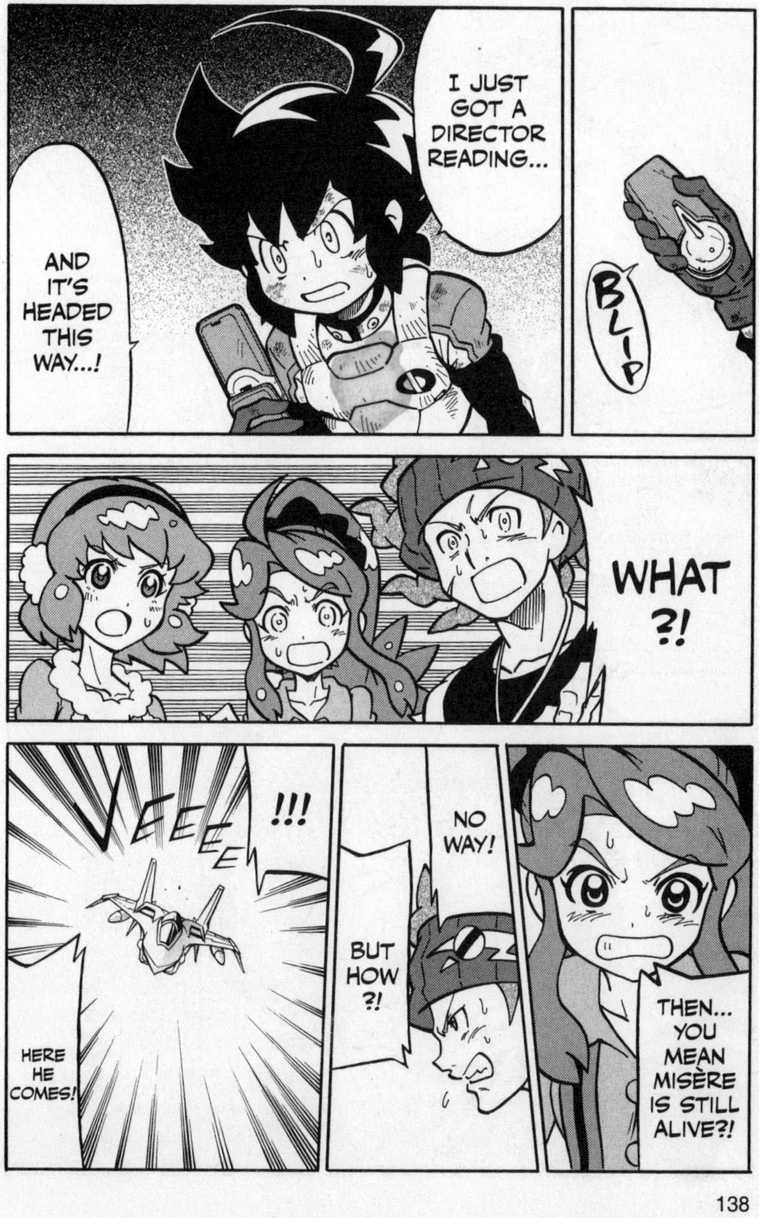
BLIP
I JUST GOT A DIRECTOR READING...
AND IT'S HEADED THIS WAY...!
WHAT?!
THEN... YOU MEAN MISÈRE IS STILL ALIVE?!
NO WAY!
BUT HOW?!
!!!
VEEEE
HERE HE COMES!

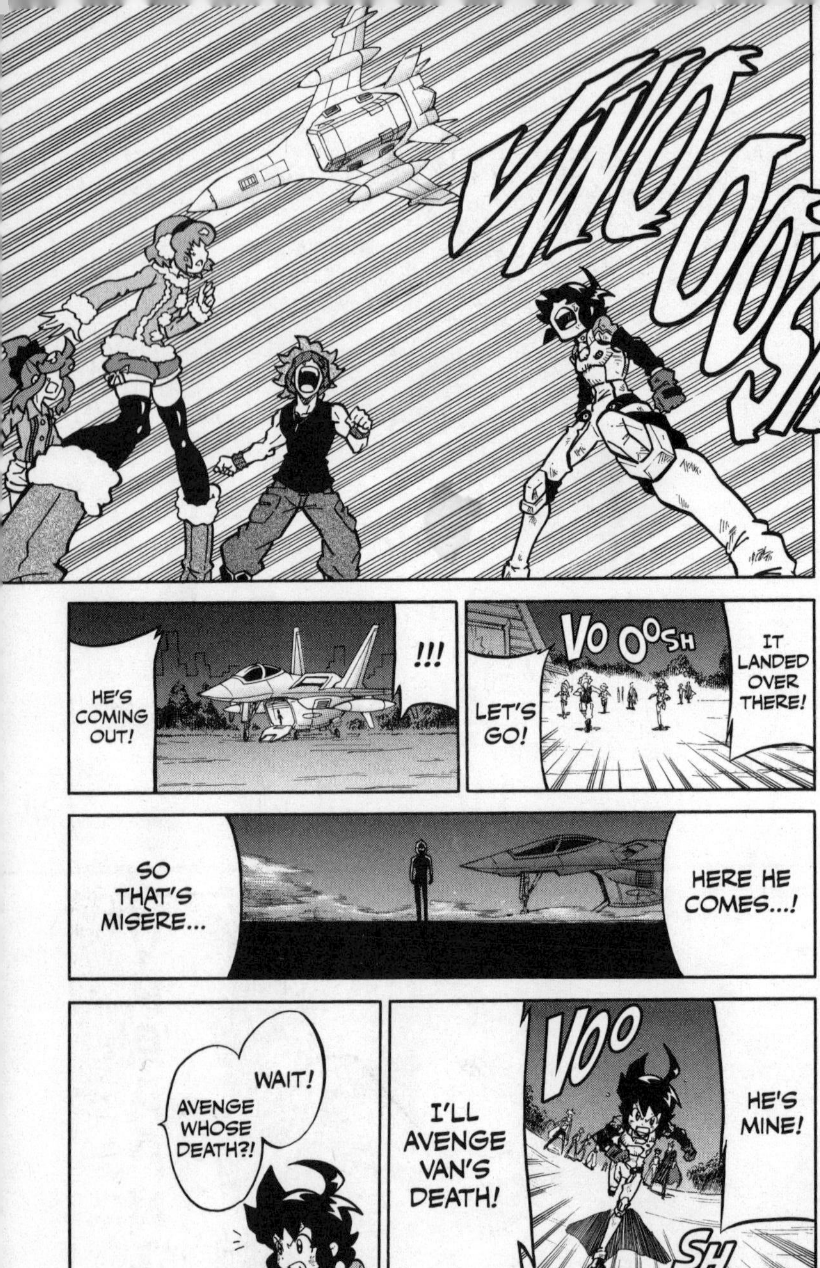
VVOOOOSH
IT LANDED OVER THERE!
VO OOSH
LET'S GO!
!!!
HE'S COMING OUT!
HERE HE COMES...!
SO THAT'S MISÈRE...
HE'S MINE!
VOO
I'LL AVENGE VAN'S DEATH!
SH
WAIT!
AVENGE WHOSE DEATH?!

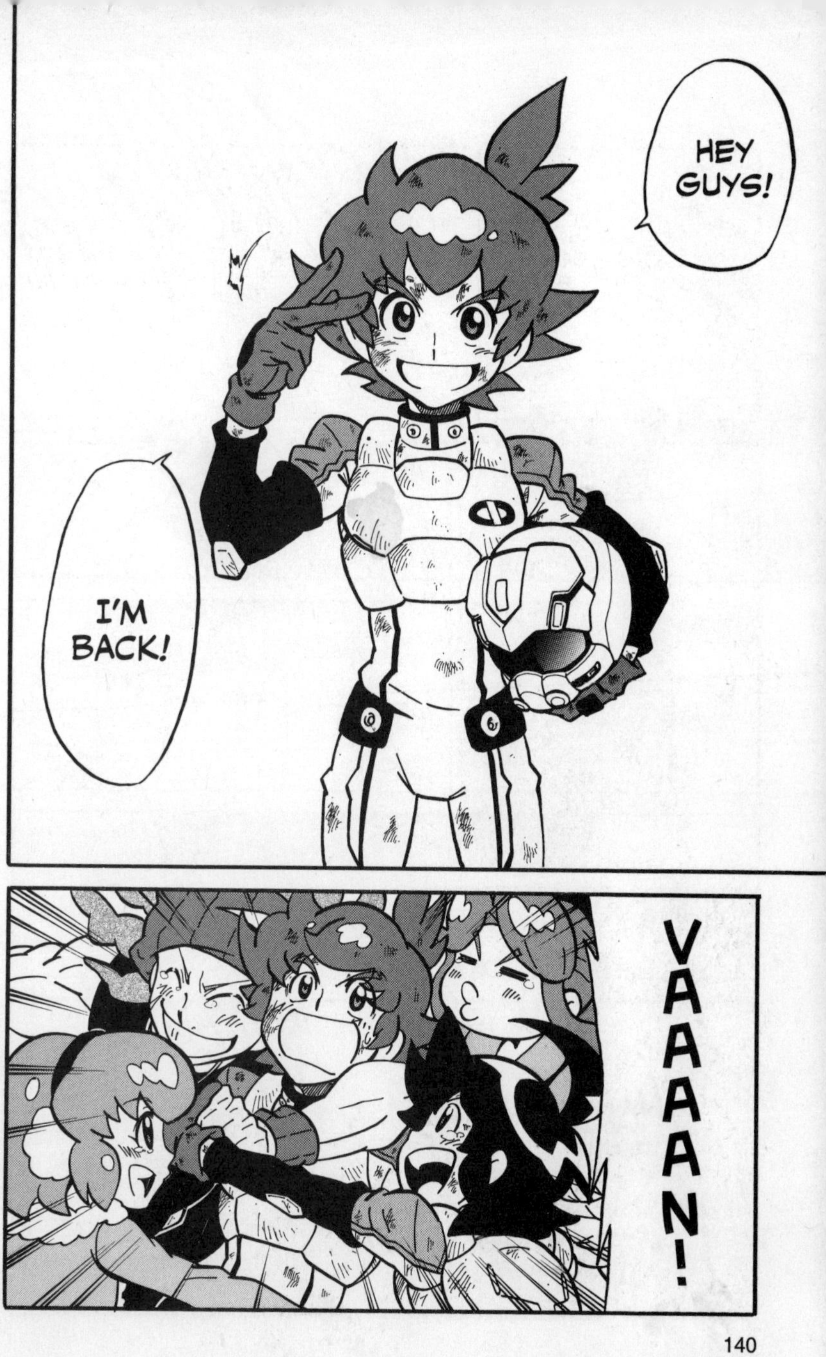
HEY GUYS!
I'M BACK!
VAAAAN!

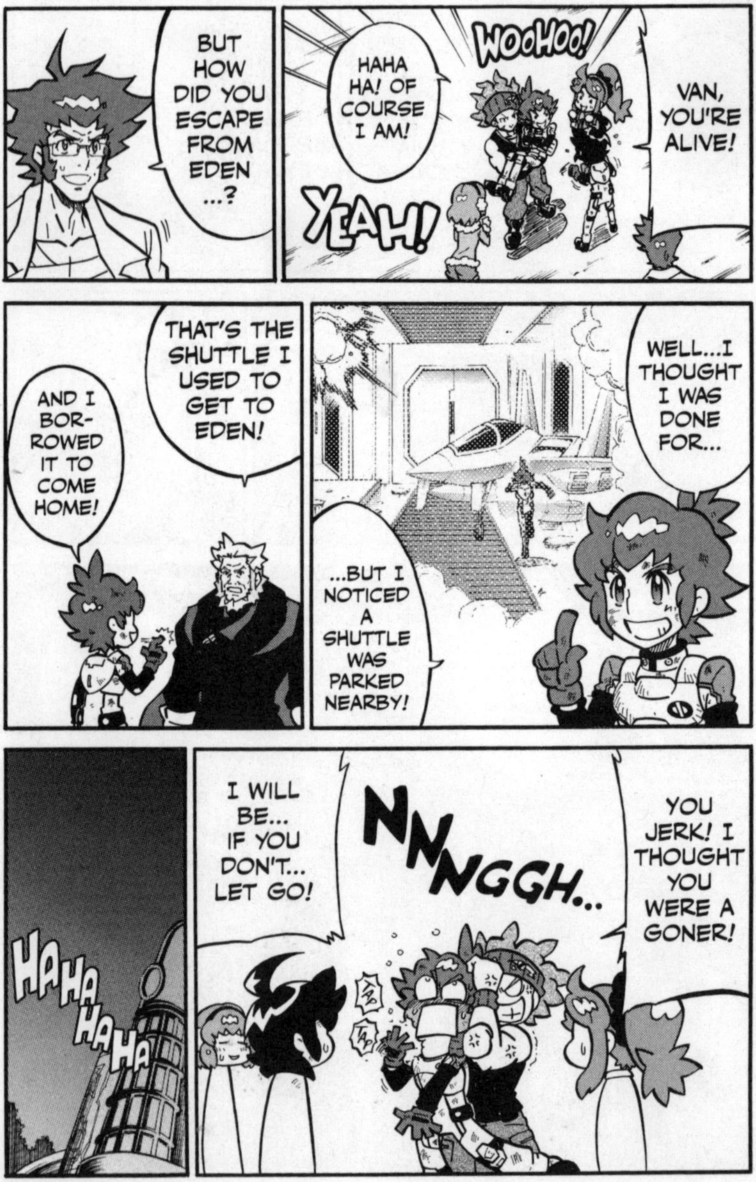
VAN, YOU'RE ALIVE!
WOOHOO!
HAHA HA! OF COURSE I AM!
YEAH!
BUT HOW DID YOU ESCAPE FROM EDEN ...?
WELL...I THOUGHT I WAS DONE FOR...
...BUT I NOTICED A SHUTTLE WAS PARKED NEARBY!
THAT'S THE SHUTTLE I USED TO GET TO EDEN!
AND I BOR-ROWED IT TO COME HOME!
YOU JERK! I THOUGHT YOU WERE A GONER!
NNNGGH...
TAP
TAP
I WILL BE... IF YOU DON'T... LET GO!
HAHA HAHA HAHA

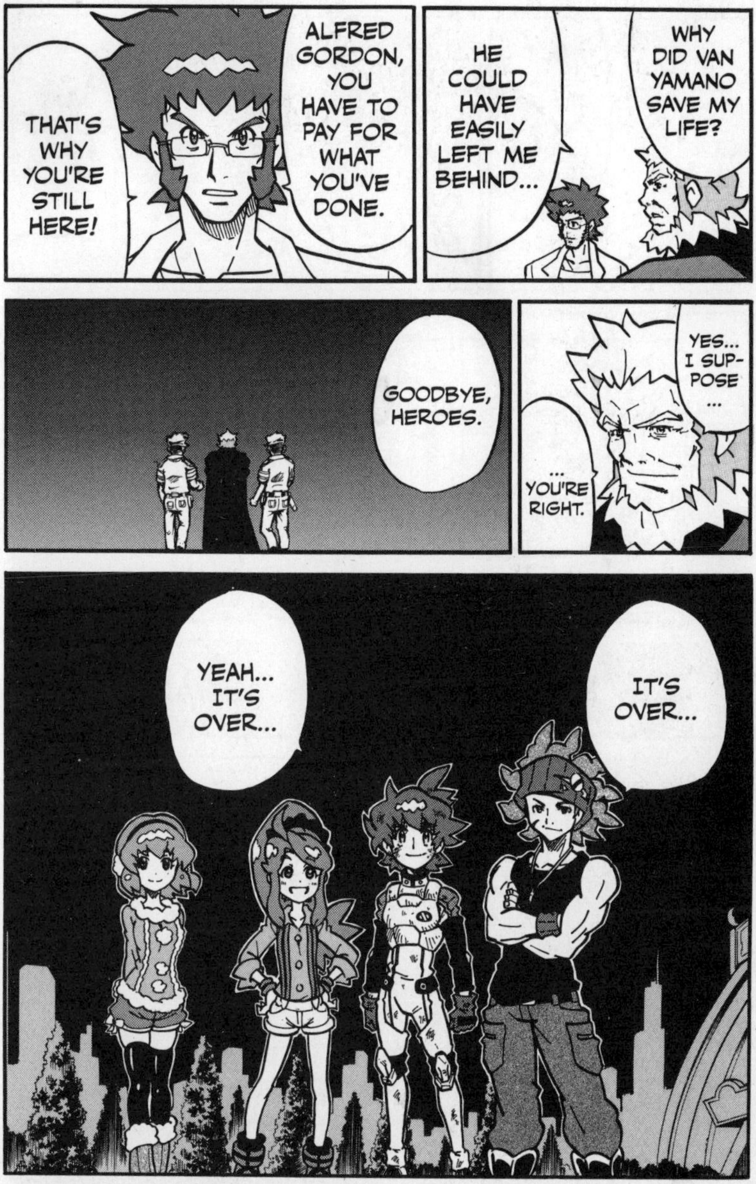
WHY DID VAN YAMANO SAVE MY LIFE?
HE COULD HAVE EASILY LEFT ME BEHIND...
ALFRED GORDON, YOU HAVE TO PAY FOR WHAT YOU'VE DONE.
THAT'S WHY YOU'RE STILL HERE!
YES... I SUPPOSE...
... YOU'RE RIGHT.
GOODBYE, HEROES.
IT'S OVER...
YEAH... IT'S OVER...

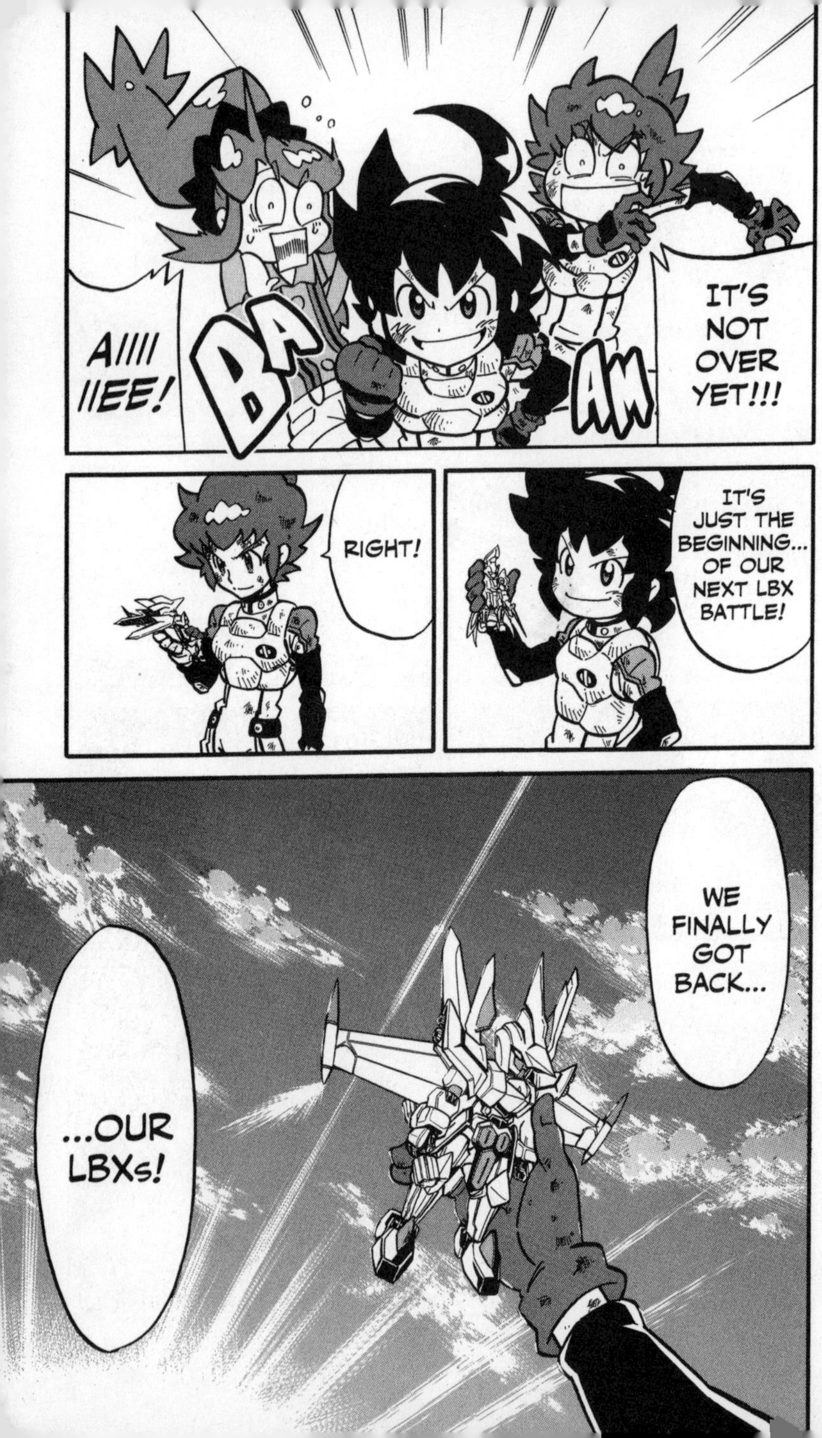
IT'S NOT OVER YET!!!
BAAM
AIIIII IIEE!
IT'S JUST THE BEGINNING... OF OUR NEXT LBX BATTLE!
RIGHT!
WE FINALLY GOT BACK...
...OUR LBXs!

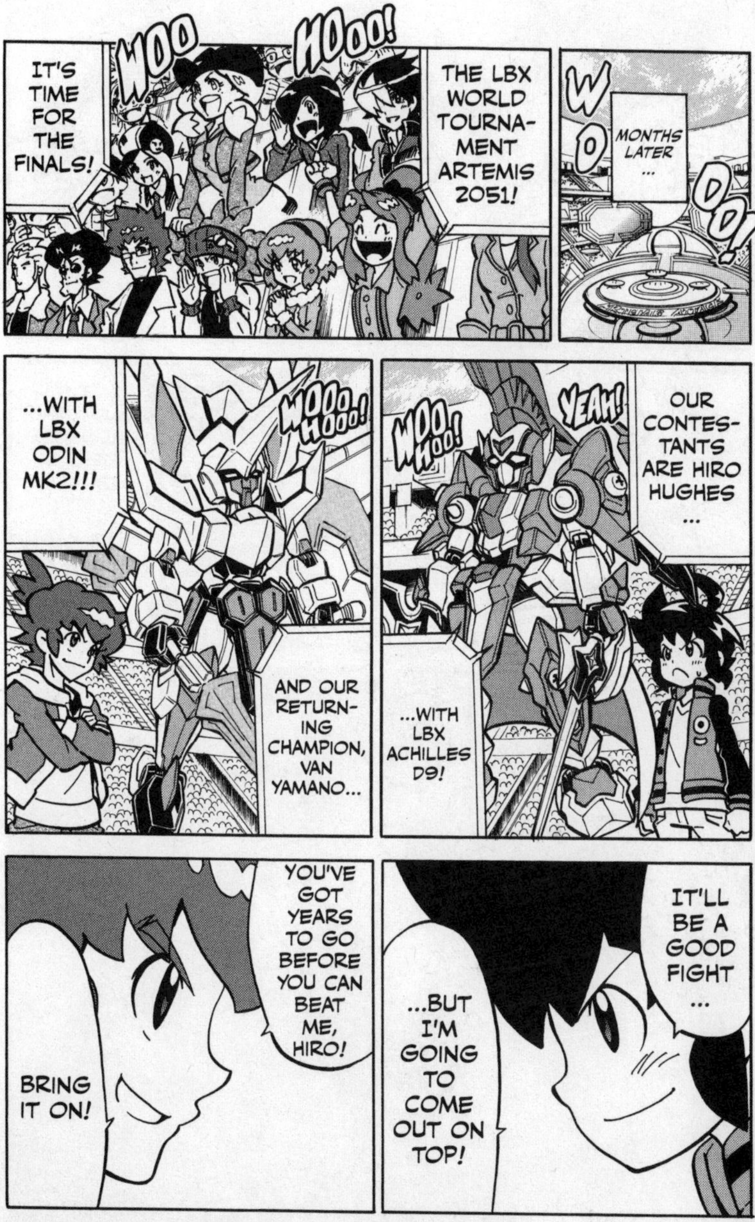
WOOOO!
MONTHS LATER ...
WOO HOOO!
THE LBX WORLD TOURNAMENT ARTEMIS 2051!
IT'S TIME FOR THE FINALS!
OUR CONTESTANTS ARE HIRO HUGHES ...
YEAH!
WOO HOO!
...WITH LBX ACHILLES D9!
WOOO HOOO!
AND OUR RETURNING CHAMPION, VAN YAMANO...
...WITH LBX ODIN MK2!!!
IT'LL BE A GOOD FIGHT ...
...BUT I'M GOING TO COME OUT ON TOP!
YOU'VE GOT YEARS TO GO BEFORE YOU CAN BEAT ME, HIRO!
BRING IT ON!

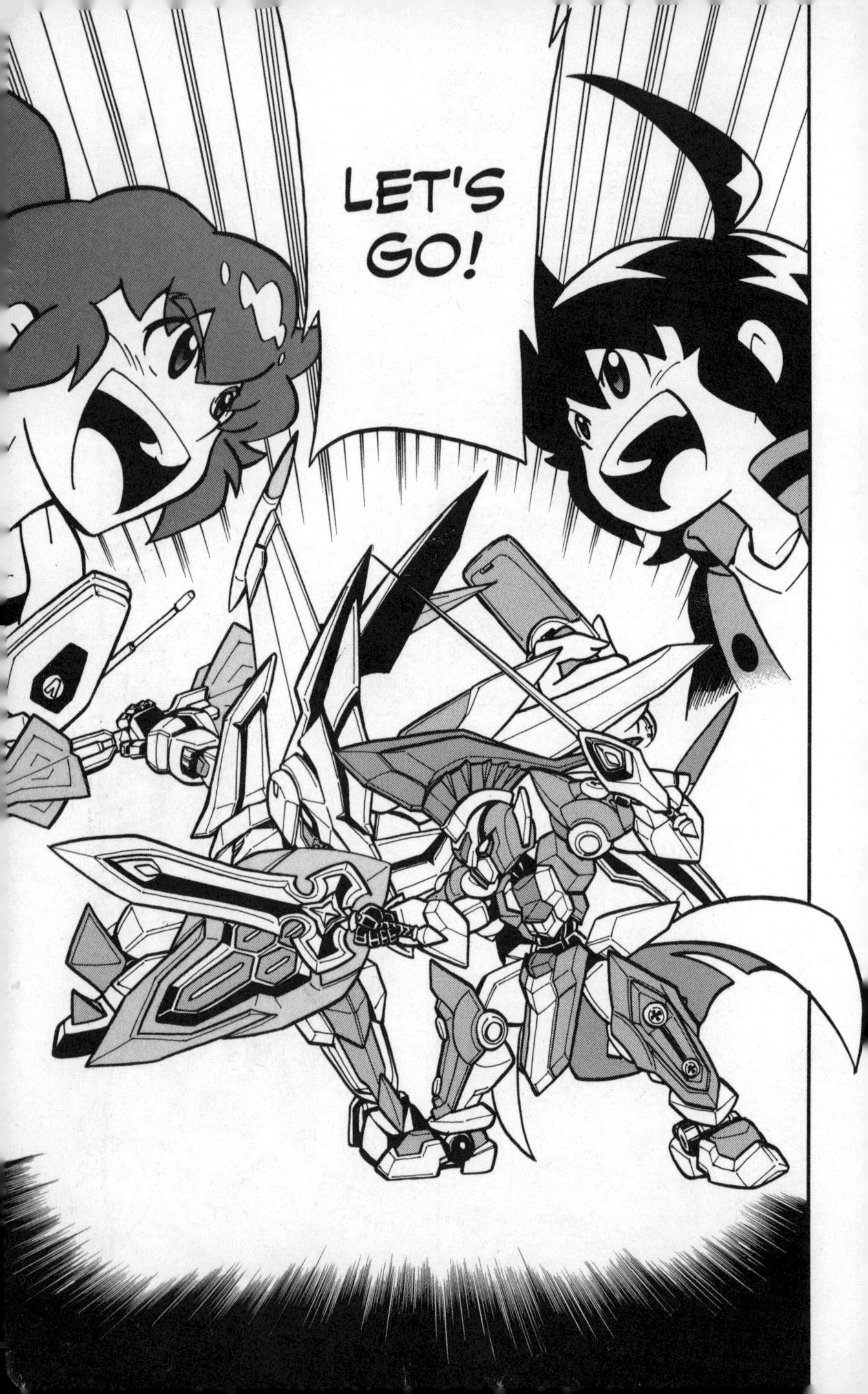
LET'S GO!

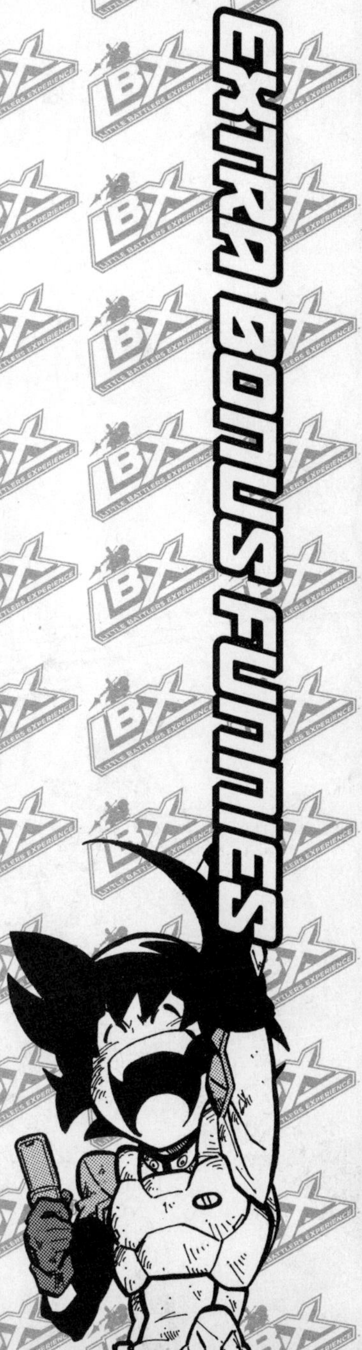
EXTRA BONUS FUNNIES

HANDS OFF!

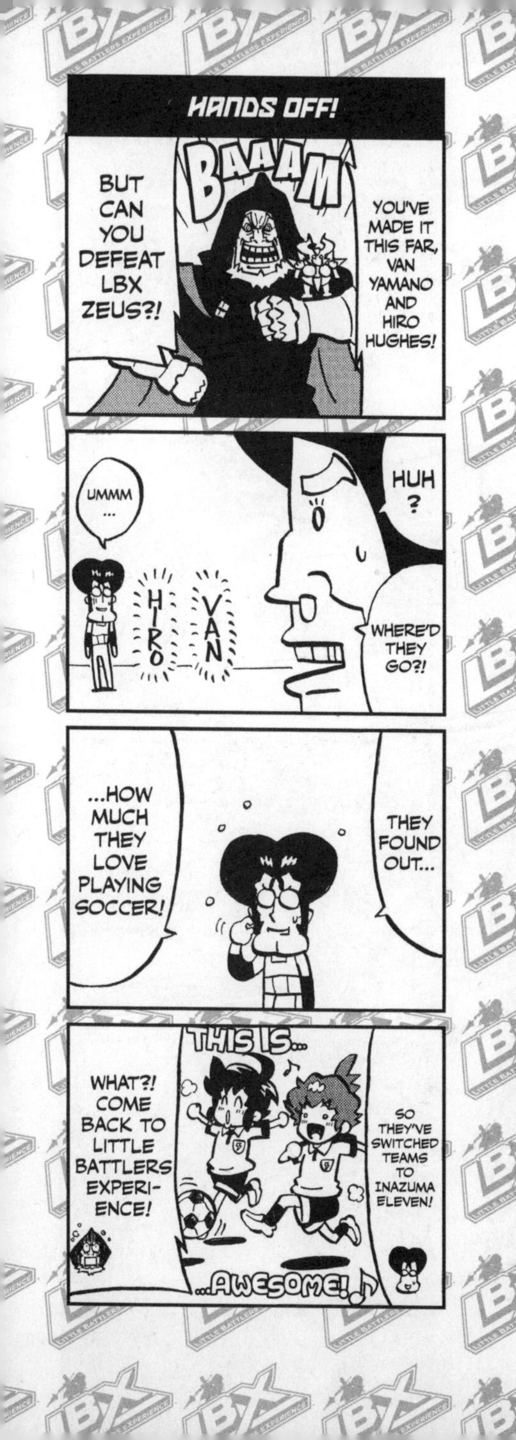
YOU'VE MADE IT THIS FAR, VAN YAMANO AND HIRO HUGHES!
BAAAM
BUT CAN YOU DEFEAT LBX ZEUS?!
HUH?
WHERE'D THEY GO?!
VAN
HIRO
UMMM ...
THEY FOUND OUT...
...HOW MUCH THEY LOVE PLAYING SOCCER!
THIS IS...
SO THEY'VE SWITCHED TEAMS TO INAZUMA ELEVEN!
WHAT?! COME BACK TO LITTLE BATTLERS EXPERI-ENCE!
...AWESOME!♪

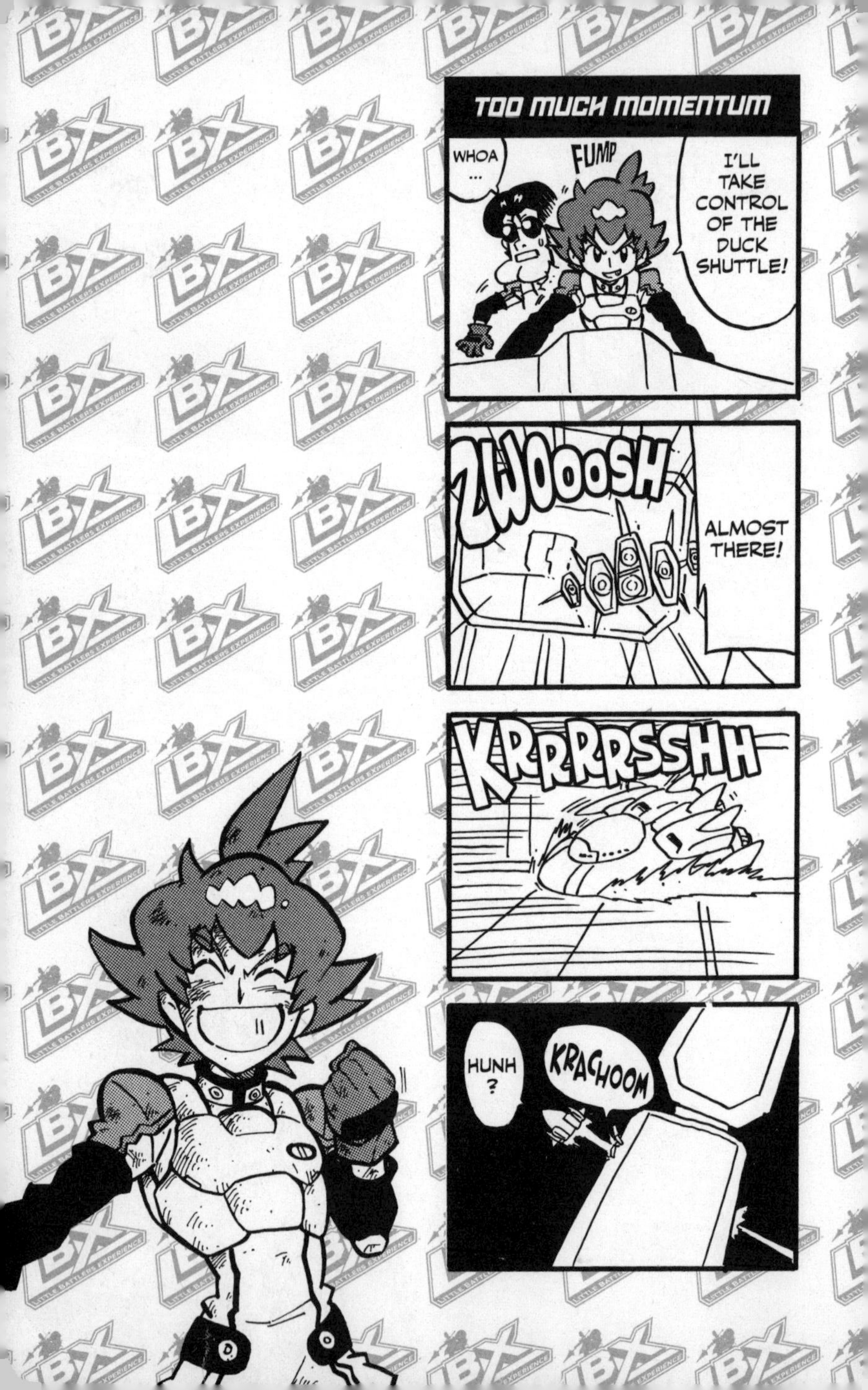
TOO MUCH MOMENTUM
I'LL TAKE CONTROL OF THE DUCK SHUTTLE!
FUMP
WHOA ...
ZWOOOOSH
ALMOST THERE!
KRRRRRSSHH
KRACHOOM
HUNH ?

CLOSE CALL

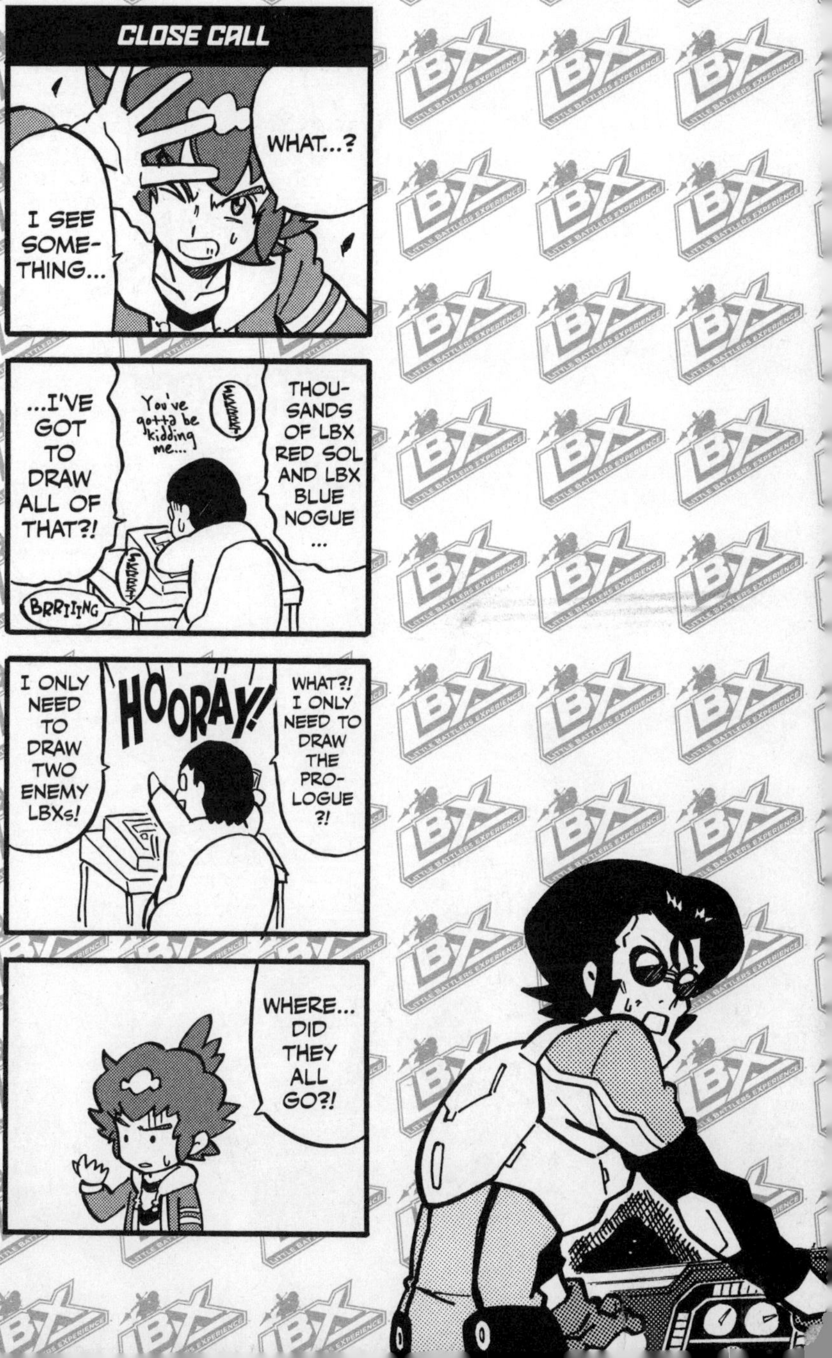
WHAT...?
I SEE SOMETHING...
THOUSANDS OF LBX RED SOL AND LBX BLUE NOGUE ...
You've gotta be kidding me...
...I'VE GOT TO DRAW ALL OF THAT?!
BRRIIING
WHAT?! I ONLY NEED TO DRAW THE PROLOGUE ?!
HOORAY!
I ONLY NEED TO DRAW TWO ENEMY LBXs!
WHERE... DID THEY ALL GO?!

UMMMM...THANKS?

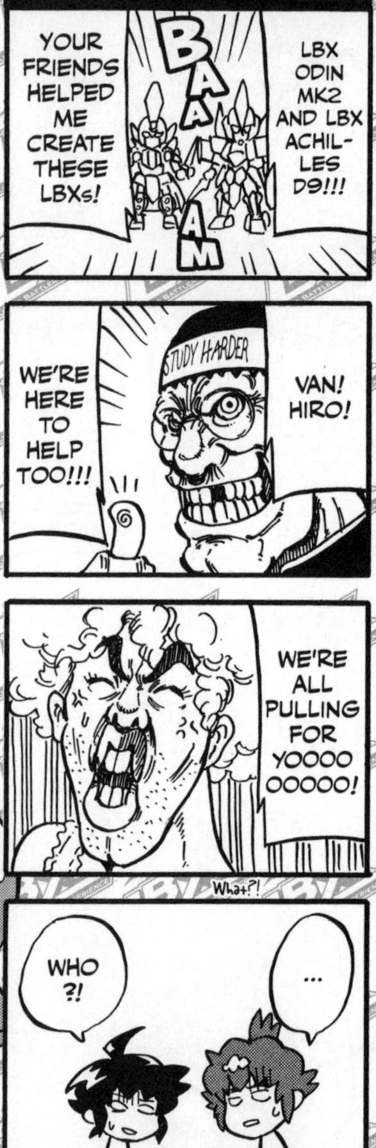

LBX ODIN MK2 AND LBX ACHIL-LES D9!!!
BAAAM
YOUR FRIENDS HELPED ME CREATE THESE LBXs!
VAN! HIRO!
STUDY HARDER
WE'RE HERE TO HELP TOO!!!
WE'RE ALL PULLING FOR YOOOO OOOOO!
What?!
...
WHO ?!

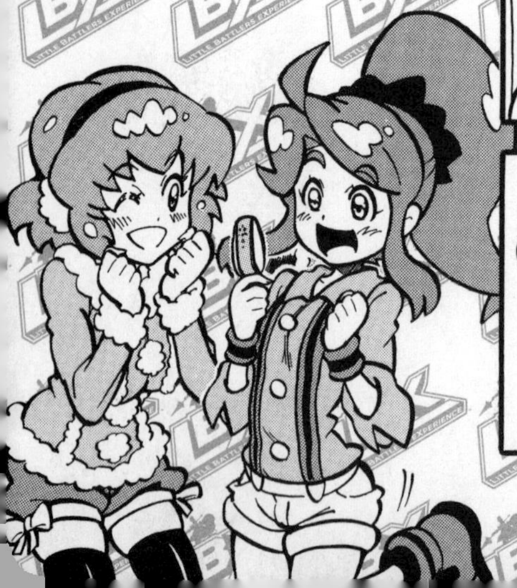

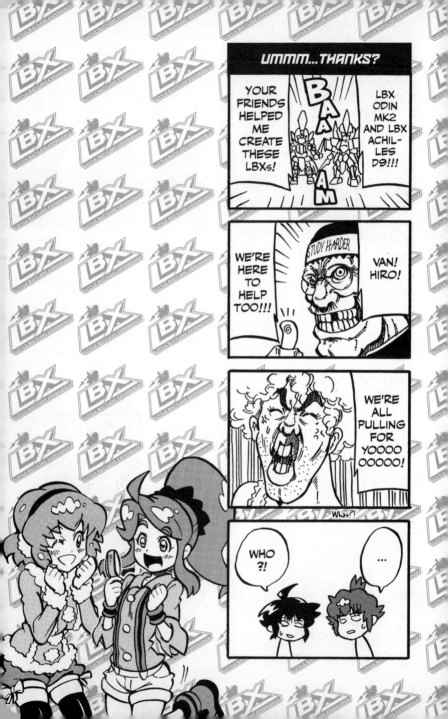

LUCKY GUY

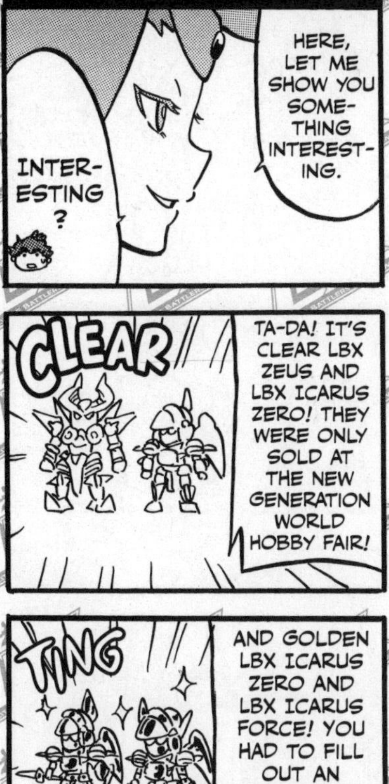
HERE, LET ME SHOW YOU SOME-THING INTEREST-ING.
INTER-ESTING?
TA-DA! IT'S CLEAR LBX ZEUS AND LBX ICARUS ZERO! THEY WERE ONLY SOLD AT THE NEW GENERATION WORLD HOBBY FAIR!
CLEAR
AND GOLDEN LBX ICARUS ZERO AND LBX ICARUS FORCE! YOU HAD TO FILL OUT AN APPLICATION TO GET THESE!
TING
TING
MAN...
NOW HE'S JUST SHOWING OFF!

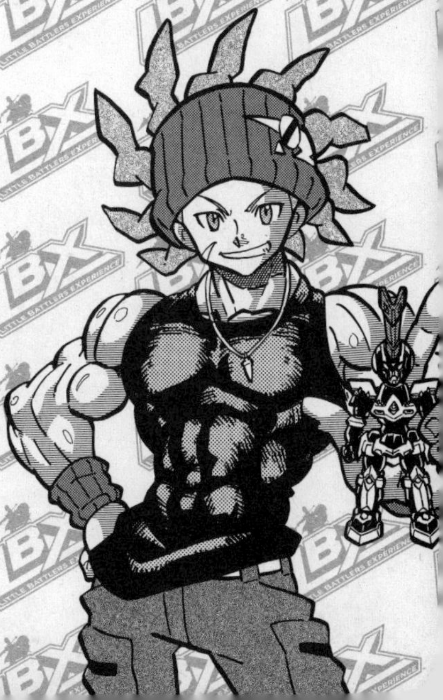

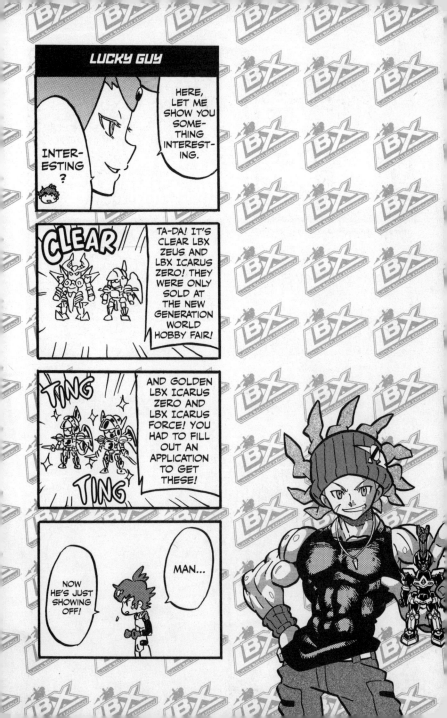

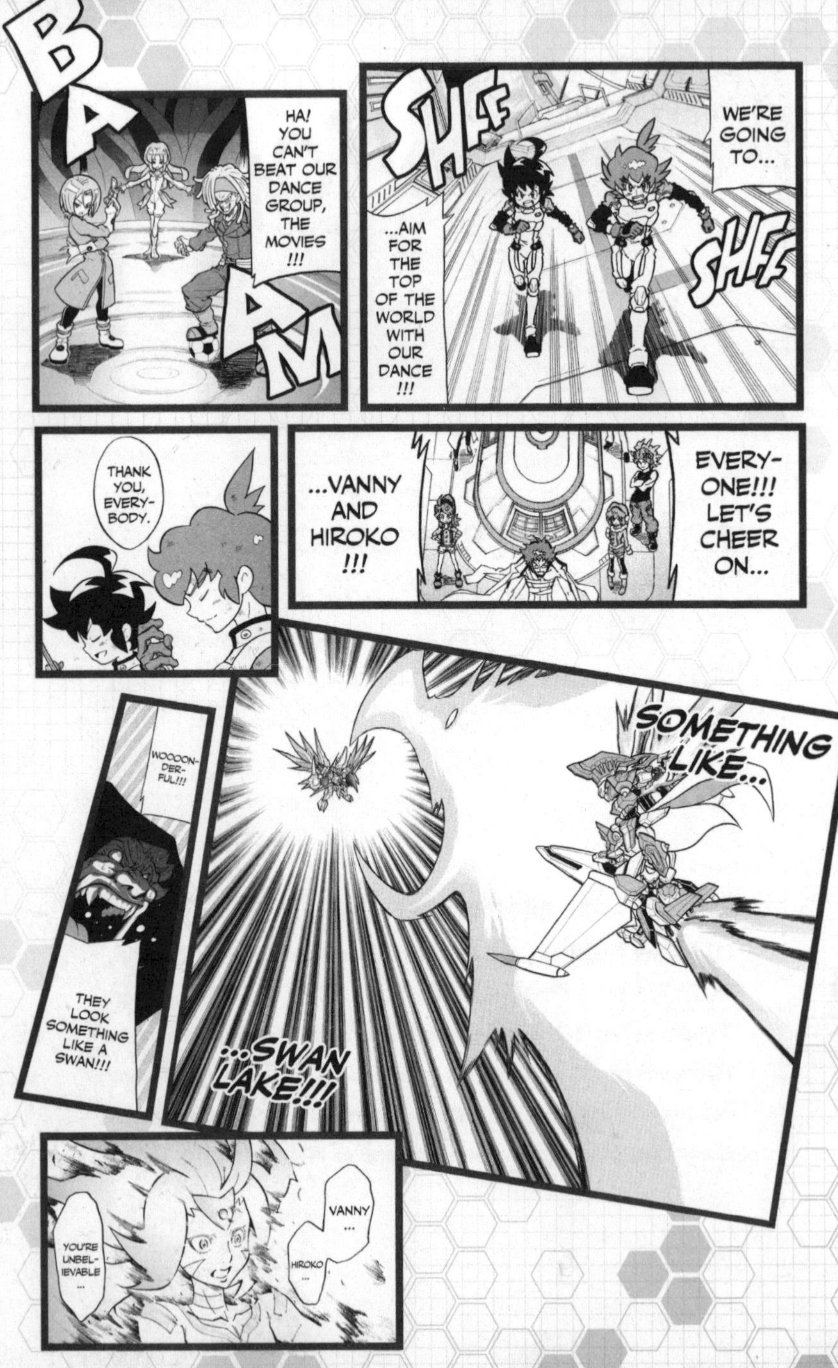
SHFF
WE'RE GOING TO...
...AIM FOR THE TOP OF THE WORLD WITH OUR DANCE!!!
SHFF
BAAM
HA! YOU CAN'T BEAT OUR DANCE GROUP, THE MOVIES!!!
EVERY-ONE!!! LET'S CHEER ON...
...VANNY AND HIROKO!!!
THANK YOU, EVERY-BODY.
SOMETHING LIKE...
...SWAN LAKE!!!
WOOOON-DERFUL!!!
THEY LOOK SOMETHING LIKE A SWAN!!!
VANNY...
HIROKO...
YOU'RE UNBEL-IEVABLE...

The next arc...

BRING

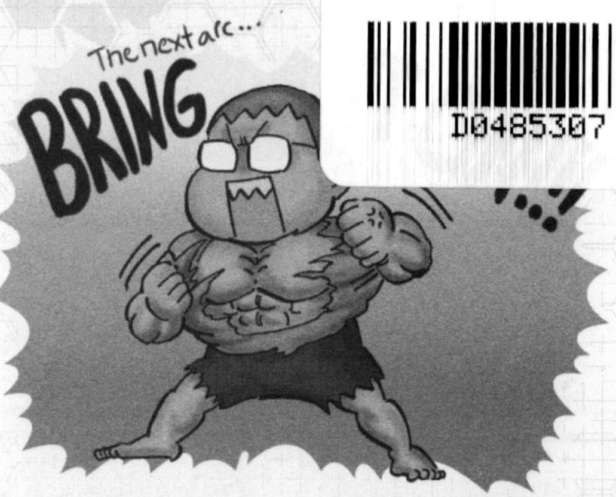

VAN AND HIRO HAVE ENTERED EDEN! AND THEIR BATTLE AGAINST GORDON BEGINS!! BUT THE TRUE ENEMY IS YET TO BE REVEALED...! HOW WILL THEY OVERCOME THIS HOPELESS SITUATION?! THE ARC HAS FINALLY REACHED ITS CLIMAX!! NOW, BATTLE START!!!

● Hideaki Fujii ●

Hideaki Fujii was born on December 12, 1977, in Miyazaki Prefecture. He made his debut in 2000 with *Shin Megami Tensei: Devil Children* (*Monthly Comic BomBom*). His signature works include *Battle Spirits: Breakthrough Boy Bashin* and many others. Blood type A.